ALEXANDER WILSON was a writer, spy and secret service officer. He served in the First World War before moving to India to teach as a Professor of English Literature and eventually became Principal of Islamia College at the University of Punjab in Lahore. He began writing spy novels whilst in India and he enjoyed great success in the 1930s with reviews in the *Telegraph*, *Observer* and the *Times Literary Supplement* amongst others. Wilson also worked as an intelligence agent and his characters are based on his own fascinating and largely unknown career in the Secret Intelligence Service. He passed away in 1963.

By Alexander Wilson

The Mystery of Tunnel 51
The Devil's Cocktail
Wallace of the Secret Service
Get Wallace!
His Excellency, Governor Wallace
Microbes of Power
Wallace at Bay
Wallace Intervenes
Chronicles of the Secret Service

a&b

The Mystery of Tunnel 51

ALEXANDER WILSON

Allison & Busby Limited
12 Fitzroy Mews
London W1T 6DW
allisonandbusby.com

First published in 1928.
This edition published by Allison & Busby in 2015.

A CIP catalogue record for this book is available from
the British Library.

10 9 8 7 6 5 4 3 2 1

Paperback ISBN 978-0-7490-1805-4
Hardback ISBN 978-0-7490-1894-8

Typeset in 10.5/15.5 pt Adobe Garamond Pro by
Allison & Busby Ltd.

The paper used for this Allison & Busby publication
has been produced from trees that have been legally sourced
from well-managed and credibly certified forests.

Printed and bound by
CPI Group (UK) Ltd, Croydon, CR0 4YY

CONTENTS

CHAPTER ONE

Simla

A jarring of brakes, and the long train gradually slowed down and stopped in Kalka station at the foot of the Simla Hills. There was the usual conglomeration of noise and bustle always associated with the arrival of a train in an Indian station. Bearers hurried about at the behest of their masters; fruit vendors, cake vendors and purveyors of chota hazri kept up the shrill cry which is so confusing to the untutored ear, and the babel of talk from the native travellers completed the din.

The door of a first-class compartment opened and a tall, lean, weary-looking man, with a small suitcase in one hand and a haversack on his back, stepped on to the platform. Immediately he was surrounded by a clamouring mob of carriers, but waving them imperiously aside he stepped up to the stationmaster, who was giving instructions to an underling, and, waiting until the official was disengaged, he enquired if there was any possibility of booking a seat in the rail motor for Simla.

'Certainly, sir,' replied that worthy. 'Will you come this way and I'll fix you up. There are not very many people travelling upwards now – all the rush is for the plains.'

They entered the office, and the matter was soon completed, the tall traveller giving his name as Major Elliott of the 'Sappers and Miners'.

'Is there time to have breakfast here?' he asked.

'Well, there is, for a hasty one, sir, but the rail motor stops at Barog about nine for breakfast and you can take your time there.'

'Then I'll wait – Thanks!'

'What about your baggage, sir? Is your servant booking it through?'

Major Elliott smiled.

'I have no servant with me,' he replied, 'and this is my baggage.'

He indicated the haversack and small suitcase. The stationmaster raised his eyebrows, but made no comment. So wishing him 'good morning' Elliott walked out of the office and strolled along in the direction of the rail motor. He stopped where the small car was drawn up, and stood for some minutes looking ahead towards where the mountains rose, which were the Mecca of so many jaded Europeans during the hot season. A look of relief came over his face, and he sighed with the satisfaction of a man who has done his duty and done that duty well.

'At last!' he murmured. 'Ten months' drudgery, and now relief and a little rest!'

He was about to take his seat in the rail motor, when a hand clapped him on the back and a boisterous voice exclaimed:

'Elliott, by all that's wonderful!'

He turned sharply, and the next moment was shaking hands with a big, burly man whose good-humoured face was lit up with pleasure.

'Hallo, Willoughby, where did you spring from?'

'I haven't done any springing,' said the boisterous one. 'I am merely a lone male going up the hills in the hope of bringing back a memsahib. But you? Nobody has seen or heard of you for a year! Where the devil have you been?'

'That is a secret,' said Elliott, 'which I am not at present at liberty to divulge!'

'Always the mystery man, eh Elliott?' grinned Willoughby. 'Righto! But having been the first to find you, I claim to be the first to hear all about your disappearance. Going up?'

'Yes, for a few days, I suppose. How long are you staying in Simla?'

'Only till Monday. Simla will be tame now the Viceroy and all the big-wigs have returned to the plains.'

Elliott gripped Willoughby's arm so tightly that the latter looked at him in surprise.

'Did you say the Viceroy had come down?'

'I did. He came down yesterday.'

'Damnation!'

Willoughby stared at his friend questioningly.

'His Excellency's movements seem to annoy you,' he said. 'You weren't going to see him, were you?'

'I was!'

Willoughby whistled and stared harder than ever.

'What a pity he didn't know!' he said sarcastically. 'He might have waited for you!'

Elliott shrugged his shoulders, then:

'Perhaps he would have done,' he said.

His friend looked as if he were not quite sure of the Major's sanity; then with a roar of laughter he gave him another pat on the back and said:

'You're the queerest fellow I ever met. Come and take your seat; we'll soon be off.'

Elliott hesitated.

'I don't know whether to go up now or carry on to Delhi,' he said, almost to himself; and then apparently making up his mind, he added: 'Oh well, there's bound to be a message, so perhaps I had better go up.'

Five minutes later the little rail motor drew out of the station, and was soon climbing up the mountains on its way to Simla.

Those who are making the journey to the famous hill station for the first time find a peculiar fascination in the trip. On all sides rise jagged heights and densely wooded slopes; now the train is climbing a steep incline, now running through a narrow tunnel, or again along a ledge from which the traveller looks down hundreds of feet into a valley below. As one rises higher and higher the panorama spread before one becomes more and more magnificent, and after a while one feels hemmed in from the outside world by the heights which rise all round. The air becomes cooler and sharper, and those who have not troubled to discard the thin clothes of the plains for something warmer begin to shiver and regret their lack of foresight. Tiny little stations are passed on the way at each of which a signalman waits to show if the line is clear. Halfway up there is a beautiful little spot called Barog, where a first-class dining room gladdens the traveller's heart and reminds him that the rarefied atmosphere has reborn an appetite which the hot weather on the plains had apparently destroyed. Sixty miles of climbing and circling the hills brings the train at last to Simla, with its steep roads, its beautiful scenery, its rickshas, which are the only means of conveyance, and its many and varied races, tribes and religions.

From Kalka to Barog neither Elliott nor Willoughby spoke much. The former appeared to be deep in thought and Willoughby instinctively refrained from breaking in upon his meditations. But as soon as they had breakfasted and had both lighted cigarettes, Elliott cast off the cloak of reserve in which he had hitherto enveloped himself, and for the rest of the journey the two friends found much to discuss, so that they were quite surprised when the motor ran into Summer Hill station, which is the official station of Simla.

'I think I had better alight here,' said Elliott. 'The sooner I get to Viceregal Lodge the better I shall be pleased.'

He shook hands with Willoughby and, renewing a promise to call on the latter and his wife as soon as circumstances permitted, stepped down from the car and made his way to the stationmaster's office where he asked for a ricksha to be sent for. This was soon procured and he was presently on his way to the Lodge.

As he left the station he noticed a tall, dark man, with a decided Semitic cast of countenance, lounging at the door of the waiting room and watching him intently. Somehow the face seemed familiar, but try as he would, he could not place it. The man, apparently noticing the interest Elliot showed in him, moved hastily away, and presently disappeared.

'I wonder where I have seen that fellow before,' muttered the sapper. 'Oh, well, it doesn't matter! It's not likely that I have been shadowed up here! Still one never knows.'

He lit a cigarette and presently forgot the Jewish-looking man in his enjoyable contemplation of the beauties of Simla.

CHAPTER TWO

A Confidential Discussion

Perched right on the top of a hill, Viceregal Lodge stands in an imposing position and the view from its many windows, is glorious. During the season it is the hub of the official and social life of the hill capital and many great national secrets have been whispered inside those walls, which have housed so many successive viceroys.

When Elliott reached it, it wore a dignified, restful aspect, which would have immediately told him, if he had not already known, that the man who controlled the destinies of the Indian Empire was not in residence. A solitary sentry stood at the gates, and he saluted the Major as though he regarded the latter's advent as rather unusual. A servant showed him into an office where two Indian clerks were seated engaged in animated conversation. They looked up at his entry and one, who appeared to be the senior, said in a supercilious tone:

'What can I do for you?'

He looked rather disparagingly at Elliott's travel-worn

appearance, which the Major was quick to notice and resent. The latter coolly seated himself.

'I am Major Elliott,' he said. 'Is there any message for me?'

The clerk seemed galvanised as if by an electric shock. He stood up and bowed.

'Sir,' he said, no longer supercilious, 'I have instructions with regard to you. Will you be so good as to come with me. Sir Henry Muir, His Excellency's Private Secretary, awaits you.'

He led the Major along a corridor, up some richly carpeted stairs, and knocked on a door halfway along another corridor. A deep voice answered, and the clerk opened the door and announced:

'Major Elliott!' and withdrew.

The sapper entered a room tastefully furnished, but which had the look of an office. It was lighted by two large windows and in the centre stood a beautifully carved desk at which a man was seated. He rose and came towards Elliott as the latter entered the room, and showed himself to be a small, alert man of about thirty-five. He wore pince-nez, but they failed to hide the keen, penetrating eyes behind them. His hair was greying at the temples and he had the bearing of a man of quick decisions and authority. He strode quickly to Elliott, his hand outstretched in welcome. 'My dear Elliott,' he said. 'At last!'

'Sir Henry Muir of all people!' said Elliott, warmly returning the hand-clasp. 'This is a greater pleasure than I expected.'

'Then you knew His Excellency had returned to Delhi?' asked Sir Henry, pushing a chair towards him and reseating himself at the desk.

'Yes, I heard it at Kalka. I almost decided to go on to Delhi, but guessed there would be instructions for me here.'

'I'm glad you came,' said Sir Henry, 'otherwise I should have been cooped up here for a few days longer and I am not a great lover of Simla.'

'Then you waited specially for me?' asked Elliott.

'I did. The Viceroy's instructions were to await your arrival and accompany you straight to Delhi. I suppose you'll want a day's rest after all your travels, so I'll make arrangements for us to leave tomorrow evening and go through by the Calcutta express.'

'I'm ready to travel tonight if you wish.'

'Nonsense! We're not altogether heartless, you know. I'll have a room prepared for you here, and no doubt you'll be glad of a bath and change right away!'

'Thanks, I shall. You must think me pretty cool walking in like a scarecrow.'

Sir Henry laughed.

'Quite a tidy-looking scarecrow. You surprise me – I expected a totally different-looking personage, and you turn up almost brand new.'

He rang a bell, and, to the bearer who entered, gave instructions in rapid Urdu. The bearer bowed and noiselessly went out. Sir Henry gazed intently at his companion, and noted the haggard, worn look on his face and the tired eyes.

'You've had a pretty thick time of it, haven't you?' he asked sympathetically.

'Well, it hasn't been a bed of roses,' replied the soldier. 'Ten months of strain doesn't improve one's looks, but I've completed the job I went to do, and that's my satisfaction.'

Sir Henry dropped his voice.

'Did you have any trouble in getting back? Any attempts to rob you?'

'No, though I've thought myself shadowed several times. Of course I was watched on the frontier, and three attempts made to assassinate me.'

'Good Lord!'

Elliott laughed.

'I remained too wide awake for them, however. But that's nothing – I expected it! I had to shoot one fellow, though, but he might have been an ordinary thief.'

'What was he?'

'A Pathan.'

'H'm! And the plans—?'

'Are quite intact and as safe as houses. I carry them in a case under my shirt, and they've never left me night or day.'

'Good!'

At that point the bearer re-entered to announce that the room and bath were ready. Sir Henry rose with his guest and walked with him to the door.

'As soon as you're ready we'll have lunch,' he said.

Elliott thanked him and withdrew.

After luncheon the two men returned to Sir Henry's study and over some excellent cigars Elliott gave an account of his ten months' wanderings.

'The plans are complete in every way,' he said. 'I went over the same ground two or three times to make certain there could be no mistake. Each pass is marked with full information as to when it is open and when not. All our defences and fortifications are down to the minutest detail. The notes contained on my report are exhaustive and I flatter myself that the map is the most complete that could possibly be drawn.'

'Splendid!' said Sir Henry. 'If all we hear about the activities of the Russian spies is true, they would possibly give a fortune to possess that case of yours.'

'Then I'm glad I'm back. But honestly I think the Bolshevik spy scare is a bit exaggerated, don't you? I did not see one man whom any stretch of imagination could convert into a spy.'

'What about the attempts at assassinating you?'

'Nothing to do with spies. You must remember that I was compelled to go into some pretty sticky places, and the folk up there regard a murder or two as deeds well done!'

'H'm, I'm not so sure that there wasn't something behind it. Did you search the Pathan you shot?'

Elliott carefully removed his cigar ash.

'Yes, but there wasn't a scrap of paper to tell me anything. One curious fact struck me, however: he had two hundred rupees on him in notes.'

Sir Henry looked at the other sharply.

'That's an interesting item,' he said; 'one does not expect a fellow of his type to carry a large amount of money about with him. He may have been paid that sum to kill you'

'Well, he failed, and I'm back in civilisation now, thank goodness.'

There was silence for some time; then Muir leant closer towards the other and spoke quietly.

'We cannot afford to take any risks even now,' he said, 'and I am going to keep as close as a leech to you all the way to Delhi. Three times during the last three months there have been attempts at burglary at the Secretariat and I am firmly convinced that on each occasion it was the work of Russian Bolshevik spies. Russia has her eyes set on India now more than she ever had, and the country is overrun with her agents.'

Major Elliott stretched back luxuriously in his chair, and smiled.

'You've still got it badly, Sir Henry,' he said. 'If I remember correctly you have always been rather prone to the Russian menace. Why should Russia, more than any other nation, hunger for India? Surely their internal troubles must keep them fully occupied without that.'

'But think what India would mean to Russia Why, this country would be a Godsend to a nation like that. The possibilities to her would be immense – stupendous.'

'I know all that, but then she is not in a condition even to consider India, much less make a grasp at her.'

'One cannot tell what Russia is in a condition to do,' said Sir Henry portentously. 'She may have resources which we never dream of, and I do think that at present there is a very decided danger from her, and that this country is full of her agents gleaning information from every possible source. I am not alone in my opinion. The Viceroy shares it with me!'

Elliott shrugged his shoulders and gazed reflectively at the end of his cigar.

'You may be right,' he said, 'and of course every precaution should be taken, but personally I think the greatest trouble India is suffering from just now is the unfortunate misunderstandings that exist between her own peoples.'

'Oh, those!' Sir Henry waved his hand contemptuously. 'They are nothing! In time the country will settle down and there will be nothing but perfect amity between all those who are now at loggerheads. I think I can speak with authority on that point.'

CHAPTER THREE

A Midnight Visit

That night the two men visited a theatrical performance at the Gaiety Theatre, and afterwards went to the Club where Major Elliott met several acquaintances.

It was late when they returned to Viceregal Lodge, and as Elliott undressed for bed he felt tired and looked forward with some degree of pleasure to a really good night's rest, a luxury which he had not enjoyed for months.

He got into bed and was almost immediately asleep. He awoke a couple of hours later with a feeling that he was in danger. He lay perfectly quiet and listened, but not a sound disturbed the stillness and presently, thinking he had been dreaming, he turned on his side. But at that moment there was a thud and he felt something touch his back. He fell rather than sprang out of bed and waited. He now heard the sibilant hissing of an indrawn breath and knew that in turning in the bed he had saved his life, for what he had felt was a hand containing a knife which had stabbed at the place where he had been lying.

For some moments there was no sound and Elliott gradually, carefully, felt for the switch of the electric light. He had just reached it when something bounded through the air, and the next moment he was fighting for his life with a practically naked creature, whose body was oiled to an extent that made a grip almost impossible. Elliott searched for and found an arm that was obviously raised to strike, then commenced a terrible struggle. Backwards and forwards the two went, their breath coming in great gasps. Two or three articles of furniture were knocked over, and presently, with a crash, they fell to the floor.

Elliott felt his hand slipping from his opponent's wrist. The latter, though apparently small, was a man of immense strength and was obviously getting the upper hand. The Major lost his hold, the arm was once again raised to strike, and at that moment the door was flung open and a flood of light lit up the scene. The intruder sprang for the open window, and as he disappeared Sir Henry – for he it was who had entered – fired. He ran to the window and looked out just as the man reached the ground by way of a tree that rose close by. Again he fired, but the dim light spoilt his aim and the ruffian disappeared. Muir quickly returned to Elliott, who was rising rather shakily from the floor.

'Phew!' gasped the latter. 'That was a near thing. I should have been a dead man if you hadn't turned up, Sir Henry.'

He sat limply on the edge of the bed. Muir walked to the door and called loudly for whisky and sodas, which presently forthcoming, he mixed two stiff drinks and giving one to Elliott, took the other himself.

'So they're still after you!' he said. 'Thank God your room was close to mine, otherwise I would never have heard a sound. That little brute was a hillman, up to all the tricks of the trade. It never occurred to me that that tree might be used as a means of entrance. Those fellows are as agile as monkeys.'

Elliott took a long drink.

'That's better,' he said with satisfaction. 'I shall be jolly glad when these plans are handed over. I didn't expect to be interfered with here!'

'The question is, who employed that little devil?'

'By Jove!' Elliott sat up stiffly. 'When I arrived at Summer Hill station there was a tall Jewish-looking fellow there watching me as though he were interested in me. Now I'd swear I have seen him two or three times before, but I can't think where and under what circumstances. It is only an idea, but perhaps he is the key to this business!'

'He probably is,' said Sir Henry thoughtfully, 'but even if we knew where he is, we could not have him arrested just because he was looking at you and you think you have seen him before. The sooner we get those plans to Delhi the better, there certainly is someone who wants them very badly. Then I am going to persuade the Viceroy to comb out India for Bolshevik spies.'

Elliott smiled.

'What a job!' he murmured.

Muir drank off his whisky and soda.

'Now,' he said briskly, 'I'm going to interview the sentry and then get the guard to search the grounds. I don't suppose we'll find anybody there, unless he, or they, are waiting to make a further attempt, in which case I hope to get them. Do you feel fit enough to come with me? I don't want to let you out of my sight between now and our arrival in Delhi!'

Elliott laughed and stood up.

'I'm perfectly fit now,' he declared. 'I'll put some clothes on and come along with pleasure.'

'Very well,' said Sir Henry, 'I'll wait until you're ready, and then if you'll come with me I'll put something warm over these things.'

Elliott laughed again and walked towards a wardrobe. As he turned Muir uttered a startled exclamation and the Major looked round enquiringly.

'You've had a narrower shave than I thought,' said the Secretary. 'Your pyjama jacket is cut right across the back.'

The sapper took it off and surveyed it ruefully.

'That must have been done when I turned over in bed,' he said. 'You see, I thought I heard a sound and lay on my back listening; nothing happened, so I decided that it must have been imagination and turned on my side, and as I turned something struck. I knew that the movement had saved my life, but I didn't know it was as close as that.'

He was soon dressed, and together the two men entered Sir Henry's room.

'We'll leave the lights on,' said the latter, as he quickly pulled on some clothes over his pyjamas, 'then if there is anybody watching, they can go on gazing at the lighted rooms until we pounce on them.'

'Sounds simple enough,' remarked Elliott. 'If only it were, we'd have a chance of getting to Delhi safely. As it is—' He shrugged his shoulders.

Muir stopped in the act of buttoning up his coat and stared.

'You're not having premonitions, are you?' he asked sharply.

Elliott laughed a little shamefacedly.

'Well, to tell you the truth I have an uncanny sort of feeling that I'm booked,' he said. 'How, or where, or when, I can't tell you, but it's there, and I'm going to make extra certain of those plans!'

Sir Henry grunted.

'Nonsense!' he snapped. 'That's sheer foolishness. I'm going to see that you get to Delhi or my name's not Muir. Come along!'

He strode to the door, and Elliott followed him. They descended the stairs, and, having let themselves out of the house, went up to the sentry at the gate and accosted him. Sir Henry asked him in Hindustani if he had let anybody pass into the grounds. The man, a smart, alert-looking Gurkha, seemed deeply hurt at such a question, and immediately replied that he had not.

'Have you noticed any suspicious-looking characters about?'

'No, sahib.'

'H'm! Call out the guard!'

This was done and Muir spoke rapidly to the sergeant telling him that he wanted the grounds thoroughly searched and anybody found in them arrested.

'If they resist, don't hesitate to use as much force as you like,' he added.

The soldiers departed eagerly on their errand. Sir Henry turned to Elliott with a smile.

'Very little will escape them,' he said. 'Come along; we'll have a look round ourselves while we're here!'

They walked to a tall pine which grew close to the house. Muir stood by it and gazed reflectively upwards.

'This is the tree your assailant came down by, and probably got up into the room by,' he said.

'It seems hardly possible that anything but a monkey could climb that,' said Elliott. 'There's no foothold at all!'

'No, but these hillmen are first cousins to monkeys,' replied Sir Henry. 'He had a jump of not quite four feet from the tree to your window. Pretty daring, you know.'

They wandered on down the slopes and searched among bushes and anywhere that looked as though it could afford shelter for a cat. But they found not a sign of a hidden man, and retraced their steps towards the Lodge. Under the tree again they stopped, and searched the ground round it. There was not even a footprint to suggest that anyone had been there, and they were about to give up their quest and go indoors, when there was a shout. The two men stood still and stared in the direction whence it had come, and presently a shadowy figure darted out from some bushes, and sped rapidly across the lawn closely followed by two others, undoubtedly Gurkhas. Quickly drawing a revolver from his pocket, Sir Henry fired, but missed, and the figure vanished down a slope.

Half an hour later the sergeant reported that the man had got away in spite of being closely followed, so giving him instructions to set a very close watch, Muir led the way into the house, and they ascended to his bedroom.

'I'm very annoyed at missing that fellow,' he grumbled. 'That's the third time and I used to think I was a good shot!'

'It would have been rather wonderful if you had hit him in that light and considering the pace he was moving at. Well, it doesn't matter much. I don't suppose he'll trouble us again tonight.'

'No, he'll probably keep well away for the time being, but he's at liberty and will be able to attempt further mischief. Dash it, I was a fool to miss him!'

He sat on his bed, and lit a cigar with an air of disgust.

'I don't suppose he's the only pebble on the beach,' said Elliott. 'If you had winged him, there are no doubt others. What I can't understand is: why are they showing this activity now? Why wasn't a more determined attempt made to get me when I was out in the wilds?'

Sir Henry shrugged his shoulders.

'They did try thrice!' he remarked.

'Yes, but they might have tried a dozen, two dozen times, and they would have been bound to get me sooner or later.'

He threw himself into a chair.

'The funny thing is, I never had the slightest doubt of my ability to get through up there. And now I'm full of absurd presentiments like a nervy girl.'

Muir rose from the bed and crossing to the other, clapped him on the shoulder.

'You've had a pretty rotten time one way and another,' he said. 'I don't wonder at your feeling a bit run down. You'll have to go in for a course of dinners and dances – in fact have a thoroughly gay time when you get to Delhi to make up for it.'

Elliott laughed.

'Not in Delhi, Sir Henry,' he said. 'I'm off to England as soon as I can get away. It's time the old country saw a bit of me again. I haven't been home since the War. Gad!' His eyes lighted up enthusiastically. 'Just think of it: a cold sharp morning, full cry across country after the hounds, with one's blood racing through one's veins in the sheer joy of being alive. Why, the very thought makes me feel young again!'

He rose and walked to the window, stood staring out a moment or two and then returned to Sir Henry.

'Away with premonitions,' he said, 'they're foolish and childish. I'm going to bed – I've a lot of sleep to make up.'

'Tumble into my bed for the rest of the night,' said the Secretary. 'I'm going to lie down on that couch by the window.'

'Nonsense, I'm not going to turn you out of your bed.'

'The couch is very comfortable and I shall be perfectly happy there. At any rate I have determined to watch over you like a guardian angel, so here in this room you stop.'

'Well, I'll have the couch.'

'No, you won't. So turn in and go to sleep!'

Elliott shrugged his shoulders and without further argument undressed and got into bed. In two minutes he was fast asleep. Muir looked at him for a minute or two and then thoughtfully took off his clothes. He took a couple of rugs from a cupboard, switched off the light, and lay down on the couch. The glowing end of his cigar shone in the darkness like a beacon light.

CHAPTER FOUR

The Deputy Commissioner

The next morning Sir Henry Muir rang up the Deputy Commissioner of Police, Colonel Sanders, and asked him to call at Viceregal Lodge. The Colonel came and was met by Muir who immediately took him into his office, where Elliott was seated reading a newspaper. The latter was introduced to the Commissioner, and the three men sat down by the desk.

'I asked you to come up here, Colonel Sanders,' said Muir, 'because I felt that this was the best place to tell you our little story.'

The Commissioner grunted. He was a morose-looking man of about fifty, with a small grey moustache, thinning grey hair and tired blue eyes. He never under any circumstances became agitated, and his general air was one of languor and boredom. But, in spite of that, he had a very sharp brain, and a reputation for shrewdness which was unequalled in the Punjab. His manner was non-committal, and people who did not know him were apt to regard him as a person with a limited amount of intelligence, and a boor.

'Major Elliott,' continued Sir Henry, 'has been away on the frontier for ten months making the most exhaustive plans of our fortifications, passes by which it would be possible for an – er – invading army to cross from Russia to India, and a general detailed survey map of the whole frontier. His instructions were to come direct to the Viceroy at Simla when he had finished and he arrived yesterday – to find that His Excellency had left the day before for Delhi.'

Colonel Sanders nodded, and looked as though he were about to suppress a fawn.

'Last night,' went on the Secretary, 'Major Elliott, who slept in a room here next to mine, had a visitant, who was obviously after his plans, and he very nearly lost his life. I heard the sounds of a struggle and went into the room, but the intruder, a hillman, escaped by climbing down a tree just outside Elliott's window. I had a revolver and fired, but missed unfortunately. The guard was called out and the grounds searched, and we almost had the fellow, but he got away. This is the fourth time Elliott's life has been attempted, but the other three attempts were made on the frontier.'

Muir ceased speaking and for a minute or two there was silence. Then:

'Russian money behind this,' grunted the Colonel. 'The whole country is under espionage now.'

'Exactly,' said the Secretary, looking rather triumphantly at Elliott.

Again there was a silence. The Commissioner got up, and walked up and down the room once or twice.

'What do you want me to do?' he asked suddenly, stopping in front of Sir Henry.

'To see that we are protected as far as possible from any further outrages between here and Delhi.'

'When are you travelling?'

'We are leaving here by the six-fifteen rail motor this evening to Kalka, and thence to Delhi by the Calcutta express.'

'Why not travel by private car to Kalka – the rail motor *can be derailed!*'

'Good Lord!' exclaimed Elliott, speaking for the first time. 'You're not very cheerful, Colonel.'

'If these people are after your plans, they'll stick at nothing to get them,' snapped Sanders. 'A private car would be safer! And leave during the afternoon so that you'll have daylight all the way!'

Sir Henry rubbed his chin thoughtfully.

'It seems to me,' he said, 'that a motor car could be more easily held up or tampered with than the rail motor.'

Elliott nodded in agreement.

'How are they to know when you are travelling if you go by road?' demanded the Commissioner.

'You may be sure that if they can find out one thing, they can find out another,' said Elliott.

'But if they discovered you were travelling by road,' said the Colonel, 'it doesn't follow that they would have time to make arrangements to interfere with you.'

Sir Henry leant back in his chair, and looked questioningly at Elliott.

'What do you say, Major?' he asked.

Elliott smiled.

'I'd feel a great deal safer in the rail motor,' he said. Muir nodded.

'I agree with you.'

Colonel Sanders helped himself to a cigarette from a box on

the table, lit it, and, holding the spent match in his fingers, looked from Muir to Elliott and back again.

'Well, you'll have your own way, but don't forget that I advised you to travel by road! You're going at six-fifteen, you say? Well, be advised in this particular – ring up the stationmaster and order a private rail motor for seven o'clock.'

Sir Henry looked surprised.

'What on earth for?' he ejaculated.

'A blind! There's bound to be a certain amount of fuss getting a special ready and these people who are so interested in you will get to hear of it somehow. Actually travel by the six-fifteen and nobody will turn up for the other. Only we three will know that it isn't wanted, and I'll explain to the railway authorities once you are away.'

'By Jove!' said Elliott, 'that's a notion.'

'I've got to save you from yourselves somehow,' growled the Colonel.

'But supposing there is no other rail motor available,' questioned Sir Henry.

'There's got to be!' snapped Sanders. 'No car available and Sir Henry Muir demanding one in the name of the Viceroy! Pshaw!'

Muir looked properly subdued.

'I'll see that every station from Kalka to Delhi is watched by the police,' continued the Colonel. 'You'll be all right going down the hill, as you'll only stop at Barog, and there'll be a special police officer on the car all the way down who'll shadow you there. That's the best I can do for you.'

Both Muir and Elliott expressed their thanks, but the Commissioner waved them aside.

'If you weren't fools,' he said, 'you'd go down in a private car. I could have sent a police car ahead and one behind you and there wouldn't have been the slightest danger. However, you'll go your own way, I suppose.'

'It's jolly good of you, Colonel,' said Elliott, 'but I don't see how we can possibly go wrong on the rail motor. There will be other passengers and your policeman. It's between Kalka and Delhi where the real danger is to be feared and, as you say you'll arrange for the police to watch every station en route, I shall be perfectly safe. I don't mind telling you that you've lifted a great load from my mind. The thanks of the Government will be due to you, if I get through all right.'

'Nonsense,' said the Colonel, 'it's my business! Now, before I go I want to see the room where the outrage occurred and look around the grounds a bit.'

'Elliott will show you,' said Sir Henry. 'I'll get through to the stationmaster at once and arrange for the special.'

'Don't let him suspect that it is bogus,' said Sanders. 'And don't be shy about it. Let your clerks know that it is a special at seven. Perhaps they'll help to give it out! Tell them you don't want it generally known and they'll blab it to all their friends!'

He followed Elliott out of the office and along to the room in which the latter had been attacked. He walked straight to the window, and gazed out.

'Is that the tree?' he asked, pointing to the tall pine that raised its stately head outside.

'Yes,' said Elliott. 'I don't know whether he came in that way, but he certainly departed by that tree.'

'H'm! A bit of a jump, but nothing to a Hillman – nothing! How did you know he was in the room?'

Elliott told him the whole story of his awakening, and the

subsequent events. Sanders listened in his usual bored manner.

'Of course it's an impossibility to lay this fellow by the heels,' he said at the end of the recital. 'Neither of you saw him clearly and even if you had all hillmen are more or less alike. And supposing I could get hold of him, a dozen of his friends would turn up with alibis. Pity you didn't get him last night. Still, it doesn't matter much; if he was finished, there would have been others!'

'Just what I thought,' said Elliott.

'Well, we'll go outside,' muttered the Colonel, almost to himself. 'Nothing to be seen, of course, but might as well go.'

They went out of the house and wandered round the grounds. It all appeared very aimless to Elliott, especially as Sanders walked along with his chin on his chest and appeared to be deeply in thought. When they came to the tree, of which the assassin had made such use, the Commissioner gazed at it as though he had never seen a tree before. Presently he looked at Elliott and asked a surprising question.

'Are you pretty strong?' he enquired.

The sapper laughed.

'Fairly,' he replied. 'Why?'

'I want you to give me a back up.'

Feeling that the suns of India had turned the Commissioner's brain, Elliott did as he was asked. At that moment Sir Henry Muir came out of the house and stopped with astonishment when he saw the Major bent double with Colonel Sanders standing on his back and gazing intently at a smooth part of the tree from which the bark had come off. Presently the Colonel jumped down and Elliott straightened up.

'Hope I didn't hurt you,' said the former. 'Hullo, Muir, fixed everything up?'

'Yes,' said Sir Henry. 'A special rail motor will be at Summer Hill station at seven sharp for us.'

'H'm! That's all right then!'

'What on earth were you two doing?' asked Muir curiously.

'Nothing much,' replied the Commissioner, 'but you're a better shot than you thought you were, Muir. Do you see that blur on the bare patch there?'

'Yes,' said the Secretary eagerly.

'It's blood, dried of course! I may be able to find a man who's been wounded. Not that I've any hope,' he added.

'Did you tell Sanders about your Jew, Elliott?' asked Sir Henry.

'No – I haven't done so.'

'What about a Jew?' asked the Deputy, who once again wore a look of boredom.

'I saw a tall Jewish-looking fellow watching me rather intently when I arrived here,' explained Elliott, 'and his face seemed rather familiar. When he saw I was looking at him he moved away.'

'H'm! Nothing in that,' growled the Colonel. 'It's not a crime for a man to look at you, and you might have seen him anywhere.'

'I know, but – by Jove!' Elliott almost shouted, and even the Commissioner looked at him with interest. 'I remember now where I saw him – the first time was in Kabul, and the second time in the railway station at Peshawar.'

'Great Scott!' exclaimed Muir. 'Then it looks as if—'

'He's a damn fool to let himself be seen,' interrupted Sanders, 'if he were following you – an absolute idiot!'

Elliott laughed with whole-hearted enjoyment at this remark.

'Give me a description of him!' went on the commissioner.

'What's the good of that?' asked Muir. 'You can't arrest a man because he was in Kabul and Peshawar the same time as Elliott.'

'No, but I can have him watched and find out his antecedents,' snapped the other.

'Well,' said Elliott, 'he was tall, quite six feet in height I should say, fairly broad, had a small black moustache, black hair, sallow complexion and large Jewish-looking nose.'

Colonel Sanders made some notes in a small pocket book.

'Eyes?' he questioned.

'I was never near enough to see much of them, but I should say they were of some dark colour and very small.'

'How was he dressed the last time you saw him?'

'Blue lounge suit, brown shoes and a white topee.'

'Pity everybody can't give such lucid descriptions when they're wanted to,' said the Colonel, and actually smiled. He closed up his book, and put it in a pocket. 'Well, I'll be off now,' he added. 'Goodbye in case I don't see you again before you go, and keep your eyes open and revolvers handy.'

He shook hands with Muir and Elliott, and, turning abruptly, strode off to the gate where his ricksha patiently awaited him.

CHAPTER FIVE

What Happened in the Tunnel

The rail motor car ran into Summer Hill station promptly to time and Sir Henry Muir and Major Elliott, who had arrived a minute or two earlier, emerged from the waiting room, where they had concealed themselves from general observation, and boarded it.

There were only two other passengers, a Captain Williams of the 107th Horse, who was known to both Muir and Elliott, and a small, sharp-featured man, whom Sir Henry recognised as one of the astutest police officers in Simla. The rail car was a small one and had only seats for ten, apart from the driver. All the seats faced in the direction the car was going. In front sat the driver and next to him was seating accommodation for two; behind these were seats for four more, and to the rear of these again were another four seats. Captain Williams was seated by the driver and the policeman was sitting by him; directly behind them Elliott and Muir took their places, the Major being on the outside and Muir sitting practically in the centre.

'Hullo, Williams!' said Sir Henry. 'Where are you bound for?'

'Lahore,' replied Williams. 'I've only had a few days' leave, but it's been a change.'

'I thought your troop was at Pindi! Have you been transferred?'

'Yes, about a week ago,' said the young officer.

He was a man of apparently not more than twenty-six or twenty-seven years of age. He had fair hair, blue eyes, good features and a pleasant, open countenance. He was extremely popular in his regiment and had innumerable friends in various parts of India. Both Muir and Elliott had known him for some years.

'We are quite a small party,' remarked Elliott. 'I thought there would have been quite a number of people travelling.'

'Most of them have already gone down, I suppose,' said Sir Henry. 'We are a safe party anyway,' he added in a whisper.

Elliott nodded, and then suddenly gripped the Secretary's arm so fiercely that the latter winced.

'There's the Jew!' said the sapper in a tense undertone.

Muir looked startled.

'Good Lord! Where?' he exclaimed.

'Over by that native with the box on his head! Quick! He's going!'

Sir Henry looked sharply at the place indicated, and was just in time to catch a glimpse of a tall, broad-shouldered man sauntering away towards the exit of the station. Just then Colonel Sanders appeared and Muir beckoned to him. The Commissioner wandered leisurely across, and at that moment the rail car started.

'Everything's all right,' began Sanders, 'I—'

'The Jew's just gone out of the station!' jerked Sir Henry. 'Was here – watching us!'

'Which exit?' snapped the Colonel.

'That one!' pointed the Secretary, and, without another word, the Deputy Commissioner turned and walked away.

The car gathered speed and had soon left Simla behind. Elliott's face was a bit pale, and he and Muir looked at each other with foreboding.

'He was smiling,' said the former, 'as though with triumph.'

'Hang him!' said Sir Henry uneasily. 'I thought our plans were going so well.' Then he laughed. 'What a couple of fools we are!' he said. 'The man may be, and probably is, entirely innocent, and not a bit interested in you or me.'

Elliott shook his head.

'No,' he said, 'that fellow has trailed me right down from the frontier, I'm sure of it. I didn't like his smile, it was so full of satisfaction.'

'Well,' said the Secretary, 'we can only keep our eyes open and look out for trouble. Have you your revolver ready?'

Elliott smiled grimly.

'I have my hand on it at this moment,' he said, 'and I am perfectly prepared to shoot at the slightest sign of danger.'

'Good! So am I!'

The two men relapsed into silence, each finding much to occupy his thoughts. The rail motor ran on, swinging around a corner one moment, the next down a steep grade and then for a little time on the level. Tunnel after tunnel was passed through, some were very short, one or two quite long. There are no less than a hundred and two tunnels between Simla and Kalka and each of them is numbered. They are cut through the solid rock, and the longest of them, No. 51, has a sharp curve in the very middle.

Daylight had almost faded as this tunnel was approached, and the driver switched on the lights without waiting for the deeper darkness within to compel him to do so. There was only one electric light in the interior of the car, which gave but a poor illumination. Captain Williams turned round and smiled at Elliott.

'They don't give one much light to read by,' he said.

'I don't suppose anybody wants to read,' said Elliott. 'There is too much vibration.'

At that moment with a shrill whistle the rail motor ran into the tunnel, and the rattle of the wheels, rendered twenty times louder by the confined space, prevented further conversation. Then suddenly the light inside the car went out, and they were plunged into complete darkness. The driver slowed down but did not stop, preferring to wait until he got out of the tunnel before trying to find out what had gone wrong. Sir Henry's voice could be heard shouting unnecessarily that the light had fused. And then, just as suddenly as it had gone out, it relit, and a moment or two later the car ran out into the open.

'What happened to the light, driver?' asked Muir, leaning forward.

'I think lamp loose, sahib.'

'Well, it had a most weird effect,' said the Secretary, and turned smilingly to Elliott.

Then suddenly the smile turned into a look of frozen horror. The Major's body was lying as though he had slipped, and his head was lolling back on the cushion. But it was not the position of Elliott's body that caused such distress to Muir; it was his face. It wore a look of startled surprise, and was deadly pale. The eyes were wide open, and staring in a fixed and grotesque manner, while there was a trickle of blood running from the corner of the mouth.

'Good God!' cried Muir, and his face was nearly as white as the other's. He leant forward and, lifting the Major's hand, let it go again. It fell back dully on to the seat, and immediately the Secretary was galvanised into action.

'Stop, for God's sake, stop!' he shouted, hitting the driver such a blow on the back that the latter looked over his shoulder with a startled countenance before bringing the motor to a sudden halt. Captain Williams and the police officer glanced around enquiringly, and both faces became suffused with horror as they saw Elliott.

'Is he ill, sir?' asked the policeman, starting to his feet.

'Ill!' almost sobbed Sir Henry, who had his hand over Elliott's heart. 'He's dead!'

'Dead!' gasped Williams. 'Are you sure, Sir Henry?'

The policeman climbed over the back of the seat and, pulling open the Major's coat, laid his ear on the latter's heart. Then he stood up and gazed down at the dead man.

'He's been stabbed!' he said. 'Look at that trickle of blood from his mouth!'

While the others watched him, he pulled the body forward, and looked at the back, and there, between the shoulder blades, was a small wound from which the blood was still oozing.

'Yes,' he said, 'he's been murdered right enough!'

'How can he have been murdered?' exclaimed Williams.

'I can't tell you that, sir, but he has. Somebody boarded the car in that tunnel and stabbed him!'

'But, man alive,' cried the cavalry man, 'there wasn't time, and why should he be murdered?'

'There's reason enough,' said Sir Henry quietly. 'He was carrying a most important document on him, and—'

'Where was he carrying it, sir?' interrupted the policeman quickly. 'Have you any idea?'

'Yes,' said Muir, and tenderly opening the dead man's coat and shirt, he felt underneath, and presently drew forth a square case, which was heavily sealed.

'This is safe enough,' he muttered; 'but why in Heaven's name was he murdered, obviously for this, when there was no chance of the murderer obtaining it?'

The three men stared at each other for a few seconds. Sir Henry put the case away in an inside pocket and buttoned up his coat. Then he looked at the police officer.

'What is to be done, Hartley?' he asked.

'I'm going back to search that tunnel, sir. You get on to Barog as quickly as you can – you'll get a doctor there. Ring up Colonel Sanders, tell him what's happened, and ask him to send somebody down to me.'

Sir Henry nodded, and Hartley stepped on to the line and immediately started to walk back towards the tunnel. The driver, who had watched everything with a look of terror, was directed to drive on as fast as he could safely do so.

At last, after what seemed to Muir an interminable time, in spite of the dangerous rate of speed at which they travelled, Barog was reached. As soon as it was known that a man had been murdered, the little station buzzed with activity. Elliott's body was carried into a small room adjoining the restaurant, a doctor was sent for, and Sir Henry immediately got on the telephone to Colonel Sanders' office in Simla.

He was not there, but had gone home, so Muir rang up the Commissioner's house and, to his relief, heard the latter's voice at the other end of the wire. He immediately related what had happened, and a startled exclamation answered him.

'Hartley is in the tunnel,' said Muir, 'and he wants you to send a man down to him.'

'I'll go myself. Are the plans safe?'

'Yes, I've got them.'

'Then get to Delhi as quickly as you can with them! Don't lose a minute!'

'But I can't leave poor Elliott!'

'You can't do anything for him, and if you don't get away with those plans at once you'll go the same way as he did.'

'Good Lord!'

'Don't say "Good Lord", but get away. I'll come on to Barog from the tunnel, and take charge of everything. Let me see, who was in the rail motor with you besides Hartley?'

'Williams of the 107th Horse.'

'Oh, yes, I remember. Tell him to stop at Barog until I arrive. Instruct him to see that Elliott's body is locked in a room, nobody is to have the key but himself, and he is to allow only the doctor to go in. Do you understand?'

'Quite!'

'Right! Now get off! Commandeer a car and don't stop for a moment until you get to Delhi and have handed those plans to the Viceroy. Good luck!'

The Commissioner rang off, and Muir hastened back to Williams, who was just about to take the doctor into the room where Elliott lay. He repeated the Commissioner's instructions to the young officer. The latter listened attentively and nodded. Then Sir Henry turned to the stationmaster.

'I want the highest powered car you have in the place,' he said, 'and at once!'

The stationmaster looked thoughtful, and stood rubbing his chin for a moment.

'The most powerful car here is the doctor's Fiat,' he said at last.

Sir Henry immediately went after the medical man; the latter was examining the body and the Secretary stood by, waiting until the examination was complete. At last the doctor concluded and turned to his two companions.

'He was stabbed by a very thin-bladed knife which has made quite a small wound,' he said. 'The blow was driven downwards with great force, and pierced the heart. The Major must have died instantaneously.'

'I don't think he uttered a sound,' said Muir. 'I heard nothing; though, of course, there was a lot of noise at the time. And now, Doctor, I have a very urgent request to make.'

The doctor looked at him enquiringly, and he explained his need. When the medical man understood the importance of the matter he at once agreed to lend the car.

'I have no driver,' he said, 'but if you—'

'Yes, I'll drive myself.'

'Then come with me; my house is close by and we'll soon get the car out!'

Muir shook hands with Williams.

'You'll keep that door locked,' he said, 'and not leave the vicinity till Sanders arrives? You may have to wait here, or in Simla, for some days. I'll communicate officially with your Colonel about any extra leave it may be necessary for you to have.'

'Thanks,' said Williams. 'Goodbye and good luck!'

Sir Henry followed the doctor out of the station, and they soon arrived at the latter's house. The car was taken out of the garage without delay, and the tank filled with petrol. Then the doctor insisted on his taking a packet of sandwiches and a flask of brandy. At last all was in readiness for his departure, so shaking the worthy medico's hand, and thanking him, Muir got into the car and started. Just outside Barog he stopped a moment, looked at his revolver to make sure that it was ready for action, felt to see that the case containing the plans was quite safe, and then, with his face grimly set, drove forward on his lonely two hundred mile journey to Delhi.

CHAPTER SIX

His Excellency the Viceroy

Sir Henry Muir never remembered clearly, in after years, that frantic race of his to Delhi. Mile after mile flew by and he sat grimly, leaning a little forward, his lips set in a desperate line, his eyes glued to the stretch of road in front of him and his hands holding the steering wheel with a grip that betrayed his thoughts. He stopped for a few minutes at Kalka station to instruct his bearer, who had travelled down with his baggage during the afternoon, to go on to Delhi by the train. Then on again.

The car seemed to respond to his mood and tore onwards, the engine purring rhythmically, beautifully; firing perfectly, as though in very exultation at its ability to eat up space.

Muir expected every moment to be stopped; that death in some terrible form would overtake him; once he glanced over his shoulder apprehensively into the tonneau and the car swerved violently. But he never slackened pace. The events of the last few hours had affected his nerves to such an extent that he almost thought of the mysterious assassins with superstitious dread; nothing seemed beyond them; they appeared supernatural, uncanny, weird; a malignant force, cloaked in invisibility, with the power to do evil at will.

It was a dark night, and the glare of the headlights threw the trees on either side into ghostly relief. Muir imagined the shadows to contain men waiting there with diabolical purpose; the wind had risen and seemed to contain the sound of fiendish, laughing voices, mocking at his puny attempts to escape them. He passed bullock carts wending their peaceful way on their lawful business, but the eyes of the bullocks approaching him, shining a brilliant green in the powerful lights of the car, looked like the eyes of devils glaring at him with hatred.

He had several narrow escapes of collision. The Indian bullock cart wending its somnolent way never worries about other traffic on the road. The driver invariably sleeps while his bullocks wander on at their own sweet will, mostly in the centre of the highway, often on the wrong side. Sir Henry approaching one bullock cart in the way, sounded his Klaxon horn loudly, viciously. The driver woke up with a start and, with shouts, turned his animals aside, but just as Muir was about to pass the bullocks swerved back across his path. He was right on top of them, but with wonderful skill he swung his car aside just in time, trod hard on his accelerator and shot by, the yoke of the oxen scraping the paintwork and his off-wheels being half an inch over the edge of the road. The perspiration broke out on his forehead and trickled down his face; he almost thought that a collision had been contrived there by those enemies of whom he knew so little.

He passed Umbala going at forty miles an hour, and the lights of the cantonments heartened him a little, braced him up. He had a great yearning to stop there, take his ease, and rest; for an utter weariness seemed to be numbing his senses and gradually overcoming him. But he stiffened himself, tore past into the darkness again, and fumbled with his left hand for the sandwiches and brandy. He took a bite at a sandwich, but it nauseated him, and unscrewing the top of the brandy-flask, he gulped down a generous peg, felt better for it, and set himself once more to his grim, stern, unrelenting race through the darkness.

He was on the grand trunk road now and there was more traffic. Several times he was compelled to slow down and he chafed inwardly at the delay, but onward he went, ever onward, and gradually he was drawing nearer to Delhi. His spirits began to rise. When he left Barog he never expected to reach Umbala, but now that he had left that city behind, he felt more hopeful and with the assistance of the brandy grew more cheerful. He took another bite at a sandwich, and this time it did not sicken him, so he went on munching until he had eaten the lot, and felt infinitely better for it.

At last, at a quarter past two in the morning, he entered the outskirts of Delhi, and turned the car in the direction of Viceregal Lodge. His whole body was numbed, and he was in agony with the cramp in his legs. For some time past he had been driving with the throttle lever, as he was quite unable to use his right foot. But he was filled with exultation, and his heart was beating rapidly with a great satisfaction at having accomplished his mission as he drove up to the gates of the Viceroy's palatial dwelling. He was challenged by a sentry, and at once made known his name. The enormous gates immediately swung back, and a man walked quickly up to him and got into the car. It was one of the aides-de-camp.

'His Excellency desired to be called as soon as you arrived, Sir

Henry,' he said. 'He had a telephone message some hours ago, telling him you were on your way.'

Muir nodded and drove on.

'Things have been happening, haven't they?' asked the other curiously.

'Yes,' said the Secretary, shortly, 'they have!'

He pulled up outside one of the private entrances and turned to the aide-de-camp.

'Will you see that this car is garaged?' he said.

'Right ho!'

Muir had to be helped out of his seat and for some minutes he was unable to stand, but by dint of much rubbing and stamping the circulation was presently restored, and he proceeded to his own little study, and immediately sent a servant to inform the Viceroy of his arrival. Then he took off his coat, sank into an armchair and a great sigh escaped him. He was beginning to doze when the servant returned, and told him that His Excellency was awaiting him in his study, so pulling himself together, he went along the corridor and entered the room where the Viceroy in a dressing gown was pacing up and down, his hands behind his back.

Lord Oundle was a tall, thin, scholarly-looking man, with a slight stoop. His hair was turning grey at the temples and his eyebrows were almost white. Beneath them a pair of deep-set eyes looked out on the world with the troubled gaze of a man of great responsibilities, who would fain put them aside and devote himself to books. He had a long thin nose and sensitive nostrils and a mouth which was almost effeminate in its beauty. The chin suggested that, in spite of the slight weakness depicted in the rest of the face, he was a man who had strong willpower, and did not hesitate to use it.

The study was a large, lofty room with three long windows. The walls were almost covered by bookshelves in which works on India predominated. On the floor was a dark green dhurri, and various oriental rugs were dotted about. There were two or three comfortable-looking armchairs, a long cane chair, a Blackwood desk of Chinese workmanship crowded with books and papers, and an inlaid cabinet in a corner of the room containing various curios presented to the Viceroy on different occasions.

As Muir entered the room, Lord Oundle turned sharply and held out his hand, which the former grasped.

'Thank God, you have arrived safely,' said His Excellency. 'Did you have any trouble on the way?'

'None at all, sir,' replied Sir Henry, and smiled wanly as he added, 'except those conjured up by my own fancies.'

'You've come through remarkably quickly – who drove you?'

'I drove myself. The doctor at Barog lent me his car . . . You have heard what happened to poor Elliott, sir?'

'I know he was murdered, but I have no details. The Deputy Commissioner of Simla rang through, and has promised to do so again about nine.'

He noticed how tired the Secretary was.

'Sit down, Muir!' he said. 'You must be thoroughly worn out.'

Muir gladly did as he was bidden, but the Viceroy continued to walk up and down. There was silence for a minute or two, then Lord Oundle stopped in front of Sir Henry.

'How did it happen?' he asked.

Muir gave him an account of the whole affair from the time Elliott arrived at Simla till he was murdered. The Viceroy listened in silence until the end, then:

'You had no idea whatever that anybody had boarded the rail car, of course?' he said.

'None. Whoever it was took advantage of the light going out to jump on, stab Elliott, and get off again.'

'It almost looks as though the light was put out on purpose.'

'That's impossible, sir. It was undoubtedly a loose lamp which was shaken out of connection and jolted back again.'

'Strange – very strange. You don't suspect the driver of being a confederate?'

'Not in the least, and besides he couldn't possibly have caused the lamp to go out.'

'No, that's true. But it's a most mysterious affair. You have the plans quite safe?'

Muir took the case out of his pocket and handed it to the Viceroy. The latter held it in his hand and contemplated the seals.

'And this cost a good man his life,' he murmured.

'Poor Elliott!' said Sir Henry with an unwonted huskiness in his voice. 'He was looking forward to handing that over, and hoped to get away to England on leave. He spoke with enthusiasm of hunting last night – Last night! Good Lord! It seems like weeks ago.'

'It must do,' said Lord Oundle sympathetically. 'You had better get to bed, Muir, and have a rest. I'll put this in the safe till tomorrow morning. The Commander-in-Chief is coming to see me at ten, and I won't open the case till he is here.'

He crossed to one of the bookcases and touched a hidden spring. The large case immediately swung outwards like a door, and showed a safe hidden behind it. This the Viceroy opened and, having deposited the precious case inside, shut the door and caused the bookcase to swing back into position again. Muir rose from his chair.

'Have you had anything to eat tonight?' asked Lord Oundle suddenly.

'A few sandwiches, which the doctor pressed on me at Barog,' replied Sir Henry. 'But I don't want to eat. I simply want to lie down and go to sleep.'

'Well, go! I am deeply grateful to you for the good work you have done tonight, Muir.'

The other smiled deprecatingly and, bidding the Viceroy 'good night', stepped out of the room, and went along to his own quarters.

Lord Oundle continued to pace up and down his study for some time. His brow was wrinkled in thought and occasionally he clenched his hands. At last he switched out the lights and went back to his own bedroom.

In spite of his fatigue Muir did not sleep readily. His mind was full of the events of the last few hours. Elliott's murder cut him to the very depths of his being; he almost felt as though he were to blame. He remembered his repeated assertions that he would see the Major safely to Delhi, that he would watch over him like a guardian angel. He intended doing all he had promised, and yet he had failed, failed dismally. The plans had arrived safely it is true and in that particular he had succeeded, but Elliott's life had been sacrificed wantonly, needlessly, or at least so it seemed to him. Why, he continually asked himself, was Elliott stabbed, when the assailant, or the man who employed him, must have known that it would have been impossible to rob the dead man of the plans. Then he wondered if there could be any other reason for the murder: had the Major drawn on himself the enmity of someone who, in consequence, desired his death? But he put that thought away; an ordinary murderer would not take the risks this one had.

No, it must have been for the plans, and yet *he* had been allowed to get to Delhi without interruption, without any attempt being made to stop him, when the man, or party of men, who had the wit to conceive the assassination must have known that he, Muir, would carry on. It was inconceivable, fantastic! Try as he would he could find no solution, and at last, worn out in mind and body, he fell into a troubled sleep.

CHAPTER SEVEN

A Surprising Discovery

Lord Oundle was at work early the next morning, in spite of his night's rest having been disturbed. Seen by daylight he looked older, more worn. There were many lines on his face, and he appeared to be a man who had suffered and whose sufferings had left an indelible mark. And he had suffered. His two sons, of whom he had been inordinately proud, had fallen in the War, and he had never recovered from the shock.

He had filled several high positions of state, and had always done his duty meticulously, conscientiously, but he was a broken man. Now his private life was devoted to his wife and only daughter, a charming girl of twenty-three upon whom he lavished a great affection.

There was a little pile of papers before him as he sat at his desk, and he read them through carefully before appending his signature, and occasionally added notes in that small, geometrically correct handwriting, which was so well known in official circles. At eight o'clock he breakfasted with his wife. Their daughter had been to a ball the previous night and had not put in an appearance and Sir Henry Muir, who, apart from being the Viceroy's Secretary, was an old friend of the family, and usually took his meals with them, was still sleeping off the effects of his frantic drive from Barog.

Lady Oundle was a stately woman, a few years her husband's junior. The shock of the deaths of her two sons had turned her hair completely white, and she also, like the Viceroy, when her face was in repose wore a look of sorrow. She was still beautiful and was generally loved for her sweet womanliness, her kindness and the great charm of her manner.

She had heard of Major Elliott's tragic death and, though she had never met the sapper, she was full of enquiries and listened with great sympathy to her husband as he related to her all that had taken place.

At a quarter to nine His Excellency returned to his study, and, lighting a cigar, sat back in his chair and waited for the promised telephone call from Colonel Sanders. Sir Henry presently came in. He was his usual well-dressed, alert self, but there were great rings under his eyes to show what he had been through.

'And how are you this morning, Muir?' enquired Lord Oundle.

Sir Henry smiled.

'I haven't had much of a night,' he replied, 'but I feel just as fit as ever now.'

'You have not had breakfast yet, have you?'

'I'm ashamed to confess that I had it in bed!'

'There's nothing to be ashamed of in that. I think you had better take things very easily today.'

Sir Henry stiffened.

'There will be no ease for me, Your Excellency,' he said, 'until Elliott's murderer is discovered.'

Lord Oundle nodded.

'God grant that he will be found,' he said. 'I fear there is a lot behind this murder, Muir; probably a great deal more than we suspect.'

'It is horrible, dastardly!' said the Secretary. 'It seems to me that the poor fellow was murdered out of pure spite! They were baulked in their efforts to steal the plans, but in sheer devilry they assassinated him.'

'I wonder!'

Muir looked at the Viceroy in surprise, and was about to ask him what he meant, when the telephone bell rang. His Excellency drew the instrument to him, and held the receiver to his ear.

'The Deputy Commissioner of police, Simla, is asking to speak to Your Excellency,' announced the exchange clerk.

'Put him through!' said the Viceroy sharply.

A moment later he heard the tired voice of Colonel Sanders.

'I am speaking from Barog, Your Excellency. I spent a considerable time examining the tunnel with Hartley – who was in the train with Major Elliott – and another man. We found not the slightest trace of the murderer. I am having the surrounding country searched and all strangers brought in, but I'm afraid there is little hope in that direction. There was nothing in the rail car to give us the slightest clue.'

'Have you any suspicion that the driver was concerned in the affair?' asked the Viceroy.

'No, I think he is quite innocent. I have interrogated him about the failure of the light in the car, but he says that it can only have been due to a loose bulb. It occurred to me that he could have switched it off; the switch is placed in front of the driving-seat, but Captain Williams assures me that he couldn't possibly have done that without his seeing it.'

'H'm! If you could only find out what happened to the light you might—'

'If I could find that out, Your Excellency, I should know more about the murder.'

'You do not think the failure of the light was an accident then?'

'No – I feel certain it was connected with the outrage. I don't know how it was done, but I'll find out!'

'I wish you every success!'

'Thank you, sir. Did Sir Henry arrive safely?'

'Yes, and the plans are here.'

The Colonel's sigh of relief could be heard from the other end.

'That's good hearing,' he said. 'Sir Henry will be coming back to Barog for the inquest?'

'Oh, yes. When will it take place?'

'Tomorrow morning at ten o'clock, Your Excellency. There are several things I want to ask Sir Henry Muir, so I shall be glad if he can come back at once.'

'Very well, I'll speak to him. Have you any theories, Commissioner?'

'None at all, sir. The whole thing is a mystery at present. I'll let Your Excellency know if anything turns up.'

'Please do! I wish you to keep in touch with me daily.'

'Very well, sir.'

The Colonel rang off, and Lord Oundle put down the receiver.

'Nothing has transpired yet,' he said. 'You'll have to go back to Barog today, Muir; the inquest is at ten tomorrow morning, and the Deputy Commissioner has several questions he wants to ask you himself.'

'I'll go directly after tiffin, sir,' said Muir, 'if that is agreeable?'

'Quite! Quite! So, if I were you, I'd rest until then.'

'I'll wait until the Commander-in-Chief has gone, Your Excellency. You may require me!'

'No doubt I shall, but I'll manage without you, unless you would prefer to wait?'

'I would, sir.'

'Very well, then.'

Sir Henry Muir went into an inner room, which he used as an office, and he was busily engaged with some work there, when he heard voices in the other apartment, and presently the Viceroy appeared at the connecting door.

'You'd better come in, Muir,' he said. 'The Commander-in-Chief is here.'

Field-Marshal Sir Edward Willys was rather a small man with grey hair, bushy grey eyebrows, and a grey moustache. He had a hawk-like nose, fierce eyes, and a humorous mouth. Although small, he was as straight as a ramrod, and his whole air was of one used to command and expecting to be obeyed. His military record was a splendid one, and his achievements during the War were such that he now held one of the most important of military posts, at the comparatively early age of fifty.

He greeted Sir Henry with a smile.

'By Jove!' he said. 'You seem to have got mixed up in a mysterious affair, Muir. But I hear you brought those plans through safely. I must congratulate you!'

'Thanks, Sir Edward,' said Muir, 'but I failed to save Elliott from being murdered.'

'Not your fault!' said the Commander-in-Chief. He always spoke in a staccato manner, almost like a machine-gun in action. 'Dastardly business!' he went on. 'I'd like to know who the assassins were.'

'So would a good many of us,' said the Viceroy. 'The Russian Bolsheviks are behind them I'm afraid.'

Sir Edward snorted.

'Nonsense!' he said rudely. 'An ordinary murder! Probably Elliott got somebody's back up and so they, or he, removed him.'

'I don't agree with you, sir!' said Muir. 'I feel certain that whoever murdered Elliott was after the plans.'

'Well, why didn't they get them?'

Sir Henry shrugged his shoulders.

'God knows.'

'The Deputy Commissioner of Simla has the matter in hand,' said the Viceroy, 'and we must hope for results from him.'

The Commander-in-Chief nodded.

'No doubt he'll find the murderer,' he said. 'A cute fellow, Sanders . . . Well, shall we have a look at these plans?'

Lord Oundle went to the safe, opened it, and took out the case, which he laid on his desk before locking up the safe again. The Field-Marshal took the case into his hands and turned it over two or three times.

'By Gad!' he said, 'Elliott sealed it enough. He seems to have had a pretty humour in sealing-wax, poor fellow.'

He handed it back to the Viceroy, who at once broke the seals and opened the case. Inside were three folded pieces of parchment. His Excellency spread them out on his desk, both Sir Edward Willys and Muir leaning over to see them. Then a great shout escaped from the soldier; Sir Henry staggered back as though he had been struck, and the Viceroy sank into his chair, his face the colour of chalk.

Each document was blank!

For some seconds the three men stared at each other in utter silence. The room seemed to have become ominously quiet; only the ticking of the great clock upon the mantelshelf could be heard and to Muir's excited imagination it appeared to be repeating, 'No plans! No plans!! No plans!!!'

At last the Commander-in-Chief shook himself as though pulling himself together after a dream.

'Somebody has rifled your safe,' he said sharply to Lord Oundle.

'Impossible!' replied the Viceroy huskily; 'besides the seals were intact, as you know!'

'Then the original case was stolen, and this one substituted for it. Muir, from the time you took the case from Elliott's pocket until you handed it to His Excellency, did you let it out of your possession?'

'No,' replied Sir Henry. 'It was buttoned inside the breast pocket of my coat, and I did not stop, except for a few minutes at Kalka when I told my bearer to go by train, and then I kept my hand over it all the time. Without the slightest doubt this is the case that I took from Elliott.'

'Then the murderer must have robbed him when he killed him!'

'Utterly impossible!' exclaimed the Secretary, almost peevishly. 'I tell you the light was only out for a couple of minutes, hardly time for the fellow to jump on the train, stab the Major, and jump off again, let alone rob him; and his clothes were not deranged in the slightest.'

Again there was silence. The Viceroy aimlessly looked inside the case and turned the papers over. Presently he spoke:

'Perhaps Elliott was robbed, and this case substituted before he reached Simla,' he said.

'He wouldn't have been assassinated then,' said the Field-

Marshal, 'unless, as I said, the murder was some private vengeance.'

'Oh, that's inconceivable, ridiculous!' exclaimed Sir Henry. He hit his forehead with his clenched fist in an agony of despair. 'If only I could see light!' he groaned.

'I don't think anything will help us now,' said the Viceroy hopelessly. 'The plans are probably well on their way to the frontier by this, if they haven't already been taken across!'

The Commander-in-Chief hit the desk a blow with his hand.

'They won't get across if I can prevent it,' he said. 'I'm going to give orders for the whole frontier to be patrolled right down to Baluchistan, and have everyone searched who passes, even if I bring Afghanistan buzzing round our ears. Have I your sanction?' he asked, turning somewhat belatedly to the Viceroy.

The latter nodded.

'Then I'll go and see about it at once.'

'Supposing they try to carry the documents over by aeroplane?' questioned Muir.

'I'm glad you thought of that,' said Sir Edward. 'I'll put the Air Force on the *qui vive* with orders to bring down any plane they see attempting to get across!'

'Rather drastic, isn't it?' said Lord Oundle doubtfully.

'Drastic ills require drastic remedies!' replied the other sententiously. 'Well, I'll be off!'

'Just a minute, sir,' said Sir Henry. 'This is all very well as far as it goes. But what if the stolen plans are not taken across the frontier at all?'

'No doubt you'll see to it that the police are put on the search,' snapped the Commander-in-Chief. 'That's your pidgin, not mine!'

'I've a great admiration for the police, and we shall see to it that they get busy at once,' said the Viceroy, 'but this seems to me to require a specialist in matters of this sort.'

'But there isn't a proper Intelligence Department out here, so the police will have to do the best they can!'

'Those plans must be recovered, and the murderers brought to justice,' said Sir Henry. Then suddenly his whole face lit up, and his eyes sparkled.

'By Jove! The very man!' he almost shouted.

The others looked at him questioningly.

'Why not cable to the India Office, sir,' he said to the Viceroy excitedly, 'and ask them to send Sir Leonard Wallace. He's a great friend of yours, too!'

'That's an idea!' said His Excellency brightening considerably. He turned to the Commander-in-Chief.

'You know him of course; he's the head of the Intelligence Department and has done some remarkable work.'

'Of course I know him; married old Kendal's daughter and ferreted out that German submarine base in Dorset during the War – used to be in the Hussars!'

'That's the man!' said Lord Oundle. 'He is now head of the Intelligence Department, and has done some wonderfully clever work.'

Sir Edward looked exasperated.

'I know all that,' he said, 'but every minute is precious, and he is six thousand miles away!'

'He can come over by air,' said Muir quickly. 'He'd be here in five or six days, perhaps not too late, and if anybody can get to the bottom of this business he can!'

'Yes, he can fly over,' said the Viceroy. 'I think I'll cable. What do you say, Willys?'

'Do so by all means. Every effort must be made to recover those documents. And now I must not stay a moment longer – I've already lost a lot of precious time.'

He took up his topee, shook hands with the Viceroy, nodded to Muir, and walked out of the room with such a martial air that one could almost hear the clank of spurs!

CHAPTER EIGHT

The Inquest

The cablegram, a very lengthy one in code, was sent to the India Office soon after the Commander-in-Chief left the Lodge. It asked urgently that Sir Leonard Wallace should be sent to India by air, in order to unravel the mystery of the disappearance of very important plans. It further pleaded for haste and secrecy.

After the cablegram had been sent, Sir Henry Muir partook of an early tiffin and then set out again for Barog. He went back in the same car that had brought him to Delhi, but this time he had a driver with him, and he himself took his ease in the tonneau. There was no furious driving now, but no time was lost en route and it had just turned eight o'clock when the doctor's house at Barog was reached.

The doctor was sitting on the veranda as Sir Henry drove up, and he looked very much surprised when he saw the Secretary.

'I thought the car might turn up today,' he said, 'but I hardly expected you back so soon.'

'No, I was not expecting it myself,' replied Muir, 'but Colonel

Sanders seemed to desire my presence here as soon as possible, so I came back in the car which proved such a blessing last night.'

He reiterated his thanks for the loan of the Fiat and told the other something of his race to Delhi.

'I think my average speed must have been over forty,' he concluded, 'and the car never jibbed once.'

'She's a good old bus,' said the doctor, 'I'm glad she served you so well.'

'What is the news?' asked Sir Henry. 'I hardly dare hope that the murderer has been found.'

The doctor shook his head

'I know very little of course,' he said, 'but I don't think there is the slightest clue. Colonel Sanders has been very busy with two other men all day long, and from the expression on his face I should say that he is one of the most puzzled men in India at the present moment. He doesn't say much, anyway!'

Muir smiled.

'No, he's not exactly communicative,' he said, then sighed. 'The whole business is horrible, mysterious and uncanny.'

'You'll put up here for the night, of course?'

'Well, that's very good of you, but I—'

'I wouldn't think of your going anywhere else. The Commissioner is going to stop here. As a matter of fact I was waiting for him to come in to dinner when you arrived.'

'Thanks; then I will. Could I have a hasty bath? I'm a bit grimy.'

'Of course!'

The doctor called a servant and gave orders.

'Don't bother to dress!' he said.

'I couldn't if I would,' replied Muir. 'I've only got this kit with me!'

He had his bath and rapidly dressed himself again, and then returned to the doctor who was still on the veranda.

'We won't wait any longer for the Colonel,' said the latter. 'He might be very late.'

They entered the dining room together, and had just started the soup, when the Deputy Commissioner walked in. He did not show the slightest sign of surprise when he saw Sir Henry.

'Hullo, Muir,' he said. 'Glad you've arrived.'

He sat down and attacked his soup with the air of a man for whom this life has very few pleasures.

'Have you made any discoveries, Colonel?' asked Sir Henry.

'Not one. I've never been so baffled in my life. Why Elliott was murdered, I don't know, and I don't suppose anyone ever will know. I've put the driver of the rail motor under arrest on suspicion, but—' He shrugged his shoulders.

'What has the driver got to do with it?'

'There's a possibility that he may have switched the light off. Williams swears that he couldn't have done so, but I'm taking no chances. He's a badly frightened man, and personally I don't think he had anything to do with it, but if he had he'll talk, so I'm keeping him locked up for a couple of days, then, if nothing happens, I'll let him go – without a stain on his character!'

'Perhaps the railway company won't reinstate him, and then—'

'Oh yes, they will! I'll see to that!'

'I suppose the inquest is not likely to bring anything to light?' said the doctor.

'Nothing at all,' replied the Commissioner. 'It will be a mere formality. Your evidence is clear enough, doctor; there's no doubt about Elliott being murdered, and as we haven't found the murderer the verdict will be the usual. Oh, dash it all!' he added irritably. 'Why on earth isn't there a clue of some sort? Even the knife it was done with might help a bit, if we could find it.'

There was silence for a time.

'Where will Elliott be buried?' asked Muir presently.

'In Simla the day after tomorrow,' replied the Colonel. 'His body will be taken up tomorrow afternoon. Poor fellow, what a beastly finish! Thank God you got those plans through, Muir – Why, what's the matter with you?'

'Oh, nothing,' said Muir hastily, giving the Commissioner a look full of meaning.

'I – I suppose the remembrance of my drive last night is still too recent to be pleasant.'

'I never expected you to get to Delhi,' grunted Sanders. 'I fully anticipated that the Viceroy would tell me you were missing when I rang up this morning. Did you have any trouble at all?'

'Not the slightest!'

'Strange!'

Conversation then became very desultory until the end of dinner, when the doctor stood up.

'Well, gentlemen,' he said, 'I've a patient to see, so I will leave you for a while. No doubt you have a lot to talk over. Help yourselves to drinks and cigars and make yourselves at home!'

He nodded and went out.

'Sensible man that,' grunted Sanders. He took a cigar and carefully lit it. 'Now, Muir,' he said. 'You have some news for me – what is it?'

Sir Henry looked the Colonel straight in the face. 'The plans have disappeared,' he said.

'What!' shouted Sanders. 'Do you really mean that?'

Muir nodded, and proceeded to give an account of the discovery that morning in the Viceroy's study. The Commissioner heard him to the end without interruption, and for once the bored look had gone from his face.

'It's incredible!' he exclaimed at last. 'Absolutely incredible! Then the documents *must* have been stolen when Elliott was murdered!'

'How could they have been?'

'God knows! You say that the case was in your pocket from the time you left here until you reached Delhi and you never stopped after Kalka! Then by some means they were taken from Elliott; but how? How? How?'

He put his head between his hands for a moment or two, and then stood up and walked about the room.

'There were a few things I wanted to ask you,' he said, 'but this has taken the wind out of my sails completely, and they'll have to wait . . . What is the Viceroy going to do about it?'

'He has cabled to the India Office, and asked them to get hold of Sir Leonard Wallace and send him out.'

The Commissioner stopped and stared at Sir Henry. 'Who the devil is Sir Leonard Wallace?' he demanded.

'You know surely – The Chief of the Intelligence Department—'

'Oh, yes, I've heard of him – He's the fellow they made such a fuss about over some German spies during the War, isn't he?'

Muir smiled and nodded.

'I think the fuss was deserved,' he remarked. 'At any rate he removed a very big menace to England's safety, and he has done a lot of good work since he was put in charge of the Intelligence Department.'

'Friend of yours, I see,' sneered the Colonel. He sat down suddenly. 'And so the Viceroy doesn't think the police of this country are capable enough for this affair, and sends for a picturesque, out-of-a-novel sort of detective to supersede me.'

Sir Henry felt annoyed, and he looked it.

'I'm surprised at your taking such a childish attitude, Colonel Sanders,' he said. 'Sir Leonard Wallace is a specialist in this sort of thing, as his reputation proves. He is coming out entirely to discover, if possible, what has become of the plans and, I hope, to get them back. Who committed the murder has nothing to do with him, except in so far as it is connected with the disappearance of the documents – that is yours, the police's, side of the case. If he assists you to discover the murderer, you should be grateful, I think. I do not understand this resentful attitude of yours!'

Sanders stared at Muir for a moment, and looked as though he were verbally about to pulverise him, but thought better of it, then:

'It will be much too late anyhow by the time he arrives in India. If, as we suspect, the Russians have Elliott's plans, then they are well on their way to the frontier by now.'

'They can't get across!' replied Muir, almost in triumph. 'The whole of the frontier has been closed by order of Sir Edward Willys, and nobody can cross without being searched, while the Air Force has orders to keep watch, and to bring down any suspicious aeroplane that attempts to get over. As for Sir Leonard Wallace, he will travel out from England by air as fast as a plane can carry him.'

'H'm!' murmured the Colonel grudgingly. 'You haven't let the grass grow under your feet in Delhi apparently.'

'I don't think that can ever be laid to our charge,' retorted Muir.

'Well, let us hope that Wallace will not come out on a wild goose chase! He's got the job of his life before him!'

'Of course you will give him every assistance, Colonel?'

'Oh, I suppose so!' He said ungraciously. 'But if he can do any more than the Indian Police, I'll eat my hat!'

'Hasty words,' smiled Muir, who had by now fully recovered his good humour. 'Remember you are dealing with the most brilliant brain in England in his particular line, and you may be called upon to eat that hat after all!'

'India isn't England,' snapped Sanders; 'and he'll find everything against him out here.'

'Oh well, he knows India pretty well, so we'll wait and see, to use a platitude . . . By the way, where is Williams?'

'In Simla! He went up this morning and will be back in time for the inquest tomorrow. Did you remember to communicate with his C.O.? He told me you were going to do so!'

'Yes – I left instructions for one of the secretaries to get through and arrange matters.'

The next morning the inquest went very much as the Deputy Commissioner had prophesied. Care was taken that no mention of the plans should be made and to the ordinary mind it appeared as though the murder was motiveless. Sir Henry told how the light had gone out, and that after it relit again and the car had left the tunnel, he turned to make some remark to Major Elliott, and discovered that he was dead; how he had ordered the rail motor to stop and had drawn the attention of Captain Williams and Mr Hartley to the dead man. Hartley described how he had clambered over the back of the seat and found the wound between the shoulder blades, obviously made by a thin-bladed knife. Captain Williams corroborated the testimony of the other two. All three witnesses agreed that the failure of the light must have been due to a loose lamp that had been jolted off and on again, and all agreed that the murderer had been waiting his opportunity in the tunnel, and had taken advantage of the mishap to the lighting to do his evil work and escape. The driver of the car, who was in a state of abject terror and almost wept as he gave his evidence, declared that the failure of a lamp through jolting was quite a common occurrence; and when sternly asked by the Coroner if he had touched the switch, swore by all the gods that he had not done so.

The doctor stated that he had been called in to examine the murdered man, who was lying in a room at Barog station, whither he had been carried from the rail motor, and found that he had been stabbed in the back between the shoulder blades, and that the blow was driven downwards, obviously by someone standing behind Major Elliott, with such force that it had pierced the heart, and death must have been instantaneous. The Coroner asked several pertinent questions and summed up the case very lucidly. The jury, without retiring, brought in a verdict that 'Major Elliott had been done to death by some person or persons unknown.'

As Colonel Sanders and Sir Henry Muir left the building in which the inquest had been held, the former looked very glum.

'I wish to Goodness you had gone down in a private car, as I advised,' he grunted.

'I wish we had, Colonel,' said Muir. 'But it's too late wishing now. I feel morally responsible for Elliott's death.'

'Don't be a fool!' said the Commissioner brusquely. 'Elliott himself was not any keener than you to go that way. Well, I suppose I had better let that driver go. You three make it impossible to hold him any longer.'

'Why?'

'Oh, with your damnable shaky lamp evidence.'

'Then you still think that the light was interfered with?'

'I do! But I'm hanged if I know how. I'm going through that

rail motor inch by inch, even if I have to pull it to pieces, to see if I can find out why the light went out. There's one thing I am convinced about.'

'And that is?'

'The murderer did not board the train in the tunnel, but was in the car all the time, hidden on the floor behind you and Elliott!'

'Great Scott! . . . And how does that theory help?'

It doesn't!' snapped the Colonel. He held out his hand. 'Well, goodbye, Muir, there's no reason for you to stop up here – you'll know how things go from the Viceroy.'

He shook hands and turned away, then swung back again.

'And – er – Muir,' he said. 'I shall be glad when the most brilliant brain in England arrives in India!' He smiled faintly and was gone.

After bidding farewell to Captain Williams – who was returning at once to his regiment – and to the doctor, Muir drove back to Delhi. He arrived there a very tired man and went to bed early that night with the intention of having at least ten hours' sleep, and he went with a feeling of great hope, for on his arrival the Viceroy had shown him a cablegram from the India Office, and it read:

Sir Leonard Wallace left early this afternoon for India by aeroplane. Hopes to arrive within five days! – DALSTON.

CHAPTER NINE

Sir Leonard Wallace

A luxurious car skirted the traffic in Trafalgar Square, swung along the Mall and up St James's Street, and presently stopped in front of an imposing mansion in Piccadilly. The door opened and a slightly built man of middle height alighted and held out his hand to assist a woman. The man gave the chauffeur some instructions and then followed his companion up the steps of the house. The door was opened by a solemn, elderly butler whose every movement bespoke dignity and importance; his white side-whiskers whispered of responsibility, and his bow was the very epitome of what a butler's bow should be. The woman, she seemed little more than a girl, smiled and passed in. The man, more leisurely, stood at the door for a moment and gazed appreciatively across the Park where the trees, in all the glory of their autumn tints, gave a warm sense of colour to their surroundings. Then he turned and walked quietly inside.

'There are many worse places than London, Sims,' he said, as he handed his coat and hat to the butler.

'Don't you think so?'

'I do indeed, Sir Leonard,' replied the man in a deep sepulchral voice.

'H'm! And I suppose the body is still upstairs?' imitating the solemn voice.

'Body, sir! What body?' A slight twitch of the left eyebrow was the only indication of surprise Sims permitted himself.

'The same old body! I've often wondered when you are going to bury it.'

The butler had by this time grasped the point, and he bowed, if possible, more deeply than ever. Sir Leonard strolled along the wide, beautifully panelled hall, and stopped by a great fireplace where a fire blazed merrily away.

'By Jove! You don't seem to be worried by coal strikes, Sims,' he remarked. 'There seems no shortage of coal in this house.'

'Certainly not, sir! I hope I always do my duty!'

'In spite of miners and the dole and Russian money and all the rest of it, eh?'

Again the butler bowed.

'You're a paragon, Sims. I wish you weren't sometimes. I suppose you were human once?'

'Sir?'

'I said, "I suppose you were human once". Yes, you were! Do you remember keeping wicket during a certain famous cricket match at Kimmeridge years ago?'

Sims actually smiled – it was a fleeting sort of a smile, but still a smile for all that.

'I have never forgotten that match, Sir Leonard, nor, if I may be allowed to say so, the exciting events that took place about that time.'

'No, I suppose not – neither have I!' He looked rather ruefully at his left arm, which to the ordinary gaze appeared quite normal except for the glove which he wore on the hand and which was seldom removed. But that arm was an artificial one! He had lost it through the exciting events mentioned by the butler. Coming home from France with a badly wounded arm, he had spent a holiday on the coast of Dorset whilst convalescing, and there, with the aid of some friends and, later on, under the auspices of the Home Office, discovered a German submarine base and the headquarters of a number of spies. Four submarines and practically all the spies had been captured, and it was when Sir Leonard and his assistants had cornered the chief of the German secret agents that he was again shot in the arm, as a consequence of which it had to be amputated.

Great excitement had been caused throughout the country by the capture. Honours were showered on Sir Leonard, who was then plain Major, and his companions, the chief of whom was his great friend Major, then Captain, William Brien. The two of them had been cavalry officers, but as a result of their work they were attached to the Intelligence Department and now several years after the War, Sir Leonard was head of the Department and held undisputed sway, with Major Brien as his second in command.

Dressed in the most fastidious taste, Sir Leonard looked the picture of indolent ease as he lounged in front of the great fire. By no means handsome, he possessed a most attractive face, with humorous curves, which the majority of people found irresistible.

He never got excited, was seldom known to lose his temper, had the most easy-going disposition in the world, and, to quote Major Brien, 'would probably light his pipe and take his ease if the end of the world had come.' His utter nonchalance exasperated some people, but offended none.

He took out a pipe now and cleverly using his artificial hand filled and lighted it.

'This old limb's almost as useful as the real one was, Sims,' he remarked. 'Anyhow we don't miss it much, do we!'

The old servitor shook his head sorrowfully.

'It was a very sad business, Sir Leonard,' he said. 'Very sad indeed I—'

'Oh, go away, you old croaker! By the way where did Lady Wallace go?'

'Up to her boudoir, I believe, Sir Leonard.'

The other nodded, and Sims turned, and crossing the wide hall as silently as a ghost, disappeared through a green baize door at the end, which obviously led to his pantry and the other domestic rooms.

Sir Leonard strolled up the wide carpeted stairs. Halfway up he stared reflectively at a beautiful stained glass window, whereon were pictured stirring events, in the life of St George, who had a penchant apparently for destroying dragons.

'St George,' murmured Wallace *sotto voce*, 'yours was a pretty straightforward sort of job – there's nothing very subtle about a dragon.'

He smiled whimsically and continued his easy way to his wife's boudoir, where he knocked gently on the door. A sweet voice bade him come in and he entered. A dazzling picture of smiling womanhood looked up at him.

Lady Wallace was just thirty and looked no more than twenty-three or four. She had the clear complexion of a young girl, glorious hair of a rich chestnut colour, which fell in natural waves round her head, big, deep, blue eyes, a slightly tip-tilted nose and a cupid's bow mouth, with scarlet lips which put the finishing touch to one of the most beautiful faces in London. And with all her beauty Lady Wallace was clever, sweet and charming, and she was as popular with her own sex as she was with her men friends. She adored her husband, as he adored her, and they were consequently an ideally happy pair, who jointly worshipped their small son Adrian, a merry little fellow of six.

She was seated now, resting, in a deep armchair in front of the fire. Her room was a perfect setting for such a woman. The predominant note was blue and silver. The walls were a pale blue, the carpet a slightly darker shade. Curtains of pale blue and silver hung before the windows and doors. The tables were Sheraton, upon which the ornaments were, in the majority of cases, silver. A few priceless etchings hung on the walls and a couple of beautiful Persian rugs lay on the floor.

She laid her head back in her chair and smiled at her husband.

'Why the knock, dear?' she asked.

'I have just been looking at St George,' replied Sir Leonard, and seated himself opposite her in the other armchair.

'What has St George got to do with it?'

'He was a gentleman!'

She laughed.

'That window seems to have a peculiar fascination for you, Leonard,' she said. 'I've often caught you staring at it.'

'It has! By the way St George didn't smoke! Do you mind my smoking in here?'

She laughed again, a silvery peal that was much admired by the maids, who all tried to copy it.

'Have you made up your mind to imitate the Saint?'

'Oh, no! He was a woman hater, and I'm not.'

She stared at him amusedly.

'St George a woman hater! That's the first I've heard of it.'

'Well, a certain type of woman. He was always killing dragons!'

'Oh, Leonard! And at your time of life? You should be ashamed of yourself.'

'What do you mean by my time of life? You'll be telling me I want a bath-chair next. Let me see, how old am I?'

'Thirty-four!'

'Good gracious! I thought I was ageing fast. It's very ancient, isn't it?'

'Very!' she smiled. 'You'll be thinking of retiring soon, dear, I suppose.' Then she looked serious. 'I almost wish you would,' she added.

He looked surprised.

'Why?'

'Well you know the horrible risks you run sometimes! Think of that affair in Egypt when—' She shuddered.

He smiled.

'That sort of thing doesn't happen very often, Molly dear,' he said. 'As a rule I sit in a large office like a staid, respectable business man and give orders.'

'Yes, but there are the other times and – I hate them!' She spoke vehemently. 'It's very wonderful to think that you are the head of the Secret Service, and at your age, but—'

'Please don't call it the Secret Service – Intelligence Department is so much nicer, and it does suggest that one has brains whether one really has or not!'

'Well, Intelligence Department then! But I'm always afraid

when you go away on something yourself, in case there is – an accident.'

He stood up, crossed to her chair and kissed her tenderly.

'Bless you,' he said. 'You're a wife in a million. But get rid of those worries, dear; I seldom go into danger.'

'I know you,' she replied. 'Oh, I know you so well.'

At that moment the door burst open and a small boy, with sparkling blue eyes, rosy cheeks and brown curly hair, ran into the room. He held a toy pistol, and pointed it at his father, and in a belt were two toy swords, while he wore a three-cornered hat upon his head.

'Hands up!' he cried. 'I am a wicked, bad pirate!'

In a simulation of terror Sir Leonard dropped on his knees by his wife's chair. He held his hands above his head and shivered.

'Don't shoot, sir,' he pleaded. 'I'm only a poor sailor man.' He looked sideways at his wife. 'I was never in greater danger than this, Molly,' he added. 'Just look at the bloodthirsty look in that villain's eye. He'll make me walk the plank; I know he will!'

With a shriek of delight the child jumped on his father, and for some minutes the two rolled on the floor to the imminent danger of several articles of furniture close by. At last Sir Leonard sat up, and perched the child on his knee.

'Now, my lad!' he said. 'The wicked, bad pirate is dead.'

'Oh no, he isn't,' said the boy. 'I'll show you, shall I?'

'Not just now! Attendez, monsieur!'

'What does that mean, Daddy?'

'Your attention, sir, if you please!'

'Is this another game?'

'Not yet! I want to know what you have been doing all the afternoon!'

'I've been in the Park with Alice, of course,' said the little fellow with disgust. 'It's not fair to a chap to let him out with a woman like that; she's got no go in her!'

His mother and father laughed delightedly.

'It's all very well to laugh,' he went on, and they laughed the more, then he brightened up. 'I met Uncle Billy and Auntie Phyllis,' he said.

'Where, dear?' asked Lady Wallace.

'Near the bandstand, Mummy – but there wasn't any band.'

'No, dear, not at this time of the year. Was Auntie Phyllis glad to see you?'

'Of course, she always is. Although she's got quite enough children of her own,' he added reflectively.

Sir Leonard laughed heartily.

'By Jove!' he said. 'I must tell Billy that,' and he went into another roar of laughter. The boy rose to his feet.

'I s'pose I must go and have tea,' he said, 'or Alice will be cross. She's very difficult that woman. If I was you, Mummy—'

'"Were", dear, not "was".'

'If I were you, Mummy, I wouldn't be afraid of her! I'd show her that I was – were – was mistress and tell her to go!'

With this parthian shot he went out of the room followed by a further burst of laughter from his parents. He was back in a minute looking eagerly at Sir Leonard.

'Daddy,' he said, 'when I've had my tea, will you come to the den and play pirates with me?' He always called his nursery 'the den', in imitation of his father's name for the study.

Sir Leonard nodded, and the child ran off with a happy laugh.

'I loved that bit about Phyllis having enough children of her own, didn't you?' said Lady Wallace.

'Rather! It was delightful! I mustn't forget to tell Billy that tomorrow. Adrian's quite right you know, dear. I think three in seven years is pretty good going!'

'Leonard!'

He laughed.

'Well, we've had one child in twelve years and he's had three in seven. Billy apparently thinks it is time something was done to improve the birth rate!'

'Oh, Leonard, how awful you are!'

There was silence for a moment. She gazed into the fire and he looked at her, devotedly, proudly, noting the warm beauty of her, the slender lines of her graceful figure, silently thanking his Creator for giving into his care such a glorious example of perfect womanhood, and wondering as he always wondered in the humility of his great heart, why she was his. Presently she turned to him, a little shyly, and put her hands into his.

'Leonard,' she said, 'it wouldn't seem fair to Adrian, if – if we had another child. He has always been just the one, hasn't he?'

He nodded, watching her face the while.

'And yet,' she continued, 'it might be good for him, if – if he had a little brother or sister, to look after.'

'I agree with you, dear.'

There was another silence. She put her head on his shoulder, and smoothed his cheek with her hand, then:

'I would love to have a little daughter – some day,' she whispered.

He took her into his arms and kissed her.

CHAPTER TEN

At the India Office

Sir Leonard Wallace walked into his office at ten o'clock the next morning, and found a pile of reports and correspondence awaiting him. He stood at the door and gazed at the collected heap of literature on his desk, and softly whistled to himself.

It was a comfortable office this. Two large windows looked out on to Whitehall. A cosy fireplace, in which a fire burnt brightly, was on one side of the room, with cupboards full of stationery on either side of it. On the opposite side were bookshelves which reached to the ceiling, and contained nearly every book of reference in existence as well as statistical reports from Scotland Yard, the Foreign Office, the Home Office, the India Office, the Colonial Office, and all the other Government departments. A carpet covered the floor, and a warm-looking rug lay in front of the fireplace, before which stood a rather ugly brass fender.

The large oak desk was placed almost in the centre of the room, with a padded swing chair behind it. Three other restful chairs stood in geometrically opposite corners.

Sir Leonard put his hat and coat in an alcove, and seating himself at his desk, looked thoughtfully at the pile before him. Then he rang a bell.

'Has Major Brien arrived?' he enquired of the clerk who entered.

'Yes, sir!'

'Then request him to be good enough to come in!'

'Very well, sir.'

The clerk went out, and a minute later the door opened and a tall, fair-haired man, with twinkling blue eyes and a small military moustache, dressed in the most correct morning garb, entered.

'Good morning, Leonard!' he nodded.

'Morning, Bill! Take a seat somewhere and have a cigarette.'

Major Brien looked at the other with suspicion.

'Why the palaver,' he asked, taking a cigarette from a box on the desk, and stationing himself with his back to the fire.

'What do you mean?'

'Why so polite? I generally do take a seat or help myself to a cigarette if I want one, don't I?'

Sir Leonard smiled.

'Yes, you always were an undisciplined sort of blighter.'

The other grunted.

'Have you any work to do this morning?' went on Wallace.

'Why?'

'Good Lord! Don't answer a question by asking one!'

'Well, you wouldn't ask unless there was something on!'

'True!' He stood up, picked up the pile of documents on his desk and, crossing to Brien, put them in his arms. The latter took them mechanically.

'What on earth—?' he began.

'That's just a little to go on with. You see Molly is coming here at eleven-thirty, and I'm going out with her, so I thought I'd better hand that little lot to you.'

'Thanks for nothing!' He put the collection down on a chair. 'If I'd known that was all you wanted me for, I would have been out, or dead, or something.'

'I knew you were in, because I saw Phyllis driving off in the sewing machine just as I arrived.'

The sewing machine was Wallace's unkind name for Brien's little two-seater.

'Well, I'll have a look at these,' said the latter, nodding at the papers on the chair, 'but I'll pay you out by making copious notes for your reference on each report!'

'Don't you dare!'

'I will! By the way a letter has come through from the Foreign Office, suggesting that for the future all King's Messengers should be detailed for duty direct from this department.'

'Oh, blow old Ainsley! He will persist in thinking that we belong entirely to him, and I'm always telling him he has no more right to us than any other department of state. We're a self-contained show and I don't want his King's Messengers.'

'Well, tell him so!'

'Bless you, I will.'

There was a knock on the door, and the clerk entered. He crossed the room and placed a visiting-card in front of Wallace, who by this time had resumed his seat.

'There's a gentleman to see you, sir,' he said.

'Has he an appointment?'

'I believe not, sir.'

'Then tell him that, I never—' He glanced at the card, and a look of interest came over his face. 'Oh, well, show him in!' he said.

The clerk went out and he handed the card to Brien.

'William C. Caxton,' the latter read. 'Isn't that the fellow who was American attaché in Russia, and wrote a series of articles for *The Times* on the Russian menace to India?'

'He is!'

'What do you want to see him for?'

'Partially because his articles interested me, and partially because of my curiosity to know why he has called.'

The door opened, and the clerk ushered in a tall, thin man, whose rugged features gave his face an air of strength. He wore a tweed suit of a slightly loud pattern, a turned-down collar and a bow tie.

He bowed slightly, and smiled at Sir Leonard.

'Sir Leonard Wallace, I believe,' he said with a strong American accent. Wallace waved his arm towards a chair.

'Sit down, Mr Caxton,' he said, 'and tell us what brought you to this extremely musty department.'

'Well, I don't know that it's musty, Sir Leonard,' smiled the American. 'You sure have a snug office here.'

'That is a blind!'

Mr Caxton appeared amused.

'It's real kind of you to see me – I understand from your clerk and the janitor that you never see people without appointment, except in a very few cases.'

'This is one of the few. I was interested to know why you came.'

'Then you have heard of me?' asked the American.

'It is our business to hear of people, and besides you can't break out into print in *The Times* without being noticed.'

'Well, I guess not. Say I'd better cut the cackle and get down to facts,' he added briskly. 'I have just got back from India where I have been touring around looking for signs of the Bolshevik menace I wrote about, in the country itself. Of course it is none of my business, but I've got a genuine love for the old country and I'm interested – Do you get me?'

Wallace nodded. Caxton leant forward impressively.

'I found signs of quite a lot of Russian propaganda work, and more by luck than by good judgment located three houses which seem to be the meeting place for Russians who are travelling about the country ostensibly as agents for merchant firms, but really to distribute pamphlets and stir up the people against Britain.'

Sir Leonard no longer toyed abstractedly with his pen. He wore an alert, businesslike air. Major Brien was also watching the American intently, and listening to every word he said with great interest.

'How did you discover this, Mr Caxton?' asked Wallace.

'I found out a lot in Russia; but when in India I made myself genial with two Indians who were employed as typists in one of the houses in question – they didn't know much but what they told me was significant, and I put two and two together. The rest I ferreted out for myself.'

'You'd be useful in this department,' remarked Brien.

Caxton smiled.

'Where are these houses?' questioned Sir Leonard.

'One is in Lahore; one in Delhi, and the other in Karachi.'

'Karachi seems an out-of-the-way place for a meeting house. Now would you mind telling me why you did not inform the Indian police?'

The other shrugged his shoulders.

'I'm an American and it occurred to me that if I went to the police they would only laugh at me and tell me to mind my own business. Then I had heard from several quarters of the state of efficiency of the British Intelligence Service and knowing that India did not possess a like department, or, if it did, a very unknown and doubtful one, I decided to take ship at once and report my discoveries to you.'

'I'm very much obliged to you, Mr Caxton, for your trouble. Can you give me the actual addresses of these three houses?'

'I can, sir. I have written them on this slip of paper for you.' He handed a sheet of notepaper to Sir Leonard.

'By Jove!' exclaimed the latter. 'You're certainly thorough. You're the sort of man I like to meet!'

The American smiled and rose.

'If I can be of any further assistance—' he began, when the telephone bell rang.

'Excuse me a moment!' said Wallace, and placed the receiver to his ear. 'Hullo!' he said, 'Colonel Wallace speaking!'

'Hold the line a moment, sir,' replied a voice. 'The India Office is on the phone!'

Wallace smiled across at Caxton.

'Talk of coincidences,' he said. 'It's a call from the India Office!'

'Well, that's mighty strange!' exclaimed the American.

Another voice came across the wire.

'Hullo! Is that Wallace?'

'It is!'

'This is Fellowes!'

'Yes, I know. One can't very well mistake your husky voice, Fellowes. Well, what's the matter? Lost one of your stamped envelopes?'

'It's too early in the morning to be facetious. I say, can you come round at once?'

'Why?'

'Lord Dalston wants to see you urgently. We have received a cable from the Viceroy. It is very important! Come now if you can!'

'Right-ho!'

Wallace put down the receiver and looked across at the others.

'We seem to be getting mixed up in Indian affairs,' he said.

'What's the trouble?' asked Brien.

'Can't tell you yet – I'm going down to the India Office to find out.'

He held out his hand to Caxton.

'Once more many thanks, Mr Caxton,' he said.

'Will you leave your address with Major Brien here, so that we can keep in touch with you?'

'Sure!'

Sir Leonard put on his coat and hat, and went out. He strolled down Whitehall, and into the India Office, and casually made his way to the Secretary of State's own room, and knocked at the door.

A deep voice shouted to him to enter, which he immediately did, and found himself in the presence of Lord Dalston and Sir Stanley Fellowes.

'Ha!' said the statesman with pleasure. 'You've lost no time, Wallace.'

'I understood from Fellowes that there was no time to be lost!'

'Quite so! Sit down!'

Sir Leonard sank into an armchair, and the burly nobleman leant back, and put the tips of his fingers together.

'Can we have your services?' he asked.

'You want a secret service man?'

'No – we want you yourself! Can we have you?'

'It depends upon what you want me for.'

'We're not cognisant of all the facts, but it seems to be a very serious matter. Read this!' He picked up a paper from his desk and handed it to Sir Leonard. 'It is a decoded cable from the Viceroy, received twenty minutes ago!'

Wallace read the following:

Most important and secret frontier plans, recently completed by Major Elliott, stolen. Elliott murdered. Very mysterious affair. Believed work of Russian spies. Can you send Sir Leonard Wallace out by air immediately to investigate. Very urgent. Oundle. Viceroy.

He handed the sheet back to Lord Dalston, who looked enquiringly at him.

'Of course, it is very sudden,' said His Lordship, 'but you are used to sudden calls in your department!'

'Yes, but this is the most sudden I have ever had.' He stood up, and walked to the window and contemplated the traffic below for a moment, then turned.

'Very well, sir,' he announced, 'I'll go!'

'Splendid,' said Lord Dalston. 'And when will you start?'

'This afternoon!'

'By Jove!' said Fellowes, who had hitherto not spoken. 'That's quick work!'

'Now, sir,' said Wallace briskly, 'will you communicate with the Air Ministry, and arrange all details about a plane. I want the two best pilots they've got, and the fastest machine, to be ready at three o'clock or soon afterwards, at Croydon. I must have two pilots, for we've got to travel at record speed and waste no time resting en route.'

Lord Dalston turned to Sir Stanley Fellowes.

'Will you see to it at once, Fellowes?'

'And don't let the Air Ministry hum and haw. Make them get busy!' added Wallace.

Fellowes nodded.

'Now I must put my own department in shape. I'll take Major Brien with me.'

The Secretary of State stood up and held out his hand.

'Good luck, Sir Leonard!' he said. 'And many thanks!'

Wallace shook hands with both, and strolled out of the room.

'By Jove!' said Lord Dalston, looking quizzically at the Under Secretary. 'That man takes things in the calmest way imaginable, and yet he arranges everything in half the time another fellow would.'

CHAPTER ELEVEN

Lady Wallace Has a Shock

Sir Leonard Wallace walked up Whitehall at the same unhurried pace, and entered his office. Major Brien was still there, and sat at the desk going through some of the documents that had been forced upon him. He looked up as the other walked in.

'Well,' he said, 'has one of the girl clerks lost her favourite teapot?'

Wallace put his overcoat and hat on their pegs, and emerged from the alcove before he replied, then:

'I'm going to leave for India this afternoon,' he announced calmly.

Brien was used to sudden journeys and the cool manner of his chief, but this took the wind out of his sails completely.

'You're going to what?' he demanded.

'Leave for India. And so are you, my son!'

This further shock was too much for Billy. He rose and grasping Sir Leonard by the shoulders propelled him to his chair and pushed him into it.

'Now explain!' he commanded.

'Well, it appears that some very important plans of the Frontier have been stolen, and a Major Elliott, who made them, murdered. The Viceroy has asked for me to be sent out to unravel the mystery, and incidentally restore the plans to his sorrowing bosom. Russian spies are suspected.'

'But, hang it all, you won't have a ghost of a chance by the time you get there – it will be much too late.'

'We shall fly from Croydon Aerodrome at three this afternoon! We are taking two pilots and shall – well, just fly!'

'Well, I'm damned!' Billy sat down heavily.

'S'sh! Remember you're not in church. Aren't you looking forward to the trip?'

'No, I'm not! Phyllis and I had made special arrangements for this week too!'

'Well, to tell you the truth, I wouldn't have taken it on if Caxton hadn't come this morning.'

'Blow Caxton!'

'Don't blow Caxton – he may have put us in the way of something big, and perhaps you and I can clear the Russian Bolshevik rabble out of India. Still, if you don't want to come, I'll take Maddison with me.'

'You're an idiot, Leonard!' said Billy wrathfully. 'Of course I'm coming!'

'Well, we've got to leave our house in order. You'd better go and fix up your little lot, and ring up Phyllis and break the news to her gently; also get your man to pack a collar and a toothbrush for you. You needn't bring him, I'll take Batty. He can look after both of us. By the way,' he added, looking at his watch, 'Molly's late, it's a quarter to twelve!'

Billy walked towards the door.

'Shall I send Maddison in to you – I suppose you'll want him?'

'Yes, do!'

A few minutes later a small, keen-eyed, grey-haired man entered the room. Until recently a detective inspector at New Scotland Yard, Maddison had been appointed to an important post in the Intelligence Department and he had proved himself to be a most able man. Sir Leonard had great confidence in his acumen, his organising ability and his general all-round excellence.

'I've a lot of instructions for you, Maddison,' he said 'and very little time to give them in. Sit down!'

When Maddison had seated himself, Wallace continued.

'I am going to leave for India this afternoon with Major Brien,' he said, 'and you will be in charge until I return!'

Maddison showed no surprise at all at the news and simply nodded.

'Some very important plans have disappeared, and the Viceroy has cabled for me. Now you know how to carry on, and I have absolute reliance in your judgment and discretion. If anything very special arises cable to me to Viceregal Lodge, Delhi. Do you understand?'

'Perfectly, Sir Leonard!'

'Good! Now for my instructions!' And for the next quarter of an hour they were deeply engaged, the one in giving orders, the other in listening and making notes. Wallace had almost concluded, when the clerk came to announce that Lady Wallace had arrived and was sitting in a waiting room.

'Tell her I'll be disengaged in three minutes,' said Sir Leonard.

In three minutes exactly he rose from his chair.

'That's all, I think, Maddison. I may be back in three weeks, I may not be back in two or three months, but everything is in order for you to carry on I think.'

'You can rely upon me, Sir Leonard,' replied Maddison. 'I hope you will have the best of luck out there.'

'Thanks. Goodbye!'

Maddison departed and Wallace rang the bell. Lady Wallace came in quickly.

'I'm so sorry to be late, dear,' she said.

'My darling, it is your privilege. But I'm afraid I can't come out after all. You see Billy and I are going to start on a flight to India this afternoon!'

'Leonard!'

'I'm not joking, dear. Something has gone wrong out there, and the Viceroy has cabled for me to go out at once.'

'Oh, my dear, how awful! And you announce it as calmly as though you were going to Maidenhead.'

He smiled.

'I don't know quite how long we shall be, but I hope to settle the business in a fortnight, and come back.'

There was silence for a moment and then:

'Oh, Leonard, this is a shock,' she said.

'I know, dear, but these things do happen and it will be a relief for you perhaps to be on your own for a little while.'

'Don't say such awful things. You know I shall miss you terribly. Phyllis and I will have to comfort each other.'

He kissed her.

'Bless you!' he said. 'You're a wonderful woman! Will you ring up Sims and ask him to tell Batty to get ready to come with me and pack a couple of suitcases with some things – only necessaries – and the majority of them suitable for the tropics, and say that lunch must be sharp at one! I'm just going along the corridor to give a few final instructions. I won't be long!'

He got as far as the door when:

'Tell Billy to bring Phyllis round to lunch,' said Molly, 'and we can all motor to – where are you starting from?'

'Croydon!'

'We can all drive to Croydon, and Phyllis and I can see you off!'

'Good idea!' he said heartily, and went out.

She immediately got on the telephone, and gave Sims the necessary orders, and was just replacing the receiver when Brien walked in.

'Good morning, Molly,' he said. 'What do you think of Leonard's latest escapade?'

'I'm awfully upset about it. I hate the idea of his going away again. It's only a month since he came back from Egypt, and you know what happened there?'

'Yes, but I don't think there's likely to be any danger in this affair, and besides he'll have me to look after him!'

She smiled.

'What did Phil think of it?'

'She just shrieked in her surprise. I told her I'd be coming along at once, so I am going home now.'

'You're bringing her to lunch, aren't you? We'll have a little farewell affair, and then drive to Croydon.'

'Yes, thanks very much. About one, I suppose?'

'Yes!'

'Right-ho! We'll be there sharp to time. Cheerio!'

'Goodbye, Billy.'

He left the room, and presently Leonard came in carrying a

large map of India. He spread it out on the desk. Molly joined him, and the two of them looked at it.

'What has happened, Leonard?' she asked. 'Is it a secret?'

'Not exactly, dear. They have had some very important plans stolen, and the officer who made them has been murdered.'

'But haven't they got anybody out there they can trust to search for the plans? Why send all this way for you?'

'Well, I suppose it's my job – it's secret service work you see.'

'I know, but surely the Indian police are capable enough, and they have a special branch, haven't they?'

'Yes, but Lord Oundle apparently thinks it is a matter for my department!'

'Well, why won't some of your men do? Mr Maddison, for instance, with another?'

'I don't know; he specially asked for me. I dare say there is a lot behind this business that we know nothing about. It sounds as though it might be interesting.'

'And dangerous! Oh, dear, am I always to go about with my heart in my mouth?'

He looked at her and smiled.

'I don't suppose there will be much danger in it,' he remarked. 'Probably it will mean my sitting down most of the time with a wet towel round my head.'

'I hope so! I shall tell Lord Oundle next time I see him that he has no consideration for a wife's feelings.'

'He'll retort in that dry way of his, that duty comes before other considerations.'

'Oh, duty, duty!' she exclaimed in exasperation. 'I'm tired of the word. I did my duty during the War like other women, trying to be brave and smile and look cheerful while my husband was fighting in France. I did my duty when you were in danger routing out those spies at Kimmeridge. But unlike other women who have had their reward since in knowing their husbands and brothers and sons are now in some safe occupation, I have to go on – doing my duty! Oh, Leonard dear, will there never be any real peace for me in my happiness?'

'You know you glory in it, darling!'

'I glory in it for your sake, because I am proud of the work you are doing for the country. But, oh, I want my husband to myself always – I want to know he is never in any danger, never likely to be killed suddenly. What should I do if that happened, dear?'

Her beautiful eyes were brimful of tears, and he kissed her with a great tenderness.

'There isn't going to be any danger of that sort this time, Molly – I feel pretty certain of that.'

'But there might be – you never know. And there will be the other times!'

'Perhaps not! Perhaps I shall just chain myself to the office when I get back and get fat and lazy like the other heads of departments.'

'Oh, Leonard, if you only would!'

'What! Get fat and lazy?'

'No, stupid. Keep to the office and let the others do the outside work under your instructions. Would you do it?'

'For your sake, dear!'

'You darling!' She flung her arms round his neck and kissed him, then stepped back and smiled. 'Wouldn't people think it was bad form of me to show my feelings so, if they had seen me then?' she said.

'Blow people! And please continue your bad form, Molly.'

'Your brother always says we are like a couple of children.'

'Well, I hope we always shall be! Can you imagine Victoria throwing her arms around his neck?'

They laughed in unison, and he returned to his contemplation of the map.

'I suppose you don't remember a certain incident that happened here?' he said, putting his finger on a spot on the map. She looked at it.

'Delhi!' she breathed. 'How could I ever forget – our wedding day! I should love to visit the place again and go into the cathedral, and just conjure everything up!'

'That's an idea!' he said. 'Why not come out and join us there?'

'Oh, Leonard, how splendid!'

'Borrow the Governor's yacht, he's not using it, and come as soon as you can! She's a fast boat, and won't take long to get to Bombay. Bring Phyllis with you. Lady Oundle and Doreen will be delighted.'

A look of real pleasure spread over her face.

'I'll go and see your father as soon as you're gone. Won't it be lovely? I feel much happier now.'

'By Jove! What an idea! I'm glad I thought of it!'

He studied the map for a minute or two longer, and then rolled it up and rang for the clerk.

'Take this back to the map room,' he said, giving it to the man, then turned to Molly.

'I'm ready to come now, dear.'

She helped him into his overcoat, and together they descended to the waiting car below, and were soon back in their home in Piccadilly.

Wallace gave a few instructions to his man Batty, an ex-naval seaman, and had a last glorious romp with his son, and then descended from the nursery just as Brien and his wife entered the hall, with Sims, looking more solemn than ever, bowing them in.

Phyllis Brien was not quite what the world would describe as beautiful, but she possessed a most bewitching pair of soft grey eyes, an abundance of wavy hair, which she had kept its own natural length, and never had bobbed or shingled in the prevailing mode, a small *retroussé* nose, very much like Molly's, a nicely shaped mouth with full red lips, delicately pencilled eyebrows, and above all charm and vivacity.

'Hullo, you two!' sang out Leonard.

Phyllis hurried forward and placed her two hands in his.

'What are you two going to do in India?' she demanded. 'Billy assures me that there will be no murder and sudden death or anything like that. Is it true, Leonard?'

'You women are the limit,' said Wallace. 'I've just been telling Molly that we are not going into any danger, and now you come bothering me! Don't you know yet that Billy and I are the most careful people in the world?'

'No, I don't!'

'Well be assured; we are! This is merely a little flying picnic we're having. You ought to be glad to be relieved of his company for a bit.'

'What's that?' demanded Billy coming up. 'Don't put Bolshevik notions into her head, or I shan't get a moment's peace in future.'

'Oh, Leonard, do be serious!' pleaded Phyllis. 'This has been an awful shock to me!'

'My dear little woman, you'll only be parted from him for three weeks, so don't worry!'

'Are you sure it will be only three weeks?' she asked eagerly.

'Of course! You and Molly are going out in the yacht to join us at Delhi!'

'What's that?' demanded Billy and his wife in one breath.

'Oh dear, how persistent you are! Molly is going to borrow the yacht and bring Phyllis out with her, and we'll all come home together.'

'By Jove!' cried Brien. 'What an idea!' He beamed all over his good-natured face.

Phyllis impulsively kissed Leonard.

'What dears you two are!' she exclaimed.

'Mrs Brien,' said a silvery voice from the stairs. 'Did I see you kiss my husband?' And Molly looked down on them.

'You did, darling!' said Phyllis, 'and I'm coming to kiss you!' Which she did forthwith.

'That's all very well,' said Molly and they joined the men. 'But a kiss is a kiss and—'

'It's the first one I've given Leonard since Billy and I were married and he was best man.'

'And then you didn't kiss me,' put in Wallace, 'I kissed you, but got none in return.'

'Yes, you did, fibber!' retorted Phyllis. 'Because I kissed you for giving me him.'

'I didn't give him to you – you took him!'

'O – oh!' she said. 'What an awful story!' She frowned a little in thought. 'But if Molly and I come to India, what about the children?'

'Bring them too, bless you!' said Leonard. 'The trip will do them good!'

A solemn voice boomed across the hall.

'Luncheon is served, my lady,' announced Sims.

Lunch was quite a cheery affair. The fact that they were following their husbands out to India made a big difference to the spirits of the two wives and when a note of despondency threatened to creep in, Wallace came to the rescue with his usual humorous nonsense. Adrian, who had been permitted to come to the table as a special favour, also helped to keep the conversation brisk and lively, and so altogether it was a very merry meal.

At half past two the car was at the door, and the four took their places inside. Adrian pleaded to come to see his Daddy off, a request which was at once granted, and he squeezed in between the driver and Batty, and proceeded to give directions, imagining that he was the captain of a ship, and the chauffeur the steersman.

Croydon aerodrome was reached in good time, and upon enquiry it was found that the Air Ministry had gone one better than expected. A large Handley-Page aeroplane awaited them which would have comfortably carried fourteen. Two of the finest pilots of the Royal Air Force, Wing Commander James Forsyth and Squadron Leader Gerald Hallows, had been provided with two very competent and experienced mechanics. There were stores on board to last the whole trip and almost sufficient petrol, and altogether, as Billy remarked, 'The Air Ministry has done us proud!'

Molly and Phyllis, now that the time had arrived for parting, were a bit glum, but Adrian was full of delight. He had never been so close to an aeroplane before, and he jumped in and out, and had twice to be hauled from somewhat perilous positions.

Wing Commander Forsyth had already flown to Karachi and back, and Wallace had a talk with him before starting. He was a fair, freckled-face young man with steely grey eyes and a determined chin. He grinned cheerfully at Leonard.

'We've had a bit of a rush, sir,' he said, 'but we got here well up to time. The old bus was ready, luckily.'

'What is the quickest time in which you can get to Delhi without taking any undue risks?' asked Leonard.

'Four days, perhaps a little less. It is just about four thousand, eight hundred miles by the route I propose to go. Of course if we could fly all night, as well as by day, we could do it much sooner, but as there would be no landing lights to guide us in the event of our having to come down, I suppose we must stick to daylight.'

Wallace nodded.

'If you'll step inside I'll show you the route, Sir Leonard!'

He led the way into the plane and produced a chart on which he had mapped out the route.

'We shall cross the Channel and head due south to the Mediterranean, follow the coast along here, cross Italy and the Adriatic, then through Greece and Mesopotamia, down the Persian Gulf to Karachi, and thence straight to Delhi. I propose to stop just south of Paris tonight. Is that agreeable, sir?'

'Quite! I am entirely in your hands; you are the captain. All I insist on is getting to Delhi as soon as possible.'

'Right! Are you ready to start now, sir?'

'Quite!'

'Very well. We'll get away at once!'

He went off to give the necessary orders and have a final look round the machine with his colleague and the two mechanics.

Leonard returned to the ladies. Batty had placed the suitcases, bedding and his own kit on board, so nothing remained but to say the 'goodbyes', which were naturally somewhat prolonged. At last they were said. Leonard lifted his small son in his arms and whispered,

'Look after Mummy, old man! And when you get back home give her a big kiss, and say Daddy sent it!'

'Yes, Daddy,' said the little fellow bravely, though two big tears glistened in his eyes.

'And don't forget that you must take care of her and bring her to India quite safely!'

'Yes, Daddy!' Then turning to his father he covered his face with kisses before he was set on the ground.

There were a few additional softly spoken and somewhat husky 'goodbyes'. Then the two men climbed, into the aeroplane.

'Right-ho! Let her go!' sang out Forsyth. The huge propeller in front was swung round twice without result, then, with a roar, the engine started, the mechanics climbed aboard and the aeroplane glided across the ground and rose beautifully into the air. Twice she circled above, while Billy and Leonard waved their handkerchiefs in response to those waved below, and then, with her nose pointing due south, the great man-made bird started on her long flight to India.

It is not proposed to weary the reader with a detailed account of Sir Leonard Wallace's trip to Delhi. Aeroplane travel is such an accomplished fact in these days that a very great number of people have experienced the delights of flying. Nothing sensational happened, and the two splendid pilots Forsyth and Hallows, with the able assistance of their mechanics, kept well up to the time that Forsyth had set himself.

At Athens and Busra they renewed their supplies of petrol and oil and in the Persian city they were almost mobbed by a screaming, smelly, altogether oriental crowd of men, women and children. It took Forsyth and his assistants all their time to prevent the children carrying away parts of the aeroplane as keepsakes. However they got away without accident and flew down the Perisan Gulf towards Karachi. Although so high up they felt the heat intensely and were very relieved when the rugged, barren shores of the Gulf were left behind and they turned the bend and came into view of the third seaport of India.

'India at last!' said Leonard, as they glided over the city and circled round preparatory to landing. 'I wonder what we are going to find here – murder and sudden death, as Phyllis said, or – what? Do you know,' he added, turning sharply to his companion, 'I have a feeling that Caxton has put the key of this business into our hands, and that Karachi may have a lot to do with the solution!'

CHAPTER TWELVE

An Episode in Karachi

One cannot fly halfway round the world in record time without causing a certain amount of interest and publicity, and although the India Office had endeavoured to keep the matter secret, it had leaked out, and when Wallace and Brien arrived in Karachi there was quite a large, well-dressed crowd waiting to greet them, as well as a collection of the lower strata of Indian humanity.

'Good Lord!' muttered Billy with disgust. 'What are we supposed to be – a triumphant air feat or a secret mission?'

'We had to take the risk of this,' he said, 'when we came by air. If we had been able to spare the time to come in a liner, we might have had a better chance, but even then I doubt if we could have reached India without our Russian friends knowing all about it – that is, if the Russians are involved in this business, and we haven't proved that they are yet!'

'Then you think they'll know what we came for?'

'Of course they will! I never had the slightest doubt on that score. Billy, my lad, we start beautifully handicapped! From the time we land at Delhi we shall be watched as mice watch cats and they will have the additional advantage of knowing us. Oh, yes; taking it for granted that we are up against agents of the Russian Soviet, they start with all the trump cards in their hands. You and I have had so many dealings with Bolsheviks in England that our names must be anathema to them, and I think we shall possibly be in for a lively and interesting time out here!'

This conversation took place just before the aeroplane glided to the earth and as Wallace finished speaking they touched the ground, and running along in the midst of the spectators came to rest gently and calmly like some great bird. Leonard waved his hand round in an eloquent gesture.

'India, the land of sahibs and snobs,' he said.

As they emerged from the saloon they were immediately taken possession of by the congratulating crowd, who behaved as though the flight had been undertaken for their especial benefit. Invitations poured in from all sides, and they were hard put to it to refuse them. Entire strangers took turns in shaking their hands and introducing themselves, and everybody appeared to be speaking at once with the result that they only caught such phrases as: 'I'm Willows of the General Staff and I met you in France, Sir Leonard, if you remember—'; 'Do give us the pleasure of dining with us—'; 'My wife and I would be delighted if you would stay the night—'; 'What a wonderful journey yours must have been—'; 'I have a car waiting here for you—'; and so on *ad infinitum*.

Thoroughly fed up, but answering with a smile here, a nod there, Leonard felt inclined to beat a hasty retreat back to the aeroplane, when a tall figure with a military air made its way through the crowd.

'I'm the Deputy Commissioner, Sir Leonard,' he said smiling.

'I had information from Delhi that you were on your way, but I did not expect you quite so soon.'

'Well, I'm jolly glad to see you,' said Wallace. 'Come into the saloon – we shall be alone there – I hope.'

The other smiled.

'You were not expecting such a reception?'

'No, I was not, I assure you, and – I'm afraid it is very rude of me to say so – I did not want it!'

'I can quite understand that.' He entered the narrow doorway at Leonard's behest and the latter was about to follow him, when he noticed a big burly man with a fair, well-trimmed beard, standing on the verge of the crowd, and, from the expression on his face, watching proceedings with the utmost contempt. The smile of sardonic amusement had no attempt at disguise about it, and it immediately occurred to Leonard that this man appeared to view things entirely differently from the rest of the crowd.

'I wonder!' he muttered to himself. 'I'll take the chance anyway! Billy,' he said, as that worthy came up, 'do you see that big fellow with the beard? Don't stare, just glance – over there—'

Billy nodded.

'Well, get hold of Batty quietly, and tell him to follow that chap wherever he goes, in a taxi or a gharri, or whatever the other uses, and to come back and let us know the address!'

'What's the game?' asked Billy.

'Tiddley-winks,' replied Wallace, and disappeared into the interior of the plane.

'No,' he repeated, as he sat in a small easy chair and invited the Commissioner to take another. 'The last thing I wanted was publicity. I am out here on a secret mission and want as much privacy as I can get.'

'So I gathered,' replied the other, 'though I know nothing about it. They're a canny lot at Delhi.'

Wallace ignored the implied invitation to talk about his mission.

'What I cannot understand,' he said, 'is how these people knew anything about it.'

'There was an article in the *Indiaman* this morning, saying that you were flying out to India on special service, and that you were travelling at such speed that it was quite likely you would arrive here today.'

'Good Lord! Isn't it amazing!' said Leonard. 'Now how on earth did they get to know that?'

The Commissioner shrugged his shoulders.

'All the same I wish you would find out, Commissioner. The *Indiaman* is a Karachi paper, is it not?'

'Yes! I'll ring up the editor and make enquiries and let you know.'

'Thanks!'

A cheerful-looking, middle-aged man looked into the saloon.

'Excuse me, Sir Leonard,' he said, 'but I should like a few words for my paper, if you can spare me the time.'

'Paper!' ejaculated Leonard. 'What's your paper?'

'He's the editor of the *Indiaman*, Sir Leonard,' said the Commissioner. 'Come in, Reynolds, you're just the very man we want.'

Taking it for granted that this meant news, the man stepped inside with alacrity.

'Sit down,' said Wallace. 'I've a very big grouse against your paper,' he went on, as the other seated himself.

'Oh, indeed, Sir Leonard,' said Reynolds. 'I'm very sorry to hear you say that.'

'I came out to India hoping to avoid publicity! Will you tell me where you got the information you printed this morning about my arrival?'

The other hesitated, and then looked questioningly at the Commissioner.

'Well, you know,' he said at last, 'we get information from all manner of sources.'

'And you print it irrespective of where it comes from?'

'No, certainly not. It must be from someone whom we know to be reliable.'

'Then you heard about my coming from a reliable person?'

'Of course!' Again he glanced at the Commissioner, a suggestion of surprise in his look.

'Well, who was it?' asked the Chief of Police.

The editor laughed.

'Really, Major Watkins,' he said, 'that's rather an extraordinary question from you, is it not?'

'By no means!' replied the other. 'I naturally desire to help Sir Leonard Wallace to find out.'

'But—' The newspaper man stopped, and stared at him.

'Mr Reynolds,' said Wallace. 'I don't understand why you are making all this mystery. Surely you do not object to giving us this information?'

'Certainly not!'

'Then who was it?'

'Why, the Commissioner, of course. I don't understand—'

'What!' cried Major Watkins, jumping to his feet. '*I* gave it to you?'

'Of course you did!'

'When?' gasped the Major.

'Why, last night! Do you not remember ringing me up and telling me?'

'No, I'm hanged if I do!' said the other with emphasis. 'You're talking nonsense.'

'There is naturally some mistake,' interposed Leonard.

'But I recognised the Commissioner's voice,' said Reynolds, a very puzzled expression on his face.

'My dear man,' said Watkins wrathfully, 'you're dreaming!'

There was silence for a moment. The Deputy Commissioner glared at the editor, who looked a badly surprised man, while Wallace glanced from one to the other of them with an amused expression on his face.

'Obviously, Commissioner,' he said at last, 'somebody rang up Mr Reynolds, and imitated your voice.'

'That must be it!' said Watkins. 'I'd like to get hold of him!' he added with emphasis.

Reynolds looked relieved.

'To tell you the truth,' he remarked, 'I was rather surprised when you – the voice rather – said, "The Deputy Commissioner speaking", because when you ring me up you invariably say, "Watkins speaking", but I took very little notice of that, the voice seemed so obviously yours.'

'I am going to find out who it was somehow or other,' said the Commissioner.

'I'm afraid you'll find it rather a job,' smiled Wallace.

'Then am I to understand, gentlemen,' asked the editor, 'that the information should not have appeared in the paper?'

'Yes, you are,' replied Leonard. 'And please see that nothing else appears; not that it matters very much now. You cannot very well contradict your report because I have arrived, but if you get any further information about me over the telephone, or otherwise, will you do your best to find out where it came from, and then tell the Commissioner?'

'I will, Sir Leonard. You may rely upon me! I am very sorry this has happened.'

'You are not to blame. I certainly would like to interview the individual who rang you up, though.'

'And so would I!' growled the Commissioner.

Reynolds took his leave soon afterwards, and Major Watkins rose to his feet.

'Now, Sir Leonard, you and your colleagues will give me the pleasure of your company at dinner and stay the night, I hope.'

'We'll come to dinner, thanks very much, but we won't stay the night if you'll excuse me. I have a lot of work I want to do and so we'll sleep here.'

'Just as you please, of course, but if you should change your mind, my bungalow is at your disposal.'

'Thanks!'

Five minutes later, Wallace and Brien, with the two pilots were on their way in the Commissioner's car to Karachi. The latter proved a very entertaining host and the evening passed quickly and pleasantly. At eleven o'clock they were driven back to the aeroplane and found Batty awaiting them. He grinned when he saw them and Leonard gathered at once that he had been successful in his mission.

'Come inside, Batty,' he said, and the ex-sailor followed him and Billy into the saloon.

Batty had been in the Navy for many years, and Wallace, on the recommendation of a naval friend, had engaged him as a personal servant on his retirement, and had never regretted it. He had found the sailor a thoroughly reliable and very useful man, and had come to regard him as a very confidential servant. Batty was not polished, but what he lacked in that quarter was more than counterbalanced by his many attributes.

'First of all, Batty,' said Leonard, 'have you had anything to eat?'

'Yes, sir,' replied Batty, and he smiled reminiscently. 'Me and the a.m.'s 'ad all sorts o' food brought to us by the audience, sir, an' we 'ad a pretty good tuck in.'

For the guidance of the reader it must be explained that a.m. means air mechanic. Batty had a fondness for abbreviations, probably culled from his long naval service.

'I'm glad to hear that,' smiled Wallace. 'Now tell me about your adventures.'

'Well, I don't know as I 'ad any adventures, sir. I'd a good look at the bloke – beggin' your pardon, man, sir, what the Major said I was to foller an' when 'e crossed to the road, I ups anchor and sets sail arter 'im. He boarded one of them shaky-looking craft they calls gharris, so I did ditto, sir, and told the Injun wot sat on the box to keep the other craft in sight. Well, sir, to cut a long story short like, 'e didn't seem to understand wot I wanted 'im to do. I tried 'im in a bit of French, sir, and then a bit o' Chinese, wot I learnt when I was stationed on the *Tamar* in 'Ong Kong. But it all weren't no use, so, as the other feller was drawing away fast, I just took the reins o' the old gee meself an' went full speed ahead.'

'What became of the driver?' asked Brien.

'Well, you see, sir, we started so sudden that 'e fell overboard and I went on without him, or thought I did. 'Owsoever when I stopped, I found 'im 'anging on the stern an' saying 'is prayers, sir.'

His hearers laughed.

'Well, and what happened?' asked Leonard.

'Oh, I gives 'im a shilling, sir, an' 'e seemed quite 'appy about it.'

'No, I mean what became of the man you followed?'

'When I was a-chasin' of 'im, sir, my 'orse went so fast that I got too near 'im like, so I 'ad to 'old the gee in. Any'ow the other craft stopped outside an 'ouse, and the bloke – man, sir – got out, and went in. 'E opened the door with a key, so I presoomed 'e lived there, an' arter I 'ad taken the name – there weren't no number – I came back 'ere.'

'I see. And where is this house?'

Batty searched in his pockets, and, at last, produced a soiled scrap of paper on which was laboriously scrawled, 'Waller and Redmond, General Merchants, Bunda Road'.

'By Jove! Billy,' exclaimed Wallace. 'I believe we are on the track. Have you got that list of addresses Caxton gave us?'

Brien nodded, and taking a pocket-book from an inside pocket opened it and produced the list. The first address was the same that Batty had written on his scrap of paper.

Leonard and Billy looked at each other, and the former laughed.

'A long shot that came off!' he said.

'You're a cute old blighter,' said Billy. 'What on earth made you suspect that fellow?'

'His smile!' replied the other. 'Thanks, Batty, you've done a good night's work. Help yourself to a whisky and soda!'

'Well, sir, beggin' your pardon, sir,' said Batty regretfully, 'but them people wot gave us the grub, weren't nowise be'ind with the liquor, an' I've taken a lot aboard, sir. Besides,' he added naively, 'there's about a dozen bottles left, includin' two or three o' rum, sir.'

The others laughed, and Batty disappeared – probably to find the mechanics and the rum.

'Billy, I'm going to have a look at this place,' announced Wallace. 'That is why I did not stop at the Commissioner's bungalow for the night – Are you coming?'

'Of course I'm coming!'

The two of them strolled across the road, but owing to the lateness of the hour there were no conveyances to be obtained there, so they walked on towards Karachi, and were lucky enough to meet a belated taxi-cab which took them to the Bunda Road. On the way Wallace told his companion about the report in the paper, and how somebody had imitated the Commissioner's voice and given the information.

'By Jove!' said Brien. 'I wonder who it was!'

'Probably the very man Batty tracked tonight, or someone connected with him.'

'But what object could they have?'

'Well, I suppose the paper is distributed throughout India or the greater part of it and that was a quick and safe way of warning their colleagues in other places that we had arrived or rather were arriving.'

'I believe you're right, but I'd like to know how they got their information.'

'Billy, I'm surprised at you! A member of the Intelligence Department and you ask that! How do we get *our* information about things?'

'H'm! Of course!'

'There's one thing we can be pretty sure of at last. It is that Russian Bolshevik spies are in possession of those plans, because the fellow Batty followed would not have come to see our arrival, and the news would not have been in the paper, if they were not very interested in us. What a bit of luck that Caxton gave us the information about this firm of Waller and Redmond!'

Billy nodded. The cab began to slacken speed, so Wallace leant out and ordered the driver to go on. He stopped the man about a hundred yards farther along, and he and his companion alighted. Ordering the chauffeur to drive on for three or four hundred yards and then wait for them, the two retraced their steps, and had presently arrived opposite the establishment belonging to Messrs. Waller and Redmond. It was a large double-storied building, and the ground floor had the appearance of a warehouse. At one side of it was a narrow lane which apparently led to the back of the premises, and from a window halfway down a light shone out into the darkness.

Wallace looked up and down the road to see if there were any people about, but it was entirely deserted, except for the taxi-cab which could be dimly seen in the distance, and he and Brien quietly crossed to the other side and made their way down the lane until they were opposite the window. There were no curtains and no efforts were apparently made to hide what was happening within, and certainly the scene looked innocent enough. There were three men sitting in what appeared to be an ordinary commercial office, while another, standing at the desk, was talking earnestly to them. Each man had a drink in his hand, or by his side, and they were all smoking cigars. It seemed as though the merchant was merely having a convivial evening with some acquaintances. Certainly an office was hardly the place for that sort of thing, but there was nothing very odd about it.

'Do you recognise the man standing?' asked Leonard.

'Yes, the fellow whom Batty tracked, isn't he?'

'M'm! By Jove, Billy, I'd give a good deal to hear what he is saying.'

He stole across the lane, and standing close beside the window, put his ear to the wall, but only a subdued murmur could be heard.

'No good,' he said, rejoining the other. 'We can only stand here and watch proceedings.'

For half an hour they remained almost without moving, and still the conversation went on within, the burly man doing the bulk of the talking, and, at times, gesturing as though driving some point home.

'Oh, hang it!' said Billy, at last. 'This is getting monotonous!'

'We've certainly had time to study their faces well. I'd give anything for a pipe, but it would be too risky.'

'That taxi-driver will soon be thinking we've run off without paying him and come to investigate.'

'Yes, I thought of that just now! Look here, Billy, go along to the car and have a smoke, and then, when you have finished, come back and relieve me, and I'll go.'

'That's not a bad notion. But don't do anything risky without me—'

'No, of course not!'

Billy crept quietly away, and Leonard was left alone. Still the conversation went on, the only interlude being the production of a small revolver by a man, sitting in a corner, who handed the weapon round. It had a curious-looking affair attached to the muzzle and Wallace was puzzled as to what it could be. The burly man took it and examined it minutely, then handed it back to the owner, who was about to put it into his pocket, when Brien came softly back.

'Billy, what is the attachment on that revolver?' asked Leonard gripping him by the arm. The other just caught a glimpse as the man put it away.

'By Jove!' he said. 'It's one of those newfangled silencers. What have they been doing?'

'Nothing much. He has simply been handing the weapon round for the others to admire.'

'H'm! I don't like that silencer; an honest man wouldn't have it!'

'Well, you'd hardly call these men honest, would you?'

At that moment the owner of the revolver rose, and picked up a topee; the others grouped themselves round him, and the big man, with one hand on his shoulder, appeared to be giving him some advice. Then he shook hands with them all and turned towards the door of the room.

'He's coming out!' muttered Leonard. 'We'll follow him and see what he is up to. Let us get out of here and hide somewhere!'

They hurried quietly out of the lane, and had scarcely time to crouch in a doorway before the man came out and set off at a quick pace up the road. The two watchers carefully started to follow him.

'Go back and discharge the taxi, Bill, and rejoin me. As he's walking we won't want it any longer!'

Without a word Brien was off. Wallace continued his tracking, taking advantage of all the cover he could find. However, the man looked neither to the left nor right, but went on as though he were in a great hurry. He appeared to be going in the direction from which they had come and at last just as Billy glided quietly up, it dawned upon Leonard where the fellow was bound for.

'I think he is off to carry out a nice little murder plot,' he whispered.

'Good Lord! That would certainly explain the silencer. But whom do you think he is going to murder?'

'Us!'

Brien gave a start and whistled softly.

'He's not!' he said between his teeth.

'No, but he thinks he is. Get behind me! Two are easier to see than one and we're getting out into the open, although it's pretty dark, thank Goodness!'

The assassin, if assassin he were, now began to show more caution. Two or three times he stopped and looked behind, and his pursuers had much difficulty in concealing themselves effectively, but there were several trees behind which they could hide, and the night was too dark for anything to be seen clearly at a distance. After going on for what seemed an interminable time they came to the open space in which the aeroplane stood.

'So I was right!' muttered Wallace. 'They must be pretty desperate!'

'And we told the girls there would be no danger!' murmured Brien.

Carefully they followed him from the road towards the great plane. When quite close to it they lay down behind a bush and watched him. A makeshift tent had been put up for Batty and the two mechanics, and the fellow warily approached this and was for some time busily engaged on the ground before the opening.

'What on earth is he doing?' said Billy.

'Goodness knows! By Jove, yes I do, though. He's stretching a cord across, so that they'll fall over and give him time to get away if they're disturbed and come out.'

Brien whistled quietly.

Presently the man rose, and went to the small door leading into the aeroplane saloon, and carefully, gently, opened it.

'Come on, Billy,' said Wallace. 'We don't want to risk letting Forsyth or Hallows get shot. Have you a revolver with you?'

'No!'

'Neither have I. Never mind, come on! Quickly does it!'

They were up, and had sped across the intervening space before the intruder noticed them. And then he swung round with his revolver levelled. Before he had time to fire, Billy had knocked his arm up, and there was a soft thud, as the weapon went off. Then there was a terrific struggle; the fellow fought like a wild cat, and it was all Brien could do with his two arms, and Wallace with his one, to prevent him from slipping away. But the noise awoke the others. There were yells and curses as Batty and his companions fell over the stretched cord, but the two pilots dashed out of the saloon, and in response to Wallace's yell, came to their assistance. Soon the man was disarmed and rendered helpless, and the mechanics, aided by Batty's sailorly advice, were busily and thoroughly engaged trussing him up, as the little sailor remarked, 'taut fore and aft!'

'A little fellow who came to murder us!' explained Brien, in reply to a string of questions.

'Take turns in guarding him!' said Wallace to Batty and the airmen. 'Don't let him get away whatever you do!'

'He won't get away, sir!' said Batty with a glitter in his eyes. 'I'll keelhaul him if he tries!'

'Doesn't seem to me he can try anything – even breathe,' laughed Hallows.

The four entered the saloon, leaving Batty and his companions with the prisoner.

'Well, I think we've had a very merry evening!' yawned Leonard. 'And now I'm going to sleep.'

Forsyth and Hallows were told a little – a very little – of the evening's adventures, as Wallace and Brien prepared for bed.

'This is a nice little keepsake!' said the latter, handing the revolver round. The others curiously examined the silencer attached to it.

'Just another specimen for our museum!' said Wallace, and went to bed.

CHAPTER THIRTEEN

An Interrogation in Mid-Air

Arising at daybreak Wallace went to visit his prisoner.

'Take him into the aeroplane!' he said to Batty. 'And don't breathe a word to anybody about his capture. If you are questioned, know nothing about it, and express astonishment.'

He repeated his warning to Forsyth and Hallows.

'I don't suppose you will be asked,' he added, 'but you might be in a roundabout sort of way. We'll take him to Delhi with us. A little trip might do him good!'

The others grinned. The fellow was duly packed inside the saloon, and Leonard contemplated him.

'Well, my man,' he said, 'you have got yourself into a nasty mess. We cannot spare the time to wait and prosecute you here, so we'll take you to Delhi with us and hand you over to the authorities there!'

All he got in reply was a baleful glance, for the fellow had been very effectually gagged.

'I suppose you find that sponge in your mouth rather

troublesome; but it will be removed as soon as we are in the clouds.'

Wallace walked out, and joined Brien who was talking to a native.

'I'm practising Hindustani,' grinned Billy. 'I don't seem to have remembered much.'

'I don't think I've remembered any, excepting whisky and soda lao and juldee!' Thereupon he promptly contradicted himself by speaking fluently, much to the Indian's delight.

'You old rotter,' said Brien. 'Fancy taking a rise out of me like that!'

'Never mind, Bill. We'll engage a munshi for you!'

There were very few people to see them off. It was too early for one thing and probably the freezing manner in which their reception had been treated had kept a good many away. But the Deputy Commissioner was there, and Wallace and Brien had a friendly little chat with him before Forsyth announced that everything was in readiness. As they shook hands:

'There is a certain house here, Major Watkins,' said Leonard, 'in which I have a deep interest. If you receive a telegram or a phone message from me giving you the address, will you immediately see that everyone in it is arrested, and anyone going in also taken into custody until I arrive?'

The Commissioner looked puzzled.

'Well,' he said, 'it is rather a serious thing to do, but, of course, if you give me such instructions I'll carry them out!'

'Good! And please keep your own counsel. You may be sure that I shall have a very good reason for such a drastic measure, and you'll get a surprise when you know the address.'

'I'm used to surprises,' smiled the Major. 'Goodbye, Sir Leonard!'

They were just about to enter the saloon when Brien grasped his friend's arm.

'The man with a beard, and one of the others, is here and he's coming across to us!'

'Probably wants to find out if we've discovered anything. Careful, Bill!'

The burly man came up to them.

'Excuse me, Sir Leonard,' he said, 'but owing to the crush I couldn't get near you last evening and hesitated to intrude on you before. My name is Waller, and I was wondering if I could ask you to do me a favour!'

'Well,' smiled Wallace, 'I am hardly going round on a philanthropic expedition, but if I can—'

'It is quite a small matter,' interrupted the other hastily. 'You are going to Delhi, I believe, and perhaps you may see Sir Henry Muir, the Viceroy's Chief Secretary?'

Leonard nodded.

'Would you be good enough to tell him that the consignment of goods he sent home per my firm was dispatched on *The City of Edinburgh*, and that I have been delayed in replying to his letter owing to pressure of business, but will write as soon as possible?'

'That's not a very difficult matter. Yes, I'll do it with pleasure!'

'Very many thanks! I must apologise for making such a request!'

'Don't mention it!' And Wallace turned away.

'I'm afraid you have not seen much of Karachi!' said the other quickly.

'I'm not very keen to see much!' said Leonard looking him straight in the face. 'The only thing I am grateful to Karachi for is that it gave me the first good night's rest I've had since I left England!'

He nodded and waved his hand to the Commissioner, then climbed aboard with Brien. A few moments later the great aeroplane rose, and was on her way to Delhi.

Billy sat down and chuckled.

'What a lot of information he received!' he said. 'I like the good night's rest touch – it was delightful!'

'We've left him a badly-puzzled man, Billy. We're not murdered as he expected and his friend has disappeared. Still, I suppose his real object was to discover if by any chance *he* was suspected, and he'll go away in happy innocence, bless his kind heart. Of course, even if he thinks we have this object,' he pointed to the man lying on the floor, 'he feels perfectly certain that it won't give anything away!'

'Rather a clever touch that consignment of Muir's. Bound to be true, of course!'

'Oh, yes. He wouldn't bring himself under suspicion by concocting such a tale. At any rate I'll give Muir the message. Untie your prisoner, Batty!' he added to his man, who was standing guard over the recumbent captive.

It took some time, for the latter had been bound by experts. At last the fellow was free and he rose to his feet very shakily.

'Sorry to have inconvenienced you for so long,' said Wallace dryly, 'but it was very necessary!'

'What is the meaning – of this – this outrage?' gasped out the other in fury.

'Oh, just a little game!' said Leonard sarcastically. 'You pretended that you came to murder us and we pretended to capture you and tie you up and now we're pretending to take you to Delhi with us and hand you over to the authorities!'

'On what charge?' spluttered the man.

'Attempted murder!'

'What absolute nonsense! I came to see you because I had a little request to make, and was set upon and man-handled in the most brutal fashion!'

'Do you generally creep quietly upon sleeping men with a revolver in your hand, attached to which is a useful little silencer, to make your requests?'

'I drew the revolver because I was attacked!'

'And tied a cord for the occupants of the tent to fall over for the same reason, I suppose?'

The fellow hesitated.

'What – what cord?' he stammered at last.

'Enough of this nonsense!' said Wallace, a stern note in his voice. 'You had better make a clean breast of the whole affair!'

'I am perfectly innocent of any of the accusations you have made against me!'

'Don't tell lies! We, Major Brien and I, followed you all the way here, first having watched you in consultation with Waller and your other friends, and the exhibition of this pretty little toy.' He held up the revolver.

The man's face blanched. He saw that the game was up, and from outraged dignity his manner changed to utter fright. He seemed to shrink in size as he stood, and both Brien and Batty, as well as Wallace, looked at him with contempt. The latter continued:

'The best thing you can do is to tell us everything; it may help you slightly in the long run: I make no promises and it is immaterial to me whether you say anything or not.'

'There – there is nothing to tell!'

'Very well! If that is the attitude you mean to take, you will also be prepared to stand your trial on a charge of attempted murder as well as being a spy in the pay of the Russian Government.'

A shivering almost as of ague overcame the man. For a few minutes he could not speak. Then,

'And if I – I – speak?'

Wallace shrugged his shoulders.

'We may consider dropping the charge of attempted murder!'

There was nothing more said for a minute or two. The roar of the engine could be heard as the aeroplane tore on her way, and a tremor occasionally ran through the machine and made the four men stagger slightly. Wallace stood gazing sternly at the spy and Brien was engaged in closely examining the silencer on the revolver and apparently trying to discover the principle on which it worked. Batty looked from one to the other and awaited results, while the captive himself stood with his head bowed down. At last he looked up.

'What do you want to know?' he asked.

'It all depends,' replied Wallace, 'upon what you can tell us. We know so much that it would be quite useless your attempting to lead us astray. In order that you may not let your imagination get the better of you, I will tell you this much: there are several places in India, which pretend to be honest commercial firms, but which in reality are the headquarters or meeting houses for spies of the Russian Government, who are in India for the purpose of creating trouble and distributing pamphlets against Great Britain to the inhabitants. I have addresses in my pocket of these places, one of which is in Karachi. Again certain plans were stolen from a British officer who was murdered, and are in the possession of the Russians! I intend to recover those plans!'

He paused and Billy looked at him in surprise. It seemed to the latter that Wallace was showing his hand rather recklessly. For a moment the spy appeared dumbfounded, then smiled.

'I am afraid you are much too late, Sir Leonard!' he said. 'Those plans are in Russia by now!'

'Did I not tell you,' said Wallace, 'that it would be useless your attempting to lead us astray? The plans I speak of are *not* in Russia nor anywhere near that country, and I happen to know where *they are!*'

Billy gasped and a look of utter astonishment came on the face of the spy. After a moment:

'There seems to be nothing I can tell you,' he said.

'Not much! A link here and there, that's all! However, it is difficult to hear distinctly now, we'll wait till Delhi is reached. In the meantime what is your name?'

'Wainwright!'

'I didn't ask you for the name you go under, I want your proper name.'

'Boris – Leopold Boris.'

'H'm! And how is it you speak English without a trace of accent?'

The man hesitated.

'Come on! If you want any leniency at all, you must answer my questions!'

'I was educated in England, and I joined the firm of Waller and Redmond in that country.'

'So there is a branch in England, is there?'

'Yes.'

'I see! Whereabouts?'

'In Clerkenwell, London.'

'I suppose Waller and Redmond are also fictitious names?'

'No! The firm was quietly bought by the present owners four years ago, and remained under its own name.'

'That's interesting! The present proprietors, no doubt, are working under orders of the Russian Government?'

After a moment's hesitation the fellow nodded.

'And the man who calls himself Waller is, of course, not entitled to that name at all?'

'No, Sir Leonard.'

'What is his name?'

A look of fear passed over the features of the spy, and he did not answer.

'Come! What is his name?'

'I would rather not say.'

'Very well! You know my conditions!' He shrugged his shoulders and turned away. 'Keep your eyes well glued to him, Batty!' he ordered, and sank into a chair.

Presently the spy spoke hoarsely.

'If he knew I gave his name away my life would not be worth a moment's purchase,' he said.

'I don't think you need fear him,' said Leonard, and languidly turned in his chair. 'He will be where he can harm nobody very soon!'

'When the firm was bought,' said the man, almost eagerly now, 'Mr Waller came out to India as the son of the old owner; letters having been sent from England to notify the people in Karachi of his coming. His proper name is—' again he hesitated; then, 'is – Dorin!'

Brien whistled, and exchanged a glance with his colleague who was smiling grimly.

'And is there a Redmond out here?' asked Wallace.

'No, Sir Leonard!'

'I see! Then Dorin, alias Waller junior, is the sole managing representative in Karachi?'

'Yes!'

'But *not in India!*'

The fellow started.

'What do you mean?'

'The managing director of the firm of Waller and Redmond that is the "Russian Soviet Limited" in India is – Who?' He shot the question at the spy almost savagely.

'Lev—' blurted out the man in surprise, then went on hastily, a look of utter terror on his face, 'I don't know – I don't think there is one!'

'So Levinsky is running things!' Wallace said to Brien. 'We're up against something out here, Billy! I won't bother you any more just now,' he added to the spy, who was white with fear and trembling like a leaf. 'You'd better sit down! Take him into the other apartment, Batty!'

Billy, standing with his hands in his pockets, looked at his friend and chief in amazement.

'You're a devil!' he said admiringly. 'But I thought you weren't going to question him till we reached Delhi?'

'Those were only a few preliminaries! By Jove, I'd like a smoke!'

'How, by all that's wonderful, do you know where the plans are?'

Leonard laughed with enjoyment.

'I don't,' he said. 'But by that bit of bluff I found out that they were still in India and a little deduction goes a long way – sometimes! And it's worth something to know the name of the leading light of these fellows out here too,' he added with satisfaction.

'By Jove, yes! You quite took him off his guard when you shouted "Who" at him. He made a pretty good effort to recover, though!'

'He did! But that Lev – was quite enough for me, thank the Lord! Levinsky and Dorin, Billy! A nice slippery pair to start with, what do you think?'

'Slippery is not the word for it! I shall never forget how Dorin tried to get away from that house in Whitechapel when we rounded up those Bolsheviks four years ago!'

'Yes, that was clever work. They must have had the business of Waller and Redmond in their hands already and when he escaped from us he came out to India!'

Billy nodded.

'Well, we've made a start,' he said. 'Things are beginning to look quite promising.'

'Don't be too optimistic, Billy! We've a long way to go yet, and with Levinsky and Dorin on the other side, it is going to be a narrow and stony way too!'

Brien shrugged his shoulders.

'We're used to treading narrow and stony paths,' he said. 'And sometimes people who spread the most stones on a path, fall over and cut themselves badly!'

'Hooray!' cried Leonard. 'Billy Brien makes an epigram!'

CHAPTER FOURTEEN

In the Viceroy's Study

At half past three the aeroplane reached Delhi, and alighted on a wide open space not far from Viceregal Lodge. As the huge machine came to a halt, a beautiful closed car drove up and stopped within a few yards of it. Sir Henry Muir sprang out, and in a moment he and Wallace were shaking hands.

'Gad!' exclaimed the Secretary. 'I have never felt so delighted at seeing anyone in my life!'

Wallace turned to Brien.

'On the face of it,' he said, 'that sounds like a compliment, Billy but it isn't – it is merely a very selfish example of cupboard love!'

Muir laughed.

'Some of it is,' he said, 'but not all.'

'He even has the effrontery to admit it, though he does try to soften the blow a bit. Muir! Muir! I expected such a lot from you, and this disappointment is very bitter!'

Sir Henry apologised with much humility.

'And now are you ready to come at once?' he asked.

'Quite! I've a friend I want to bring with me, and as I do not wish any of the interested crowd to see him more than necessary, you must not mind if he makes a sudden dart from the aeroplane to the car. Billy, get inside and keep your revolver handy!'

Brien obediently entered the machine, and Wallace returned to the aeroplane, leaving Muir standing between the two with a somewhat puzzled expression on his face.

Leonard accosted the spy who was waiting in the saloon with Batty standing guard over him.

'Now, my man!' he said, 'put that topee on and pull it well over your eyes. There is likely to be one or two of your pals standing among the people who have collected, so walk hurriedly, with your face as hidden as possible, to the car, and get in. It is no use your making any attempt to escape, for I shall be standing watching you with this neat little Browning in my hand and Major Brien is doing ditto. So, march!'

The man obeyed and, walking quickly to the limousine, got in.

'Now, Batty, you wait here! There'll be another car along for you and the baggage presently, no doubt, and don't say a word to anyone about our prisoner! If you are asked any questions be as astonished as you like, and warn the mechanics!'

'Aye, aye, sir!'

Leonard rejoined Muir who was speaking to Forsyth, having conveyed an invitation to stay in Viceregal Lodge to him and his companion from the Viceroy.

'I'm ready if you are, Muir!'

'Then we'll go at once!'

Sir Henry glanced curiously at the spy as the car rapidly covered the distance to the Lodge, but asked no questions and no information was given him, till the car stopped, then

Wallace startled him by asking for a safe place, within the main building, where the man could be securely locked up. However, he at once took them to a room that might have been made for such a purpose. The only window it had was high up in one of the walls and even then was too small for a human being to squeeze through. The door was thick and not only locked but had bolts on the outside, and within there was only a table, two chairs and a small couch.

'The very place.' said Wallace. 'In you go, my man, and thank your lucky stars for the many blessings you have received!'

The door was locked and bolted. There had been no servants or officials about during this interlude, Leonard having asked Muir to see that all the bearers, who had awaited their coming, were sent out of the way.

'I do not want anybody else to know of my prisoner, Muir,' he said as they walked away from the room. 'At least not at present, and if there are any more keys, will you get hold of them at once and give instructions that nobody is to go to that room?'

Sir Henry nodded.

'I'll see to it at once,' he said, 'but I'm burning with curiosity!'

'You'll know all about it soon. In the meantime, as soon as Batty arrives, I want a bath and an entire change of clothing, and from the look of Brien I should imagine he does too!'

They had not long to wait for Batty and their belongings, and, in the meantime, Muir informed them that the Viceroy and Lady Oundle were at a garden party and would be back about six. They partook of a light tea in Muir's sitting room and Wallace resolutely refused to 'talk shop' as he called it until he had changed.

Both Leonard and Billy sought their baths like ducks discovering a stream of water after a particularly dry season.

The former revelled in his to such an extent, and sang and splashed so loudly, that the bearer who had been allotted to him as his particular servant thought the new sahib must be surely mad. He started laying out garments, shaking his head doubtfully the while. He was in the midst of this occupation when Batty, who had been engaged in another room, came in and saw him.

'What the 'ell do you think you're doing!' cried the sailor. 'Take them 'ands away from the clothes, d'you 'ear?' He pushed the bearer away with no gentle touch. 'Don't you lemme catch you pawin' Sir Leonard's clothes again with them dirty 'ands – they don't look as if they'd been washed since you was a nipper. Sink me, if this ain't coming it a bit too thick. 'Ere 'op it and likewise get out, or I'll train me fore-chasers on to you quick!'

The man stood and stared at him in utter amazement, then broke into a flood of voluble Hindustani.

'It ain't no good you attempting to excuse yerself. I know the artful ways o' you gents with yer conjurin' tricks and black magic. Now 'ook it and 'ook it quick!'

The bearer still protested excitedly, so Batty took him by the shoulders and pushed him out of the dressing room, through the bedroom, and left him in the corridor outside, where he shook an admonitory forefinger at him and left him.

When Wallace emerged from the bathroom he found the sailor still fuming with indignation.

'What's the matter, Batty?' he asked cheerfully.

'Matter enough, sir,' replied that worthy. 'I found one of them black 'eathens pulling your clothes about. I think 'e was trying to steal summat!'

Leonard laughed heartily.

'He was only a bearer, Batty,' he said, 'sent to look after me, help me to dress, and so on!'

The other looked at him indignantly.

'What about me, sir?' he asked. 'That's my job, an' I ain't goin' to 'ave none of them creepin' fellers takin' my place. An' there's another o' 'em squattin' on the mat outside.'

'But you're in India now, and you should be pleased to find somebody to do your work for you.'

'Well, I ain't, sir, an' that's a fact!'

'What did you do with him?'

'Pushed 'im outside with 'is mate. 'E couldn't even talk English.'

'You'll have to learn Hindustani!'

'Not me, sir. English is good enough for me, an' if these blokes don't speak it, well they ought, that's all I've got ter say. It ain't natural to speak in that outlandish lingo.'

Wallace laughed, and continued his leisurely dressing.

'You'll get used to them in time,' he said.

He soon afterwards rejoined Muir, and found that Brien had preceded him.

'Have you been imagining you were swimming the Channel?' asked the latter.

'Why?'

'You've been a dickens of a time, and I heard a most unholy splashing coming from your bathroom.'

'When I wash myself, Bill, I do the thing properly; not in the way beloved of Irishmen!'

Muir laughed.

'It's good to hear you two again,' he said. 'It makes me feel younger!'

'Dear old granddad!' said Brien. 'How lightly the years sit upon your bent old shoulders!'

'Now for business!' said Leonard briskly. 'It's time you told us the facts of this case, Muir. All I know is that some very important plans have been stolen and a man murdered, and that the Viceroy has sent for us to recover the plans.'

At that moment a secretary entered the room.

'His Excellency has returned!' he announced. 'He desires you to come along to his study, gentlemen, if you feel you are rested sufficiently!'

They immediately followed Muir into the Viceroy's private study, where they found Lord Oundle eagerly awaiting them.

'Wallace!' he exclaimed, shaking hands warmly. 'And Brien! I don't think I have ever welcomed two men so gladly before!'

'Almost the exact words Muir used,' said Leonard, 'and I told him it was a case of sheer cupboard love; but of course I would not think of accusing Your Excellency of such a thing!'

Lord Oundle laughed.

'I am afraid that even in my case there is a selfish motive,' he remarked. 'We have got ourselves into a hole, and want you to get us out. Have you told them, Muir?'

'I was just about to do so when Your Excellency sent for us.'

'Then perhaps you will tell them the story now.' He turned to Wallace. 'I am very anxious that you shall hear everything without a moment's delay, and I must express my thanks for the extraordinary speed you have shown in getting here.'

'That is due to our very expert pilots and mechanics,' said Leonard.

'I shall have an opportunity of thanking them presently,' said His Excellency. 'Sit down, both of you, and help yourselves to cigars or cigarettes!'

'I'd prefer a pipe, if I may?' said Wallace, and the permission being granted, he carefully filled and lit a pipe, without which he never moved.

'You use that arm of yours very cleverly, Wallace,' remarked Lord Oundle. 'Now, Muir, perhaps you will relate the extraordinary events that led us to summon Sir Leonard from England.'

'First of all, Muir,' put in Leonard, 'I'd like to ask a question or two! Were you in personal touch at all with the officer who was murdered?'

'I was with him when it took place!'

'H'm! Have you any idea whether or not he had the plans on him at the time?'

'I am perfectly certain he had. My narrative will put the whole facts of the case before you.'

'Carry on then, and please omit nothing, even the smallest detail!'

Sir Henry nodded, and commencing from the time that Major Elliott came to him at Simla, and relating every incident that happened until he returned to Delhi after the inquest, he gave a very lucid and concise account. He even described the man whom Elliott half suspected of watching him at Summer Hill station and his own fears and doubts on his headlong drive to the Viceregal Lodge at Delhi. None of his hearers interrupted him. Wallace smoked away as though he were not very interested, and indeed somewhat bored by the story, while Lord Oundle kept his eyes on the latter's face, and appeared slightly disappointed and disturbed by the apparent lack of interest he saw there. Brien who had been smoking a cigar, allowed it to go out after a while, and seemed utterly absorbed in what he heard.

At length Muir finished, and Wallace rose quietly to his feet and knocked the ashes from his pipe into an ash-tray. He smiled at the others.

'So Colonel Sanders arrested the driver of the rail motor,' he said, and chuckled. 'What I can't understand is why he did not arrest you, Muir!'

'Arrest me!' exclaimed the indignant Secretary.

'Yes! You were sitting next to the murdered man, and it would have been easy for you to have stabbed him, and nobody would have suspected you of taking the plans!'

'But, my dear fellow, you don't mean to say—'

Wallace laughed outright.

'Poor Henry's got the wind up!' he exclaimed. 'I am only saying what the Colonel might have done. To my mind it would have been just as sensible as arresting the poor wretched driver.'

The Viceroy leant forward over his desk.

'Surely you have not already evolved a theory,' he asked.

'Nothing tangible enough to be called a theory,' replied Leonard. 'But I am quite certain the driver had nothing to do with the light going out! May I have a fast car at seven o'clock in the morning? I've a lot to do in Simla tomorrow.'

'Of course,' replied Muir, who by now had recovered from the shock he had received. 'I suppose you will want to interview Captain Williams and Hartley!'

'No, I don't think so – not yet anyway. Where can I find Williams if I want him?'

'Lahore Cantonments! He belongs to the 107th Horse!'

'Right! Make a note of that, Billy!' He walked to the fireplace, and although there was no fire there, planted himself with his back to it, and refilled his pipe.

'I have several very important questions to ask,' he said,

'and please be as accurate as possible in your replies. First of all, though, I am going to tell Your Excellency something and you, Muir, which will interest you. The Commander-in-Chief did a very good day's work when he closed the frontier so effectively, and that is probably the reason why the plans are *still in India!*'

The Viceroy and Sir Henry looked at him in amazement.

'Are you sure of that, or is it merely conjecture?' questioned the former eagerly.

'I *know* they are still in the country, and I know that they are in the hands of Russian spies. Furthermore I have a pretty good notion how they were stolen!'

'God bless my soul!' gasped the Viceroy, while Billy, forgetful of the presence of His Excellency, exclaimed, 'Well, I'm damned!'

'Now, Muir,' said Wallace briskly, 'what were Major Elliott's exact words about safeguarding the plans after that midnight attempt to steal them?'

'He said that he had an uncanny feeling that he was doomed, and that he was going to make extra certain of them!'

'Ah! Now where were you exactly when he said that?'

'In my bedroom!'

'I see! Could anybody have overheard you?'

'I don't think so!'

'Nowhere where anybody could have been hidden in the room?'

'Well, I didn't search, but there were three cupboards where a man could have hidden himself. I don't think anybody would have risked that!'

'Have you a veranda outside your window?'

'No! It is a sheer drop of about twenty feet to the grounds below.'

'What about the door – could a conversation be heard through it?'

'Yes, I suppose so! And, now I come to think of it, we left the door ajar!'

'Just so! Nothing very extraordinary about that. Who was in the building besides yourselves?'

'Nobody! There were of course several bearers, chowkidars and other servants still living in the compound.'

'None of them, you are quite certain, were in the house at the time?'

'Oh yes, one – my own bearer – who had supplied us with whisky and sodas.'

'How long have you had him?'

'Ever since I came out, about two years ago!'

'Has he served you faithfully?'

'Very!'

'Is he with you here?'

'Yes, would you like to see him?'

'Not just now, thanks.'

Wallace lapsed into silence, and the others looked at him curiously.

'Why do you attach so much importance to that remark of Major Elliott's?' asked the Viceroy.

'Oh, it is merely a whim of mine,' replied Leonard with a smile. 'Just another question, Muir. Elliott's dead body was left in a room at Barog station until Colonel Sanders arrived, you say. Had anybody but the doctor access to that room?'

'Only Captain Williams, who, as I told you, had the key, and was left with orders to admit nobody but the doctor, until the Deputy Commissioner arrived.'

'Could anybody have got in through the window?'

'There was no window!'

'H'm! . . . The doctor is above suspicion?'

'Of course,' Muir laughed. 'He is an Englishman, and besides Elliott was dead then, and I had the case which was supposed to contain the plans!'

'Yes, quite! Well, I don't think I will bother you with any more questions just now, thanks very much. And now,' he added, smiling at the Viceroy, 'I think it is high time I paid my respects to Her Excellency and Doreen!'

'Certainly! I'll take you along to them,' replied Lord Oundle, 'but you have aroused my curiosity with your questions.'

'Your Excellency will pardon my not satisfying it at present, I hope?'

Lord Oundle nodded and smiled.

'You are a mysterious fellow, Wallace,' he said.

'I'll give you one little item which may be news to you,' said Leonard. 'This country is overrun with Russian spies, who are doing their best to undermine British authority. An article appeared in the *Indiaman* about our arrival on a special mission in India, and I am firmly convinced that it was put in by a Russian agent, as the Bolsheviks are intensely interested in our trip.'

The Viceroy looked thunderstruck.

'I did not see the article,' he said, 'and how dare the editor publish it without authority?'

'He thought he had authority, for the man who rang him up and gave him the news said he was the Deputy Commissioner of Karachi, and imitated the Commissioner's voice!'

Lord Oundle and Sir Henry Muir looked at him in wonder.

'Furthermore,' went on Wallace, 'the man you have so kindly

locked up for me in this building, Muir, is a Russian Bolshevik spy, who was sent to murder Brien and me at Karachi. I want him kept here till I have asked him a few questions!'

The Viceroy walked to the door as one in a dream, and held it open for Wallace.

'After you, Your Excellency!' said Leonard politely, and followed Lord Oundle out of the room.

CHAPTER FIFTEEN

Batty Changes His Tactics

Lady Oundle and her daughter Doreen were unaffectedly glad to see Sir Leonard Wallace, and, in a slightly lesser degree, Major Brien. They had been friends for many years and, apart from that, the two ladies felt as though they had, in some intangible way, been brought closer to their own country by the arrival of Wallace and his companion, who had actually been in London only four days before.

The Vicereine had travelled to many parts of the world with her husband, but she was essentially a home-loving woman and England to her was home. She often longed for the time when they could return for good. India as a country she admired very much, and she liked the majority of Indians with whom she came into contact, but all the same it was a species of exile, even though she was in India as the Vicereine and she counted the days to the momentous occasion when she would step on English soil, never to leave it again.

Lady Doreen Spencer was like her mother in a great many

ways, but she was still very young, and India to her was a glorious adventure. She had come out half expecting that she was coming to a semi-civilised country; that she would be thrown amongst all kinds of strange and fearsome people, and meet with exciting and hairbreadth adventures. If the truth were told, the real India had come more as a shock than as a revelation. The culture, the refinement and the courtesy of the average people she met had surprised her, and it took her some time to readjust the views she had formed during her schooldays. But she found the country a very beautiful one, and she was never tired of expatiating on the delights which she discovered every day, and although she had been out a very short time, she spoke Hindustani almost fluently. She was a pretty girl, full of life, but quite unsophisticated, and Lady Oundle never made any attempt to curb her naturally high spirits. She knew that on occasions her daughter could be most dignified, and she lavished all her affection on this sole-surviving child.

As Wallace and Brien entered the drawing room where the two ladies awaited them, Doreen rose from her chair with a cry of delight. She hardly gave Leonard time to bow over her ladyship's hand before she had put her arm through his, and begun to ask him eagerly about his journey. After a while he raised his arms in mock surrender.

'My dear Doreen,' he said, 'your questions are laying me out flat. Before I have time to answer one you have asked me half a dozen more. Now will you take them one by one in regular order, and I will endeavour to reply to them!'

'Please don't bring your officialdom into this room!' she said. 'I'll ask them as I want to! Anyhow, I am not really interested to know how you got here, or what you did on the way. What I wish to know is: first, how's the Earl?'

'Topping! At least he was the last time I saw him!'

'Splendid! He's a dear old man, and I'm very fond of him. What I can't understand,' she added, 'is how on earth he ever got a son like you!'

Lord and Lady Oundle laughed, and Leonard made a wry face. Billy grinned at his friend in amusement.

'If you say things like that to Leonard,' said Lady Oundle, 'I'll tell him what you confided to me when you heard he was coming—'

'Oh, you dare not!' exclaimed the girl with a sudden vivid blush.

'Do tell me, Lady Oundle!' said Wallace. 'She deserves it, whatever it is!'

'Oh, I'll spare her this time.'

'I don't care if you do tell him!' said Doreen obviously inviting her mother to speak.

'There you are,' said Leonard. 'She wants me to know!'

'Well, she said that if you had not been married to Molly, she would love to have you for her husband!'

'My sentiments exactly!' returned Wallace. 'But we've known this for a long time, haven't we, Doreen? Do you remember the day we made love to each other, and Molly would not get jealous?'

'Don't tell tales! What will Daddy think of me if you reveal my dreadful past like this! And that brings me to a very burning question – How is Molly?'

Leonard went into an enthusiastic discourse on Lady Wallace which was terminated by his companion withdrawing her arm from his and pouting.

'Did you ever hear anything like that?' she said. 'The deceitfulness of man! One moment he is making love to me and the next going into rhapsodies over his wife.'

There was a general laugh, in the midst of which she turned to him again.

'I do think it is mean of you not to have brought her with you.'

'She's coming!' replied Leonard. 'In fact, she must be well on her way by now.'

'How perfectly ripping!' exclaimed the girl with dancing eyes, and both Lady Oundle and the Viceroy voiced their pleasure. 'When will she arrive?'

'I'm not quite sure! I half expected to find a cable awaiting me here. She and Phyllis are coming out on the yacht!'

'Phyllis too! I'm so glad! I hope all the babies are coming as well, Major Brien?'

'They are,' replied Billy with a blush, 'but don't talk as though there is an army of them!'

'Well, there almost is!' she returned, and amidst the laughter of the others Billy blushed again. 'What about Adrian?' She turned to Leonard. 'He is coming too, I hope?'

'Of course,' said Wallace indignantly; 'He couldn't be left behind!'

For some time the coming of Molly and Phyllis was discussed, and many plans for their entertainment spoken of by Lady Oundle and Doreen. At length the gong summoned them to their various rooms to dress for dinner, and Wallace and Brien walked along to their apartments together.

To his surprise, the former found that Batty had apparently changed his tactics. As he dressed, Leonard discovered that he had two bearers waiting on him, while Batty stood by with serious mien, and directed them. He smiled quizzically at his man-servant.

'What is the idea, Batty?' he asked.

'Idea, sir?'

'Yes! I thought you would not allow these "black heathens" to look after me?'

'Well, sir – beggin' yer pardon, sir,' replied Batty apologetically, 'I found that if they didn't do nothin' for you, they'd be 'angin' round lazy like, and it don't do no one no good no'ow to be lazy, so I thought I'd better let 'em work, and just watch that they did it all right, sir – 'ang round in the offing, so to speak, sir.'

'I see!'

''Ave I your approval, sir?'

'Oh, quite!'

Batty looked mysterious, and then a grin gradually spread over his face.

'Wot do yer think, sir?' he asked with a half suppressed chuckle. 'If it ain't the whole bloomin' – beg pardon, sir – if it ain't a bit of a joke like!'

'Well, what is it?'

'They've been and given me one o' these 'ere black angels to look arter me!'

'You've got a bearer, have you?'

'Yes, sir! Take me oath on it, sir! I wish I 'ad a wife now,' he added.

'What on earth for?'

'Well, sir, 'er an' me could laugh at me 'aving a servant for many a long day, sir.'

Leonard chuckled.

'What are you going to do with him?'

'I'm blest if I know. I've took me boots off four times and made 'im clean 'em, and I've brushed me 'air six times, so as 'e could 'and me the brushes every time. Swab me decks – beggin' yer pardon, sir – I've never been so tickled to death in me life!'

Wallace was still laughing to himself as he went down to dinner.

Forsyth and Hallows had arrived, but there were no other guests, with the result that an informal note was struck, and dinner, in consequence, was quite a bright function. The Viceroy became almost jovial and Lady Oundle confided to Wallace that she had not seen him looking so happy for a very long time. Doreen sat between the two airmen, and by the end of dinner, it looked as though one, at least, had fallen a victim to her charms. The gaiety was further heightened by the arrival of a cablegram for Leonard during the meal which informed them that Molly and Phyllis had embarked at Marseilles that day, and were sailing at once.

When the ladies had left the room, and the men had drawn their chairs closer together, the Viceroy thanked Forsyth and Hallows for their expert airmanship, which had enabled Sir Leonard Wallace and Major Brien to reach Delhi in such a remarkably short space of time. He invited them to stay at Viceregal Lodge for a few days before returning, and informed them that both Sir Henry Muir and he would do their best to entertain them. The airmen expressed their appreciation of his kindness, and told him that they had received instructions to hold themselves under Sir Leonard Wallace's orders in India as long as he required them, and not to return to England until he ordered them to do so.

'By Jove!' exclaimed Wallace, on hearing this. 'The Air Ministry have been very good. Why didn't you tell me that before, Forsyth? I was thinking of taking a touching farewell of you tonight!'

Forsyth laughed.

'I thought you knew, Sir Leonard!'

'This gives me furiously to think,' murmured the other, and immediately lapsed into thought. Presently he looked at

Muir. 'Would it be possible for an aeroplane to land in Simla?' he asked.

'Yes,' replied Muir. 'There is a fine open space between the hills where football matches are played, called Annandale.'

'That seems very nice; what do you say, Forsyth?'

'It sounds ideal, sir.'

'Good! Then we won't want the car, Lord Oundle, after all. We'll fly there tomorrow morning. Perhaps Muir will furnish Forsyth with a map of Simla, and anything else he wants?'

Sir Henry eagerly expressed his willingness to do everything in his power to help.

'I am very grateful to the Air Ministry,' said Wallace with satisfaction. 'They have made our job a good deal easier. There is just one thing more I should like to ask you to do, Muir, before we join the ladies: will you send a wire to the Deputy Commissioner to tell him of our arrival, and ask him to meet us at Annandale . . . By the way, how far is it from here to Simla?'

'About two hundred miles,' replied Lord Oundle. 'Then we'll be in Simla at nine-thirty tomorrow morning! That all right, Forsyth?'

The airman smiled.

'Quite, Sir Leonard!'

'Good! Then I'll leave the rest to you, Muir!'

At eleven o'clock that night Sir Henry, Brien and Wallace were seated in the latter's sitting room discussing events.

'When did the murder take place exactly, Muir?' asked Leonard, puffing a cloud of smoke from his pipe.

'At about seven o'clock on Monday last!'

'And this is Saturday. That is, the plans have been in the hands of these people for five days! In that time they could have been taken across the frontier, but the frontier was closed. Tell me!' he added suddenly. 'How long would it take to get from Barog to Karachi?'

'Well, the usual way would be via Lahore, though a slightly quicker route might be by way of Bhatinda. In any case it would take about two days.'

'I see! That means to say that a man leaving Simla or Barog, with the plans on Monday night, would not reach Karachi until Wednesday night?'

Muir's eyes opened wide.

'Then you think that—?'

'I think that obviously the plans will have to go to Russia by Karachi and the Persian Gulf, as they cannot cross the frontier.'

Sir Henry rose to his feet in a state of great excitement.

'I never thought of that,' he groaned. 'And I might have done something to stop them. They have probably gone by now.'

'They had not gone this morning!' announced Wallace.

'How on earth do you know?'

'By an aptitude for watching faces, and asking leading questions! Still I don't like taking chances! There is only one thing I am worried about – When do the boats leave Karachi for Busra?'

'I don't know,' said Muir. 'Just a minute and I'll find out for you.' And he hurried out of the room.

Wallace walked up and down with his hands behind his back, and his teeth clenched over his pipe.

'There's a chance that we may have been beaten after all, Billy,' he said. 'A boat might have left today and then—! That fellow showed me pretty clearly by his face that the plans were still in India this morning, but he might have been hiding the fact that they were going today!'

'I see what you are driving at,' said Brien. 'But they might have been *posted* to Russia.'

'By Jove! That's another notion! I wish Muir would hurry up – it will be damnable if we have been just a bit too clever!'

Sir Henry came back into the room as though he had been running.

'Well?' said Wallace, quite eagerly for him.

'The ordinary boat leaves on Wednesday; the mail on Friday!'

Leonard stood deep in thought for a moment, then he smiled.

'Good!' he said. 'I think we've still got a chance!'

'But,' said Sir Henry in agitation, 'if the plans were taken by boat from Karachi, they might have gone either on Wednesday, or yesterday!'

'Not on Wednesday certainly – there would not have been time; and I feel pretty certain that there would not have been time to catch yesterday's boat either.'

'Why not?'

'My dear Muir, I am only working on a theory, and I am not going to say any more until I've been to Simla. Apart from that I tell you that my prisoner gave away the fact to me, quite unintentionally, that the plans are still in India. Now we must make certain that they do not go by next week's boats!'

'Do you want me to do anything about that?'

'No; Billy and I will see to it. There is only one possibility now by which we may have been beaten, and that is, as Billy suggests, the post. But I don't think they would dare send them that way, and there again my captive's accidental confirmation of my remark that they are still in India precludes that worry. However, Muir, it may come to the post next week, and, if so, I shall have to get you to see that every blessed letter, or package, going up the Persian Gulf is examined before it goes.'

Sir Henry nodded.

'But,' said Billy, knocking the ashes out of his pipe, 'they might post the plans to a confederate anywhere in the world – Europe Africa, Australia or America – and the recipient could take, or send them on! What then?'

Wallace looked at him grimly for a moment, and then a smile gradually came over his face.

'Have a heart, Billy!' he said. 'And now I'm going to have a few words with the spy. Give me the key, Muir!'

Sir Henry handed it over.

'Shall I come along?' he asked.

'No, if you don't mind. I do not expect to get much out of him, but he is more likely to talk if there are only two of us!'

They left the disappointed Muir standing at the door, and walked along to the room in which the Russian was imprisoned.

'Now,' said Wallace, when he and Brien had locked themselves in with the captive, and the former had seated himself on one of the two chairs, 'I told you the conditions on which I would drop the attempted murder charge, so perhaps you will give me a little information!'

'There isn't much you don't know already,' the fellow answered sullenly.

'No, not much, it is true! I want to hear how much *you* know about the stolen plans.'

'Nothing!'

'Come, that tone won't do! If you are going to be foolish, Major Brien and I will not waste any more time over you, and you'll be handed over to the police at once.'

'What if I am? It won't make any difference to me whether I

am charged with trying to murder you, or as a spy!'

'Oh, yes it will – very much difference! If you are merely found guilty of being a spy, your sentence will be quite a small one, especially if I mention that you were only a tool. On the other hand, a conviction for attempted murder as well as espionage will mean years of imprisonment!'

The man looked from one to the other.

'I did not want to kill you,' he said; 'they forced me to go!'

'Pshaw!' exclaimed Billy in disgust. 'It's no use your cringing, it will not help you!'

Wallace raised his hand.

'Just a minute!' he said to Brien, and then turned to the spy 'We are not really interested in your feelings. If you are going to answer do so, if not we'll leave you!'

'I'll answer if I can!' replied the man. 'But I dare not mention names.'

'First of all, then, the plans were stolen on Monday night! When are they to be taken to Karachi?'

The fellow hesitated, then,

'They are expected there on Tuesday night!'

'I see! And will be sent on up the Persian Gulf, I suppose, by the boat that leaves on Wednesday.'

The spy nodded.

'Where are they now?'

'You said you knew!'

'Quite so! I want confirmation!'

'You can't fool me like that!'

'I am not trying to fool you! All I want is the exact place!'

The man looked at him earnestly for a minute or two, and then a sly expression crept over his face.

'I do not know the exact address,' he said, 'but the agent who has them is in Simla somewhere.'

'You're telling lies!' snapped Leonard sternly. 'They are in Lahore and you know it!' He bit his lip and looked at the other intensely. The spy became utterly confused, and made feeble efforts to pull himself together, but it was apparent that he was a beaten man. Brien, looking on in amazement, heard his friend murmur, 'Thank Heaven!'

'Come on, Brien!' he said. 'We'll leave this fellow to his meditations. He has not a very rosy future to look forward to!' And rising he took Billy's arm, and walked with him to the door.

'Just a minute!' pleaded the spy in a strangled sort of voice. They turned. 'I only tried to mislead you because I was worried about what the others might do if they found I had given them away. But you know so much that it does not seem to matter what I tell you!'

'No – it doesn't!'

'Well, they *are* in Lahore!'

'Yes, and will be taken from there by the Karachi mail on Monday night?'

'Yes!'

'By whom?'

'That I cannot tell you!'

'Are you quite certain?'

'I swear it!'

'And the address where the plans are at present hidden is?'

'I dare not tell you!'

'Is it Messrs. Ata Ullah, Lohari Mandi Street?'

'My God! You're a devil!'

'Then it is?'

'Yes!' The spy closed his eyes as though utterly weary.

'What was the name of the man who stole them?'

'I don't know!'

'Do you know how they were stolen?'

'I heard that Major Elliott was murdered, but how the plans were taken from him, and who took them, I swear I do not know.'

'H'm! Well that will do, I think! You'll be kept here for the present, so you have nothing to fear!'

Wallace walked to the door and opened it. Brien passed through; he followed him and, having locked and bolted the door again, set off hurriedly for his own rooms, with the mystified Billy close behind. Once in the sitting room he threw himself into an armchair, helped himself to a whisky and soda, and signed to Brien to do the same.

'I'm just bubbling over with questions!' said the latter, as he mixed himself what Americans call a high-ball.

'For the Lord's sake don't ask them, Bill,' replied Leonard, wearily filling his pipe.

'Well, just one then! Was it all bluff, or do you really know something?'

'A good deal was bluff, but I had formed a theory which events have almost substantiated. Tomorrow, in Simla, I am expecting that theory to be confirmed beyond all doubt. If it is not, then we shall be beaten!'

'But you have information enough now to enable us to recover the plans!'

'Quite so! But it is not the plans I am worrying about now so much as the copies that may have been made!'

'By Jove, yes!'

They lapsed into silence. Presently Batty entered followed

by the two bearers. The latter knelt down and each took off one of Wallace's shoes, and replaced it with a slipper – the ex-sailor watching them approvingly the while. When they had finished and risen to their feet, he pointed to the door.

'Jao – juldee,' he commanded and the bearers departed. Then he turned to Wallace. 'That's 'Industani for 'op it quick, sir!' he explained.

CHAPTER SIXTEEN

Re-enter Sanders

Nobody seeing Sir Leonard Wallace strolling round the aeroplane the following morning, in his neat grey suit and white topee, would have taken him for the head of that great organisation which spreads its tentacles to so many parts of the world, and which is Britain's eyes and ears – the Secret Service – unless they had personal knowledge of that fact. He always gave the impression of being an idler, who loved to dally his way through life and found something to amuse him everywhere. He seldom, if ever, hurried and yet he was always on the spot; he gave decisions without hesitation, almost as though they were mechanical, yet behind his easy-going, happy-go-lucky exterior a wonderful brain directed his actions, and was hardly ever at rest – a brain which Muir described rightly as one of the most brilliant in England.

The responsibility of being the chief of what was perhaps the most important government department, would have turned most men white and hurried them to premature graves, but it never worried Wallace. No matter how intricate the situation, how desperate the position, he never turned a hair, and that was why worried statesmen stared at him in amazement when discussing international problems with him. The British Cabinet placed the utmost reliance in him, and his confidential department worked under his orders quietly, silently, never sleeping, always alert.

Few people know of the enormous staff employed by the Intelligence Department. Under Wallace were men and women in almost every civilised country in the world, and a great number of them owed their success as secret agents to his astuteness. From these people was derived the information which was used by Great Britain to combat foreign plots, and which enabled her to deal with the delicate situations which constantly arose. Then again was the office staff, consisting mainly of ex-officers of the Army and Navy, who dealt under Sir Leonard's and Brien's orders with the many documents relative to the intrigues of foreign governments and the juggling that continually goes on in the inner circle of international diplomacy. Major Brien's chief duties concerned this side of the department, but, as ever, he and Wallace were almost inseparable, and whenever possible the latter took his great friend with him on what he called his 'outdoor duties'. Billy had not the quick perception, the imagination and inventiveness that gave Leonard the wonderful faculty of following a thing through, as though he had been actually present, and he did not possess that unerring instinct where secret enquiries were necessary; but he had the same dogged determination, though Leonard's was the determination of a terrier, and his the obstinacy of a bulldog, and like his great friend, once he had set his mind on a certain course, he kept grimly on and never deviated until the end was attained. He also was an expert on the routine work of the department, and Wallace left a lot of that responsibility upon his shoulders in consequence.

A most fascinating volume could be written dealing entirely with Wallace's department; its many ramifications and activities, the night side of it, the postal department where correspondence which was suspected could be opened and copied; the hundreds of agents living in all parts of the world, ostensibly in some profession above any suspicion, but really as the Secret Service men and women of Great Britain; and the connection that exists between it and the Special Branch at New Scotland Yard; but this account deals only with Wallace's adventures in India. He appeared to regard the loss of the plans as a very ordinary affair, though to Sir Henry Muir, and even to Billy Brien the problem of their disappearance seemed beyond explanation.

As Leonard strolled round the aeroplane admiring its lines and complimenting the two mechanics on the result of their cleaning and furbishing – for the machine shone in the early morning sun until the onlookers were compelled to turn away with watery eyes – Muir followed him round, hoping to get him to talk and thereby expound his theories, but all to no avail. Wallace appeared to be thinking of anything but the loss of the plans, and replied to Sir Henry's questions in monosyllables, or with remarks on some totally different subject.

The Secretary had a great admiration for the head of the Secret Service and although very little information was ever permitted to leak out about the activities of that department, he had, owing to his position, heard of one or two of Leonard's exploits which struck him as being almost incredible. It was, therefore, very disappointing to him to find himself prevented from attempting to follow the workings of Wallace's mind, and at last he ceased to ask questions and indeed became a trifle irritable. Leonard immediately noticed this and smiled.

'Billy!' he called. 'Come here! I've an object of curiosity to show you!'

Brien left Forsyth and Hallows with whom he had been chatting, and strolled across to them.

'What's the trouble?' he asked.

'Our little Henry is sulky, because I won't answer his questions!'

'Good Lord! Did you call me across just to tell me that?'

'M'm! I thought you'd be interested and perhaps alarmed!'

'Don't worry about him, Muir!' said Billy to the Secretary. 'He's like that! He won't even answer *my* questions! Between you and me, he's more puzzled than any of us, but he pretends he has a theory – it's merely bluff!'

Wallace grinned cheerfully.

'That's it,' he said. 'Just bluff!'

'Well, we've given you a needle to look for in a bottle of hay this time,' said Sir Henry.

'Yes, I must say you've found a pretty little problem for us to unravel!'

'Absurd job to give anybody,' grunted Billy, 'and almost impossible after this lapse of time.'

'Your tempers will be pretty well tried if you have much to do with Sanders!' said Muir, who still appeared to rankle under a sense of injury.

'Who's Sanders?' asked Wallace, then, 'Oh, I know, the Deputy Commissioner at Simla?'

'Yes! A very choleric old bird! When he heard you were coming out, he got annoyed and called you a picturesque, out-of-a-novel detective.'

Billy and Leonard laughed heartily.

'I shall like that man,' said the latter.

'Are you ready, Sir Leonard?' asked Forsyth, joining them.

'Yes, quite!' replied Wallace. 'Now listen to me, Muir,' he added seriously, and looking round to see that he was not overheard. 'There's another and very important job I want you to do, so consider yourself a Secret Service man for the time being!'

'And the Lord help you if you make a mistake!' put in Brien.

'Dry up, Billy!' said Wallace. 'Don't frighten the man! I want you to go straight to the Chief Commissioner of Police from here. Don't wait to have breakfast first, and if he's still in bed, pull him out. Tell him to give orders for a strong squad of men of the Special Branch or CID, to stand ready day and night in all the large cities to raid certain premises at a moment's notice. I expect to put my hands on a list of addresses sooner or later, from where Russian Bolshevik propaganda work is carried out, and when I do, I'll phone to him *every address* with orders to raid it at once. Do you understand?'

Sir Henry nodded, his eyes sparkling with excitement.

'Tell him to get his orders through immediately as secretly as he can, and to have a reliable man always handy at the telephone.'

'What am I to say if he wants to know all about it?'

'Tell him to do what he's told first, and ask questions afterwards!' replied Leonard tersely. 'And now, for goodness' sake don't bungle it!'

He made Muir repeat his instructions before he was satisfied, then:

'Keep the whole thing absolutely secret, and see that he does too! All the big towns, mind, and as many of the small ones as he likes. Tell him not to spoil the ship for a ha'porth of tar. And when the raids are carried out nobody going in or coming out is to be allowed to escape, and all documents and every scrap of paper taken to police headquarters. He needn't bother about Karachi – I've already arranged things there, and that is my special province. Now, cheerio, Muir, and be careful! Expect us back when you see us! We might come back tonight, and we might not be back for days!'

Sir Henry shook hands, and getting into his car drove away at once.

As the plane rose in the air, Billy turned to his companion with a grin.

'Muir's delighted with his job,' he said. 'He feels himself one of us now! By the way, why this thusness about the raiding squads?'

'Because I hope to raid that place in Lahore during the next twenty-four hours, and we might find a list of addresses of other places there.'

'Then you think there are more than Caxton's three?'

'Yes, rather! Don't you?'

Billy nodded.

'And I suppose you want it to be done quickly in case they are warned?' he asked.

'Exactly!'

It was not long before they sighted the hills, and in a couple of hours' time they found themselves flying over towering masses which sometimes appeared to be only a few feet below them, and anon over beautifully wooded valleys that seemed to drop to an incredible depth. Some of the hills were covered with vegetation, others looked barren and ugly and as bare as the human hand. In the distance could be seen snow-clad peaks, gleaming brilliantly in the sunshine. They were among the Himalayas, that great range of mountains which boasts of the highest peak in the world.

Bungalows and houses appeared in view far below looking like tiny toy houses left about by a careless child. In some cases, where the bungalows were surrounded by well-kept gardens, the whole had the fascinating appearance of the popular Japanese garden decoration at one time found gracing the centres of so many tables in English and Continental homes.

The curious formation of some of the hills interested Wallace and Brien immensely. There were a few which looked like extinct volcanoes, others were almost grotesque in their shape, while one, spread below them, had the curious appearance of a giant's face, with puckered eyebrows, thick lips, large hooked nose and closed eyes.

Presently Simla was in sight, and rows and rows of white houses could be seen spreading up the hillside, with here and there the sun glinting on a window and causing a bright shaft of light to shine in their eyes. The narrow, snake-like mountain railway was observed twisting its way upwards, and right ahead were the deeply wooded slopes of Jakko which is crowded with monkeys, and where the sightseer can watch a withered ancient priest feed them for the sum of a few annas, from the old Hindu temple on the pinnacle.

Neither Leonard nor Billy had been to Simla before, and though they had been stationed in India with their regiment previous to the outbreak of war, their only acquaintance with hill stations was with Ootacamund in the south and Darjeeling in Bengal.

Forsyth, who was piloting the machine, took no risks in landing. He circled round Viceregal Lodge and Summer Hill station several times before he eventually glided down and came to rest on the large sports ground known as Annandale.

As Wallace and Brien stepped down from the machine, a bored-looking man with a sandy moustache turning grey, and blue eyes that had a look of weariness in them, walked towards them. He gazed from one to the other, and then said:

'I am Sanders, the Deputy Commissioner here!'

'How do you do, Colonel!' said Leonard heartily. 'My name's Wallace. This is Major Brien, my very capable second in command!'

The trio shook hands, Leonard languidly, Billy energetically and Sanders as though very bored at such a ceremony. For a second or two there was silence, and in that small space of time Wallace had formed a complete opinion of the Commissioner. That this opinion was favourable was evident from the smile with which he favoured the man who had met them.

'I have just stepped out of a novel, Colonel Sanders,' he said, with a twinkle in his eyes.

'You've what, Sir Leonard?' asked the other in surprise; then a look of understanding spread over his face and he actually blushed. 'Do you mean to tell me,' he blurted out, 'that Sir Henry Muir repeated to you what I had said?'

'Yes; I think he was a little piqued with me at the time!'

'Well, I'm not going to apologise, Sir Leonard, but—'

'Apologise! Good gracious, no! I regard it as a compliment! I've stepped out of my novel to find the plans and restore them to the Government! You want the murderer of Elliott. I have a feeling we may do a lot together!'

The two steadily regarded each other, and then they both smiled, and in that moment a friendship was born which was destined to last.

'I have some rickshas waiting here,' announced Sanders.

'Thanks,' said Leonard, and called to Forsyth. 'I think we'll be ready to depart about two,' he remarked, 'so you'd better go and enjoy yourselves until then!'

'Not much enjoyment in Simla now,' grunted the Colonel.

'Forsyth and Hallows will find it if there is any,' said Brien, and

Forsyth grinned. Batty came up and saluted respectfully.

'Any orders, sir?' he enquired.

'No! Go and do anything you like until two,' said Wallace, 'but be here sharp at that hour. And don't get into any scrapes in the Bazaar, or you might find yourself left behind in jail and coming up before Colonel Sanders tomorrow morning.'

Batty departed indignantly.

'Now, do you want to visit Viceregal Lodge?' enquired the Commissioner.

No, thanks! I'm not a bit interested in it. I want to see this famous rail motor and I should like a few words with your man Hartley.'

'Right!' replied Sanders. 'We'll go straight to the station, and we'll probably find Hartley awaiting us there. I thought you'd want to speak to him, so I told him to go to the station, so that you could see the motor and interview him at the same time!'

'Colonel,' said Leonard, as he got into his ricksha, 'you're a man after my own heart!'

The Commissioner directed the coolies, and soon the trio were being hauled up the long steep slopes that led to the railway station. It was slow work and the laboured breathing of the men as they pulled his vehicle up some particularly steep incline moved Wallace to pity. At last they reached their destination, and he alighted gladly.

'Poor beggars!' he said to the Commissioner. 'What a beastly life to lead!'

The Colonel shrugged his shoulders.

'It is their job!' he replied, and led the way into the station. The stationmaster saw them and hurried up.

'Good morning, Sloan!' said Sanders. 'Where's Mr Hartley?'

'In that siding, sir, standing by number six.'

They walked along the platform, and found Hartley near a rail motor car. He was introduced to Wallace and Brien, and saluted respectfully.

'Is this the car in which the murder took place?' asked Leonard.

'Yes,' replied the Commissioner, and the four of them gazed at it in silence for a moment.

'An innocent looking object,' murmured Billy.

'And a most puzzling one, too,' grunted Sanders. He turned to Wallace. 'I suppose Muir has told you the whole story, Sir Leonard?' he questioned,

'Muir was concise, lucid and dramatic!' replied Leonard. 'He told me everything so clearly that I was able to picture it. Tell me!' he added. 'What is your theory about the light suddenly going out?'

'I felt certain that the loose bulb business was all wrong,' replied Sanders, 'and I had the whole car examined by electrical experts to see if it would have been possible for anybody to interfere with the lighting in the tunnel. But they declared it would not be. Hartley here is one of the maniacs who consider that the lamp must have been loose and thus the shaking of the car temporarily caused the light to fail,' he added.

Wallace looked at the police officer.

'Doesn't it strike you as a most remarkable coincidence,' he asked, 'that it should go out at the identical time that the murder was committed?'

'Well, no, sir! My idea is that the murderer was waiting in the tunnel to kill Major Elliott in any case, and that the failure of the light helped his purpose!'

'That's Muir's theory!' murmured Billy.

'Oh, but it's weak – weak!' growled the Commissioner.

'It is!' nodded Wallace. 'Very weak indeed!'

'I am convinced,' went on the other, 'that the fellow was concealed in the car all the way, and that he did not jump on in the tunnel. He certainly jumped off there after he had murdered Elliott!'

'That is rather immaterial,' said Leonard. 'At all events it's the plans I'm after, and according to Muir's story there was no time for them to have been stolen when the murder took place.'

'There was not, sir,' said Hartley with decision.

'But supposing Major Elliott had them in his breast pocket! It would have been easy to have abstracted them!'

'No, sir. His coat was buttoned up with four buttons and it would have been impossible for the murderer to stab Major Elliott, unbutton his coat, take out the plans, and then button the coat up again!'

'H'm!'

'I still have my suspicions that the driver was connected with the business somehow,' said Sanders. 'Both Captain Williams and Hartley swear that he couldn't have switched off the light without their seeing him do it, but, I don't know—' He shook his head doubtfully.

'Why couldn't he?' demanded Wallace.

'Well, sir, he would have had to stretch right across Captain Williams to reach the switch,' replied Hartley.

'Ah! That brings me to my little theory.'

'Your theory?' asked Sanders.

Leonard smiled.

'Yes! You see Muir was so exact in his description of everything that I was able to form a little idea of my own.'

'Well, I'm hanged!' exclaimed the Colonel, and then turned and swore at some native loungers who had approached and were watching the four with curiosity.

'Where is this switch?' asked Wallace.

Hartley pointed it out to him. It was placed just in the centre of the dashboard, and was an ordinary electric light switch, though a trifle larger than the usual household variety. He entered the car, and sat in the driver's seat.

'Get in, Hartley,' he said, 'and sit where Captain Williams sat!'

The policeman got in, and sat by his side. Brien and Sanders watched them curiously. Leonard leant across and touched the little knob. In doing so his arm brushed Hartley's knee.

'H'm!' grunted the Colonel. 'I never thought of testing it like that. Certainly, the driver could not have switched off the lights without Williams, at least, knowing. Well,' he growled, 'I suppose I shall have to accept the idea that the light was jolted off and on again, and put it down to coincidence!'

'By no means, Sanders,' said Wallace, stepping lazily out of the car. 'The whole thing *hangs* on the failure of the light, and my little theory is strengthened. Now with your permission we'll test it. Then, perhaps, I shall be able to tell you who stole the plans!'

CHAPTER SEVENTEEN

A Startling Demonstration

Wallace's statement seemed to startle his three companions, for they gazed at him for a moment or two in surprise, then:

'What do you want to do?' asked the Commissioner.

'Go down to the tunnel where the murder was committed,' replied Wallace, 'in this car and, if possible, with the same driver!'

'I don't know about the same driver,' said Sanders, 'but the rest can be arranged no doubt. Go and talk to Sloan, and fix it up, Hartley!'

The policeman hurried off, and Wallace leant on the car with his arms folded and looked inside.

'This is where Elliott sat, isn't it?' he asked, and the Colonel nodded.

'Yes,' he said, 'and my theory is that the murderer lay on the floor there.' He pointed to the floor space just behind the seat that had been occupied, by the murdered officer, 'and at the appointed time rose up and stabbed him!'

Wallace shook his head.

'Rather daring if he did,' he said. 'There are several stations on the way down, are there not?'

'Yes.'

'Well, I don't think he would have risked discovery in that bold manner.'

'Whoever he is, or they are, and I believe there are several of them, they don't hesitate at risks, as witness the attempt on Elliott in Viceregal Lodge!'

'I suppose you never found the fellow who got in that night?'

'Not a trace!' replied Sanders gloomily, 'though I combed the bazaar and all the native houses in the district thoroughly for any man with a bullet wound.'

'Oh, I didn't know he was wounded!'

'Yes, found blood on the tree he came down by from the room. Muir might have caught him if he'd been a bit smarter.'

Wallace smiled, and for a time there was silence.

'By the way, Colonel,' asked Billy presently, 'what became of the white man whom Elliott suspected of watching him? Didn't you follow him from here?'

'I followed him from Summer Hill station, and had him closely watched. He was staying in one of the best hotels, and left the next day. My men traced him all the way to his destination. He is a perfectly innocent and respectable member of society, and a highly valued commercial traveller of a very reputable firm which has branches all over India.'

'I seem to be getting a testimonial of him,' murmured Brien.

'Where did he go to?' asked Leonard, carefully filling his pipe.

'Lahore!'

Billy whistled, and Wallace stopped in the act of striking a match, and looked quizzically at the Colonel.

'All roads lead to Lahore!' he said.

'What do you mean?'

'Nothing much! We're taking a little joy ride, or rather I should say flight to Lahore, when we've finished here.' And he went on with the careful ceremony of lighting his pipe. That finished, and puffing out a cloud of smoke:

'What was this highly respectable gentleman like?' he queried.

'You seem very much interested in him, Sir Leonard!'

'I am – very much interested.'

'I was at first, until he turned out to be such an entirely innocent sort of fellow.'

'Why?'

'Well, because Elliott had seen him in Kabul and Peshawar, and at the time that struck me as suspicious, but, of course, his being a commercial traveller accounted for his moving about so much.'

'But not with Major Elliott,' said Billy.

'Oh, that was merely an accident. But you want a description of him. Well, he is very tall, quite six feet in height, and rather broad; has black hair, which he keeps brushed right back without a parting and allows to grow rather longer than usual; a small black semi-military moustache, sallow complexion, thick eyebrows, and a big heavy Jewish nose.'

'That nose: will I ever forget it!' said Leonard quietly.

'Do you know him?' asked Sanders in surprise.

'Oh yes, I know him well – and so does Brien! Billy,' he said to his second string, 'remove the moustache and crop the hair closer, and whom do you find?'

Brien thought deeply for a moment or two and muttered the description to himself, then:

'Great Scott!' he exclaimed. 'Levinsky!'

'You've hit it – our dear old friend, Levinsky.'

The Commissioner was watching them in amazement.

'You've made a mistake,' he said; 'his name is Silverman!'

'Oh, well,' said Leonard, shrugging his shoulders, 'one name's as good as another! What is the name of the very reputable firm he belongs to?'

'Campbell and Brown!'

'The famous wine and spirit merchants? Well, certainly Mr Levinsky – Silverman is adept at getting in with the best people.'

'Look here, Sir Leonard' said Sanders irritably. 'Do you know something about this man?'

'A good deal,' replied Wallace, puffing away contentedly. 'Brien and I have had two or three quite exciting little passages with him, although the last was three or four years ago.'

'Then he is not altogether what he appears to be?'

'No – not altogether. For your private ear alone, I may inform you that he is one of the most dangerous men in the world!' Sanders started. 'He is one of the chief, in fact I should say *the* chief spy of the Russian Soviet Government.'

'Good Lord!' groaned the Commissioner. 'And I let him slip through my fingers!'

'Don't worry about that! I'm glad you did for if you had arrested him – and, I can assure you, you would have found it the most extraordinarily ticklish business – you might have upset my arrangements. I am out here, Colonel Sanders,' he added, in a sterner voice, 'not only to recover those plans, but to try and rid India of this Russian menace and I assure you that the country is simply overrun with spies and agents of the Russian government who are doing their best to undermine British rule.'

The Commissioner digested this statement for some time. Brien interrupted his thoughts.

'Where does Levinsky live when he is at home?' he asked.

'He has a bungalow in Davis Road, Lahore,' replied Sanders.

'We must remember that,' said Leonard, 'though it is very unlikely that we shall ever catch him there. By the way, Sanders,' he added, 'is it possible for you to poach on other people's preserves?'

'What do you mean?'

'Well, we are going to Lahore from Simla, and there may be one or two happenings there that I should like you to be in. Can you come with us?'

'That is Rainer's district, and I couldn't very well act officially there,' replied the Commissioner regretfully, 'but, by Jove! I'd like to come.'

'You're after Elliott's murderer, are you not?'

'Yes, of course!'

'And I suppose can go anywhere on that duty? Well, I can't hand over the actual murderer to you, but I think I may be able to put you on to an accessory to the crime!'

'You can?' asked Sanders in startled surprise.

'I didn't say I can – I said I think I may be able to.'

'That's good enough for me! I'll come with you!'

'Good!'

Just then Hartley hurried back followed by the stationmaster, and the driver of the rail motor.

'Sorry I've been so long, sir,' he said to Sanders, 'but the driver was off duty, and it took a little while to find him.'

'Is the line quite clear, Sloan?' asked the Colonel.

'Quite, sir. And I'll see that it is kept clear until you are back. I suppose you'll be here before the twelve-fifteen leaves?'

'Oh, yes, we're only going to tunnel 51.'

'I see, sir!' And the stationmaster turned away.

'Perhaps though,' went on Sanders to Wallace, 'you wanted to go to Barog, Sir Leonard, and interview the doctor there?'

'No, thanks. All I am interested in in Barog is the room where Major Elliott's body was placed, and that, I believe, was only a small apartment with no windows and one door?'

'Yes!'

'And Captain Williams had the key of that door, and only he and the doctor could get in until you arrived; isn't that so?'

'Yes!'

'I might want to see the doctor some other time, but I don't think I shall. So let us start!'

The driver, who was the same man who had driven the motor when Major Elliott met his death, was in a condition of high nervous tension, and watched the four almost in a state of dread. They all boarded the car, and presently were running down the hill. Colonel Sanders pointed out the spot where he had started to trail the Jewish-looking commercial traveller as they passed Summer Hill station, but Wallace appeared to have lost all interest in the matter in hand, and sat blowing out clouds of smoke from his pipe, and gazing abstractedly at the scenery. One after another they passed the little wayside stations, stopping a minute or two at Tara Devi where the Colonel got out and gave a message relative to his departure from Simla to one of his subordinates whom he found waiting there. Several tunnels were passed through, most of them merely gaps that they were through in the twinkling of an eye, others a trifle longer, and one or two that nearly earned the name of tunnel.

At last tunnel 51 was reached and Hartley was directed to stop the car as near the exact spot where the light had gone out as he could remember. He did so and they came to a halt.

'It was just about here, sir,' he said to Wallace, who got out and looked curiously round the dark, vault-like place in which he stood. The brilliant headlights of the car, which had been switched on when they entered the tunnel, illuminated the surrounding gloom, and caused weird shadows to appear. The walls, which were dripping with moisture, showed, in places, creeping, slimy-looking things, which, startled at the light, scuttled into crevices out of sight. Leonard noticed that at interval lamps were placed, but they gave a very feeble illumination.

'I suppose these lamps hardly make any difference at all?' he said to Hartley, who had accompanied him.

'No, sir, they are very poor, and there are really not enough of them.'

'Put the lights out!' ordered Wallace in Urdu, and the driver immediately obeyed, with the result that there was only a glimmer of light in the tunnel. 'No,' he went on to his companions, 'they only throw a radiance for a few yards. All right!' he shouted again. 'Switch them on!'

He walked back to the car.

'Now, Hartley,' he said, 'get in and direct him to go on as far as the spot where you think the light went on again. Don't go too fast, for I am going to walk!'

The policeman obeyed, and the motor moved on, with Leonard walking by its side. Then it stopped once more.

'Just about here, sir,' announced Hartley.

'Just over three hundred yards! What pace were you going at?'

'When the lights went out, the driver slackened down, sir. I should say we were moving along then at about ten miles an hour!'

'Therefore you were only in darkness for just over a minute!

That proves that it would have been utterly impossible for Elliott to have been robbed as well as murdered. Now for my demonstration!'

He directed the driver to back right out of the tunnel again. About thirty yards outside he made him pull up.

'Now,' he said to the others. 'Will you sit where Elliott sat, Sanders, and you next to him, Billy, in Muir's seat. I am going to sit where Captain Williams was, next to the driver, and you, Hartley, sit in the same seat that you occupied on the fatal occasion, that is by me!'

They obeyed in silence, each of them very puzzled.

'Now, Hartley,' he said, 'we are reconstructing the whole affair. Watch carefully, and you two behind, hold my hands.' He put both hands over his shoulders, and Brien and Sanders grasped them in dumb amazement. Then he spoke to the driver in his own language.

'Whatever takes place,' he said, 'do not become frightened, but carry on. Don't stop the car until I give the word, do you understand?'

'Yes, sahib!'

'Switch the light on! . . . That's right! Off you go!'

The car started, and, gathering speed, plunged once again into the tunnel. The rattle of the wheels, and the echo from the confined space seemed to the three, who were puzzling over Wallace's actions, to hold a sinister note, as though some malignant force were at work. Then suddenly without the slightest warning the light went out, and they were thrown into almost complete darkness. Leonard felt the tightened grip of the hands that were holding his; Hartley ejaculated, 'Great Heavens!' while Sanders could be heard swearing above the roar of the motor. The driver gasped in terror and slackened speed, but the man who controlled Great Britain's

Secret Service shouted to him to carry on, and, almost blubbering in his fright, he obeyed. Then as suddenly as it had gone out the light flared on again, and presently the rail motor ran out of the tunnel, and, at Wallace's command, stopped.

'All right, you two,' he said over his shoulder, 'you can release my hands now!'

They did so, their own clammy with perspiration. Hartley sat back in his seat and mopped his brow. All three looked quite shaken, while the driver sat crouched over his controls almost fainting with terror. Wallace smiled cheerfully round on them, and pulling out his pipe commenced to load it.

'A bit theatrical, I'm afraid,' he said, 'but very effective!'

'Effective.' grunted Sanders. 'Why I almost felt the murderer's knife go into my back!'

'I don't like these conjuring tricks, Leonard,' said Billy. 'How the devil was it done, and why did you make us hold your hands?'

With great care Wallace lit his pipe, still smiling at his agitated companions. Then he ordered the driver to get out of the car and go for a stroll for a minute or two. The man was nothing loth, and, descending, went to a grassy knoll, and throwing himself down, covered his face with his hands.

'I don't suppose he understands much English,' said Leonard, 'but he may do, and I want no eavesdroppers to what I am going to say. I appear to have broken his nerve altogether,' he added. He won't want to drive through that tunnel again!'

'Oh, he'll recover,' said Sanders, lighting a cigarette with fingers that were riot quite steady. 'Now tell us how it was done, Sir Leonard.'

The latter turned to Hartley.

'I asked you to watch carefully,' he said. 'Did you?'

'I did, sir. But I had no idea what to watch for.'

'Have you any idea why the light went out?'

'Not the slightest, sir.'

'Did you notice any movement on the part of the driver?'

'No, except his hands on the levers.'

'Nothing else at all?'

'No, sir.'

'Any movement on my part?'

'No – you crossed one leg over the other, that's all I noticed, sir!'

'Ah! And that's the whole simple trick! I asked you two behind to hold my hands, so that you could not accuse me of tampering with the switch. But in crossing my legs I deflected it with the toe of my boot and put the light out, and I only had to depress it to put it on again! That's how it was done the first time – the whole matter being cunningly arranged beforehand!'

'Good God!' ejaculated Sanders. 'You are not suggesting that – that Williams—!'

'I am! And Williams is the man I had in mind when I said I might be able to put you on to the accessory to the murder!'

The Commissioner gasped.

'But – forgive me, Sir Leonard – the man is an Englishman, and a first class soldier. He is very highly spoken of by all who know him.'

'No doubt! I found out in Delhi – never mind how – that he passed out of Sandhurst six years ago, having previously been educated at an English school and a military academy in Germany. Muir's description of the tragedy was so graphic that, as I have already told you, I was able to picture everything, and when he mentioned about the switch and how you had arrested the driver on suspicion of having touched it, I got an idea that Williams could have worked it in the way that I did. You see Muir had described exactly where everybody was sitting! I must say he was wonderfully clear and complete in his whole description. So I decided to come here and put my theory to a proper test, and in the meantime made a few enquiries about Williams from Army Headquarters!'

'It is almost grotesque!' said Sanders. 'Captain Williams of the 107th Horse a Russian spy.'

'I think by the time we have routed them all out, you'll find many even more creditable people amongst them. Probably on enquiry into Williams' ancestry you'll find he's not English after all.'

'I've known the man and liked him for years, and I would as soon have believed that I was a spy myself,' muttered the other.

Wallace shrugged his shoulders.

'But there seems no sense in it,' went on the Commissioner. 'How could the plans have been stolen?'

'My dear Colonel, just think a bit! After the attack on Elliott in Viceregal Lodge, he and Muir talked things over in Muir's bedroom previous to their going down and searching for the miscreant. The door was left ajar, and anybody listening outside could have overheard their conversation. There were many bearers still in the compound, any one of whom could have crept into the house. Muir's own bearer was actually in, having supplied them with whisky and sodas. I ascertained that he speaks and understands English. I have not questioned him or shown any suspicion of him at all yet, in case there were others who might send out warnings. At all events the conversation between Elliott and Muir was listened to; Elliott was heard to say that he would take extra precautions about the safety of the plans, and from that time he was undoubtedly watched. He, no doubt, took the plans out of the case in which he carried them, hid them on some other part of his person, and substituted a few pieces of parchment, and resealed the case. All this was seen by a watcher and reported to Levinsky, who was, without doubt, the prime mover in the whole business. It was arranged that Elliott should be murdered, and when Williams was to switch off the light and switch it on again to give the assassin time to do his work and escape – no doubt they have several of those agile natives in their pay – and thus everything was conceived exactly as it happened. They knew Muir would take possession of the case; they guessed he would rush to Delhi with it, and that left only Williams to look after the dead man. He was bound to be taken to Barog, as none of the tiny stations in between possessed a doctor or facilities, and they knew also that you would be communicated with, and that you would insist on Williams taking charge until you arrived. So the latter just searched Elliott, and helped himself to the plans at his leisure. If there had been others travelling in the rail motor, the task of guarding Elliott's body would still have devolved upon Williams, for he was a friend of the dead man and of you and Muir. Oh, it was all very cleverly conceived, Sanders!'

'Clever – damnably clever!' said the Colonel. 'My God! It was more than clever – it was fiendish.'

'You are dealing with people who see a long way ahead and stop at nothing! And now I think we'll return – I'd rather like a drink!'

'You'll lunch with me, of course!' said the Commissioner.

'We will, Colonel! Thanks very much,' And Billy, who had listened to his friend with rapt attention, nodded. The driver was called, they shunted in a siding, and were soon speeding back up the hill.

'Those man-holes could conceal three or four men,' remarked

Leonard to Hartley, as they passed through tunnel 51 again.

'Easily, sir,' replied the policeman, 'and that's where the murderer hid himself and waited, of course!'

Wallace nodded.

Colonel Sanders sat next to Billy Brien in a state of stupefied silence most of the way up. He roused himself just before they reached Simla, however, and turned to his companion.

'Sir Leonard Wallace is a marvel – a damned marvel!' he blurted out.

Billy grinned, and selected a cigarette from his case.

'I found that out many years ago!' he said.

CHAPTER EIGHTEEN

Batty Has an Adventurous Morning

Batty watched his employer being pulled slowly up the hill, and shook his head doubtfully.

'Don't know as I'd like to sail in one o' them there craft,' he remarked to Woodhouse, one of the mechanics.

'They're all right,' replied the other. 'I've been in them in China many a time!'

'So've I,' said Batty, 'but there it's all plain sailing. There ain't no bloomin' big 'ills like these 'ere and they 'as sedan chairs for the 'ills any'ow. I s'pose,' he added thoughtfully, 'they ain't thought o' sedan chairs in these parts yet. China is a go-a-'ead country compared with this one. Fancy 'aving rickshas to go up 'ills almost like the sides of an 'ouse! Why, it ain't natural. Just s'posin' you was in one, an' the blokes in front let go – you'd be in a nasty mess, wouldn't yer? You'd turn a complete someysault and end up on the ground with the blinkin' craft a-top o' yer.'

Woodhouse laughed.

'Bless me!' he said. 'You've got plenty of imagination!'

'Me an' the guvnor 'as to 'ave imagination in our job!' replied Batty placidly. 'Where'd we be if we 'adn't, I'd like to know? . . . When was you in China, mate?' he asked after a pause, during which Woodhouse had looked at him with amusement.

'Just after the war, for a couple of years.'

'Do yer know 'Ong Kong?'

'Not much! I was stationed in North China, and only called there on the way up and back.'

Batty grew reminiscent.

'It ain't 'alf a bad place,' he said, 'when yer knows all the ins an' outs of it.' He winked at his companion. 'I were stationed there aboard the *Tamar* for three years, an' there wasp' nothin' ter do, but swab decks an' stand yer watch. Sink me, but the old ship looked a perfect picture, wot with 'er gleamin' brass fittin's an' white sides; an' yer could 'ave 'ad yer food off the decks any time o' day. Yer see when we got fed-up like, we just did a bit o' polishin' on our own!'

'Didn't you ever go to sea?'

'No, o' course not!' said Batty indignantly. 'She was the guardship – one o' the old men-o'-war!'

'I see.'

'So we spent a lot o' time ashore, an', my word, the things we seen!' He paused in ecstatic remembrance.

'Well, what did you see?' asked the mechanic impatiently.

Batty looked at him a moment as though he were about to answer his question, then shook his head. 'No,' he said, 'you're too young!'

Woodhouse burst into a roar of laughter.

'Young,' he gasped; 'me young! Why I've seen some things that would make your hair stand on end!'

The ex-sailor removed his topee, and ran his fingers through his declining locks.

'I ain't got much now,' he said, 'but I've never knowed it stand up yet, except when the gals 'ave been chummy like! Did you ever see a Chink gal?' he asked.

'Of course!'

'Some of 'em ain't 'alf saucy when they gets to know yer! There were two, daughters of an old bloke wot used ter supply the ship with vegetables, name o' Jelly Belly; an' 'e looked it too! Don't think that was 'is right name, but that's wot 'e called 'isself! They was two o' the tightest little craft that ever sailed, an' I ain't no mean judge neither. My word, I almost got 'itched up to them too!'

'What the both of them?'

'Yes, they was twins! An' the old man use' ter 'elp things along – 'im and me was great pals!'

'How did you escape?'

'Wot d'yer mean, escape?'

'Get off without marrying the girls?'

'Well, yer see, I ain't a marryin' man, an' I 'appened to get transferred to Singapore just when the wind was all a-blowin' up nice an' fresh like. Blow me, but it took me all me time to get away when I'd said goodbye. They 'ung on ter me, one to starboard, an' t'other ter port until I thought I'd miss me ship!'

Woodhouse smiled.

'It seems to me you've been a bit of a gay dog in your time, Batty.'

'I can't complain,' grinned the latter. 'Well, as the guvnor's given me shore leave, I'll go an' 'ave a bit of a look round. So long!'

He strolled off and up the hill. Presently he came to a place where the road forked – that on the right-hand side looked to be a worse slope than the one he had already come up and as Batty had very little liking for hills, he took the other, which appeared more level. It turned out to be a very twisting, narrow thoroughfare, with sudden dips and occasionally lengthy climbs. When he reached the top of one of these, he paused, and looked round him.

'Talk o' switchbacks,' he muttered, 'they ain't in it with this. But the scenery ain't bad, considerin'. Somebody 'ad a job cuttin' this 'ere road out!'

The view he had from where he stood was certainly glorious. On his right were tree-clad heights that seemed to reach to the heavens, while on the other side there was a steep slope, also covered with trees, dropping hundreds of feet to a sunlit valley below. The trees round him were of all sorts, shapes and sizes, most of them in the glory of their autumn colouring of brown, orange and gold. The hill on which Batty's road wound its sinuous way was semi-circular in shape, so that it was possible for him to look straight across the valley at the heights of Jakko and a little farther along at the wooded peak where Stirling Castle nestled. Why the large house so named is called a castle it is hard to tell, for it is not at all like one, and the name 'Stirling' is also very difficult to account for, but it is likely that the building was once owned by a patriotic Scotsman, who had a love for Stirling and its famous castle, and so named his house.

Turning from his contemplation of Mount Jakko, Batty leant on the rather weak wire railing that guarded the edge of the road, and gazed across country at the rugged hills and fertile valleys which stretched before him for miles. In the distance, just visible, were snow-covered mountains, rising to tremendous heights, which must have been fully fifty miles away, at least; and as Batty had heard that the river Sutlej rose somewhere in that direction he was very interested, inasmuch as he had once been on a cruiser named after that river. He became engrossed in thought, and it was only when he began to feel very chilly that he pulled himself together and decided to move on.

As he did so four native women came into view along the road ahead of him. Batty had no intention of being rude, but he had never seen any creatures like these before – he just stood still and stared. Each of them carried a basket full of earth upon her head, which she balanced without any apparent effort. Two of them wore bright yellow shawls and the other two scarlet, while all had on trousers of a dirty brown colour, and were, like all coolie women of their type, barefooted with jangling, heavy rings round their ankles. In their ears hung large ornaments which caused those appendages to take grotesque and ugly shapes and there were rings through their noses, in two cases so large that they hung down below their mouths.

The women might have been of four generations from the look of them, for the eldest was a wrinkled old hag, who walked along with difficulty, while the youngest was a mere girl. The sight of a stoutish, jolly-looking white man standing in the middle of the road with his hat at a jaunty angle, and staring at them with his mouth open, caused them great surprise, for they do not expect the white sahibs to be interested in them.

Batty was right in front of the old woman, and he politely stepped aside to allow her to pass. She moved aside at the same moment and thus they still confronted each other; so back they both went politely, and back again, still facing each other, as people so often will in trying to pass. Then they both came to a halt and gazed enquiringly one at the other, while the other three women looked on in dismay, thinking the white sahib was going to visit some dreadful punishment on their companion. But they had a surprise. Batty swept off his hat and bowed.

'We seem to have decided to 'ave a little dance, ma,' he said, 'what is it to be – a foxtrot or the Charleston?'

At once there was a perfect babel of chatter and shrill laughter, and the sailor became confused.

'This is no place for a 'ealthy man-o'-war's man,' he said. 'We don't seem to 'ave 'it it off exactly, so with your leave, ladies, I'll just sheer off. No 'arm meant.'

He looked back just before he turned a corner, and they were still standing where he had left them, talking in their shrill voices, and screaming with laughter.

'S'truth!' he exclaimed. 'I s'pose they *are* females, but they're the rummiest looking females I ever seed, an' shiver me timbers, they carry enough top 'amper to sink any ordinary craft.'

He found the path rather tiring, and paused to rest several times. At last he reached nearly to the top, and then discovered a tunnel that appeared to lead to a busy district, for he could see a couple of shops and crowds of natives at the far end. He went through, and, emerging at the other side, found himself in the midst of a howling mob of street vendors of all kinds, while Indians jostled him on every side, and smells of the rare oriental bouquet assailed his nostrils, much to his discomfort. He screwed up his nose, and looked intently at a shopkeeper who was squatting in front of a stall containing a collection of gaudily coloured wearing apparel. The native looked hard at the sailor's screwed up nose.

'Ah!' he said brightly. 'You want hand'chiefs – I got!'

'Keep 'em!' said Batty shortly, and walked on.

He became thoroughly confused by the mixture of noise and smells, the barking of dogs, and the crowds of men and women round him. At last espying a man who wore a red fez cap, and looked intelligent, he buttonholed him.

''Ere, mate,' he said, 'where can I get an 'air cut, savvy?'

The other looked puzzled, and then a smile brightened his face. 'Napi, eh?' he asked.

'Look 'ere, young feller, me lad, don't you be rude, see! I may call my 'ead a napper, but I didn't say as you could!'

Taking no notice of his remarks the man in the fez took him by the arm, and led him to a small individual who was crouched by a doorway, crooning to himself in a weird variety of cadences, He wore a bag, such as tram conductors carry, slung over his shoulder.

'Napi,' announced Batty's conductor, and turning on his heel strode away.

The sailor looked at his retreating back, and then at the small man, who had stopped chanting, and had produced a stool upon which he motioned Batty to sit. The latter looked doubtfully at it, but obeyed, and a dirty cloth was put round his neck, while the operator asked him something in Hindustani.

'Napper!' replied Batty, and touched his head. The fellow nodded, and, producing a large pair of scissors, proceeded to business. 'Well I'm blowed!' continued the sailor aloud. 'I allus thought napper was a English word, but it seems to be 'Industani for 'air.'

'No, sare,' said a voice. 'Napi allo – samee Hindustani for hairdlesser!'

Batty looked up with astonishment, and discovered a Chinaman standing by watching him with interest.

'Why, swab me decks, John, if this ain't a surprise. Fancy finding a Chinaman in these parts!'

John smiled broadly.

'Me making plenty tlade,' he said. 'Comee India side thlee four times catchee pidgin!'

'Well, I'm glad to see yer. It's years since I were in China! 'Ere can you speak the lingo?'

'Yes, sare! Plenty too muchee spik Engleesh, Hindustani, and Amelican!'

'Then tell this bloke not to cut muchee off topside, savvy?'

The Chinaman repeated the instruction, and soon the operation was finished. With the assistance of his new found friend, Barry paid the napi and they departed together.

'You come lookee see my shop!' said John. 'Got plenty plesent for memsahibs.'

'I ain't out to buy anythin', an' I've 'ad about enough of this 'ere city. Besides I ain't got no memsahibs!'

However, he was persuaded into visiting the Chinaman's shop, and in spite of his assertion that he had not come to buy anything, left it, half an hour later, with a kimono, two ivory statuettes, a carved pencil case, and a black wood walking stick:

'The least you can do arter planting these 'ere things on me,' he said to the smiling John, 'is to stand by an' pilot me to Annandale.'

The Chinaman politely took him part of the way, and showed him the road leading to his destination.

'Too muchee easy looksee now,' he said. 'Walkee down hill, and findee Annandale bottom side.'

'Well, thanks very much, John! You've been a pal, an' it's done me good to run up agin a Chink once more.'

The two shook hands solemnly.

'Me knowee plenty Blitish sailormens. Allo time plenty good chop.'

''Ow d'yer know I was a sailor?'

'Velly clever man me! Plenty time talkee talkee sailormen – allo time knowee!'

'You're a cute old bird. Well, so long!'

Batty had almost reached the bottom of the hill, when he was arrested by the sight of a native crawling through the bushes. The aeroplane stood quite close to a mass of shrubbery, and it was towards this that the fellow was creeping. Whoever was guarding the machine was apparently inside the saloon, for there was no one to be seen. Batty at once decided that the man could be up to no good, so taking every precaution he followed. The native was apparently too intent on his purpose to suspect that he himself might be followed, and the ex-naval man was able to get quite close to him. Then he hid behind a tree and watched proceedings.

Having reached the shrubbery the fellow lay for some time looking about him, then rising suddenly he ran rapidly forward and dived under the plane. He appeared to put something there, and scraped handfuls of grass and earth round it. Then he darted back to the shrubbery, and, at that moment, Batty – dropping his parcels, with the exception of the black wood stick – sprang; at the same time shouting a warning. The native made a dash for liberty, and would have got away had not the sailor thrown himself at full length, and, catching the other by the ankle, pulled him to the ground. The miscreant was immediately up again, but Batty was upon him, and he turned with a snarl, at the same time pulling an ugly looking knife from somewhere on his person, and striking. The movement was so rapid that the sailor had barely time to skip aside: as it was, his left sleeve was split from shoulder to wrist. But he had not forgotten his stick, and, as the man partially lost his balance from the force of his blow, Batty swung it with deadly precision; the heavy black wood caught the intruder on the left side of the head, and he went down with a gasp and lay still.

Woodhouse, who had heard Batty's hail, came running up.

'Phew!' he said. 'You've laid him out all right. What's he been up to?'

The seaman described the whole business, and lifting the native between them they carried him to the door of the saloon, and laid him on the ground outside it.

'Better see wot 'e put under the aeroplane! said Batty.

Woodhouse promptly crawled underneath and looked. 'My God!,' he gasped. 'Fetch a pail of water – quick!'

The sailor was ever a man of action, and he acted now. Darting into the saloon, in less than a minute he reappeared with a bucket full of water. Woodhouse, with a face as white as a sheet, dropped the small cylindrical object he held in his hand into the pail.

'Wot is it?' asked Batty, curiously.

'A bomb!'

The two looked at each other in horror for a moment. 'We'd better tie this bloke up, afore 'e comes round.'

Woodhouse nodded, and they made a very good job of it. Then Batty went back and retrieved his parcels. He sat on the ground and slowly filled his pipe.

''Ave yer got a bit o' chalk, mate?' he asked.

The mechanic looked at him in surprise, but went off, and presently returned with the required article.

'Now mark the figure one, on that bloke's forehead, and two on the bucket!'

Woodhouse did as he was directed.

'What's that for?' he queried.

'Exhibit number one, and exhibit number two!' He held up the stick, and looked at it lovingly. 'I thought that there John Chinaman was trying to make a bit out o' me,' he remarked, 'but, swab me decks, 'e never did a better day's work in 'is life!'

CHAPTER NINETEEN

Wallace Has a Narrow Escape

Green, the other mechanic, was the next member of the party to arrive back from sightseeing. He was a man of few words, but deep thought, and when the phenomenon of the trussed-up native had been explained to him, and he had looked inside the basket, he stood in silence, apparently philosophising on the occurrence.

Forsyth and Hallows came back in rickshas, loaded with parcels. They had been curio-hunting. Batty repeated his tale for their benefit, and the two airmen looked at each other. Forsyth smiled a trifle grimly.

'I don't know altogether what is on,' he remarked to Hallows, 'though I could make a fairly good guess; but things are certainly happening.'

'They are!' agreed Hallows, with deep conviction.

At five minutes to two Batty and Woodhouse were just clearing up the debris from a hearty meal, when Wallace, Brien and Sanders made their appearance. They strolled across the field deep in conversation, and it was not until they were close to the machine that they noticed anything unusual. Then Billy's eye fell on the captive.

'Who on earth is that?' he asked.

His companions followed the direction of his gaze, and Batty cleared his throat preparatory to another recital – he was word perfect by now, and was enjoying himself immensely.

'It was like this, sir,' he commenced, addressing himself to Wallace. 'I was just sailing down the road, 'aving 'ad a look round, so to speak, when I saw this bloke – beg pardon, sir – er – native, sir, crawling through the bushes. "Now," I ses to meself, "that don't look no'ow 'onest," an' it struck me that—'

'Never mind what struck you, Batty,' interrupted Leonard. 'Tell us what struck him, for he looks as though he has been very much struck!'

The sailor looked hurt at the interruption, but went on.

'Well, sir, to cut a long story short—'

'That's exactly what I want you to do!'

'I follered 'im through the bushes, sir, an' watched 'im crawl under the aeroplane, an' put somethin' there. As soon as he done that, back to the bushes 'e come, an' I grappled him, sir. 'E almost got away – 'e's as slippery as a eel – but I pulled 'im down by the leg. 'E drew this 'ere knife an' stabbed at me, but I just got out o' 'is way in time, and 'e only cut me sleeve. I sloshed 'im one across the 'ead with this stick, wot I bought from a Chinaman who—'

'He's certainly made a mess of your sleeve,' interrupted Wallace. He took the knife, and looked at it, then passed it on to Sanders who examined it with interest. Billy held the stick in his hand and weighted it.

'No wonder you put him to sleep, Batty,' he said, 'this is a remarkably heavy piece of wood, and you caught him right on the temple.'

Batty smiled with satisfaction.

'What did he put under the plane?' demanded Wallace.

Without elaboration, and with an eye to dramatic effect, Woodhouse replied.

'A bomb, sir!'

'A bomb!' ejaculated Brien, and Sanders swore. Even Leonard looked slightly startled.

'What did you do with it?' he asked.

'Exhibit number two, sir. In the bucket, sir!' replied Batty.

The three examined it.

'You had better send it to police headquarters, Colonel,' said Wallace, 'and have it examined. And as for this fellow,' he continued, 'we might get some information out of him. I think he must have made a mistake in the time, and placed the bomb too soon or else he got too nervy to wait. Throw some water over him, somebody, and bring him round!'

Willing hands procured water, and, in a few seconds, the man looked like a drowned rat. Batty had certainly made no mistake when he struck the blow, for it took some time to revive him. In the meantime Sanders turned to Wallace.

'Can I borrow one of your men to go to headquarters?' he asked.

'Certainly!' was the reply. 'Here, Batty, take the Colonel's message!'

'Aye, aye, sir!'

Sanders handed him a card, having scribbled a few words on the back.

'Take this to Mr Hartley, and tell him to come down to Annandale immediately with two Indian policemen.'

'Better make it a detachment!' said Wallace laconically. 'There may be an attempt to rescue this devil, for fear he gives anything away.'

'Do you think so?'

'I do.'

The Commissioner's face looked grimmer than ever, as he turned and gave additional instructions to the ex-naval man. Two rickshas were still at the gate.

'Get into one of those rickshas – I'll direct them!' added the Colonel.

Batty piously raised his eyes upwards, and muttered a prayer, while Woodhouse grinned, and winked at him. Sanders saw him off and returned to Wallace.

'I suppose your man won't make a mess of my orders, Sir Leonard?' he asked anxiously.

'Batty never makes a mess of anything! Now, as this kind-hearted fellow is beginning to come to his senses, I think that it would be a good idea if you did a little questioning now, because I am very doubtful if you will ever see him again!'

'Oh, nonsense!' said the Commissioner brusquely, then apologised. 'But hang it all, Sir Leonard,' he added, 'I've actually taken your advice, and sent for a detachment of police, and he couldn't get away from them!'

'He might get away from an army; at least his soul might, if he's got one. Anybody could take a pot shot at him from among the trees and escape quite easily!'

'Good God! You don't mean to say—'

'I mean to say that if he is likely to give away any information that is at all dangerous to his employers, they will not hesitate to attempt to rescue him, or, if that is too risky, exterminate him to prevent his talking.'

'How are they to know he has been captured?'

Wallace leisurely started to fill his pipe.

'Of course they know,' he said. 'I daresay they are watching us now. In fact we had better get into the saloon, and you can question him there, in case they try pot shots at him now.'

'Good Lord! You're making me feel that I have got mixed up in a sensational novel!'

'Well, I stepped out of one, so probably I brought a little of the atmosphere with me.'

The Colonel reddened, then smiled.

'I shall never be allowed to forget that unfortunate remark of mine,' he said.

At that moment something struck Wallace's topee with a thud, and it flew off his head.

'What the devil was that?' gasped Hallows.

'Get under cover, all of you – quick!' commanded Wallace. 'Green and Woodhouse, carry this fellow into the saloon. Billy, bring Batty's exhibit number two.'

They all obeyed his orders in a state of bewilderment. Leonard picked up his topee, and quietly followed them into the interior of the aeroplane.

'We're safe enough here!' he said. 'They won't dare to come out into the open, and I don't think a bomb could be thrown near enough to do us any damage!'

'Do – you – mean – to – say—?' roared the Colonel.

'Quietly, Sanders, quietly! You mustn't get excited at a little thing like that. They've put two nice air-holes in my topee!'

He showed the others where a bullet had entered the front of the helmet, and gone out at the back, probably missing his head by less than half an inch.

'Stupid to aim at the head,' he added reflectively. 'The body presents a much better mark.'

Billy was as white as a sheet of paper.

'And I told her you wouldn't be in any danger,' he muttered. He drew his revolver. 'I'm going to rout those fellows out – who's coming?'

An eager reply came from Forsyth and Hallows, and the two mechanics.

'Don't be a fool, Brien!' said Wallace brusquely. 'You'd be in the open, and they could pick the lot of you off without your ever seeing them, and with hardly a sound. They specialise in silencers apparently, though on a rifle, or rifles, this time. Well, we've discovered that the Russians still have some of their emissaries up here – perhaps they expected us! In fact, I am sure they did. Friend Levinsky may even have returned for the occasion himself. I hope Batty got through safely!' he added anxiously.

Colonel Sanders was growling the most blood-curdling threats to himself, and Brien sat down with a look of grimness on his face that was seldom seen there. The prisoner had moved once or twice, but had not fully revived. Now suddenly he groaned, and, opening his eyes, gazed with a look of hatred at his captors, when he became aware of his position.

'Now's your opportunity, Sanders!' said Leonard. 'Put the fear of death into him, and you may learn something.'

'Can't put the fear of death into these fellows,' grunted the Commissioner. 'He's a Mahsaud!'

'Ah! I thought I recognised the peculiar shape of that knife!'

'Undo his bonds, but leave his hands tied,' commanded the Colonel, and the two mechanics did his bidding. 'Stand up!' he snapped at the prisoner in his own language.

The latter obeyed sullenly, but shakily, and stood glaring from one to another like an angry wolf. The Commissioner questioned him rapidly. He asked who had employed him, what he was doing in Simla, if there were any more of his tribe concerned in the outrage with him, and a host of other questions, but the fellow maintained an absolute silence. Then Sanders tried threats; he told him that he would be tried, and sent to many years' imprisonment, but if he replied to the questions he would escape with a small sentence; he even told him that he would shoot him out of hand himself if he did not speak. But it was no use, not a word would the man say. The Colonel tried cajolery, promised a free pardon, even a reward, still with the same result.

Then an idea occurred to him. He knew that he could not frighten men of this type with the fear of death or imprisonment or even torture; but he knew that they feared anything that appeared to them unnatural, and flying like a bird was not a human sort of thing to do according to them. So he told the fellow that he would be taken up in the clouds in the flying machine when the sahibs went, and looked eagerly for a fruitful result. It seemed that he was about to get it too, the man's face became overshadowed with fear, but then, with a look of fatalism, he shrugged his shoulders and spoke for the first time.

'If the sahibs desire to take me among the clouds, I cannot refuse to go,' he said.

'Damnation!' snapped Sanders, and sat down.

Wallace grinned.

'He's an obstinate sort of bird!' he remarked. 'Hadn't you better search him?'

'There's hardly likely to be anything useful on him, but we might try. Have a look!' he added to Green.

The mechanic hesitated, and looked with disgust at the man, whose scanty, filthy garments were enough to repulse any decent-minded individual.

One of Sir Leonard Wallace's greatest characteristics was that he never expected a man to do a thing he would not do himself, and he acted on it now. Rolling up the sleeves of his jacket he started to search the captive. Immediately Green and Woodhouse followed his example, the former looking a little shamefaced. And they did it thoroughly, practically stripping the fellow naked. They found very little on him, and certainly nothing to give them any clue to his employers. Round his upper left arm was a dirty-looking bandage; Leonard gazed at it intently for a minute or two, and then took it off.

'Hm! I thought so,' he remarked. 'We've made one discovery, Colonel!'

'What's that, Sir Leonard?'

'This is the fellow who got into Elliott's Viceregal Lodge!'

'How do you know?' gasped Sanders, starting to his feet.

Wallace pointed to the place where the bandage had been.

'A bullet wound!' he said.

'By Jove, yes! And in the right place too!'

'What do you mean by the "right place"?'

'I found a smudge of blood on the tree by which he had to climb down from the window. And as he would have been compelled to put his arm round it to slide down, this part must have touched it, and left the patch of blood.'

Wallace nodded.

'Well, you've got two charges of attempted murder against him.'

'And perhaps one of murder! He's very likely the fellow who murdered Elliott in the rail motor.'

'You've got to find that out.'

The other nodded grimly, then looking straight at the native, who still remained philosophically calm, he said:

'You are in a very serious position. You will be tried on three charges, two of attempted murder, and the other of having murdered a British officer, Major Elliott, in the little rail motor that goes between Simla and Kalka!'

The fellow gazed at him almost with dignity.

'It is a lie, sahib! When the Major sahib was killed I was lying on my bed of pain with a bullet in my arm.'

'You will find that difficult to prove.'

'The people of the house where I was lying will prove it.'

'Then who killed the Major sahib?'

'I do not know.'

'You lie, you dog!'

'I do not lie – it is the truth!'

For a moment the Colonel thought deeply, then:

'You are without doubt the man who attempted to murder the Major sahib at the house of His Excellency the Viceroy.'

'It is useless to deny it,' the native replied with a shrug. 'The sahib knows!'

'And for what purpose?'

'I came not to kill him. I desired the packet of papers he carried with him, but when he awoke, I feared to be discovered so I tried to end his life. but he was lucky,' he added with regret.

'Who was your companion?' added Wallace, speaking for the first time.

'I had no companion, sahib!'

'That is a lie, for he was seen in the gardens!'

'The sahib knows too much!' with another shrug. Wallace drew Sanders aside, and spoke in English, in a low voice.

'That was mere conjecture on my part about the companion,' he said, 'but now we know he had one. No doubt they lived in the same house, and as this fellow is willing to give the address in order that the occupants can prove that he was lying there ill when the murder was committed, and thus clear himself of that charge, you had better have them all pulled in by the police and force them to say who this other is. Probably he was the actual murderer.'

Sanders nodded.

'I'll tell Hartley to get the address and act at once!'

'Get it now and make sure!'

The Colonel looked slightly aggrieved at this, but turned to the prisoner again.

'I think,' he said, 'that there is no doubt that you committed this murder!'

'Sahib, I swear I did not – it can be proved!'

'So you say, but how?'

'I have told you that the people of the house where I was lying sick will prove it to you.'

'And who are these people?'

The man hesitated.

'Well, if you do not give their names and addresses you will hang.' And Sanders turned away.

After a pause the fellow spoke again.

'I must tell you, to prove that I did not do the murder!'

'Well?'

He gave some names and an address which Sanders carefully noted down.

'The lowest district in the Bazaar,' he grunted.

'Keep a copy for your own reference,' said Wallace.

The Commissioner looked at him quizzically.

'You believe in taking precautions, Sir Leonard!' he said.

'Only a fool neglects them!' was the reply. He turned to the mechanics. 'Untie his hands,' he said, 'so that he can put his rags on again!'

The native's hands were unbound, and he was ordered to dress himself, which he did, watched carefully the while by Woodhouse and Green.

'Batty's a long time,' said Brien. 'It's nearly three!'

'Yes,' replied Wallace. 'I am beginning to get a bit anxious about him. Is it far to headquarters?' he asked the Colonel.

'No; he should have been back before this.'

Without taking any undue risks, Billy went to the little door, and looked out but could see no signs of anyone on the road. Ten minutes passed in silence, and Wallace was just about to speak when Brien called out:

'Here they come!'

A procession was descending the hill. First came Batty, sitting in a ricksha like a conqueror in his chariot, then came Hartley, also in a ricksha, followed by a detachment of police looking very smart in their khaki uniforms, and blue and red turbans. The sailor and Hartley dismounted at the gate, and marched across to the aeroplane at the head of the police.

'Sorry I've been so long, sir,' said Batty, 'but Mr Hartley was out!'

'We were getting a bit anxious,' said Wallace, 'and I'm glad you've got back safely!'

'Oh, it wasn't as dangerous as it looked, sir. The craft wobbled a bit, and she made 'eavy weather up the second 'ill, but we got up all right.'

'What are you talking about?'

'The ricksha, sir!'

Wallace laughed.

'I wasn't thinking about the ricksha,' he said.

'We've got a prisoner for you, Hartley,' said Sanders.

'So I understand, sir. Mr Batty told me what had happened!'

'He is the man that broke into Viceregal Lodge, and almost murdered Major Elliott there. Here is the address where he lodged. We have discovered that he had a companion. Arrest everybody living there, and hold them under the strictest surveillance until I return! Do you understand?'

'Perfectly, sir!'

'Have the bomb thoroughly examined by an expert. Keep a strict guard over this fellow, and look out for trouble on your way back. There are friends of his watching in the neighbourhood. Sir Leonard Wallace was shot at a little while ago.'

Hartley pursed up his lips in a whistle. Batty threw his topee on the ground, and started to roll up his sleeves.

'The swabs!' he roared. 'Where are they?'

Leonard laughed.

'Don't worry about them, Batty! You'll probably have plenty of fighting yet!'

The sailor picked up his topee regretfully.

'I'd like to 'ave got at 'em all the same,' he said.

'Well, Hartley,' said Sanders, 'I think that's all. If you

have anything urgent to communicate ring up the Deputy
Commissioner's office at Lahore.'

'Very well, sir!'

He took possession of his prisoner, the knife, and the bomb.
The man was placed in the centre of a double row of police and
marched away. The others watched the procession file out of the
gate and up the hill.

'Well, now I think we'll be off,' said Wallace. 'Next stop Lahore,
Forsyth, and land on the racecourse! But fly in the direction of
Delhi for twenty miles or so. I don't want our destination to be
known if it can be helped.'

Five minutes later the machine rose in the air, without any
further trouble having taken place, and after flying towards the
south-west for twenty-five miles, she turned with her nose pointed
towards Lahore.

CHAPTER TWENTY

A Surprise for Captain Williams

The aeroplane alighted on Lahore racecourse just before six o'clock. There were half a dozen syces exercising polo ponies in the far corner, and they stared in amazement at the unusual sight, while the ponies resented it, and shied in fright.

'I had better explain to the steward about our taking possession of the course before we do anything else,' said Sanders. 'Then where do you want to go?'

'To the Deputy Commissioner wherever he is to be found!' replied Wallace.

'Goodness knows!' said the Colonel. 'I don't know his habits very well, but, if he is pious, he'll be in church!'

Leonard smiled.

'And if he's not?'

'He'll probably be at home, calling for the first whisky and soda! Anyhow we'll go there and see – I'll ring up for a car, if I can borrow a phone somewhere handy!' And he was off.

'Useful man, Sanders!' remarked Billy, as he filled his pipe.

'Very. Well, Forsyth, what are you and Hallows going to do? We shall not leave here till the morning and perhaps not then!'

'We thought of looking the RAF mess up, and making ourselves at home there. Have you any objection, Sir Leonard?'

Wallace rubbed his chin thoughtfully.

'You have probably guessed by now that we are on a special mission – it was supposed to be a secret one, but isn't!' He added dryly: 'Of course you realise that you are under the orders of the Secret Service?'

'We could hardly fail to know that, sir,' smiled Forsyth,

'Well, I don't want everybody to know that we are in Lahore, if I can help it. But I suppose we have been well watched in spite of our precautions, and certainly your fellows at the depot here will have noticed the arrival of a strange aeroplane. So I don't suppose you can do any harm by going to see them. I tell you what! Fly there and put up for the night! Tell them any old yarn you like, but don't let anybody know that we are here on any particular business.'

'We didn't know you were, Sir Leonard!' said Hallows quietly and significantly.

'Good lad! Here comes Colonel Sanders, back with the steward I presume! We'll tell them you are going to the depot! Be ready to start away at any time after daybreak in the morning!'

'Very well, sir.'

Sanders came up accompanied by a little rotund man who was looking sadly perplexed. The Colonel beckoned Wallace aside.

'This fellow rather resents our being here, and I am sorry now I suggested the racecourse as a landing place,' he said. 'He has asked me a whole string of questions, but I did not tell him who we are or anything about our business. I thought there would not be the slightest objection to our alighting here! Of course I'll use my authority if you wish!'

'No, don't do that! Forsyth and Hallows are flying to the RAF depot, and they'll stop there for the night!'

The Colonel sighed with relief.

'I fear I made a mistake – I hope it has no unfortunate consequences!'

'I hope not,' replied Wallace grimly, and then strolled across to the steward. 'We seem to have made a mistake in landing here,' he said pleasantly. 'Sorry to intrude. Can you direct those gentlemen to the Royal Air Force depot, and they will fly there. We'll go into Lahore by car!'

He indicated the airmen. The little man, glad to be relieved of the responsibility of sheltering a strange aircraft on the holy of holies of such a sacred place as the racecourse, nodded brightly, and proceeded to give minute directions to the pilots. The others said 'Good night', and strolled towards the gates, followed by Batty, who had been ordered to accompany them, with two suitcases.

By the time they reached the exit, a car, which the Colonel had ordered, awaited their coming, and the three of them got in. Sanders gave the chauffeur the address, and soon they were speeding along Jail Road, down Race Course Road, and presently ran up a broad avenue, and stopped before a large bungalow.

A sharp-featured man in a dark suit was reclining in a cane chair on the veranda, and by his side was a tray containing whisky and sodas.

'He's not pious,' murmured Leonard, as the man rose, and came down the steps to meet them.

'This is a surprise, Sanders,' he said, holding out his hand to the Colonel.

'A pleasant one, I hope,' grunted the latter. 'We want to talk to you. Can you take us somewhere where we cannot be overheard?'

'Certainly. Come this way!' said the other looking curiously at the Colonel's companions, and leading the way along a broad hail, and into a tastefully furnished sitting room. Batty dismissed the car and waited on the veranda. The host ordered a bearer to bring drinks.

'The slogan of India!' said Wallace. 'Whisky and soda; lao juldee.'

Sanders immediately introduced Mr Deputy Commissioner Rainer to Leonard and Brien, and as he shook hands with Wallace, the Commissioner looked at him with great interest.

'I had a code message from Delhi this morning, Sir Leonard,' he said, 'relative to a squad of men standing by day and night for word from you to conduct a raid at some address to be given.'

'I'm glad the message has been circulated,' replied Wallace, 'but there was no necessity to give any names. However—'

The bearer entered and supplied the four men with drinks, then withdrew. Rainer closed the doors.

'We shall be quite unheard here, Sir Leonard,' he said, 'and I am entirely at your service.'

'Do you know a firm of the name of Ata Ullah in Lohari Mandi Street?' asked Wallace abruptly.

'Very well. It is a large stationery and printing business!'

'Apparently, yes; but in reality the headquarters of Russian Soviet agents who are occupied in flooding this country with propaganda, and endeavouring to turn the people against Great Britain.' And he gave a short, concise account of the Russian activities in India.

The other whistled in astonishment.

'I have reason to know that the plans that were stolen from Major Elliott are there at present,' Wallace continued, 'and the fact that the place is a stationery and printing business strengthens my belief that several copies are being made of them; hence the delay in Lahore.'

'But I thought you said that Williams had them?' put in Sanders.

'Williams certainly had them, but he handed them over either to Levinsky, or to someone else, to be copied.'

Rainer gazed at them in amazement.

'You don't mean *the* Captain Williams who was with Elliott when he was murdered, Sir Leonard?' he asked.

Wallace nodded.

'Yes,' he replied. 'I have only circumstantial evidence against him, but it is very good evidence all the same, and I have no doubt whatever that he is a Russian agent, and stole the plans!'

'Good Lord!' ejaculated the other weakly, and mixed himself another drink. 'Why,' he went on, 'he has been a friend of ours for some time, and only last evening had several dances with my daughter at the club.'

'I'm sorry, but there you are. Now the sooner those premises are raided, the surer we shall be of getting the plans, and the copies as well. The originals, I know, are to be taken to Karachi by the mail train that leaves here tomorrow night, so the raid must be conducted *tonight*!'

'Tonight!'

'Yes! Are your men in readiness?'

'Quite!'

'Where are they?'

'At the Anarkali police station!'

'Is that far from Lohari Mandi Street?'

'No, only about ten or twelve minutes' walk!'

'Splendid! Now please describe this street to me!'

Rainer did so, and Wallace listened carefully. At the end of the recital he smiled.

'You remind me of Kipling,' he remarked. 'What was it he called the City of Lahore – the City of a Thousands Nights, wasn't it? I suppose we can be pretty certain that the place will be thronged at all hours of the night!'

'Oh yes – it never sleeps!'

'Well, I'm sorry to disturb your Sunday evening, Mr Rainer, but matters are urgent. Will you go along to the Anarkali police station and see that all these men of yours proceed to Lohari Mandi Street in the guise of bullock drivers, tonga wallahs and anything else you like, singly and in twos, and that they are all in the neighbourhood of Ata Ullah's at ten o'clock. It is now seven, so there are three hours. I also want three or four of your best native detectives to proceed in some good disguise to a bungalow known as "Outram" in Davis Road.'

'Why, that's Silverman's place!' exclaimed Rainer.

'Quite so! His proper name is Levinsky, and he is one of the most trusted spies in the service of the Russian Government, and a very dangerous man to boot.'

'Good Heavens!' The local Commissioner looked dumbfounded. 'First Williams, now Silverman! I shall suspect everybody for the future!'

'Not a bad idea!' said Wallace. 'Now, Billy.' He turned to his second in command. 'I want you to act in conjunction with the detectives. Remain near Levinsky's bungalow in as powerful a car as Mr Rainer can place at your disposal. You must arrange some system of signals with the detectives, so that they can warn you of his movements. He may have a copy, or copies, of the plans there, and, if he is warned, try to get away with them. In that case you must follow him to the ends of India, or the world, if need be!'

Billy nodded.

'And what are you going to do?' he asked suspiciously.

'First of all I'm going to take a hurried run out to the Cantonments with Colonel Sanders and help him arrest Williams. Then I am coming back, and I am going to disguise myself as a native, if Mr Rainer will be good enough to lend me a room where I can be entirely private.' The Commissioner nodded. 'I will then proceed to Lohari Mandi Street and – listen carefully, Rainer! – I will blow three blasts on a whistle at ten precisely, and at that signal your men must get into Ata Ullah's and arrest everybody in there. Is that quite understood?'

'Yes, Sir Leonard! I shall be there myself, and keep in the background until you whistle!'

'Good! But don't let yourself be seen and recognised.'

'Of course, you would choose the most dangerous and interesting job for yourself!' grumbled Billy.

'I have an idea you may find yours the most exciting of all before you're through with it. If nothing happens wait by the bungalow until I join you. And now, Rainer, will you take Major Brien with you to the police station, so that he can get to know the detectives, and they him. And explain things to them for him – I haven't had time to get a munshi for him yet.' He grinned slyly at Brien.

'What about darkening your face, and getting some native clothes, Sir Leonard?' asked Sanders.

Wallace smiled.

'Batty has everything in a suitcase outside. And I'll take him with me to dry-nurse me,' he added to Billy, who grunted.

'You must have some dinner!' said Rainer.

'Thanks, there won't be time for that, but perhaps you will give orders for a few sandwiches to be given to my man who will keep them for me, until I get back from the Cantonments. What about Mrs Rainer? You'll have to make some excuse to her!'

'She and my daughter are out, luckily, and won't be back till late, so that saves explanations.'

'Splendid! And now we'll be off to visit Williams, if you're ready, Sanders!'

'Just one more drink before you go, Sir Leonard,' pressed Rainer.

It was drunk in silence, then Wallace and his host shook hands.

'Everything is quite clear?' asked the former.

'Perfectly!'

At that moment they heard the sound of a car drawing up outside, and the slam of a door. Presently a figure passed the window.

'Williams, by all that's wonderful!' exclaimed Sanders.

'You have been saved a journey, Sir Leonard,' said Rainer.

'This is most obliging of Captain Williams!' murmured Wallace. A bearer showed the cavalry man into the room.

'By Jove!' he exclaimed, 'I seem to have interrupted quite a gathering! Hullo, Colonel Sanders, how are you? Hope I don't intrude, Mr Rainer!'

'By no means! In fact, Sir Leonard Wallace and Colonel Sanders were just about to call on you!'

Williams started slightly, and looked curiously at the Chief of Great Britain's Secret Service.

'Permit me to introduce you!' went on Rainer, and he presented the young officer to Wallace and Brien almost with a touch of cynicism.

'Of course I know you very well by name and reputation, Sir Leonard,' said Williams hastily, to cover the confusion caused by Wallace bowing formally, and apparently not noticing his outstretched hand. 'But I did not think I should ever have the pleasure of meeting you!'

'I am glad to know it is a pleasure, Captain Williams!' replied Leonard, smiling slightly.

'You'll excuse my running away,' put in Rainer, 'but I have some rather important business to attend to with Major Brien. Make yourself at home, Williams. I believe Sir Leonard and Colonel Sanders have quite a lot to talk to you about!'

'I think I can guess what it is,' said the other ruefully. 'But Colonel Sanders knows all I can tell him about Major Elliott's murder. As a matter of fact,' he added, 'I really came to take Miss Rainer for a spin in the car.'

'Sorry, but she's out with Mrs Rainer, and won't be back till late.'

'Ah! That's disappointing! Then, Colonel Sanders, I am at your service!'

'Good!' said Sanders brusquely.

Rainer and Brien took their leave and Williams sat down. Wallace filled his pipe slowly, and the Colonel stood with his back to the mantelshelf with an expression on his face that would have done credit to *Weary Willie* himself. In many respects Wallace and Sanders possessed similar temperaments, but while one was almost invariably cheerful in his apparent languor, the other was usually glum.

'Help yourself to a drink, Captain Williams!' said the former.

'It isn't my house, or my drinks; but we were told to make ourselves at home, and, there is no reason why we shouldn't!'

Williams smiled. Leonard's manner amused him, and he found it difficult to associate this man with the great reputation he had acquired.

'I hope you are not going to cross-examine me like a prosecuting attorney, sir,' he said, helping himself to a liberal peg, and splashing soda into the glass.

'Oh, no! There are just a few questions I want to ask.'

'Have you come out to India purposely to solve the mystery of Elliott's death?'

'How do you know that I was not already in India?' asked Wallace lazily.

The other showed the slightest confusion. His hesitation was only momentary, however.

'I didn't,' he said, 'but naturally, I *thought* you had come out specially.'

'Oh! It occurred to me that you had seen the announcement of my arrival, by aeroplane, in the *Indiaman*!'

'It is a paper I seldom read!'

'No, I suppose not! It is rather a rag – generally full of Russian Bolshevik plots against India!'

Williams started perceptibly this time, and the hand that held his glass shook slightly.

'You seem to have studied it fairly carefully, Sir Leonard,' he said.

'It is my business, more or less, to be *au fait* with opinions expressed in newspapers on international matters. And now, Captain Williams, there is just a little information I want about this very sad business. The murder is Colonel Sanders's department, and professionally I am only interested in it inasmuch as it concerns the robbery of very important plans.'

Williams's start of surprise was very well done, if it was put on.

'But surely,' he said, 'Sir Henry Muir took them safely to Delhi! He certainly removed the case from Elliott's body and drove to Delhi from Barog with it!'

'He took the case certainly, but there were only a few pieces of parchment in it. What I want to know is, where are the real documents?'

'Good Lord, Sir Leonard! You surprise me! I certainly thought—'

'I don't really want to know what you thought, Williams!' He puffed a cloud of smoke towards the ceiling and watched it spiral its way upwards. 'The question is, what did you *do* with them?'

If a bomb had exploded in the room, Williams could not have shown greater consternation. His glass slipped out of his nerveless fingers and its contents ran unheeded over the carpet; for a moment he grasped the arms of his chair as though in pain, then he started to his feet.

'What – what do you mean?' he gasped. 'What have I to do with them?'

'Don't get excited, man! It's bad for one!' Leonard approached a little closer to his victim. 'As a matter of fact,' he said, 'I *know* what you did with them; how you obtained them, and the clever little trick you adopted to switch the light out in the interior of the rail car, but I think a confession from you might help you later on!'

The man was ghastly, beads of perspiration standing out on his brow. He made several attempts to speak, but could only utter inarticulate sounds. At length he pulled himself together.

'You're mad! Absolutely mad!' he shouted hoarsely. 'You are

214 THE MYSTERY OF TUNNEL 51

actually accusing a British officer of having been accessory to Elliott's death and acting the part of a spy.'

'I am! And that's the pity of it, though I know you only entered the Army with the object of being useful to your paymasters of the Russian Government. Come! What's the good of being a fool! Why, your face gives you away, apart from all my evidence! You took the real plans from the murdered Major's body, when you were left alone with him at Barog! Oh, it was all arranged very nicely and, I admit, cleverly.'

Williams swayed backwards and forwards, and grasped at the back of a chair to steady himself. Wallace turned to Sanders.

'There's your man, Colonel! You had better take charge of him!'

The Commissioner stepped forward, but as he did so, Williams pulled himself together with a mighty effort, and drew a small bottle from his pocket.

'You may think yourself very clever, Sir Leonard Wallace,' he almost screamed, 'and only the devil knows how you discovered everything. But you haven't got me, and neither you nor your vulture Sanders will *ever* have me.' And with an hysterical laugh he took the cork from the bottle, and was about to drink the contents, when:

'Stop! Don't be a fool!' commanded Wallace, and he held a wicked-looking Browning revolver pointed at the other. For a moment Williams hesitated, then:

'Do you think you can frighten me with a revolver?' he panted. 'One way's as good as another,' and he raised the bottle to his lips. There was a deafening report and, as the smoke cleared away, Williams could be seen holding the shattered remnants of the phial in his fingers, with a look of utter stupidity on his face. Then he moaned, and slipped in a dead faint to the floor.

'My God!' gasped Sanders. 'What a shot!'

'You'd better make certain of your man, Colonel,' said Wallace calmly, and stepping forward he took the broken bottle from Williams's fingers and sniffed it.

'H'm,' he muttered. 'Cyanide of potassium!'

CHAPTER TWENTY-ONE

The Raid

At half past nine that night a tonga, containing two Indians, drove with shouts and warnings from the driver down the famous Anarkali, where almost anything from a drawing pin to a suite of furniture can be bought in the various shops which line its narrow way. Crowds of people thronged the road; motor cars here and tongas there, not to mention bullock carts and cyclists, filled up all the available space, until it would appear to the casual observer that nothing could move. But the tonga in question continued on its way with only an occasional slackening of speed, the driver apparently having no regard for life or limb whatever.

At length one of the gates leading into the city proper was reached; the passengers descended from their precarious seat, and having paid the fare, walked through the archway, and found themselves in the midst of a jostling, shouting crowd.

Both were small men, but whereas one was stoutish and jolly-looking, the other was slight and gave the impression of having a lazy disposition. They each wore the wide voluminous trousers generally affected by Mahommedans, shirts overhanging their nether garments and almost reaching to the knees, and longish black alpaca coats that buttoned up to the neck. The slight man wore a beautifully rolled turban, but his companion had on a red fez which was stuck jauntily on the side of his head and gave him a rakish appearance.

They strolled quietly along in the unhurried manner of most Indians, and presently came to a place where the way forked. For a moment they hesitated, as though not quite certain of their route, and then took the left-hand road. It could hardly be called a road, so narrow was it. The houses on each side appeared almost to touch and only a very small strip of sky could be discerned between them. But Lohari Mandi Street is one of the busiest commercial districts in the whole of the city of Lahore and although the hour was late, business was apparently still as brisk as at any time during the day.

The two Indians were obviously in search of somewhere, for they looked at each shop as they passed, reading the names with interest. At last they came to one where the slight man muttered 'Ah!' They still walked on, however, and halted about twenty yards farther on.

'What do we do now, sir?' asked the fat man in a hoarse undertone, and in unmistakable English.

'Shut up, Batty!' was the whispered reply. 'Stand here, and pretend to hold a conversation with me; fling your arms about and try to look earnest!'

Batty scratched the side of his head and looked puzzled.

''Ow can I 'old a conversation, an' shut up, sir?' he asked.

'Talk in Hindustani, or, if you can't, just open and close your mouth, and pretend to!'

'All I know is juldee and jao, sir, so—'

He was interrupted by a perfect torrent of Urdu from the other, who gesticulated freely as he spoke, and was apparently trying to impress his companion. Batty just gazed in fascination with his mouth open, and Wallace, for he it was, stopped in the middle of his rapid discourse to whisper.

'That's all right! You look like a fool trying to grasp a point from a learned man, and the attitude suits you beautifully.' And on he went with his voluble chatter.

One or two passers-by paused inquisitively to listen, and heard the slight man telling the other that he was a fool to allow his wife's relations to interfere in his domestic bliss. A wizened-looking span, standing by, heard all this, and, looking sympathetically at Batty, shrugged his shoulders and went his way.

'Oh, thou fool! Thou son of a thousand fools,' continued Wallace loudly. 'If I had a woman like thine, I would lock her up and beat her until she obeyed me. Then if she still obeyed not, I could cast her to the jackals, and her mother, and her brothers, and her sisters with her. Thus would I obtain peace and take unto myself a wife who gave me domestic happiness.'

'Thou bast spoken wisely,' put in a tall, fierce-looking man, who had stopped to listen to the last bit with great interest. 'If thy friend cannot keep his women-folk obedient to his wishes, then he is no man, but only a woman himself.' And spitting with disgust, the stranger passed on.

'Wot did 'e say, sir?' asked the irrepressible Batty in his husky whisper.

'That you're not a man, but a woman!' smiled Wallace.

'Well, I'll be—!' began the sailor, forgetting in his indignation the part he was playing. A hand like steel was placed over his mouth.

'Cease thy cursings, thou fool!' almost shouted Wallace, as an excuse for his forcible action. Then removing his hand, he added, 'Bring not down upon thyself the wrath of Allah!'

He took Batty by the arm, and led him a little farther on.

'Thou art indeed a thrice cursed fool, Batty!' he said in English. 'You nearly gave us away then!'

'Sorry, sir, but that there swab—'

'Never mind the swab,' He looked at his watch. 'Five minutes more; I hope everybody is ready!'

They turned and retraced their steps. As they did so, a white man came along the street with an Indian companion. His was a tall, commanding figure, and as Wallace caught sight of him, he whistled below his breath.

'Levinsky himself!' he exclaimed, and stood still.

The tall man looked round him suspiciously, and then went into the house they were watching.

'With a little bit of luck, Batty,' whispered Leonard, 'we are going to make a coup of coups tonight. Come on! We won't wait any longer now.'

He strode to the door of Ata Ullah's establishment, followed closely by his henchman. Immediately drawing a little silver whistle from his pocket, he blew three shrill blasts on it.

The effect was magical. Men appeared from everywhere running towards the establishment. Two bullock drovers who had been quarrelling a little way down the street ceased their quarrel at once; a beggar who had been sitting outside the door stopped his wailing chant for alms, and jumped to his feet. In a moment the place was swarming with men; tonga wallahs, bullock drovers, beggars, fruit and cake vendors all pressed into the shop with an alert, businesslike air, and thence all over the house.

Wallace had not waited to see if he were followed, but ran through the shop, knocking over bundles of papers as he went, and upsetting a man who tried to bar his progress. Batty with a roar like a bull joined him; together the two went from room to room, and then up a rickety staircase, which shook violently as they ascended it. Here they met with more opposition, two men with lathis awaiting them at the top, and aiming deadly blows at their heads; but lathis meant nothing to Leonard and the sailor. They dodged the blows and an upper-cut from the former, with a full-blooded punch from the latter, placed their two opponents *hors de combat* in a groaning, gasping heap of mixed humanity.

Up here there were several rooms, some of which contained stacks and stacks of papers – others full of books and stationery material of all kinds. In one long room were several printing presses, but they met with no further opposition.

'Where the devil has Levinsky got to?' panted Wallace. He opened a door at the end of the printing room.

'Ah! Another flight of stairs!' he muttered. 'Come on, Batty!'

These stairs were narrower, but much firmer than the others, and appeared to lead to the living apartments. There were five rooms in all, and at the end of a corridor a locked door, in front of which hung a bead screen, pulled them up.

'Probably the women's quarters are behind this,' said Wallace, 'but this is no time for ceremony.'

He lifted his leg, and crashed his foot with great force against the door. Batty followed his example, and in a few seconds, they broke their way in. As Leonard had guessed, they were in the part of the house devoted to the women-folk. Half a dozen females looked at them with terror and one or two screamed when they saw Batty. He certainly looked rather a terrifying object. He had become very hot during his recent exertions, and had wiped the perspiration from his face, with the result that he had rubbed some of the paint away, and now had a curious piebald appearance.

'Very sorry to intrude, ladies,' said Wallace, 'but it cannot be helped!'

They searched the zenana thoroughly, but found nobody but women and a few children about. Then they returned to the other rooms, all of which were unoccupied.

'Dash it!' said Leonard. 'The blighter has got away!'

''Ere's a trapdoor out 'ere, sir,' said Batty, who had wandered into the corridor. 'P'raps 'e's gone on the roof.'

Wallace immediately joined him, and looked at the square framework above them.

'There ain't no ladder, though,' added the sailor.

'They, or he, might have pulled it up. Give me a back, Batty! I'm going through if I can reach.'

The man obligingly bent his back, and, with the assistance of the wall, Wallace climbed on to it, and gradually stood up. Then the sailor slowly straightened himself to enable the other to get on to his shoulders. It was a ticklish operation, but, by leaning against the wall, Leonard managed it, and at last stood on his companion's shoulders. He could just reach the trapdoor, and, pushing at it, found it moved easily.

'This is where I miss my other arm,' he muttered. 'Batty, I've got my fingers through, and I'm going to hang on with my hand. Get hold of my legs – I'll stiffen myself – and push me upwards!'

'Aye, aye, sir!'

Wallace got a good grip, and then swung his legs free of the ex-sailor's shoulders. Batty immediately gripped them by the ankles and, by slow degrees, pushed him up. It was a feat of strength for

Wallace to hang on with one hand as he did, but in spite of his slight build he had muscles of steel, and at last he managed to get his whole forearm through the opening and rested it there. Then with a swing of his legs that would have done credit to any acrobat, he had one foot resting against the side of the trap. A few seconds later and he had wriggled entirely through on to the roof.

''Struth!' exclaimed Batty to himself admiringly. 'I'd like to see another man wot could 'ave done that. The skipper's a bird and no mistake.'

The roof was covered with debris of all sorts, and Wallace tripped over various things before his eyes became accustomed to the darkness. Then he made a thorough search, and found that it would have been easy for anyone to have escaped that way, by running over the roofs of the adjoining houses. He turned back to the trapdoor with an exclamation of disgust. He had just lifted it preparatory to descending, when there was a thud close to him.

'H'm! There's somebody about with one of those delightful silencers on his gun!' he murmured to himself, as he dropped behind a large weather-worn packing-case. 'Now I wonder from what direction that bullet came?'

He proceeded to consider the position. If he found out where his assailant was, he might have a chance of getting him, and the only way to find out would be to see the flash when he fired. The question was, how to get him to fire without endangering his own life.

'If I stand up,' he muttered, 'I'll probably see the flash all right, but I should also leave a widow and one child so that's no good.'

At that moment the trapdoor close to him began to rise.

'Go back, Batty!' he commanded.

'It is I – Rainer!' replied a voice.

'Well, don't come up!' said Wallace. 'Unless, of course, you are tired of this sad world, and want to commit suicide.'

'Why?'

'There is someone up here with a revolver, and attached to it is a silencer, which these people specialise in.'

'Whereabouts is he?'

'My dear man, that's what I would like to find out. I suppose he is placed up here to cover Levinsky's retreat.'

'Levinsky! Was he here?'

'He was. He entered about two minutes before I blew the whistle. And with his usual agility he's slipped through my fingers.'

'Then it must have been his car I saw standing near the Lohari Gate.'

'Good Lord! Then, man alive, send some men there! You may be in time to get him yet.'

'I'll go myself.' The trapdoor went down with a bang as the Commissioner descended.

Then an idea occurred to Leonard by which he might discover where the watcher was. Near him was a pile of old sacks and it struck him that in the darkness the fellow could not possibly see anything clearly; thus if he bundled up the sacks together, and pushed them through the trap, they might be mistaken for him.

He immediately acted on the idea. He made the sacks into as large a bundle as he could, then pushed up the trapdoor with his foot, and held it there. That part of his scheme accomplished, he raised the sacks above the packing-case, and cautiously looking over the top, with his head as far from the bundle as possible – he had previously removed his turban – he began to move it towards the opening, at the same time keeping a sharp look-out. The scheme was successful for as he was pushing the bundle through the trap there was a flash from the roof of the next house, and another, and two distinct thuds. Wallace let the bundle drop through and the trapdoor crash into place. Then quickly he drew his revolver.

'Now, my lad!' he said. 'I know where you are, and if I mistake not, you'll make a dash for safety.'

He was right. A shadow rose from the place whence the flashes had come, and moved across the roof. Taking deliberate aim at the lower part of it, Leonard fired twice. There was a cry of agony and a crash as some heavy body fell. At the same moment the trapdoor was raised again and Batty appeared.

'Are yer all right, sir?' he called, and got a surprise, when he heard Wallace's voice reply close to him.

'Yes, I'm all right, Batty, but the other fellow isn't! Come up if you can.'

The sailor immediately climbed on to the roof.

'Mr Rainer sent for a ladder, sir,' he explained; then added: 'I was comin' up just now, sir, when a pile of dirty sacks fell on me 'ead, an' they made me sneeze so much that I couldn't get no breath back for a minute or two.'

Wallace laughed.

'I pushed those through, Batty,' he said. 'I thought you might be cold waiting there. Sacks are warming, you know.'

'I don't want no warmin', sir, beggin' yer pardon, sir; I'm 'ot!'

'Well, come along, and help me to get that fellow down. He's groaning enough to wake the dead.'

They crossed to the other roof, and between them managed to get the wounded man down the ladder and into a room where they laid him on a couch. Wallace examined him carefully, and found that one bullet had gone through the fleshy part of the thigh, and the other had lodged behind the knee.

'He's not very badly hurt!' he said. 'It won't be long before he is quite all right again.'

He took the revolver with its silencer attachment from the man.

'We shall be getting a regular collection of these things,' he said. 'Now, Batty, just keep an eye on him, while I go and have a look round. I'll send someone to relieve you!'

'Aye, aye, sir,' replied the sailor, and added: 'He's the bloke – beggin' yer pardon, sir – man wot came into the 'ouse with the tall feller, ain't he?'

Wallace gazed at the captive for a moment or two.

'I believe you're right, Batty,' he said, and went out of the room.

Batty, left alone with the groaning man, looked at him reflectively. By this time he had rubbed most of the paint from his face, and did not look quite so fearsome an object as he had done.

'If I 'ad me way,' he murmured, 'you'd be 'ung for tryin' to pot the guv'nor. Don't yer know as 'e's the most vallyble man in England? An' you goin' playin' about with a revolver as if 'e was a cove that didn't matter, like you! Shiver me timbers, but you blokes ain't got no sense o' proportion, none whatsomever, no'ow!'

The man groaned.

'Oh, stow it!' grunted the sailor. 'You ain't 'urt, an' you take it from me, that you're a bloomin' lucky bloke an' ought ter be full o' gratitood, not makin' a fuss. The guv'nor could 'ave killed yer easy only 'e's such a blinkin' 'umane feller that 'e never kills unless it's necessary. I never seen a shot like 'im, 'e never misses nowise!'

'Sahib, I am sorely hurt!'

'Oh, so yer speak English, do yer? Well, that's summat in yer favour!'

'I was compelled against my willings to shoot at the other sahib!'

'I've 'eard that tale afore. An' now against yer willings you'll go to the lock-up!'

'My master he make me stop, and say shoot if sahib comes. And what could I do but obey him?'

'Yer could 'ave told 'im ter go to the devil nice an' polite like. Where's he gone?'

'God knows!'

'An' so do you!'

While this conversation was taking place, Wallace went down the stairs, and found the whole building in the hands of the police. Everybody who had been discovered on the premises had been taken to the Anarkali police station under a strong guard. As he reached the lower floor he met Rainer who had just returned. The latter failed to recognise Leonard at first, and when he did passed flattering comments on the disguise.

'It was no good,' he added ruefully. 'The car had gone when I reached the gate with my men.'

Wallace nodded.

'He's the most slippery customer! Our only hope now is that he will go to Davis Road, and if he gets away from there, he'll be followed by Major Brien.'

'Will he know that you're after him?'

'Not exactly, but he's not the man to take any risks. In fact he may not return to his bungalow at all, and in that case we'll have a devil of a job to find him again . . . Have you discovered anything of interest here?'

'I have two European, and two Indian sergeants on the job. Shall we go and see if they have come across anything?'

'Yes!'

The two went into one of the inner rooms, which had apparently been used as an office. Here two khaki-clad Englishmen were busily engaged in sorting out correspondence, circulars, handbills and a multitude of other literature. They looked up as Rainer and Wallace entered and saluted.

'Have you found anything, Fielding?' asked the Deputy Commissioner of the elder of the two men.

The sergeant smiled grimly.

'There is enough seditious stuff here, sir, to inflame the whole of India,' he replied.

Wallace and his companion glanced through some of it. In the majority of cases it was in Urdu, and as Leonard could not read the language it was translated to him. There were stirring calls to clear the country of the English oppressors; instructions to Communists of the inner circle with regard to the procuring of arms, sowing discontent among the troops of the Indian Army, and generally raising a state of unrest in the minds of the populace. There was a whole pile of documents relative to the glories of Communism, couched in laudatory terms respecting the beauties of the ideal government as practised in Russia, and describing how the Soviet were prepared to help the Indian people with money, men and guns to drive the British into the sea.

'Great Scott!' exclaimed Rainer. 'What a haul!'

Wallace nodded.

'I believe there are places like this all over India, and I think there is likely to be a list of them here somewhere. You haven't come across one?' he asked Fielding.

'No, sir,' replied Fielding, who had taken some time to realise that the Indian gentleman with his chief was in reality an Englishman and the famous head of the British Intelligence Department.

'Where are Majid and Feroz Din?' enquired Rainer.

'In the next room, sir, searching the cupboards.'

The Commissioner read a few more extracts for his companion's benefit, and then a tall, smart Indian policeman entered the room carrying three sealed packages. He saluted gravely and addressed Rainer.

'These packages, sir, we found in the safe, which has been forced open.'

Rainer took them. They were heavily sealed, and two were addressed to people with Russian names, one in Paris and the other Berlin. The third envelope was blank. The Commissioner tore them open, and the contents caused him to whistle. Wallace smiled slightly.

'Photographic copies of Elliott's plans,' he said. 'Now we're well on the track. Did you capture Ata Ullah himself, or whoever is the head of this business?'

'No,' replied Rainer. 'Either he was out, and will, therefore, have been warned, or else he has got away with Silverman.'

'Probably the latter,' said Leonard. 'Let us go to the private apartments upstairs; we may find something there!'

Rainer nodded and handed the three packages to him.

'You had better take charge of these, Sir Leonard,' he said. 'If any of you find a list of addresses, or the original of these documents,' he added to the three policemen, 'bring them up to us!'

They ascended the stairs, and went into the room where Batty still guarded his prisoner.

'By Jove! I quite forgot about your man, Batty,' said Leonard. 'Has he said anything to you?'

'Nothin' of importance, sir,' replied the sailor, and he repeated the conversation he had had with the wounded Indian.

'H'm! As I thought – he is merely Levinsky's jackal!' He turned to the prisoner, and asked him, in his own language, if his master had been accompanied by another.

'Yes, sahib!' replied the fellow at once.

'Who was he?'

'Ata Ullah, sahib!'

Wallace stood in thought for a moment, then he asked Rainer to send for a doctor to attend to the man's wounds and to have him removed. The Commissioner called down to one of his assistants and gave the necessary orders. He and Wallace made a systematic search of the apartment, even removing hangings and carpets, and looking in the most unlikely places for the list of addresses and Elliott's original plans. In one corner stood an oriental desk, and this they examined first, but it appeared to be quite innocent of any suspicious papers. Aided by Batty who had been relieved of his duty, and to whom Leonard explained what they were searching for, they went through the other rooms on that floor; nothing, however, came to light. Twice one of the policemen below brought up lists of various addresses that had been found, but in no case were they the lists they were after. At last they desisted.

'We haven't been as successful as I hoped,' said Leonard to Rainer. 'I'm afraid all those other places will be warned, and make a clean sweep of everything.'

'Still you've discovered enough here, Sir Leonard, to give us a good chance of cleaning up India, and we'll be on the *qui vive* for the future.'

'Yes, I know, but I hoped to do the job thoroughly while I was about it. I'm going to have another look at that desk!'

He returned to the front room, followed by the other two. Going carefully all over the desk he tapped it, and presently was rewarded by a hollow sound in one of the solid looking legs.

'There's a secret recess here,' he said. 'Fetch me something to split it open, Batty!'

The sailor was off at once, and Wallace and Rainer examined the leg to discover how it opened.

'If there is a cavity in there,' said the Commissioner, 'it has been very cleverly conceived!'

He was thoroughly excited by now, and when Batty returned with a crowbar, he could hardly suppress his impatience as Wallace aimed blow after blow at the powerful desk. For some time it resisted the onslaught, but at last the leg began to give, and the three men, turning the desk upside down, pulled with their united strength until it came away in their hands.

Inside was a narrow cavity, and Wallace drew out a small exercise book, which had been rolled up and kept in place by an elastic band. He opened it, and looked eagerly through the contents, which were in English.

'Here we are!' he said with satisfaction. 'Thirty-five addresses including this one, and the places I know of already in Karachi and Delhi. Probably written by Levinsky. Come on, Rainer, we'll get to a phone at once, and ring up the Commissioner at Delhi!'

They hurried downstairs, Rainer stopping only a minute to give further orders to Fielding. There was a powerful car outside, and threading its way through the gaping crowd which had collected, and along the narrow street, where its mudguards very nearly touched the houses on both sides, it carried them out of the city, up the Anarkali and presently stopped in the courtyard of the police station. Wallace was soon on the phone and after a wait of ten minutes, during which he almost lost his calm in his impatience, he was speaking to the Commissioner's office at Delhi.

He read out the list of addresses, and insisted upon the man at the other end repeating them to him as he copied them down. Then he gave peremptory orders that the deputy commissioners in each town mentioned should be immediately communicated with, and ordered to raid those addresses as already directed. The official at the other end repeated the instructions to ensure of there being no mistake, and Leonard rang off.

'That's that,' he said. 'Now we'll go to Davis Road, and see what has happened there!'

The car carried them to their destination, and they stopped some distance from Levinsky's bungalow, and walked along the road. There was no sign of Billy anywhere, and presently Rainer gave a low whistle. Almost immediately a man who, from his dress, looked to be a bearer, sauntered up to them, and saluted the Commissioner.

'Well, Abdul, where is the Major sahib?' asked the latter.

'At half past ten, your Excellency, a car drove up containing Silverman sahib and another man, and passed into the grounds of the bungalow. Hakim was lying by the porch, and saw the sahib enter the bungalow hurriedly, and go straight to the telephone in the hall.'

'Of course, he sent out warnings,' grunted Leonard to Rainer. The detective, who understood English, smiled slightly.

'It was of no use, sahib,' he said, 'because the Major sahib had previously given orders that the telephone wires should be cut.'

'Well done, Billy!' murmured his friend.

'What happened?' asked Rainer impatiently.

'After five minutes Silverman sahib finding that he could not get a reply to his call threw down the receiver in a fit of anger, and dashed into a room. He quickly returned, and jumping into the car, they drove away rapidly in the direction of the Cantonments. The Major sahib had been warned at once, and he followed, taking Hakim and Juggat Lal with him. But before going, he ordered, me to remain here and inform your Excellencies that as soon as he had news, either Juggat Lal or Hakim would ring up and inform you.'

'Is the telephone call coming through to my house?' asked Rainer.

'Yes, sahib. I gave him your number!'

'Good! Do you want to search his bungalow, Sir Leonard?'

'No! Just order your men to take possession of it, and make a systematic search tomorrow. We'd better get back to your place as soon as possible.'

Rainer gave the detective orders to keep watch over the house until he was joined by others, for whom he would send directly when he arrived home; then he and Wallace returned to the car and drove off.

'You must be pretty famished, Sir Leonard,' said the Commissioner.

'I'm more thirsty than hungry,' replied Wallace. 'I think a whisky and soda is indicated. Batty must be pretty dry too,' he added. Batty, sitting in the front of the car with the driver, overheard and smacked his lips.

'Indicated is the word,' he murmured to himself. 'Swab me decks if it ain't.'

CHAPTER TWENTY-TWO

A Desperate Chase

Brien, waiting in a powerful Buick, almost opposite Silverman's bungalow, but up a dark lane that completely hid the car from view, found time pass tediously. However, during his years of service in the Intelligence Department he had become used to this sort of thing; he made himself comfortable, and spent the time smoking and wondering if his friend and chief was having any success. He was also a trifle anxious, for he realised only too well how Wallace, in spite of his assertions that there was no danger, went into the most desperate situations without the slightest hesitation; almost invariably, in fact, as though he were walking into a lady's drawing room. But Billy also knew that there was nobody in the world more wide-awake than his friend, in spite of his lazy air certainly nobody who had a more uncanny instinct of the proximity of danger; this knowledge comforted him somewhat.

It is doubtful whether there could have been a greater friendship than that existing between the two men. They had known each other since early boyhood, and had always been inseparable. Each understood the other perfectly. Marriage had made no difference, but rather had caused a friendship between their wives which had become almost as great as theirs. Billy had an unbounded admiration for his brilliant chief, and was never happier than when he was helping him to unravel some knotty problem of Secret Service work. Their years of close association had made, not lessened, Brien's continual amazement at Leonard's extraordinary astuteness, his almost weird powers of deduction and his utter nonchalance in all situations. Wallace, on the other hand, admired the solid worth of his chum; his keen grasp of detail, and above all the bulldog courage which made him cling on tenaciously to any task on which he had set his mind. They fitted into each other like a jigsaw puzzle, and it had been the same all through their lives.

One of the first things Brien had done on arriving in Davis Road was to order Abdul, the detective, to cut the telephone wires connected to Silverman's bungalow. It occurred to him that if Silverman or, to give him his correct name, Levinsky, was in the house, he could not then be warned of the raid, while on the other hand, if he did find out, it would prevent or at least delay his warning others.

Billy had smoked his second pipe, and was about to knock the ashes out, when a car, with great gleaming headlights, ran into the drive across the way, and stopped in front of the bungalow. Immediately came three flashes from an electric torch, and he sat up, alert and eager. This was the signal he had been waiting for. Abdul glided up.

'It is Silverman sahib!' he whispered in his quaint English. 'Anodder man are with him, and waiting in motor. It looks they are not stopping here!'

'Where are the other detectives?' questioned Billy.

'Hakim hiding by house, sahib; Juggat Lal here.'

The latter appeared apparently from nowhere, and grinned. Billy got out of the tonneau, and sat by the driver.

'You stop here, Abdul, and wait for Wallace sahib and the Commissioner sahib. I'll take Hakim and Juggat Lal with me. Tell your chief and my chief that as soon as I have news, I will leave Hakim or Juggat Lal behind to telephone to the Commissioner's house. Do you understand? What is the telephone number?'

Abdul told him. At that moment the car opposite was away again, and turning into the main road, tore in the direction of the Cantonments.

'Get in, Juggat Lal!' ordered Brien.

A moment later Hakim ran up, and was directed to take his place by his companion's side. Then the great car started, and was soon in full cry after the other, with dimmed headlights.

On through the night they raced. Levinsky had a good start, and was already some distance away, but the powerful Buick was gradually eating up the space between. The driver, a bearded Sikh policeman, crouched over the wheel, with his foot pressed down hard on the accelerator, and his eyes glued ahead at the ray of light that indicated their quarry's position.

Soon they were on the Mall with its beautifully macadamised surface, and the car hummed with all the freedom of a perfectly-running engine. Presently the lights of the Cantonments came into view, were passed, and left behind, almost as though they were merely the chimera of a distorted imagination. It was unlikely that Levinsky had as yet discovered that he was being chased, but Brien, expecting that every moment he would find out, urged his driver on to greater efforts, not knowing what speed the other car might be capable of.

Half an hour went by, and they were right out in the country, while the distance between the two machines had decreased to a matter of thirty yards or so. It was not till then that the occupants of the other car in front discovered another close behind them. Levinsky stood up and looked back – Billy could just discern him gazing over the hood. Then he sat down, and a little while afterwards the motor ahead began to draw gradually away.

'By Jove! He can move,' growled Brien to himself, and then ordered the lights to be switched on to their fullest extent, deciding that it was useless to attempt to cloak their purpose any longer.

A great beam of light shone out and brought Levinsky's car into bold relief. Then commenced a desperate chase. At times the distance between seemed to be lessening, at others it was undoubtedly widening, and on they went, through village after village, past farmhouses and sleeping caravans, swerving round bullock carts and other vehicles that travelled by night. Brien fingered the revolver in his pocket, and watched the other car with a steadfast, almost unblinking gaze waiting for the slightest movement of aggression on the part of Levinsky or his companion. It did not come for a long time, the Russian probably not being as yet certain that the people following him were actually after him for any other purpose than in an effort to race him.

They passed through Montgomery still at the same reckless tearing pace, and were once more out in the open with no company but the stars in the canopy of the sky overhead, a few trees on either side of the road, and for miles round the flat expanse of sandy waste which indicated the proximity of the Sind desert. Billy leant back and spoke to the detectives.

'What was the name of that town?' he asked.

Juggat Lal showed a line of white teeth in a broad smile,

but made no reply. Apparently he had no English; but Hakim understood and answered.

'That Montgomery, sahib,' he said.

'Where does this road go to?'

It took the detective some time to frame his reply; then:

'Him going Karachi, sahib!'

Billy whistled softly to himself. So Levinsky was heading for Karachi! At least it appeared so. 'Then,' thought Brien, 'it is very likely that he has had news of the raid and is making a desperate attempt to get to the seaport town with the plans.' The Secret Service man leant back in his seat with satisfaction. Lahore is over eight hundred miles from Karachi, he was close behind the Russian, and it was inconceivable that the latter could get away from him, especially as he had all the forces of law and order on his side and could call on their aid if necessary. Besides Levinsky was bound to stop before long for petrol, if for no other reason.

Apparently Levinsky thought the same for, of a sudden, he stood up and looked back, and casting all pretence and caution to the winds, raised a revolver and fired. But the brilliant lights of the car blinded him and his shot was a very sorry attempt. He disappeared from view again, but a moment later reappeared wearing a pair of sun goggles. This time his shot was better aimed and the bullet splintered the windscreen. Both Brien and the driver were covered with fragments of glass, but, except for a cut or two, escaped injury.

'This won't do,' muttered Billy, and standing up he took deliberate aim and fired. Levinsky got a fright and a flesh wound in the left shoulder at the same time, and bobbed out of sight immediately. There was intermittent firing for some time after this, but the Russian was at a disadvantage. In order to take aim he was compelled to show himself, and every time he did so, a bullet from Brien passed uncomfortably close to him. Then he tried shooting with his revolver resting on the folded hood and trusting to luck that a shot might take effect, but the bullets either went too high or too low, although one occasionally came very close. At last he gave up shooting altogether, and apparently contented himself with bestirring his driver to greater efforts, for the car drew away an appreciable distance.

'He must carry a lot of petrol,' muttered Billy. 'I'll put a bullet through his tank presently.' He leant back to Hakim.

'What is the next town or village?' he asked.

'Next town, sahib.' The detective thought a moment. 'Khanewal,' he added triumphantly.

'We'll slow down there, and Juggat Lal must jump off and ring up the Commissioner's house at Lahore, and tell him where we are and in which direction we are going. Do you understand?'

'Understanding, sahib!' replied Hakim, and conveyed the instructions to his companion.

At one-thirty they reached Khanewal and, slowing down to fifteen miles an hour, Juggat Lai jumped off, and disappeared in the darkness. They immediately picked up speed again, but the delay, short as it had been, had enabled the other car to get quite a long distance ahead, a distance that it might take hours to make up. They lost sight of it for a few minutes, too, and taking one of two roads, Billy feared for a little while that his quarry had taken the other, which he found out afterwards led to Multan, but to his relief, as they turned a corner and came out into the open again, he could just discern the other car in the distance.

The Sikh set himself to make up the difference, and they tore onward, the finger on the dial of the speedometer registering sixty-four miles an hour for some time. Just after half past two they got within appreciable striking distance once more, and raced through Lodhran on the tail of Levinsky's car. Here both machines had to negotiate a road that was under repairs and Levinsky got a little farther on, but half an hour later at Samasata there could only have been four or five yards separating the two motors. Then, instead of going straight on, the Russian dived into a series of side streets, and swung round corners so suddenly that in following him the other car all but collided with houses and various other obstacles. The Sikh showed amazing skill, bringing the car round on two wheels, almost in its own length, and avoiding accidents by a hair's breadth on numerous occasions. At one corner, however, they skidded badly, and some time was lost before they were once more on the tail of their victim, which had now run into the open road once more and continued on its headlong way.

'I'm fed up with this,' muttered Billy, and urged the driver to catch up the other fellow at all costs. Mile after mile was traversed and, at last, just as they were approaching Dera Nawab they were within ten yards once more. Then standing up Brien took careful aim, and put two bullets into the petrol tank of the other car.

Not satisfied with that he fired at the tyres and with his third shot there came an explosion; the car wobbled dangerously, and lurching across the road turned completely over in a ditch. Brien's driver avoided a collision by another display of skill, and drew up a little farther on. Billy and Hakim immediately jumped out and ran back, both of them holding revolvers at the ready. But they met with no opposition. They found the driver lying unconscious quite ten yards away, but of Levinsky and the man who had been with him there was no sign.

With the headlights of his own car shining full on the wreck,

Brien searched for the bodies of the two men, but all to no purpose. They had disappeared as completely as though the earth had swallowed them. He sat down in the ditch and groaned.

'What a fool I am!' he said. 'Now I know why they led us that dance round all the side streets.'

He got up presently, and examined the driver of Levinsky's car, who appeared to be very badly injured.

'We can't leave the poor beggar here,' he said to Hakim, 'and as we are going back to that last town, we'd better take him with us.'

With the help of their chauffeur they got him into the car, and drove back to Samasata. Brien sent Hakim to watch the station, first having made enquiries about the whereabouts of the residence of the Superintendent of police.

It was a quarter to four when the car drew up in front of the Superintendent's bungalow, and Billy sent the chowkidar to find his master. The latter appeared, after a delay of five minutes, in a dressing gown and a vile temper. As soon as he saw the other he demanded in unmistakable tones to know why he had been disturbed, but his manner soon changed when Brien informed him who he was and showed him his authority.

'Come inside, Major!' he said. 'And forgive me for being a trifle brusque!'

Billy smiled, and followed him into a small office. He gave him an account of his night's adventures, and described how he had been fooled. The other listened to him in amazement.

'What do you want me to do?' he asked at the end of the recital.

'Have the whole place searched as far as possible for Levinsky!' He gave a rapid description of the Russian, which the other noted down. 'I don't know who his companion was,' he added, 'and I don't suppose he matters much, but Levinsky *must* be caught.'

'It shouldn't be difficult,' replied the Superintendent, 'there are only half a dozen Europeans here, and a big fellow would be more conspicuous than ever.'

Billy smiled grimly, but made no reply. The Superintendent immediately got on the phone to police headquarters and gave the necessary orders.

'Now will you get me through to the Deputy Commissioner's house at Lahore?' asked Brien when the other had finished.

In ten minutes the connection was made, and Billy heard Rainer's voice at the other end of the wire.

'This is Brien speaking,' he said. 'Is Sir Leonard there?'

'Yes. You've just caught him. Hold the line!'

'Hullo, Billy!' said Wallace's voice, almost at once. 'I was just going. Have you got your man?'

'No, he's given me the slip!' And Brien described how Levinsky had escaped him.

When he had finished:

'Bad luck!' said Leonard. 'Where are you now?'

'At Samasata.'

'Well, look here, I'm just off to the Cantonments, and as soon as it is daylight I'll come to you in the aeroplane. If in the meantime you pick up the trail follow it through, and leave a message for me.'

'Right ho! Did you get my previous message?'

'Yes, thanks. I decided to follow you as soon as I knew the direction you had taken. Levinsky has got the original plans with him, so he must not be allowed to get away.'

'I could kick myself for letting him slip me.'

'You couldn't help it. It was a jolly clever ruse on his part. I would have been done just the same. Cheerio!'

Billy hung up the receiver with a feeling of gratitude to his friend. But would he have been done just the same, he wondered, and decided that Wallace's quick mind would have seen through the trick at once. He drove off to the station, leaving the damaged driver with the Superintendent, who rang up for an ambulance. On enquiry Brien had found out that the mail train from Karachi had already gone through, but that a passenger train was due to leave for the same destination at five o'clock.

He found Hakim shivering on the cold, draughty platform, and was informed that nobody answering to Levinsky's description had put in an appearance. Billy hid in a waiting-room and waited for the Karachi train to come in. It seemed to him his only hope that Levinsky would elect to travel by that train, but as the minutes passed he was filled with doubt, and he could hardly bear the suspense of waiting. Then, an idea occurring to him, he went to the stationmaster's office, and borrowed the telephone. He rang up the only three garages in the town in turn, and after some time got through to each. He asked if a car had been hired recently and received a reply in the negative in every case – a railway clerk very obligingly doing the actual talking for him. The knowledge that Levinsky had not hired a car cheered him very little. There were many other ways of obtaining one, and it seemed extremely doubtful that the Russian, knowing that he was being sought, would risk detection by appearing on a station platform and going by train. Billy sighed for Leonard's acumen and his uncanny ability to put himself in the place of others and think as they thought. He went through every means of escape for Levinsky he could think of, but quite failed to find any satisfactory idea that might help him.

He strolled back to the waiting-room, and idly stopped to watch some natives who were apparently having an argument on the up-platform. Standing by them was a tall burly Pathan, who appeared to be rather amused at the storm of chatter and invective that was going on at his side. There seemed to be something familiar about this fellow, but for the life of him Billy could not remember having seen him before. He was a fine figure of a man, with long hair hanging below his turban, and a large moustache and straggling beard, which had been dyed a deep red colour.

'What a disguise that would be for Levinsky!' Billy murmured. 'The red beard would have been the sort of master touch Levinsky would have delighted in.'

Then with what, he declared afterwards, was the most brilliant flash of inspiration that had ever come to him in his life, there came recognition; he felt that he could almost see beneath the beard, beyond the dark colouring of the man on the opposite platform. What gave him this feeling he could never tell. But he was absolutely certain in his own mind that this was Levinsky himself.

What was to be done! He could not go across and apprehend a man simply because he thought he was Levinsky in disguise. The fellow might turn out to be a perfectly harmless native. But with the thought firmly fixed in his mind that this was in truth the Russian spy, Billy dared not let him out of his sight. He hurried back to the stationmaster's office, speaking to Hakim on the way and directing him to watch the Pathan.

'What train are those people on the other platform waiting for?' he asked the clerk, who had already proved himself so obliging.

'Most of them for number sixty-five, sare; the slow train for Bhatinda and Delhi.'

'Is it due now?'

'It is overdue by twenty minutes!'

'Thanks!'

Returning to Hakim, Billy instructed the latter to hurry across to the other side, to take a ticket for Bhatinda and get into the same carriage as the Pathan, and watch his every movement.

'I must not go by the train myself,' he added, 'as I should be recognised, but I'll follow in the car, and I'll get to every station before you. I'll remain in hiding, but shall be watching carefully and, if he still retains his seat, wave a cloth gently out of the window and I'll know. If he gets out make no sign to me, but follow him. Do you understand?'

At first Hakim did not, but on Billy's repeating his orders, a smile of understanding lit up the detective's features, and he immediately went off to get his ticket. Brien continued to watch the Pathan, and presently noticed the latter looking covertly in his direction, he pretended to take no interest in the other platform and glanced up and down his own, as though in expectation of seeing somebody.

At length the Bhatinda train ran slowly into the station and stopped. The argument between the natives ceased, and there was the usual scrambling and pushing for seats. The Pathan entered a compartment almost opposite Billy, and, glancing idly at the train, the latter had the pleasure of seeing Hakim force his way into the same compartment and sit close to the man he had gone to watch. After a wait of ten minutes the train drew out of the station, and the last glimpse Billy had of the Pathan showed him with a cynical smile on his lips.

Billy hastily telephoned to the Superintendent of police and left a message for Wallace. Then, having ascertained where the train made its first stop, he jumped into his car, and was rapidly driven to Chistien. It was broad daylight when he arrived at the small wayside station, and he had a long tedious wait of nearly three quarters of an hour before the train, which certainly lived up to the title of slow, ran in. Watching from behind a window of the first class waiting-room, Billy saw Hakim leaning out of his compartmen-, and aimlessly waving a dirty-looking rag to and fro. Staying there until the coast was clear, he again telephoned to the Superintendent at Samasata, then re-entered the car and went on toward MacLeodganj Road. On the way the engine developed some obscure trouble, and it was half an hour before the driver located it; while he took another twenty minutes putting it right.

Eventually they got away again, and tore in reckless fashion along the uneven, bumpy road. Billy was thrown backwards and forwards on his seat, but he hardly noticed it, so intense was his fear lest he might miss his man. At last they came in sight of the station, and saw the train standing there. At the same time Billy became aware of the distant drone of an aeroplane engine, and looking behind, and upwards, he could just discern a tiny speck in the sky.

'God grant it is Leonard!' he muttered.

The car ran into the station-yard, and he jumped out before it had stopped, dropping his topee in the process. Not waiting to pick it up, he ran into the booking office. From there he could see very little of the train, so he made his way round to a deserted space, which adjoined the platform, and from where he judged he would be able to see the entire line of carriages. This piece of ground was more or less hidden from the road, and seemed to be used for depositing rubbish. A high railing separated it from the platform, and Billy was about to pull himself up and look over, when he heard a sound behind him. He turned and just caught a glimpse of the Pathan, when something crashed down on his head.

Flashes of fire seemed to be shooting all round him, he felt himself falling rapidly through space, then everything became black.

The roar of an aeroplane engine sounded louder and louder until all other sounds seemed to have become merged in one vast cataclysm of noise.

CHAPTER TWENTY-THREE

Wallace Follows the Trail

Mrs Rainer and her daughter had long since gone to bed, when the Commissioner and Wallace arrived back at the bungalow. They found Sanders sitting moodily over a cigar and a whisky and soda in the drawing room. He greeted them with a grunt:

'What's the trouble, Colonel?' asked Leonard. 'You don't look like a man who has done a good evening's work? You haven't lost Williams, have you?'

'No, he is safely locked up! But I've had a telephone message from Simla, which is the very deuce.'

'What has happened?'

'Hartley phoned me that they were marching their prisoner up the hill from Annandale, when three mad bullocks dashed down into them and in the confusion the fellow got away.'

'H'm! I thought an attempt at rescue would be made. So they tortured bullocks to do the trick, did they? Poor beasts!'

Sanders stared at him.

'Blow the beasts!' he growled. 'I've lost my man!'

'Never mind! Perhaps you'll get the other!'

'Oh, Hartley raided the house right away, and took six men and women into custody, among them a Mahsaud.'

'Probably the murderer, so why grumble?'

'Hartley is a fool!'

Rainer laughed.

'I can see poor Hartley having a bad quarter of an hour when you get back, Sanders,' he said.

'And he deserves it. I would have gone tonight only I was too late for the train. Can I have a car in the morning to take me back?'

Rainer nodded.

'What are you going to do with Williams?' he asked.

'Leave him under your care for the present. Isn't that what you want me to do, Sir Leonard?'

'Yes,' said Wallace. 'He'll be safer here!'

'How did you get on tonight?' asked the Colonel, after a pause, during which each of them was busily occupied in munching sandwiches and sipping their whisky.

Leonard and Rainer gave him an account of the night's doings between them, and when they had finished he whistled.

'There is an address at Simla, which I did not send through to the Commissioner,' added Wallace. 'I left it for you to raid when you get back. Here it is!'

He took the exercise book from his pocket, and read out the address in question, Sanders writing it down in his pocket book almost with an air of grim triumph.

'A most respectable firm,' he said. 'I'll make them more respectable!'

'You're properly on the war-path tonight,' smiled Rainer. 'Have another drink?'

'No, thanks; I'll go to bed. I want to be away as early as possible. When do you expect to hear from Major Brien?' he asked Leonard.

'Haven't the slightest idea. A call might come through at any time now.'

'He's been gone for nearly three hours,' said Rainer. 'I wonder which direction they've taken!'

'To make a guess,' said Wallace, 'I should say Levinsky is undoubtedly heading for Karachi. If it were only daylight I'd follow in the plane, though it would be a bit risky. Levinsky is such a tricky beggar that he might be heading for anywhere.'

'You'd better have a rest, Sir Leonard,' said the local Commissioner. 'Go and lie down; I'll call you when a message comes through!'

'No, thanks. I'll just rest in this easy chair if you've no objection. But there is no necessity for you to stay up.'

'Oh, I'll stay with you, sir, of course. Come along, Sanders; I'll show you your room; then I'll return!'

Sanders shook hands warmly with Wallace before following his host.

'I hope it will not be long before I have the pleasure of meeting you again, Sir Leonard,' he said.

'I'll look you up before I leave India,' replied the latter, and the two parted.

Rainer presently returned with a smile on his face.

'Your man is making himself thoroughly at home in the dining room,' he said. 'He has made remarkable havoc of a pile of sandwiches placed there for him, and looks perfectly happy.'

'Batty has the faculty of making himself at home wherever he is. By the way has he got into his own clothes yet?'

'Yes, and I should think by the shiny look of his face that he has been scrubbing it with soap.'

The two men lapsed into silence and conversation was very desultory for some time. At last the telephone bell rang, and Rainer immediately took down the receiver.

'This is the Deputy Commissioner of Lahore speaking,' he said in Urdu. 'Who is that?'

'Juggat Lal, Your Excellency, I am telephoning from Khanewal.'

'Yes. What is the news?'

'The Major sahib left me here to tell you that he is following Silverman sahib. He is going in the direction of Samasata!'

'I see. Is he close behind the other car?'

'Yes, Your Excellency. For a time there was firing, and the windscreen was smashed; but the Major sahib was too good a shot for the other to dare expose himself for long.'

'Very well, Juggat Lal. You had better return to Lahore by the first train you can catch.'

'It shall be done, Excellency.'

Rainer hung up the receiver and repeated the conversation to Wallace.

'You are right, Sir Leonard,' he said. 'Your man is undoubtedly making for Karachi. But with Major Brien so close behind him, he hasn't a ghost of a chance of escaping.'

'I shouldn't be so sure of that,' said Wallace. 'Although on the face of it one would not give a penny for his chances, he is such a slippery fellow that it is difficult to tell what he will do next.'

'But he'll have to stop for petrol before long, and, even if he can keep on for a few hours longer, daylight will make things hopeless for him. By Jove, sir, it was a stroke of genius on your part to have Major Brien waiting in that car for him.'

Leonard shrugged his shoulders.

'Now that we know where Brien is,' he said, 'I shall follow in the aeroplane as early as possible. Perhaps we shall be able to leave before daybreak. At all events I'll run up to the Cantonments at half past four. So go and lie down and get some sleep, Rainer. I'll remove this make-up, and then rest in here.'

'Are you sure you'll be all right, Sir Leonard?' asked the other anxiously.

'Quite, thanks!'

They walked along the hall, looking in the dining room on the way. Batty was lying on a settee, with his hands crossed over his stomach, and, from the rhythmic sounds which issued from his half-open mouth, there was little doubt but that the sailor was sailing somewhere in the ocean of dreams. They smiled at each other and proceeded on their way.

Bidding Rainer 'good night', Wallace entered the little room he had used earlier in the evening and soon had removed all traces of his disguise, and dressed himself in his own clothes. He put the three photographic copies of the plans in a small attaché case inside the suitcase, and locked it. Then packing away the clothes he had worn, he fastened the suitcase, and carried it into the drawing room. Here he made himself comfortable in an armchair, and placed the case on the floor with his feet resting on it. In five minutes, to all intents and purposes, he was fast asleep.

At a quarter past four, Rainer entered the room followed by a bearer with tea and toast. Leonard welcomed him with a smile.

'This is very thoughtful of you,' he said. 'You'll be glad when I have gone.'

'Not at all, Sir Leonard. I have thoroughly enjoyed our association, and your methods have been an object lesson to me.'

'Thanks for the compliment! Is Batty about yet?'

'Yes. He's out in the pantry drinking tea.'

At that moment the sailor appeared at the door.

'Mornin', sir!' he said touching a forelock.

'Good morning, Batty. Have you slept well?'

'Yes, thank ye kindly, sir. I could have done with some more, though,' he added.

'No time for sleep these days, Batty. You'll have to make up for it when the excitement is over. Take this suitcase out to the car, and don't let it out of your sight!'

'Aye, aye, sir!'

'Where is the other?'

'Who els answered aboard, etc.'

'Good!'

Batty lifted the suitcase, and taking it out to the car, placed it on the seat next to the driver's, and sat on it.

'Don't know if this is strictly correct,' he muttered. 'The skipper said, "Don't let it out o' your sight." I can feel it, but it ain't in sight.'

He scratched his head, then, after a moment's thought, stood up, lifted the case and, sitting down again, placed it on his knees.

'Now, yer lubber,' he said, 'I've got me peepers fixed on yer, an' I'd 'ave ter go blind afore yer could slip yer cables.'

Wallace was about to go out to the car when the telephone bell rang, and he stood by as Rainer lifted the receiver to his ear. The latter listened a moment, then 'Yes, you've just caught him. Hold the line.' He handed the receiver to Leonard. 'Major Brien is at the other end,' he said.

Leonard listened to Billy's description of how he had lost Levinsky with mingled feelings. After he rang off he told the Commissioner what had happened.

'This makes it all the more imperative that I should get away at once,' he added. 'Will you communicate with me at Delhi if anything happens, and if I am not there, leave a message. See that Williams is most carefully watched, and that he has no chance of committing suicide!'

'Very well, Sir Leonard.'

Wallace warmly bade the Commissioner 'goodbye', and soon he and Batty were speeding to the Cantonments. The driver, who appeared to be half asleep, caused Batty a good deal of anxiety by the erratic way in which he steered the car.

'Belay!' he roared, as they mounted the path. 'Not so much to port, yer swab. Keep her nice and steady, not like a windjammer in a West Injun 'urricane!'

However, they reached the Royal Air Force depot without accident, and it took some time to find Forsyth and his companions. A sergeant on duty at last discovered where the two pilots were sleeping, and Wallace roused a servant and sent him to convey his salaams to them.

In three minutes Forsyth appeared in his dressing gown, followed by a sleepy-eyed Hallows,

'Sorry to disturb you,' said Wallace, 'but things have happened which make it imperative for us to get off as soon as possible. Can you get away now?'

Forsyth looked at the sky.

'I'll get the C.O. to give us a few flares, sir,' he said, 'then we'll be all right. Come in for a minute, Sir Leonard! It won't take us long to dress.'

The airman was as good as his word, and in a remarkably short space of time quite a number of men were hurrying about preparing flares and running the huge machine from the hangar in which it had been housed.

The C.O. was apparently keen to do all he could for his distinguished visitor, and the depot became a regular hive of industry. At last everything was in readiness, and Wallace thanked the keen-eyed airman, who, on being roused by Forsyth, had risen from his bed without a grumble and shown such promptitude and readiness to aid them.

The flares cast weird ghostly shadows across the ground, but there was ample light to take off by and, as soon as Forsyth had been carefully instructed as to the direction of Samasata, they were off. The aeroplane rose into the air without the slightest mishap and sped at tremendous speed towards the south-west. Gradually the dawn broke, and objects below became clearer until at length the rising sun spread his rays in a golden glory over the countryside.

At a quarter past seven they reached Samasata, and glided to the ground just as a man on a motorcycle drew up. He asked for Wallace, and introduced himself as the Superintendent of police. He repeated the conversation he had had with Brien, and described the measures he had taken to apprehend Levinsky.

'So far we have had no luck, sir,' he added, 'but Major Brien has gone off on the trail of a man dressed as a Pathan whom he suspects of being the Russian in disguise.'

'Have they gone on towards Karachi?'

'No, sir. It appears that the fellow is making for Bhatinda, or perhaps even farther.'

'Bhatinda! That is in the opposite direction, isn't it?'

'Yes. I have had two telephone messages from Major Brien, one from the railway station here and the other from Chistien.'

'What were they?'

'He first told me to tell you that he suspected this Pathan of being his man, that he had sent a detective to travel with him and keep a watch on him, and that he himself would go by car and stop at all stations where the train was due, having arranged a system of signals with the detective.. Then as soon as he was certain that his suspicions were correct, he would arrest him.'

'Good! And the other?'

'He informed me from Chistien that the Pathan was still in the train, and that he (Major Brien) was going on to MacLeodganj Road. This second message only reached me about a quarter of an hour ago.'

'Have you any idea what time the train will reach there?'

'Yes, sir; I looked it up. It was twenty minutes late here, so can hardly get there before nine.'

Wallace called Forsyth.

'Do you think you can get to MacLeodganj Road by nine?' he asked.

'How far away is it, Sir Leonard?'

The Superintendent replied.

'About a hundred and sixty miles,' he said.

'Then we can do it easily,' said Forsyth.

'Splendid!' said Wallace. 'Follow the road, Forsyth, and we will probably sight Major Brien!' He turned to the policeman and held out his hand. 'Thanks very much,' he said. 'I shall be obliged if you will keep within telephone reach for the next few hours – I may want your aid again.'

'Certainly, Sir Leonard. I'll be waiting.'

He told Forsyth the direction he was to follow, and in a couple of minutes the aeroplane flew above the narrow white strip which indicated the road to Bhatinda. They passed Chistien not more than a thousand feet up, and travelling at a very high speed.

Wallace, with a pair of powerful field glasses focused on the road, kept watch and at length had the satisfaction of seeing a tiny dot moving along ahead of them. At the same time he caught a glimpse of a railway station, and knew it to be MacLeodganj Road. A train was just drawing into the station.

'Apparently we all arrive together,' he murmured.

They were soon very close to the station, and Forsyth circled around to find a landing-place. As he did so Wallace saw Brien jump out of the car, and run into the building, only to emerge a moment later and go to a piece of waste ground close by.

The aeroplane dropped lower and lower – Forsyth had found his landing-place – and passed over the top of the station building not more than twenty feet from it. Tasmond, looking downwards, saw Billy; saw him turn; saw his hand upraised as though to ward off a blow, and then sink into an unconscious heap, as a heavy implement wielded by a burly looking Pathan descended on his head.

The plane touched the ground, rose slightly, bumped, and then glided along for a few yards and came to rest. It had hardly stopped when Wallace, closely followed by Batty, dashed from the saloon towards the station.

Just before they reached it they saw the Pathan run towards what was obviously Billy's car. He brought down the Sikh driver, who was standing by it, with a blow from the deadly-looking instrument he held in his hand and turning dealt in the same summary fashion with a small man who was following him. Then jumping into the car he started it and was away. Wallace tried a shot, but he was too far off to do any damage.

'We'll get him yet, Batty,' he said. 'Go back for the mechanics! Major Brien is lying hurt in the station yard.'

He just glanced at the fallen forms of the driver and the other man, and saw at once that their turbans had saved them from serious injury. Billy was in a worse condition, the blood streaming copiously from an ugly wound above the right temple.

Staunching it as best he could with his pocket handkerchief, Wallace watched his friend with anxious eyes.

'Levinsky, you brute,' he murmured. 'I'll be more than even with you for this. You have taken on a greater debt than you'll ever be able to pay!'

CHAPTER TWENTY-FOUR

Levinsky Loses His Nerve and His Liberty

Billy was carried to the aeroplane. Green and Woodhouse procured water and bandages, and after some time succeeded in stopping the flow of blood and bringing him round. In the meantime the driver and the detective – for Levinsky's third 'victim' was Hakim – had recovered their senses, and the latter described to Wallace how he had followed the Pathan from the train and had been just too late to prevent him from attacking Brien; how he had wrestled with him, but had been overpowered and almost throttled, but still followed him until the Russian turned on him and knocked him out.

'You and the driver had better return to Lahore as soon as possible,' said Wallace. 'I will give you a letter to the Deputy Commissioner.'

He wrote a hurried note on a page of his notebook, explaining what had happened, and gave it to Hakim. Then returning to the aeroplane he found that Billy had regained consciousness, though still very dazed and weak.

'I seem to have made a pretty mess of things,' said the latter with a rueful smile.

'Mess! Good Lord, you've done wonders! I think it was brilliant the way you picked up the trail again and followed Levinsky.'

'But I understand he has got away.'

'Not for long. We'll soon overhaul him. And then I hope that we shall get him and the plans at the same time. After that we return to Karachi and wipe up Dorin and Co.' He called to Forsyth and Hallows, 'Follow that road and it can't be long before we come up with Levinsky. Fly low and turn him into a ditch; anything you like, so long as you do not finish him altogether. I reserve for myself the *coup de grâce*.'

He spoke so grimly that the two airmen gazed at him curiously, and even Billy looked up with interest.

'Why this vehemence?' he asked.

'I have a double score to settle with Levinsky now!'

'You mean—?'

'I mean nothing,' replied Wallace, almost irritably. 'Come on, let us get away. There's no sense in giving him too long a start.'

He helped Billy into the saloon, and in a few minutes the aeroplane was flying not more than a hundred and fifty feet above the road. In half an hour they sighted the car tearing recklessly along, and soon were right over it. The proceedings that followed can only be likened to a cat playing with a mouse.

For a time Forsyth was baulked in his attempts to get lower by the trees that lined both sides of the road and by the proximity of telegraph wires, but at last they came to an open space where there were no trees and where the telegraph wires meandered away from the roadside. The airman immediately took advantage of this and descended until he was flying not more than ten or a dozen feet above the car.

It takes a man of iron will to keep his nerve when driving a car with an aeroplane fifty or sixty feet above, but when that aeroplane is only a few feet up it is almost impossible. The roar of the engine is terrible in its intensity, and the whirr of the propeller causes such a blast of wind that it would sweep anything but an exceptionally heavy object away.

Levinsky proved himself almost a superman. He clung tenaciously to the wheel and, crouching over it, drove on with only an occasional wobble in his head-long course. Once he cast a malignant look upwards, but the watchers above could see the sweat of a great fear covering his brow. Still he hung on desperately, striving to reach a belt of trees about a mile ahead where he knew the aeroplane would be compelled to rise higher, and where he could possibly abandon the car and escape into the woods. But Forsyth sank lower and still lower until the runners of the aeroplane were hardly more than a foot above Levinsky's head. Then the suction of the propeller started to act. A sensation as though some gigantic magnet was drawing him upwards came over the Russian; a groan of agony broke from his lips as, clinging with all his strength to the steering wheel, he felt as though his arms were being torn from their sockets. He could not keep his seat, his body seemed to be gradually rising, the car behaved in a drunken manner, lurching from one side of the road to the other. Then the tortured man's resistance broke and, with a cry of fear, he swerved the machine into the ditch, where it turned over and threw him several yards away. He was not much hurt, but his nerve was temporarily shattered, and he lay where he had fallen, trembling as with the ague, his breath coming in great sobs.

Forsyth brought the machine to earth as near as he could, and Wallace and Brien alighted and walked over to the prostrate man. They had watched his efforts to escape with grim interest and had seen how frantic his terror had become, but there was no pity on Wallace's face as he stood regarding him and listening to his laboured breathing. He merely ordered Batty to bring some water and, when it had arrived, threw it over the Russian, who presently ceased trembling and after a moment or two shakily sat up.

'Well, Levinsky,' said Leonard, 'we meet once more. I hope you appreciate your somewhat novel adventure!'

'You inhuman brute!' gasped the spy vindictively. 'You coward!'

'Many thanks for the pet names. Coming from such a gentleman of virtue, they are indeed worthy.'

'You will suffer for this. I may be in your power now, but it will not be for very long.'

'Dear, dear! That will be disappointing. Well, we cannot hold a friendly meeting here, so I suggest that you accompany us back to the aeroplane.'

'By what right do you interfere with me? I am a perfectly respectable agent of a well-known firm, and you have nothing against me.'

'And you are not the prime mover of the Russian Bolsheviks in India, of course; neither is your name Levinsky?'

'My name is Silverman, and I know nothing of Russian Bolsheviks.'

'Billy,' said Leonard seriously, looking at his companion, 'we must have made a mistake. This gentleman is a harmless commercial traveller, who makes himself up as a Pathan the better to sell his firm's goods, and hits you on the head to impress you with their worth.'

But Billy was in no mood for humour. His head felt as though it were splitting.

'What's the good of telling us a yarn like that, Levinsky?' he said. 'You know us, and you also know that we know you. You escaped us once some years ago, but we've got you now, and we've got you *for keeps* this time.'

The spy stood up and bowed ironically.

'It does me good to hear such optimism, Major Brien,' he said. 'As you say, it is rather useless keeping up this pretence, so I will drop it and bow to the inevitable. It is certainly a relief to be able to remove these things.'

He took off his turban and the wig, then gradually pulled the beard from his face – apparently a somewhat painful process, to judge from the grimaces he made.

'Now I am at your service, Sir Leonard!'

'Then first you can hand over any arms you have on you.'

The spy took a revolver from among the folds of his clothes, and gave it to Batty, who was standing by him.

'Anything else?' asked Wallace.

'No,' was the reply.

'You'd better search him, Batty. I daresay he is lying.'

He was. Batty conducted his search thoroughly and found a long ugly-looking knife. The Russian merely shrugged his shoulders.

'It is a pity you discovered that,' he said.

Nothing else was forthcoming, so he was taken to the aeroplane, and ordered into the saloon.

'What about the car?' asked Billy.

'We'll leave it here and it can be collected in due course by the police. The Superintendent at Samasata will see to that.' And

Wallace gave orders to Forsyth to return to that town.

On the way back Levinsky showed no concern whatever over his capture. He seemed to have entirely recovered from the shock he had received to his nerves and actually attempted to enter into conversation, but he received no encouragement whatever from either Wallace or Brien.

'I do not seem to be popular,' he remarked to Batty.

'Stow it!' replied the sailor shortly, and so he lapsed into silence.

Samasata was reached just after noon, and the aeroplane alighted on the same open space that had been used as a landing-ground earlier in the morning. Wallace sent one of the mechanics for the Superintendent of police, then he looked grimly at Levinsky.

'Now we'll talk!' he said.

'Certainly, Sir Leonard. As a matter of fact I am tired of keeping silent.'

'Before going further, I want Major Elliott's plans which are concealed on your person.'

'Plans! I know nothing of any plans!'

Leonard regarded the spy fixedly for a minute or two.

'Listen to me, Levinsky,' he said. 'I am in no mood for any fooling, and I warn you that if you try it on I will show you no mercy. Give me those plans.'

'I have no plans of any sort, I assure you!'

Wallace turned to Batty.

'Tear every shred of clothing from that fellow's body,' he said, 'and examine it!'

The Russian stiffened, and stepped back as the sailor advanced towards him.

'Just a moment!' he said. Wallace stopped Batty by a motion of his hand. 'I suppose it is no use my continuing to deny any knowledge of the plans you are after,' went on the spy; 'but before you put upon me the indignity you threaten, I'll admit this – I know where the plans are, but I give you my word that they are not in my possession.'

'Carry on, Batty!' said Wallace and lit a cigarette. The ex-naval man immediately laid hands upon Levinsky, and commenced to pull his clothes off. With a cry of rage the latter tore himself away and stood fiercely facing the sailor, his hands clenched, and a look of hatred on his face.

'You dare!' he shouted.

Leonard drew his revolver, and held it lightly in his hand.

'If you resist,' he said, 'I shall be under the painful necessity of shooting you like the dog you are, and it is just as easy to search a dead man as a living one. Which is it to be?'

'Shoot away, you coward!' ground out the other.

'Right-ho!' He raised the revolver, and pointed it between the Russian's eyes. 'I'll give you a chance,' he continued. 'Go in and continue your work, Batty, and keep low, for if he makes the slightest effort to stop you, I'll fire!'

The sailor caught hold of the spy once more. For a moment it looked as though the latter intended to make a fight for it, in spite of his danger. He glared at the firm, grey eyes looking steadily along the barrel of the revolver, then with a shrug and a sigh he dropped his arms.

'You'll pay for this insult!' he said.

Leonard put the revolver in his pocket, but did not reply. With no gentle touch Batty removed the garments of the supposed Pathan one by one and, examining them carefully, threw them on the floor. Brien picked them up and subjected them to a further scrutiny. At last the spy stood practically naked, but there was not a sign of the plans. Wallace went carefully through the heap of clothes himself, with no result.

'For once in a way, Levinsky, you appear to have told the truth,' he said. 'Now perhaps you will tell me where the plans are!'

'No!'

Wallace's eyes narrowed.

'It looks,' he said, 'as though you and I are going to quarrel.'

'I feel certain we are,' said Levinsky insolently. 'Won't you try your famous shooting trick again?'

'Put your clothes on! I have nothing more to say to you just now.' And he turned away.

The Russian seemed to think deeply for a moment, then:

'I suppose that I had better admit that I am beaten,' he said. 'The plans are in the pocket of the car I stole, next to the driving-seat.'

At this surprising change of front Brien looked at the spy curiously, and Batty with contempt. Leonard, however, merely turned and smiled quizzically at the fellow.

'Levinsky,' he said, 'you seem to have an almost constitutional dislike of telling the truth . . . Keep him well covered, Batty, and don't hesitate to shoot if he makes any aggressive movement. I'll send in Green to help you tie him up.'

And turning on his heel he left the saloon followed by Brien. He beckoned to the mechanic who was standing nearby, and sent him in to Batty's assistance.

'What makes you think that Levinsky is lying about the plans?' asked Billy. 'Isn't it very likely that he shoved them into the pocket at the last minute in the hope that he could escape from us, go back later, and obtain them?'

'No! Such simplicity is not the Levinsky way. I don't think he has done us yet, but he very nearly succeeded, and I could kick myself for not being more careful.'

'You're talking in riddles,' grumbled Billy. 'What is the big idea now?'

'Simply this. In our eagerness to catch Levinsky we have entirely forgotten that he had a companion with him in the car that you chased. That companion escaped from you with the Russian at Samasata, and it seems obvious to me that while Levinsky disguised himself as a Pathan and went towards Bhatinda, the other man has gone on to Karachi with the plans.'

'Good Lord! . . . But why disguise himself if he meant to act as a decoy? I might not have recognised him.'

'He intended to get away if he could, but probably thought that if you did recognise him in his get-up, you would be all the more certain that he had the plans. Levinsky thinks of every possibility. He only made one mistake, and that was in not anticipating that we could fly after him. The trouble is – and no doubt it occurred to him at once – that we do not know the other man by sight. I suppose you would not recognise him again?'

'I never saw him – who is he, anyway?'

'Ata Ullah, the proprietor of the place we raided in Lahore.'

Presently the Superintendent of police arrived, with Woodhouse sitting on the pillion of his motorcycle.

'I understand you have caught your man, sir,' he said.

'Yes, but unfortunately the other fellow must have got away with the plans. I suppose you have made no arrest?'

'No, sir. I raked the district where the two of them disappeared, but there wasn't a person who was unable to account satisfactorily for his movements, and they were all residents of Samasata.'

'Nevertheless, somebody gave the two shelter. However, it

can't be helped. I intended handing Levinsky over to you, and sending him under a strong escort to Delhi, but I have changed my plans – I shall take him on to Karachi with us. By the way,' he turned to Brien, 'you were waiting for a Karachi train that left at five, weren't you?'

Billy nodded.

'When does that train reach Karachi?' Wallace asked the Superintendent.

'About noon tomorrow, sir; it is very slow and stops everywhere. There is a mail through at two, though, which gets to Karachi at nine in the morning, but it does not stop here.'

'Is there anywhere on the line where a passenger in the slow train can change into the mail?'

'Yes; at several places, but the express actually catches up the other at Rohri.'

'Well, it's pretty certain, I think, that the man we are after will change into the mail train somewhere or other, so he will be in Karachi at nine. As none of us have the vaguest idea what he is like, will you ring up Mr Rainer at Lahore, and get a description of him, and then telephone it through to Major Watkins at Karachi?'

'Very well, sir. What is his name?'

'Ata Ullah.'

The Superintendent made a note.

'Is there anything else, Sir Leonard?' he asked.

'Tell Major Watkins that we are on our way and hope to reach Karachi before dark!'

Wallace called Forsyth and asked him if he required any petrol or oil, and was assured that the aeroplane had enough to take them to Karachi.

'Can you get us there tonight?' asked Leonard.

'Yes, sir,' replied the airman, 'if we start soon.'

'We'll start immediately.' Shaking hands with the Superintendent, Wallace and Brien stepped into the saloon, and found that Batty and Green between them had tied up Levinsky so securely that he had the appearance of a trussed fowl. He glared malignantly at Wallace, but said nothing, and the latter merely looked at him as though he were a piece of useless lumber.

A slight defect found in one of the struts caused a delay, but Green and Woodhouse did not take long to put it right, and a quarter of an hour later the aeroplane was devouring space once more, with her nose set in the direction of Karachi. If Levinsky felt any curiosity as to his destination, he did not show it and indeed appeared for a long time to be asleep. He was given some food, which he at first refused but hunger apparently getting the better of him, he later fell to with a hearty appetite and consumed all that was put before him, his hands having been released to enable him to use them.

Billy, who had had no sleep at all the previous night, occupied the journey in making up the deficiency, and his example was followed by Batty, but Wallace, who seemed to be able to do with little or no sleep, spent his time in apparently deep thought.

Daylight was rapidly fading when at last Karachi was sighted. The aeroplane landed in the same open space as before, and then for the first time Levinsky spoke.

'Where are we?' he asked.

'Karachi,' replied Brien, without thinking.

'Idiot!' growled Wallace, under his breath. 'It wasn't necessary to let him know.'

'Sorry,' said Billy penitently, and Leonard smiled.

'We just had enough petrol to do it,' announced Forsyth, as they emerged from the saloon.

'Well, see about further supplies as soon as possible,' said Wallace, 'for we may have to leave again early in the morning. Here comes the Commissioner, I think; he'll see that you are fixed up!'

Major Watkins drove up in his car and gave a hearty greeting to the two Secret Service men.

'You're back sooner than I anticipated, Sir Leonard,' he said.

'Then you expected us?'

'Well, I had a feeling that you would come. Have you had any luck?'

'I raided a house in Lahore, and found a list of addresses of places all over India where Russian propaganda was being carried on. All except two were raided last night in consequence.'

'I suppose one of the two is here?'

'Yes!' Leonard took the exercise book from his pocket, and opened it. 'I want you to enter this house tonight, arrest everyone in it, and take possession of all the documents found there!'

'Where is it?'

With a smile Wallace handed the book to him, and pointed out an address.

'Great Scott!' exclaimed Watkins. 'Why this is one of the most reputable firms in Karachi! I would have staked a year's pay on the respectability of Waller and Redmond.'

'We seem to spend our time surprising deputy commissioners, Bill,' chuckled Leonard. 'Nevertheless,' he added to the Major, 'Waller and Redmond are not at all respectable; in fact the general manager who goes under the name of Waller is one of Russia's most trusted Secret Service agents, and his proper name is Dorin. He is second only to a fellow called Levinsky, who has been directing proceedings in India.'

'You amaze me,' said the Commissioner. 'Where is this Levinsky?'

'In the aeroplane tied hand and foot,' replied Wallace.

'Good Heavens!'

'I want to take him to Delhi, with Dorin as a companion. I would have sent hint before, but unfortunately some plans, which were stolen by his myrmidons, and which he had in his possession, have so far evaded us. They are on their way to Karachi, and will probably arrive by the mail train at nine tomorrow. The man who is bringing them is called Ata Ullah and I believe you have a description of him?'

'Ah, yes! It was telephoned from Samasata.'

'Good! Will you see that a couple of men are waiting at the station in the morning and that Ata Ullah is carefully watched. He will probably take the plans straight to Dorin and we will be waiting for him. But if by some chance he hands them over to somebody on arrival, both he and the other person are to be arrested immediately.'

'I understand,' said the Commissioner. 'Now about this raid!'

'The sooner it is accomplished the better. It is getting quite dark now, and I should think we will be likely to find Dorin and Co. at home. Besides I do not want them to get suspicious, and the news of our arrival will have reached them before long. If you'll drive us into the town, Brien and I will keep watch until you and your men arrive.'

'Well, we'd better be off at once, Sir Leonard.'

'Yes. But talk to Forsyth first, will you? He wants some petrol.'

The Commissioner strode over to the airman, and made a note of his requirements, then rejoined the others. Wallace sent the two mechanics to keep a careful watch on Levinsky, and told Batty to come with him. Major Watkins caught a glimpse of the prisoner as Leonard gave him instructions.

'Good Lord!' he exclaimed. 'Why it is Silverman!'

The recognition was mutual.

'How do you do, Major,' said the spy cheerfully. 'It appears that I am no longer to sell you wines and spirits!'

The Commissioner walked to his car as a man in a dream.

'Who would ever have thought,' he said, as he took his seat, 'that Silverman was in reality a Russian spy. Why the man has sold me stuff for years and—' He mopped his brow. 'Phew!' he ejaculated.

CHAPTER TWENTY-FIVE

Batty Averts a Tragedy

At Wallace's suggestion the Commissioner dropped them at the commencement of the Bunda Road and went on to fulfil his part in the arrangements. It was now quite dark and Wallace and his friend, followed by Batty, strode along quite openly, as there was very little risk of their being seen and recognised. They reached the building devoted to the activities of Messrs. Waller and Redmond and, after looking round cautiously to note if they were observed, walked along the lane that led to the back of the premises and halted opposite the window through which they had watched Dorin and his associates plotting their assassination on their first visit to the seaport town. As before there were no curtains to hide what was going on within. Dorin was seated at the desk busily engaged in writing in a huge ledger, while an Indian clerk standing in a corner was sorting a pile of papers that looked like bills.

'Friend Dorin always seems to surround himself with an atmosphere of innocence,' whispered Wallace. 'Anyone would think he was posing for a picture depicting a great captain of industry at work!'

'Posing is the word,' muttered Billy.

For ten minutes they watched, and still the clerk sorted and Dorin wrote. At the end of that time two Europeans entered the office hurriedly, and from their manner it was obvious that they were greatly excited. One of them spoke rapidly, and with much gesticulation to Dorin, who after a moment held up his hand to silence him, and turning to the clerk apparently ordered him from the room, for the man bowed and went out. Then indicating chairs to his visitors the general manager of Waller and Redmond leant forward in an attitude of attentive interest. Apparently he was much concerned by what he was told, for he presently rose from his seat and walked about, his hands clasped behind his back in agitation. Then he too spoke rapidly and, opening a drawer in his desk, took out a revolver and put it into his pocket.

'Our arrival is known, Bill,' said Wallace. 'This is where we act!'

He walked down the lane and into the road, followed by his companions.

'You and Batty stop here,' he said, 'and bring Watkins and his men in as soon as they arrive!'

'What are you going to do?'

'I intend to join the little gathering in Dorin's office. No doubt he will be glad to see me as I can assure him that I delivered his message to Muir.' And without waiting for any further remarks from Brien, he entered the open door of the establishment.

Two or three Indian clerks were about, who looked at him curiously as he made his way to the door that led into the office. One of them, he who had been sorting papers, intercepted him.

'Excuse me, sare,' he said. 'Mistah Waller is engaged. Perhaps you will wait?'

'He is not too engaged to see me,' said Leonard, and pushing past the fellow, he opened the door, and found himself confronting the three men within.

Dorin looked at him with amazement, in which there was mingled a slight tinge of fear. The other two stared at him with their mouths open.

'Dear me!' murmured Leonard. 'You seem to be busy, Mr Waller. I hope I do not intrude.' He carefully closed the door.

'By no means,' replied the other, recovering himself rapidly. 'For a moment I did not recognise you, Sir Leonard.' He placed a chair. 'Please be seated!'

Wallace sat down.

'I was afraid I would not find you at home,' he said. 'I wanted to tell you that I delivered your message to Sir Henry Muir.'

'Thank you very much; that is indeed good of you!' He looked significantly at the other two, who got up from their chairs and began to move in a careless fashion so as to place themselves between Wallace and the door. 'But,' he went on, 'this is hardly the place in which I can give you a proper welcome, Sir Leonard. I have a suite of rooms upstairs, and I shall be honoured if you will come up there with me.'

'I'm perfectly comfortable here, thanks,' said Wallace. 'I shall be going in a minute or two.'

Dorin smiled.

'I was hoping that you would pay me a prolonged visit,' he said.

'On the contrary, I want you to pay me, or rather the Government of India, a lengthy visit. I have a great friend of yours awaiting you, and he is anxious for you to accompany him to Delhi.'

Dorin glared at him.

'You mean—?'

'I mean Levinsky, who is my prisoner, Monsieur Dorin!'

'My God!' said the Russian; then, 'Tie him up and gag him – quick!' he called to his companions, and drew his revolver.

Leonard stood up quickly, but he held an ugly little Browning in his hand.

'I think not,' he said. 'Drop those revolvers, all of you!' he added. 'I have the advantage of covering you, and the slightest movement will mean death.'

For a moment there was intense silence. Nobody stirred, and the tick of a small clock on the desk sounded so loud as to be almost menacing. Each man there felt that perhaps the clock was ticking out his last seconds on earth. Leonard with his back to the wall, stood softly poised on the balls of his feet, ready to spring either way if necessary, and with his revolver held steadily in his hand. Dorin stood by his desk crouching slightly forward, while the other two, one in the act of drawing a revolver from his pocket, and the other with his held ready in his hand, stood transfixed, almost as though they had become paralysed. The picture was grim in its intensity; the Angel of Death appeared to be standing by with naked sword ready to strike.

At last a sound from the outer office relieved the tension, and someone sighed.

'Put your revolvers on the desk!' commanded Leonard.

Dorin, with a shrug, obeyed. One of the others appeared to be following his example, but suddenly swung round, and fired point blank at Wallace. The latter, however, skipped aside. At the same moment his revolver spoke, and his assailant, with a cry of agony, clapped his hand to his side, and fell in a crumpled heap upon the floor. The third man immediately flung his weapon on the desk.

'Now,' said Leonard, 'things are a trifle more even. Sit down, Dorin, and you too!' he added to the other. 'My men will be here in a minute or two to take possession of you. It may interest you to know that the power of the Russian Soviet is broken in India, and that this rendezvous of your agents was left to the last, as all tit-bits should be. It may also be interesting for you to know that our first capture was Leopold Boris, whom you sent to murder us.'

Dorin swore.

'I should have shot you when you first arrived,' he said. 'I might have known that you would have caused an upset, and I could have done it without much risk.'

'Yes, by using one of those silencers of yours, when you stood on the edge of the crowd that welcomed us.'

'Then you knew all the time that—'

'It looks obvious, doesn't it? And now you see what comes of leaving things to others. Let this be a warning to you!'

'Curse you! I always heard that you were a cold-blooded devil!'

At that moment there was the sound of shouts and cries in the outer office, and the trampling of many feet. Presently the door burst open, and Billy and Watkins, with Batty and a couple of policemen in close attendance, burst into the room.

'Thank God, you're all right,' said Brien. 'I began to think that something had happened to you.'

'Nothing ever happens to me, Billy,' said Wallace. 'Have a look at that fellow on the floor, some of you. He's pretty badly hurt!'

For a moment everyone's attention was off Dorin, and in that moment he acted. Pressing a button in the wall behind him, the part of the floor on which he stood appeared to collapse, and he suddenly disappeared from view. Wallace fired, but was just a fraction of a second too late, and the trapdoor sprang back into place with a crash. Dorin had vanished.

'Damn!' said Leonard with emphasis. 'Arrest everybody on the premises, and take possession of everything, Watkins,' he commanded in rapid tones; then: 'Come on, Billy, and you, too, Batty! We're going to follow Dorin.'

He stood on the spot that the spy had occupied, discovered the button, pressed it unhesitatingly, and found himself precipitated to the regions below. He landed on something soft, and the trapdoor sprang into place. He moved a little to one side, and a second later Billy landed beside him, followed in his turn by Batty.

They were in an evil-smelling cellar as far as they could judge, for there was not a vestige of light anywhere.

'Light a match, Billy,' ordered Wallace, 'and let us see where we are, but be careful. Dorin left one revolver upstairs, but he may have another with him!'

'I have an electric torch,' said Billy. In a moment the dungeon-like place was brilliantly illuminated.

It was a small, dirty apartment, the walls of which were covered with damp, and the floor by a pile of straw. In one of the walls a narrow cave-like opening was discovered and, after making certain that Dorin was hiding nowhere in the room, the three of them entered the tunnel. Billy led the way with his torch, closely followed by Wallace and Batty. There, was just room for a tall man to walk upright, and carefully the three of them made their way along. After a while Brien pulled up so suddenly that Wallace walked into him.

'What's the trouble?' enquired the latter.

'Look!' said Billy grimly, and gazing over his shoulder, Leonard saw a dark hole in the ground, and could faintly hear the sound of rushing water. Billy held his torch downwards, and looked over the edge.

'I can't see the bottom,' he said. 'It must be pretty deep, because the water sounds so far away. What do you think it is?'

'Might be an underground river, or a sewer, or something. Very interesting at other times, but not at all now. The question is, how are we to get over the hole. Is it far across?'

Brien flashed his light ahead.

'No,' he announced, 'about five feet. Move back a bit and give me room – I'm going to jump it!'

'Are you sure it is only five feet? I don't want you to jump to eternity.'

'Yes, it's not more!'

With a slight run Billy cleared the hole, and landed safely on the other side.

'There's a plank here,' he said. 'Wait a moment, and I'll push it across!'

He did so, and held the light so that Wallace and Batty could see where they were going. When they had joined him:

'Obviously Dorin removed it,' said Leonard, 'in the hope that, if he were pursued, we should oblige him by falling over.'

'You don't think he escaped down the hole somewhere?'

'I shouldn't think so. Let us get on, we're wasting time here.'

They got on. After a while Billy stopped again with a grunt.

'What's the matter now?' asked Wallace.

'Either Dorin did escape down the hole, or we have made a mistake somehow. I'm up against a blank wall.'

He flattened himself against the wall and Leonard squeezed to his side. Together they examined their surroundings, but there was no sign of an aperture.

'This may be a hidden door worked by some spring,' said Wallace. 'The question is where to find the spring.'

Once more they conducted a minute scrutiny of the wall in front of them, but their efforts were unrewarded. Then Billy examined the ground to see if there was any sign of a trapdoor. But they appeared to have struck a veritable *cul-de-sac*.

'Then he must have gone down the hole,' decided Brien, 'but how?'

'Wait a minute,' said Wallace suddenly. 'Shine the light on the roof!'

They immediately noticed a trapdoor just over their heads.

'That's the way he went.'

'But how could he get up?' asked Billy.

'There's nothing very difficult about it for a tall man, and besides there was probably a rope hanging ready. You can reach it easily – Push the door up.'

Handing the torch to Batty, who kept it focused on the roof, Brien reached up and pushed at the trap, but although he had no difficulty in getting his hands to it, and exerted all his strength, he could not move it. At last he desisted.

'It's fastened,' he said.

'Hang it!' exclaimed Leonard. 'We seem to be done after all. Let me get on your shoulders, and have a look at it!'

With the help of Batty he was presently seated on Billy's shoulders. His head touched the trapdoor and, holding the torch in his hand, he inspected every inch of it, but found nothing to show how it was fastened.

'It may just have an ordinary bolt on it, or work like the other one,' he said. He ran his hand round the edge and then suddenly, without any warning, the door came downwards, and with such force that it knocked him off Brien's shoulders on to Batty, who caught him with great dexterity. For a moment he stood rubbing his head.

'Are you hurt?' asked Billy anxiously.

'Not much!'

'How did you find the way to open it?'

'Well,' whispered Leonard, 'I don't know whether I found it or if it was found for me. I rather incline to the latter belief.'

'What do you mean?'

'S'sh; not so loud! I mean to say that I think it was opened from above. Of course I may have touched something that released it, but I don't think so. Stop here, Batty, and, if after ten minutes we have not returned or called to you to follow us, go back for assistance.'

'Aye, aye, sir!'

'I don't know how the other trapdoor opens from below, but you'll have to try and find out.' Then in a louder voice, he added, 'Well, I don't know how I opened it, but it is open, so come along, Bill. Let me get on to your shoulders again!'

He soon clambered through the opening, and Billy drew himself up and joined him. They found themselves in a small untidy room, furnished poorly in the native fashion. It was unoccupied and unlighted, and the only door, a solid-looking affair, was closed. Wallace flashed the torch round, but found nothing of interest.

'Somebody seems to have been using paraffin in this room rather carelessly,' said he sniffing. 'Well, there's nobody here, so let us get on, but go carefully, old chap!'

They crossed to the door, and found it resist their efforts to open it.

'Blow it!' said Billy disgustedly. 'We're done after all.'

'Let us try and break it open!'

Together they threw themselves against it, but hardly made an impression. There was nothing solid enough in the room to use as a battering ram, and presently they looked at each other ruefully.

'As you say, we are done,' remarked Leonard. 'Dorin must be well away by this. The only thing to do is to return, and hope that we shall catch the blighter later on.'

At that moment the trapdoor shut with a bang.

'Good Lord!' exclaimed Billy. 'We're caught!'

They hurriedly crossed to the spot, and examined it, but the trap fitted so neatly into the floor that it was hard to see it. There was nothing to show them how it worked and, although they made a careful examination of the wall in expectation of finding a button similar to that which had controlled the trapdoor in the other house, they found nothing. Then for the first time they both became aware of a faint crackling sound, which momentarily became louder, and a smell of burning.

'The fiend has set the place on fire!' exclaimed Brien.

'That accounts for the smell of paraffin,' said Leonard grimly. 'We have walked into our own crematorium!'

The crackling grew louder, smoke came in under the door, and presently the room was thick with it. Then a tongue of flame showed, and the door was seen to be on fire.

'This place will be a furnace in a moment with all the paraffin that is about,' said Wallace. 'We've got to force our way through the trap, or be roasted alive!'

They jumped on the trapdoor, singly, and then together; they crashed the rickety-looking table on to it with such force that it was smashed to pieces, but there was hardly a dent in the object of their attack. Then throwing himself on the floor, Leonard shouted to Batty below, and presently heard a faint voice replying.

'Go and get that plank of wood from over the hole,' he yelled, 'and try and smash this trapdoor open, and for God's sake hurry! Do you hear me?'

'Aye, aye, sir!' came back faintly.

Wallace rose from the floor, and looked at Billy. Tongues of flame were eating farther and farther through the door, and presently one side of the room was blazing. The smoke had become so thick that they were finding the greatest difficulty in breathing, and the heat was terrible. The paraffin-saturated furniture caught fire in an incredibly short space of time, then the door crashed down, and, in a moment, the room was a furnace.

Gasping, choking, burning, the two friends clasped hands.

'It's a rotten finish, old chap,' gulped Wallace hoarsely, 'but we've had a good innings. I wish I could have seen Molly and the little chap first.'

'And I Phyllis and the kids,' whispered Billy. 'Well, it's just fate, and as we've lived together, so we die together.'

And the two stood holding hands in a firm grip. Two British gentlemen prepared to face death, as they had faced life, cleanly and without a tremor of fear. Faintly to their ears came the sound of Batty belabouring the trapdoor with the plank, and through his agony Leonard smiled.

'Good old Batty!' he gasped, and then sank to his knees as the fumes overcame his senses. Sobbing in his effort to obtain breath, Billy dragged his great friend as far from the actual flames as he could, and then collapsed himself.

The walls began to crumble in, the skin on the bodies of the two men started to blister with the heat, their clothes to smoulder, and their hair to singe. Then, when it appeared that it was only a matter of time before all that would he left of them would be charred remains, Batty's plank came clean through the trapdoor. The crash roused Wallace from his semi-conscious state. He looked at the plank with almost unseeing eyes, but with his last remnants of sense he noticed that the fastening had been exposed to view, and dragging his revolver somehow from his pocket with his nerveless fingers, he put it right up against the catch, and tried to smile; but the result was a horrible caricature, on account of his blistered face and hairless eyelids.

'My last shot!' he croaked, and fired.

There was a deafening report, but wonder of wonders, the trapdoor shivered a moment, and then fell downwards with a crash. Wallace gave an almost horrible cackle in his efforts to express his relief, and feebly shook his companion. Brien raised his head in drunken fashion.

'We're saved, Billy,' gasped Leonard. 'Go down.'

'No, you go first!' choked Billy.

But even in this crisis Leonard insisted on his companion seeking safety first. Aided by him, Billy dragged himself somehow through the hole, and fell to the ground below. The whole room was in flames now, and as he painfully drew himself inch by inch to the opening, Wallace knew that his clothes were on fire. He felt himself grasped in Batty's strong arms, and then the sailor pulled him through and, throwing himself on his beloved master, extinguished the flames.

Somehow the two men, aided by the herculean efforts of Batty, and more than half-unconscious, staggered along the underground passage; somehow they reached the room under Dorin's office. But once there Wallace swayed giddily, and would have fallen had not Batty's arms been about him. He caught sight of Billy's face in the rays of the flash lamp which the sailor held in one hand.

'Oh, Billy!' he gasped chokingly. 'You do look a freak.'

And with a feeble cackle of laughter he sank into complete unconsciousness.

'Well, you're not a picture postcard,' replied Billy hoarsely, and sitting down on the ground he gently rolled on to his side and followed suit.

CHAPTER TWENTY-SIX

The Arrival of Ata Ullah

Major Watkins was a very thorough man and, as soon as Wallace and his two companions had disappeared below in chase of Dorin, he set to work, and searched the whole establishment with great care. First he had the wounded man removed to hospital in the charge of two policemen and a young doctor, and then sent all the prisoners to headquarters in a motor van, which was waiting. After that, assisted by a dozen detectives, both English and Indian, he examined the premises from top to bottom. So particular was he that scarce a pin escaped his notice, and the result of his thoroughness was that all manner of secret hiding places were discovered, in which were collections of the most inflammatory documents, denouncing British rule and promising Bolshevik aid to drive the British out of India, and form an ideal republic under the aegis of the Russian Soviet.

Every scrap of literature was removed to headquarters, there to undergo further and more careful examination, and at last the

Commissioner had cleared out the whole place and was left alone in the building with a subordinate.

He was in two minds whether to wait for Wallace and his companions to return, or to leave the establishment and await them at the police station. He decided on the latter course, and was taking a final look round the office, when he heard a muffled knocking coming from below. He immediately crossed to the button in the wall – taking care to stand away from the trapdoor – and pressed it. The trap fell at once and he kept his finger on the button to prevent it returning to its place.

'Hullo!' he called. 'Is that you, Sir Leonard?'

'It's all of us, sir,' replied Batty's voice. 'Sir Leonard and Major Brien is unconscious, an' I want someone to 'elp me get 'em aloft.'

'What has happened?' gasped the Commissioner.

'They almost got burnt to death, sir. Can yer get a ladder?'

With an exclamation of mingled sympathy and anger, Watkins sent his assistant to find a ladder. There was one in a storeroom close by, which was soon pushed through the opening, its weight preventing the trapdoor from springing back into place. The Major and the policeman descended to Batty's aid, and the three between them with great care lifted the inert bodies through the opening and into the room above. When he saw the blistered features and burnt clothes of the two men, Watkins started back in horror.

'Good God!' he exclaimed, and ordered his subordinate to telephone for a doctor immediately, then he turned to Batty. 'What in Heaven's name has happened?' he asked.

The sailor gave a graphic description of all that had taken place and Watkins listened, his anger growing stronger every moment.

'The fiend!' he cried, at the end of the recital. 'The utter fiend!'

The doctor very soon put in an appearance, and the Commissioner explained what had happened. The former conducted a rapid examination.

'They are both badly burnt,' he said, 'but I don't think it is very serious. Sir Leonard is in the worse condition. We had better get them to hospital immediately. What I fear most is shock.'

'We'll take them to my bungalow,' said Watkins. 'Send for an ambulance at once, Halliday!'

The policeman hurried off, and the doctor looked gravely at the Commissioner.

'Where is Waller?' he asked.

'He is responsible for this business,' replied Watkins grimly. 'He is a Russian spy, and it was while searching for him that Sir Leonard and Major Brien were trapped and almost burnt to death.'

'Good God!' exclaimed the doctor, and for some moments afterwards he repeated to himself in tones of absolute amazement, 'Waller a spy! Good God!'

Presently the ambulance arrived. Wallace and Brien were rapidly conveyed to the Commissioner's house, where they were at once put to bed in the same room and a nurse sent for. The doctor immediately cleansed and bandaged their burns, and then set about restoring them to consciousness. Billy was the first to regain his senses, and he stared round him in a wondering sort of way, before he remembered the events of the evening; then he shuddered and sat weakly up in bed.

'Where is Sir Leonard Wallace?' he demanded in a voice which seemed to him to come from a long way off.

'Here!' replied the doctor, endeavouring to push him back on to his pillows.

'Is he very badly hurt?' asked Billy in a tone of great anxiety.

'Pretty badly, but he'll soon be all right again.'

'Thank God!' muttered Billy, and sank back with a great sigh of relief.

At last Leonard came round, and he too lay for a time gazing at the ceiling in a perplexed sort of way. Then he saw the Commissioner, and tried to smile.

'Hullo, Watkins!' he whispered. 'Where am I, and what has happened?'

'You've been badly burnt, Sir Leonard!'

'Oh, yes. I remember now. Is Major Brien all right?'

Yes, he is in the next bed to you.

Wallace looked round.

'Hullo, Billy!' he said. 'By Jove, you've got enough bandages on you!'

'So have you! I can only see your eyes and mouth, and your right hand's completely hidden.'

Leonard regarded his bandaged hand.

'Why all this?' he asked.

Watkins looked at him with a smile in which a great relief showed.

'Your hand and face, and some parts of your body are almost raw,' he said. 'You must have been in the middle of the flames for a minute or two. Major Brien isn't so badly burnt as you are.'

'Well, that's something!' replied Wallace. 'But it's just my luck that this hand should be burnt. I wouldn't have minded the artificial one. By the way,' he added suddenly. 'Where's Batty? He saved our lives!'

Batty was sent for, and both Wallace and Brien tried to thank him, but the moment was fraught with emotion and they found it difficult to express themselves. Batty wiped something away from his eyes with the back of his sleeve.

'I only did my dooty, sir,' he said. 'An' I'd like to know wot she'd 'ave 'ad ter say to me, if I 'adn't 'auled you out, sir.'

'Well, Batty, neither Major Brien, nor I, nor she, will ever forget it.'

'That's all right, sir! Don't make such a fuss about it! I'd like ter get 'old o' the swine wot trapped you!'

'That reminds me,' said Leonard to Watkins. 'We've got to get on his track again. So I'm going to get up!'

'Excuse me,' said the doctor, 'but you're going to do nothing of the sort.'

'Oh, and who are you?' asked Wallace.

'I'm a doctor, and this lady is a nurse.' He brought forward a capable-looking woman in a nurse's uniform.

Leonard looked from one to the other.

'I am very glad to see you, Nurse,' he said, 'but I assure you I don't want any nursing.'

'You will, for several days, Sir Leonard,' said the doctor.

'Nonsense, man! I'll be all right tomorrow.'

'I'm afraid I must forbid you to move for some time.'

'Oh, well, we'll see,' said Leonard, smiling painfully. 'I'll stop here tonight anyhow to please you, and we'll continue the argument in the morning. In the meantime, Watkins,' he added to the Commissioner, 'do everything you possibly can to get Dorin. Have the docks and stations guarded, and the whole city searched! He must be caught if possible.'

'I have taken every precaution,' replied the Commissioner, 'and the whole neighbourhood of the house that was burnt is being searched at this moment.'

'Good! I suppose there wasn't anything left of that house, was there?'

'I don't know yet, Sir Leonard. I am waiting now for the report.'

Wallace gave orders to Batty to return to the aeroplane and inform Forsyth and Hallows of the events of the evening. He also asked the Commissioner to send a party of policemen to take Levinsky to the jail and keep him there for the time being. The doctor then decided that he had spoken quite enough, and insisted upon giving him a sleeping draught, which he took after protesting feebly. Billy was also made to swallow the same mixture, and presently the two of them were fast asleep.

The doctor called early the next morning, and found that the twain had just awakened. He examined them with care, and with the nurse's assistance dressed their burns. Then he stood at the end of Wallace's bed and smiled.

'I have never met anybody with such iron constitutions as you two gentlemen possess,' he said. 'Why, the shock you received would have killed most people; and here you are, apart from the burns, very little the worse for your ordeal.'

'I am glad to hear it, Doctor,' said Leonard. 'Therefore, you can have no objection to our getting up?'

'I couldn't think of it,' replied the doctor. 'You must have at least three days in bed.'

'Nonsense! I have far too much work to do to laze about in bed. Please don't argue, but just send Batty to me!'

The doctor protested, but in vain. Wallace had made up his mind to rise, and nothing could alter his determination; at last the medical man shrugged his shoulders and gave in.

'You are taking a very grave risk,' he said, 'and must not hold me responsible if any ill effects ensue.'

'Bless you!' said Leonard cheerfully. 'I shall never blame you whatever might happen. I think perhaps it would be wise if Major Brien stopped in bed, though.'

Billy snorted, and sat up.

'Not on your life!' he growled.

'Well, you'd better wait a minute or two, Sir Leonard,' said the doctor. 'I think Major Watkins and your airman are rather anxious to see you.'

'Send them in,' said Wallace impatiently. 'I have an appointment soon after nine, and I don't want to miss it. What is the time now?'

'Twenty past eight,' replied the doctor, and went to call Watkins and Forsyth.

The two entered the room with very serious countenances. Watkins expressed his delight at hearing that Wallace and Brien were so much better, and Forsyth started to make sympathetic enquiries, but Leonard interrupted him.

'I can see that both of you have something unpleasant to report, from the look on your faces,' he said. 'What is it?'

Forsyth looked at the Commissioner, who nodded, and the airman turned to Leonard.

'I am sorry to have to tell you, Sir Leonard,' he said, 'that your prisoner has escaped from the plane!'

'What!' exclaimed Billy, and Wallace swore.

'You remember, of course, that you left Woodhouse and Green to look after him?' went on Forsyth, and his two listeners nodded. 'Hallows and I stopped there until all the petrol and oil, which Major Watkins had ordered, was aboard, and then went into Karachi. We returned just before midnight and found Green lying seriously wounded outside the saloon, while Woodhouse was inside unconscious from a blow on the back of the head. He came here with me so that you could question him, but he knows very little.'

'Bring him in!' commanded Wallace tersely, and as Forsyth left the room, he turned to Major Watkins, 'Why wasn't I informed of this before?' he demanded.

'You were asleep, Sir Leonard, and the doctor gave orders that you were not to be disturbed.'

'Oh, damn the doctor!' exclaimed the other, then smiled. 'That's a bit unreasonable,' he added, 'but think of the time that has been lost!'

Woodhouse followed Forsyth into the room. His head was swathed in bandages and he looked rather pale.

'Well, Woodhouse,' began Leonard, 'tell me what happened!'

'There isn't very much to tell, sir,' replied the mechanic. 'Me and Green had been sitting with the prisoner, and having a quiet hand of nap together, and Green just went outside to fetch something. I was sitting with my back to the door, and presently I heard footsteps. I didn't look round, because I thought it was Green coming back; the next moment something hit me on the back of the head, and that's all I know, sir.'

'H'm! You didn't hear the sound of a scuffle outside before you were attacked?'

'No, sir.'

'How was Green injured?' enquired Leonard, turning to Forsyth.

'Stabbed in the back, sir.'

'Then he doesn't know anything about his assailant either. Is he very badly hurt?'

'Pretty severely,' replied Watkins, 'but he'll recover all right.'

'Thank God for that,' said Leonard fervently. 'I suppose he has been taken to hospital?'

Forsyth nodded.

'Batty arrived soon after we did,' he said, 'and I sent him to fetch an ambulance. I saw Green half an hour ago. He has recovered consciousness, but has no idea who stabbed him.'

Wallace lapsed into a brown study for a moment or two.

'All right, Woodhouse,' he said, at length. 'You had better go and rest.'

The mechanic walked to the door, then turned.

'I'm sorry, sir—' he began.

'Good Lord! You weren't to blame,' said Leonard. 'I'm very sorry that you had such an unpleasant mishap.'

Woodhouse looked relieved and went out

'Of course it was Dorin,' said Leonard. 'By Jove he had a fairly successful night last night. And I blame myself,' he added. 'If I hadn't mentioned to him that Levinsky was a prisoner, we would still have had the latter. What a fool I am!'

'Don't be an ass,' said Billy disrespectfully. 'How could you know that Dorin was going to escape?'

'One should always be prepared for eventualities,' replied his chief. 'Anyhow we've got to make a big effort to retake these two, and in the meantime,' he turned to Watkins, 'you had better send a few more men to watch for Ata Ullah's arrival at the station, in case he is spirited away somehow.'

'I've already taken precautions, Sir Leonard,' replied the Commissioner. 'As soon as I heard what had happened, I gave orders that the station, and all approaches leading to it, should be guarded by squads of plain clothes men, with a full description of this fellow. Further, fearing that perhaps Dorin and Levinsky would get away by car and intercept him at Jungshahi or Pipri, I telephoned to both those places and ordered them to be closely watched.'

Leonard held out his bandaged hand, which Watkins touched very gingerly.

'Thanks, Major,' he said. 'No man could do more!' Then he added briskly, 'Send Batty in to me – I must dress and get along to Waller and Redmond's premises to receive Mr Ata Ullah – if he comes!'

'You think there might still be a doubt of his arrival?' queried Brien.

'There is always a doubt when trying to checkmate Levinsky and Dorin, Bill. I have staked a lot on this last throw, and if we don't get those plans this morning, we shall be very nearly – though not quite – beaten.'

Watkins and Forsyth left the room, and soon afterwards Batty entered. He was all solicitude, and he helped Wallace and Brien to dress with the tender care of a young mother fussing over her first child.

When they were dressed the nurse looked in.

'I'm glad I haven't many patients like you two gentlemen,' she said. 'I should go grey in a week.'

'Sorry, Nurse,' said Leonard. 'I'd very much like to be nursed by you for a month, but the calls of duty have decided otherwise.'

She smiled and proceeded to give them advice, which was presently augmented by the doctor.

As they stood waiting for the arrival of the car which was to take them to their destination, the two regarded each other.

'We do look a pretty pair!' said Billy. 'I must say that with those bandages round your head and face and on your arm, you have a most interesting appearance.'

'I've certainly had the most complete singeing I've ever had in my life, and I am wondering what colour your moustache will be when it grows again that is, if it ever does.'

Billy fingered his upper lip lovingly.

'I feel a bit naked there now,' he admitted.

Batty came in to announce that the car was waiting, and offered the assistance of his arms, but they both refused and made their way to the door without support. They found themselves very shaky and weak, however, and once Wallace would have stumbled, had not the sailor caught him and thenceforth insisted on helping his employer to the car.

They were rapidly driven to the Bunda Road. Curious heads in the windows of neighbouring shops and houses watched them alight with Major Watkins and enter the open door of the establishment which had flourished under the name of Waller and Redmond. In spite of the extreme reticence of the police, knowledge of the raid had leaked out, and once or twice a crowd started to collect and stare open-mouthed at the building, only to be moved on by the plain-clothes policemen under orders from the Commissioner, who took every precaution to prevent Ata Ullah scenting danger and making his escape.

Once inside the office Leonard sank into a chair and smiled wanly at the Commissioner.

'It is extraordinary how quickly one's strength departs,' he said.

'I am amazed that you have any left at all, Sir Leonard,' replied the Commissioner. 'You both must be made of iron.'

'Good Heavens!' exclaimed Billy suddenly, and the other two stared at him in surprise. 'Didn't you tell me,' he went on excitedly to Wallace, 'that you had put the photographic copies of those plans in one of your suitcases?'

Wallace nodded.

'Then, man alive, don't you realise that they may have been retaken by Levinsky and Dorin last night!'

'They couldn't have been.'

'Why not?'

'Because I took the precaution of taking them out of the case, and pinning them to the inside of my waistcoat before I left the aeroplane. I also pinned them inside this suit while I was being dressed this morning, which shows that your powers of observation are not yet fully developed, my son.'

'Phew!' said Billy. 'For a moment I felt hot and cold all over.'

'Please don't talk about being hot,' complained Leonard. 'It takes my mind back to the incidents of last night; and why, oh why, Bill, will you persist in regarding me as an infant in arms?'

Brien grinned.

'For a moment, I admit,' he said, 'that I thought the infallible Sir Leonard Wallace had blundered.'

'Infallible be hanged. If I were I shouldn't be sitting here trembling in my shoes in case Ata Ullah fails to turn up.'

'You don't look as though you were worried!' scoffed Billy.

'Nevertheless I am!'

Whatever Wallace's real feelings were, it could be easily seen as time went on that his companions were agitated. Half past nine came, and still there was no sign of the seditionist. In the outer office waited two native policemen, dressed as clerks, with instructions to send Ata Ullah in as soon as he arrived. Although they knew nothing of the great issues hanging on the arrival of the Indian, they apparently found the waiting very tedious, for the three men in the inner office could hear one of them pacing up and down as though he were on beat. The monotonous sound presently got on Billy's nerves.

'I wish that fellow would keep still,' he growled.

'Hullo, Bill, feeling jumpy?' asked Leonard.

'We're not all cold-blooded beings like you,' retorted Brien.

'I think I'll ring up the station and find out if the train is delayed,' said the Commissioner, and immediately did so.

He was told that it had arrived ten minutes before, and he was imparting the information to his companions, when there was the sound of voices outside and then came a knock on the door.

'Come in!' sang out the three, almost in one breath, and a policeman looked in.

'Ata Ullah, Excellency!' he announced.

A sigh escaped from Leonard, and Billy murmured, 'Thank the Lord!'

'Show him in!' said the Commissioner; and the officer withdrew.

There was a second's pause, after which the door opened again. A small elderly man, with a greying moustache and wrinkled face, clothed in the height of Indian fashion, and wearing a spotless white turban, stepped in. He gazed in astonishment at the two bandaged men, and from them to the Commisioner.

'Which of you three gentlemen is Mr Waller?' he enquired in perfect English.

'None of us,' replied Major Watkins. 'I am the Deputy Commissioner of Police for Karachi and district, and this gentleman' – he indicated Wallace – 'is Sir Leonard Wallace, the Chief of the Intelligence Department of Great Britain!'

A great gasp of fear burst from the trapped man. He looked wildly from one to the other, and his hand went mechanically to a certain part of his coat.

'Yes, Mr Ata Ullah,' said Leonard. 'We want those plans. But sit down, and let us talk!'

With the perspiration breaking out in beads on his forehead, the Indian sank slowly into a chair.

'I am at your mercy, gentlemen,' he murmured.

CHAPTER TWENTY-SEVEN

The Plans at Last

The shock which Ata Ullah had received on finding himself in the presence of the very men he had striven so hard to avoid was almost too much for him. For some minutes he sat hunched up in his chair, breathing in a slow, laborious way, as though it were a great effort; and overcome every now and again by violent trembling fits, rather painful to witness. Wallace regarded him almost with pity, and waited patiently until he had become somewhat calmer. At last with an effort he pulled himself together, and Leonard started to interrogate him.

'Just as a matter of interest,' he said, 'I should like to know how you became involved in this Russian campaign against Great Britain. You will find it to your advantage to answer my questions straightforwardly and without hesitation. You are in a very serious position, and will gain nothing by further duplicity.'

'I recognise that, Your Excellency,' replied the man in a low voice, 'and all I can do is to throw myself on your mercy.'

'Well, answer my question!'

'I first got to know Mr Silverman about six years ago, after the riots which had taken place in the Punjab. He entered my house of business one day and had a long conversation with me. At that time I was in a very bad position financially, and was almost on the verge of bankruptcy. He astonished me by the knowledge he appeared to have of my affairs, and ended by offering to finance me on condition that I obeyed his orders implicitly. Such an offer was wonderful to me then, and I accepted it.'

'I see. So he started you on this propaganda work.'

'Not at once, Excellency. He left India for nearly two years, and I was allowed to carry on my ordinary business in peace, with only an occasional letter from him to remind me of our compact.'

'Was that compact in writing?'

'Yes, in the form of a letter from me to him, by which I bound myself to his service. I agreed that if I failed to carry out his instructions in any one particular, he could take the business entirely out of my hands without warning.'

'What did you receive in return?'

'My affairs were put on a firm financial basis, and apart from all profits, I have been receiving a sum of rupees six thousand a year from him.'

'That is, from the Russian Soviet?'

Ata Ullah bowed his head in assent.

'Where was Levinsky during the two years he was absent from India?' went on Wallace.

'In England, Excellency.'

Wallace looked at Brien and smiled.

'That was when we had our first encounter with him, Billy. So he had already commenced his activities out here.'

Brien nodded, and Wallace resumed his questioning.

'When he returned to India,' he said, 'did he immediately commence on his propaganda work?'

'I believe so, Excellency, but it was only by degrees that I was involved in it, until I found myself unable to withdraw.'

'Did you try?'

Ata Ullah was silent for a moment, his hands clasping and unclasping nervously.

'I regret to say that I did not,' he confessed at last. 'I regarded it from a business point of view.'

'Did you not realise the risk you ran?'

'Mr Silverman always assured me that there was no risk if I were careful, and I was so thankful for my release from debt that I seldom thought of it.'

There was a slight pause, then:

'Do you know what Levinsky – or, as you continue to call him, Silverman – was doing in India before you first met him?' asked Leonard.

'He was engaged upon the same enterprise.'

'Oh! But not on such a large scale, I presume?'

Ata Ullah looked round as though terrified of being overheard, then he lowered his voice to almost a whisper.

'Perhaps on an even greater scale, Your Excellency,' he said. 'I found out only last year that it was entirely due to Russian influence that the disastrous riots occurred in the Punjab which nearly had a very serious result.'

'What!' exclaimed the Commissioner.

'It is true, sir. I came across notes on the riots in a pocket-book he gave to me containing certain instructions.'

'This is very interesting,' said Leonard. 'What else have you to tell us, now that you are being so candid?'

'There are two hundred and seventy Russian agents in India, all engaged upon the work of undermining British influence.'

'Two hundred and seventy!' Leonard whistled. 'Have you a list of these people, and where they can be found?'

'No, Excellency, but Mr Silverman – I mean Levinsky – carried one about with him.'

'I must remember that when I meet Levinsky again.'

'He didn't have it on him when we searched him,' put in Billy.

'No, you're right. Probably it was left in his clothes at Samasata. By the way,' he added, turning again to Ata Ullah, 'where did you go when you escaped at Samasata?'

Without hesitation the Indian gave an address then Leonard asked him if there was any other information he could give about the activities of the Russians, which they did not already know. And he repeated for Ata Ullah's benefit what he and Major Brien had discovered. The seditionist was very much surprised at their knowledge, and looked startled when Wallace produced the exercise book in which were contained the list of addresses of the buildings devoted to the activities of the spies.

'There is very little, Excellency,' he said, 'which I can tell you apparently, except that the communal disturbances are mostly due to the Russians.'

'I don't see how they can be of any advantage in undermining British rule,' said Brien.

'It is hoped, sir,' replied Ata Ullah, 'that a great outburst of feeling can presently be caused between the Hindus and Muslims, which will keep the Government and troops fully occupied. Then under the cloak of that rising, the movement will start which is intended to drive the British out of India.'

'Well, you've certainly told us something,' said Wallace. 'And now I come to the plans which were stolen from Major Elliott between Simla and Kalka. We know you have them on you, and I have three photographic copies of them in my possession. I want an honest reply to this question: these copies were made on your premises – Were there any more than three executed?'

Ata Ullah looked him straight in the face.

'No, Excellency,' he said. 'It was thought that three would be sufficient; the originals, of course, making a fourth.'

'Very well. Hand them over.'

For a moment the Indian hesitated. Then with a sigh he slowly opened his coat and an under-garment and presently produced a package, which he handed to Wallace. The latter took it, opened it and examined the contents. After a while he looked up.

'They are complete!' he announced. Then he looked gravely at Ata Ullah. 'Do you realise,' he said, 'that a British officer was foully murdered for these?'

'I do, Your Excellency. But I knew nothing of the means taken to obtain them until afterwards. And if I had I could have done nothing. I was merely a catspaw.'

'Perhaps, but you have become involved almost beyond forgiveness. You have been helping to set a train for an explosion that might have meant another world war, and the sacrifice of thousands of lives, merely in order to save yourself, a puny little pawn on a gigantic chessboard, from financial worry. If you had not acted the traitor, and had behaved like a man, your reward would probably have been far greater than that which you have obtained from the Russian Soviet. As it is, you have lost everything. Don't you realise that under British rule everything possible has been, and will be, done for the benefit of India and her people? If the Russian Bolsheviks ever stepped into Great Britain's shoes,

God help this country. Every man and woman and child of you would be ground down in utter slavery. You have only to study their methods in their own country. By Jove! You and those of your race with you in this movement must be madmen, if you have any love in you for your country. If you have not, then you are the very worst type of scoundrel, and you are selling yourselves and your fellows for a mess of pottage.'

It was seldom that Leonard spoke so feelingly, and Billy looked at him in surprise. Presently Ata Ullah spoke.

'Excellency,' he said, 'do not judge me too harshly! I and my countrymen have always been led to believe that Russia merely favoured our independence; that they wished to see a republic established in India on the lines of their own ideal government. There was no question of their taking possession of India, but merely of acting as protector, until we could guard ourselves from invasion and outside interference. I may have been disloyal to the British Government, but I have not been a traitor to my country.'

'And do you actually believe that?'

'Certainly!'

'Then God help you for fools, if there are any more like you!' Leonard rose to his feet. 'Well,' he said, 'you have been frank, and by your willingness to answer straightforwardly have saved us a certain amount of trouble, so I will not be too harsh with you. You will go back to Lahore under arrest, and will stand your trial, but I'll make things easier for you than I would have done if you had not tried to be honest, and perhaps in the course of time, if you prove yourself loyal, you may even be allowed to re-open your establishment.'

The man's eyes filled with tears, and he stammered his thanks. He was handed over to the policeman outside, who took him away to the police station. Then Leonard smiled at his two companions.

'Do you realise,' he said, 'that it is nearly half past ten, and we haven't had any breakfast yet? The doctor did not forbid Brien and me to eat, did he, Major?'

'Not to my knowledge,' replied Watkins, and led the way to the car.

'Well, we've got the plans,' said Leonard, as he settled himself in his seat. 'But I shall not be satisfied until Levinsky and Dorin are under lock and key. Then we'll go back to England, and try and grow some more hair, Billy.'

After they had made a very good breakfast, the doctor arrived on the scene, and entreated them to take things easily, at least for that day. At first Leonard refused, but at last consented to take just one day of rest.

'After all,' he said to Billy, when the worthy medical man had left, highly satisfied with his partial victory, and they were alone with the Commissioner, 'one day won't make very much difference now. We have the plans, and I have a feeling that Levinsky and Dorin will hang round until there is no longer any chance of their recovering them. So we may get the blighters yet. You are continuing your investigations of course, Watkins?'

'Naturally! I shall go along to the office in a few minutes, and direct proceedings from there, unless you wish me to stay here.'

'No; I'd rather you were on the spot! Ring us up if you want us, or have anything to tell us.'

'Certainly I'll ring you up if I have any information for you, Sir Leonard,' replied the Commissioner, and rose from his chair; 'but I am not going to want you. You promised to rest for today, and rest you must.'

Wallace smiled.

'You and the doctor are nothing but bullies,' he said. 'However, we can do with a rest. Do you realise, Billy,' he went on, 'that we have only been in India for three days, and a bit?'

'Good Lord!' exclaimed Billy. 'It seems like months.'

'It seems like a fairy tale,' said Watkins, 'when one considers what you have accomplished in that time.'

He presently took his leave, and the two friends were left alone. Long cane chairs were placed on the veranda for them, and for the rest of the day they rested there, alternately sleeping, smoking and talking, while Batty ministered to their wants like an old hen fussing over a brood of chicks. Forsyth and Hallows came to see them and spent some time in their company. They learnt that Green was progressing favourably, but would not be able to leave hospital for at least three weeks.

During the course of the morning a long telegram arrived from Colonel Sanders in which he informed them that the Mahseud, who had been captured in the house at Simla, had confessed to the murder of Major Elliott, that the address given him as the headquarters of the Russians in Simla had been raided, and three white men and a host of seditious literature taken, and that they had recaptured the other native who had escaped from Hartley.

'That's good reading,' said Wallace with satisfaction. 'Sanders has something to beam over now.'

'It would take a lot to make him beam,' muttered Billy. 'He always looks and behaves as though he has had a broken love romance.'

'Perhaps he has,' smiled Leonard, 'but I think it is more likely to be the Indian climate and curry.'

'I wonder how he knew we were here.'

'Easy enough to find out. He probably rang up Rainer at Lahore and got the information from him. Well, there's one thing we've been very lucky in, and that is our dealings with the Indian police. It would be hard to find three more capable men than Sanders, Rainer and Watkins. If all deputy commissioners are on a par with those three, India is a very fortunate country.'

Billy nodded.

'I like Rainer immensely,' he said. 'He is really a very charming man. By the way,' he added, suddenly changing the conversation, 'I wonder where the girls are now!'

'Let me see, they left Marseilles on Saturday! Then they must be nearly at Port Said by now. It will take the yacht about eight days from there to Bombay, so we can expect them to arrive on Thursday week.'

'I hope we are a bit more presentable when they arrive,' said Billy. 'As it is they will get rather a shock.'

'I'm afraid they will. It won't be nice to find two hairless husbands awaiting them, but it cannot be helped. And our burns will not be healed much by then either.'

The Commissioner returned at five o'clock and reported a very busy day. No trace of either Levinsky or Dorin had been found, but every precaution had been taken to prevent their getting away either by boat, train or car, if they had not already done so.

The three were discussing the possibility of recapturing the two spies, when Leonard looked keenly at Billy.

'Do you think you feel fit enough to undertake a long journey?' he asked.

'Where to?' asked Billy in surprise.

'Delhi! I think that the sooner the plans are handed over to the Viceroy the better. I suggest, therefore, that, if you feel well enough to make the trip, you should leave here early in the morning with them.'

'I shall be all right,' replied Billy. 'But why not both of us?'

'Because I want to recapture Levinsky and Dorin, and I have an idea that they will hang about here for a time, so I won't leave Karachi until all hope is gone. And, as I may want the aeroplane, I hope Watkins can arrange to let you have a couple of cars.'

'Certainly,' replied the Commissioner. 'That will be easy enough.'

'But why two cars?' asked Billy.

'I am not taking any further risks, so I am going to request Mr Commissioner to give you an escort of half a dozen policemen. Also I shall send Forsyth with you as an extra aide in case of trouble. How far is it from here to Delhi?' he asked Watkins.

'Seven hundred and fifty miles,' replied the latter.

'Is it a good road?'

'Fair.'

'Then by not overdoing things you should reach Delhi by Friday morning. I suppose there are decent hotels on the way where you can sleep and have your meals?'

'I suggest that it would be safer if Major Brien had his meals at police depots, and also slept there,' said the Commissioner. 'I'll send messages through to say he is coming, and make arrangements for him.'

'A jolly good idea,' said Wallace. 'Then perhaps you will get to Delhi without mishap, Bill.'

'Why not lock me up in a cell at night,' said that worthy, 'since you are so bent on putting me under police supervision?'

'It would be wiser!' replied his chief, and so seriously that Brien thought he meant it and started to protest, much to the amusement of Watkins. 'I don't think there is much risk of your being held up,' went on Wallace. 'You must get away without our friends Levinsky and Dorin knowing anything about it. And as they probably imagine we are too ill to do anything just yet, I don't think they will expect such a move. If they are keeping a watch at all, it will be on the aeroplane.'

'There is no necessity to send Forsyth with me,' said Billy, 'you may want him.'

'I shall have Hallows, so I'll be all right. At any rate Forsyth will be able to give you a hand with your bandages, and see that they are kept clean, if he does nothing else.'

The matter was fully discussed, and Forsyth was sent for and given his instructions. Then leaving all arrangements to the Commissioner, Wallace and Brien retired to bed.

Batty saw them safely tucked in and contemplated them with satisfaction.

'I don't know as I ever seen two gentlemen pull theirselves together arter a bad doin' like you an' Major Brien, sir,' he said. 'But all the same if I could only lay 'longside that craft wot did it, I'd give a year's pay an' rations. An' swab me decks – beggin' yer pardon, sir – but 'is own mother wouldn't know 'im when I'd done wiv 'im!'

CHAPTER TWENTY-EIGHT

A New Discovery

Brien left for Delhi early next morning accompanied by Forsyth. His car got away from the Commissioner's bungalow very quietly and unobtrusively, and was met outside Karachi by another car containing the escort of policemen. Two of the latter changed over, and this arrangement was adhered to all the way to Delhi. Billy was under the most rigid surveillance. Whenever he moved from the car for meals, or any other purpose, he was accompanied by a bodyguard, much to his chagrin and Forsyth's amusement. Major Watkins had given implicit orders, and they were obeyed to the letter. It was no use Billy protesting – if he did so he was met with a bland smile, and a shrug of the shoulders from the stalwart sergeant in command; so he gave it up and resigned himself to his fate. But he afterwards remarked that he felt like a particularly evil criminal going to execution.

Nothing untoward happened on the way, and the weary journey was almost as uninteresting as it was tiring. Forsyth had secretly hoped for a scrap, as he put it, and great was his disappointment when on Friday morning the two cars, covered with thick dust, arrived at Viceregal Lodge without having had the slightest suspicion of trouble from any quarter.

Sir Henry Muir met them, and gasped with astonishment and dismay when he saw the heavily bandaged figure before him. But Billy refused to answer any questions until he had gone straight to the Viceroy's study, without waiting for a bath and change of clothing, and had handed over the documents in his possession. He insisted upon Lord Oundle examining them carefully before putting them away in the big safe; then with a sigh of satisfaction and utter weariness he sank limply into a chair.

The Viceroy, seeing the condition he was in, insisted on his having a rest before telling them of his and Wallace's adventures, and sent for a doctor to attend to him. A wire was dispatched to Wallace to announce the safe arrival of the plans, and Billy gladly went to bed and slept till the evening. Then, seated in an easy chair and wrapped in a dressing-gown, he told the whole story of the chase after the plans, the smashing of the Russian power in India, the manner in which Dorin and Levinsky had eluded them, and how he and his chief had almost been burnt to death.

Lord Oundle, Sir Henry Muir and Sir Edward Willys – for the latter was present – listened in amazement, and when Billy had finished his recital, there was a dumbfounded silence lasting several minutes.

'By Gad!' exclaimed Sir Edward at last. 'You two are marvels. The whole thing sounds like an Edgar Allan Poe story.'

'Don't include me as a marvel, sir,' said Billy. 'Sir Leonard Wallace thought out everything – I only acted under his orders.'

'And you acted damn well,' replied the other. 'When shall

I have the pleasure of meeting Sir Leonard? I want to see what manner of man this is and shake him by the hand.'

'You won't see him until he has got hold of Levinsky and Dorin,' replied Brien. 'If they haven't already escaped, he'll get them. And I am afraid it will be some time before you can shake him by the hand.'

'Why?'

'He was more badly burnt than I, and his hand is likely to be in bandages for some time.'

There was a murmur of sympathy.

'You'll find him a very unobtrusive man in his ordinary life,' said the Viceroy to Sir Edward. 'And you'll never get him to talk about himself.'

'I don't want him to talk about himself,' replied the Commander-in-Chief, 'but I confess I have a great curiosity to see him.'

'You'll get a surprise, sir,' said Billy. 'He always gives people who do not know him the impression that he is too languid to bother about anything. In fact he is, as Lord Oundle says, a most remarkably unobtrusive fellow away from his work, and even then he very seldom appears to bother. I have never seen him excited, and it is a very rare event for him to be annoyed.'

'You only make me the more anxious to meet him.'

'Well, I hope you will very soon, Willys,' said the Viceroy. He proceeded to tell Brien that both Sanders and Rainer had furnished reports which gave some idea of the progress Wallace was making in his investigations. He also said that owing to the foresight Leonard had shown in arranging for the various raids throughout the country, and the rapidity with which he had caused them to be carried out, they had been uniformly successful. Stacks of the most seditious literature had been discovered, over forty Russian spies had been captured at the various depots, and the addresses of almost two hundred others found.

'Altogether,' wound up the Viceroy, 'the whole thing has been a most amazing success. I little thought, when I cabled for Wallace, that he was going to bring to light this deadly plot against Great Britain. He deserves the grateful thanks of the British Government, and the Government and people of this country, for preventing a terrible disaster.'

Billy grinned.

'If you start thanking him when he arrives,' he said, 'he'll die from embarrassment. He absolutely loathes thanks for anything, and notoriety makes him as timid as a schoolgirl.'

'He'll have to put up with it this time,' said Sir Edward. 'We can't have him doing all this and then running away to his burrow like a rabbit.'

The doctor came to announce that too much talking was bad for his patient; so, protesting vehemently, Billy went back to bed. Before going, however, he saw Lady Oundle and Doreen for a little while, the two of them being all concern and sympathy. They insisted on his having every comfort that they could devise and altogether, as Billy grumbled to the grinning Forsyth, made him feel that he was a baby in long clothes and that they would next offer him one of the rubber comforters, beloved of babies of tender age, and generally known as 'dummies'.

Sir Henry Muir was greatly amused over Sanders' change of attitude. He told Billy how the Commissioner for Simla had gone into rhapsodies about Wallace while talking to him on the telephone.

'Considering Sanders' remarks before Wallace arrived in India,' he said, 'it was a most extraordinary turn round. Why, some of his statements almost sounded like hero-worship!'

Billy laughed.

'Good old Sanders!' he said, and presently fell asleep.

In the meantime Wallace had been far from idle. He had spent a quiet morning after Brien had left, but in the afternoon accompanied Watkins to his office, and personally searched through some of the documents which had come from the house at Bunda Road in the hope that information respecting other hiding places of Dorin and company would come to light. He also questioned the prisoners captured on the premises, putting them through a severe cross-examination, but nothing transpired, and he returned to the Commissioner's house, still without the slightest clue as to the whereabouts of his elusive foes. He and the Major discussed the matter till the doctor arrived and pleaded with Wallace to go to bed; which he did, but still continued talking to Watkins, who sat on a chair by the bedside. The latter, having thoroughly combed the whole city, gave it as his opinion that both Dorin and his companion had escaped out of Karachi on the night of Levinsky's rescue, and suggested that they would probably make for Bombay and try to board a ship there. But Leonard pointed out that the police had been warned at Bombay, and that the two spies would suspect that and in consequence would not dare to show themselves there. He repeated the conviction that they were still in Karachi waiting in the hope that chance would give them an opportunity of recapturing the plans. How correct he was in his surmise events were to prove.

After breakfast the next morning he lay in a long chair on the veranda, smoking furiously and thinking deeply; apparently quite oblivious to the presence of the Commissioner or anybody else. Eventually the Major recognised that it were best to leave him entirely alone, and stole quietly away. He met Batty in the hall and told him that he thought Sir Leonard did not wish to be disturbed.

'Bless you, sir!' said the mariner, 'I know the signs. Sometimes, when 'e 'as a bit of a corker to unravel, 'e sits for hours an' don't say a word, an' then nobody dare interrupt 'im an', if they did, like as not 'e wouldn't 'ear 'em. 'E's probably putting 'isself in the place o' them blokes an' tryin' to think with their minds.'

'I can see you have a great admiration for Sir Leonard,' said the Commissioner.

'Admiration ain't the word, sir. 'E's the best man wot ever drew breath, an' as for brains – my word, but 'e's just a bloomin' marvel, beggin' yer pardon, sir. An' there ain't nothing 'e can't do! 'Ave you ever seed 'im shoot?'

'No, I'm afraid I haven't.'

'That's pity, sir. Swab me decks, but it's a fair treat. 'E never seems to take no aim, an' 'e just plunks 'is bullet where 'e wants it. 'E seemed to miss when that there bloke Dorin went down the trap t'other night, but I wouldn't mind bettin' that 'e 'it 'im somewhere. No,' wound up Batty, with the air of a judge summing up, 'yer can't get away from it – there ain't no man in the world that is a patch on Sir Leonard Wallace, with all respects to you, sir; and 'is missus – beggin' yer pardon, I mean Lady Wallace – is just the right lady for 'im. She's the kindest 'earted, and most 'andsome woman wot I ever knowed.'

The Commissioner smiled at Batty's enthusiasm.

'You're a lucky man to serve such people,' he said. 'And they are very lucky to have such a faithful henchman.'

'I don't know about the 'enchman, sir, but you've 'it it when you say I'm lucky. An' now, if yer don't mind, sir, I'll just go on to the veranda an' stand by in the offin', ready to lay 'longside if the guv'nor gives me an 'ail.'

He saluted and went outside. Major Watkins stood looking after him for a moment.

'Thank God, there are still men left like that,' he murmured, and sending for his car was driven to his office.

Leonard spent nearly an hour and a half deep in thought, while Batty paced up and down the other end of the veranda, as though he were on watch. Then the former roused himself, and without looking round called quietly to the sailor.

'Aye, aye, sir!' replied the latter, and was immediately by his employer's chair.

'You and I are going on a little expedition this afternoon, Batty,' said Leonard. 'I have an idea that our friends Levinsky and Dorin may be hiding in that underground passage, so we'll search it together. In the meantime get me some sheets of the thickest paper you can find, a large envelope, and some sealing wax!'

'Aye, aye, sir.'

Batty disappeared to procure the necessary materials. He soon returned, and under Wallace's directions folded up the paper so that it fitted exactly into the envelope; then stuck the latter down.

'What have you done with my signet ring?' asked Wallace.

'Carryin' it aboard, sir, since I took it off your finger when you got burnt!'

'Well, give it to me!'

The sailor produced a large red handkerchief, which, was rolled in the shape of a ball, and carefully unrolling it brought forth the ring.

'Now put five large seals on the back of this envelope!'

Batty was ever thorough, and the seals he put on were enormous. Leonard pressed them down with the ring, on which was the crest of the noble house of Westcliff. When they had finished, the envelope presented a most official appearance.

'Now get a pen, and as I can't write, you'll have to write for me!'

Batty drew a fountain pen from his pocket and under Wallace's instructions wrote in a large sprawling hand,

'To His Excellency The Viceroy, Viceregal Lodge, Delhi.'

'That's that!' said Wallace, with satisfaction. 'You're a fisherman, Batty! What do you think of this for bait?'

The sailor scratched his head.

'Don't see what good that would be for bait, sir,' he said in a puzzled voice.

'Well, you might later on. If our investigations come to nothing this afternoon, I am going to fish tonight with this!'

Batty only scratched his head the more.

After tiffin Wallace announced his intention of searching the underground passage, and the Commissioner shook his head dubiously.

'Do you think you are strong enough yet, Sir Leonard?' he asked.

'I'm all right. The only thing that annoys me is that with all these bandages on my hand, I couldn't use a revolver properly if it became necessary.'

'I don't think you'll find anybody down there. I have had the whole place thoroughly examined.'

'I know, but I'd like to have a look myself, if only for the sake of curiosity. Perhaps you would like to come too?'

Watkins said he would, so the three of them presently drove once more to Dorin's late premises at Bunda Road and entered the building, which was still under the supervision of the police. The trapdoor in the office had been removed and a ladder was in place, so they descended to the regions below without difficulty. Watkins had brought a powerful electric torch with him, and he switched it on and gazed curiously round the cellar.

'I wonder what they used this place for?' he said.

'Goodness knows!' replied Wallace. 'Nothing probably. But the passage was obviously meant as a way of escape in case of emergency.'

'And they would have all got away when we raided the house, if you hadn't already entered the office?'

Wallace nodded.

'That's why I didn't wait,' he said. 'I was afraid there might be something of this sort. The office, with its one innocent-looking door, looked too much of a trap for Dorin to use it with equanimity unless there was another outlet somewhere.'

He went carefully round the walls, tapping them with the butt end of a revolver, and listening for a hollow sound.

'No hidden retreat here,' he announced at last. 'These walls are solid.'

They made their way along the passage, examining every foot of the walls on either side, and eventually came to the hole in the ground, which the police had carefully planked over. They removed the planks and looked down.

'I'd like to go down there,' said Wallace, 'and have a look round.'

'You couldn't possibly get down in your present state,' said the Commissioner. 'And besides it's unlikely that there can be any hiding place down there.'

'There might be, and I loathe leaving any of this place without searching it. I think I'll have a try – Batty, go back and see if you can find a stout rope!'

The sailor departed, and Watkins spent the time until his return in protesting against Wallace exerting himself in any way in his weak condition.

'My dear man,' said Leonard, at last, 'I'm going, so don't make a fuss. You and Batty can easily let me down on the end of a rope – I'm not heavy.'

'But how on earth are you going to hold on to the end of the rope. Your only hand is too badly burnt to enable you to hold anything?'

'You can tie the rope round my waist!'

'It seems to be so aimless, and such an unnecessary risk, Sir Leonard. There's only a sort of underground stream down there.'

'Probably, but why this hole? Somebody made it, and it was made for a reason.'

'Well, let me go!'

'No, I want to see the place for myself, and then I'll be satisfied.'

The Commissioner shrugged his shoulders.

'I don't know what the doctor will say,' he said.

'We'll spare the poor man's feelings by not telling him.'

After that Watkins relapsed into silence until Batty returned with a coil of thick rope; then once more he pleaded with Leonard to let him descend, and Batty also asked to be allowed to go down; but it was of no use. The two of them reluctantly tied one end of the rope securely round Wallace's waist, and taking the flash lamp in his bandaged hand, he was carefully lowered over the edge, first having instructed them to pull him up when he tugged on the rope. Almost at once his foot touched what appeared to be an iron bar in the side of the wall, and descending a little farther he found another, and then another. He brought the rays of the lamp to bear on the wall and discovered that there was a rusty iron ladder fixed there, starting about four and a half feet from the top. He announced his discovery to the others; thereafter his descent was much easier.

After he had gone down about twenty-five feet he found himself over a rushing, bubbling torrent that sounded like a cataract in that confined space. There was a ledge of rock about two feet square at the bottom of the ladder, and he stood there gazing round him. There was not much to see but water and damp, mildewed walls. Suddenly, however, he noticed a narrow opening in the wall almost at his side; cautiously he crawled through, to emerge without warning into a large cave-like apartment, the sight of which pulled him up short and made him look round him with astonishment.

The floor was covered with straw, and two native beds – on which a heap of bedding proclaimed that they had been recently occupied – stood on one side of the room. Three large biscuit tins stood by the side of the beds, and a pile of clothing, both Indian and European, was lying on the top of a wooden packing case stamped with the name of 'Waller and Redmond.' The room, or cave, was unoccupied. Leonard was unable to go any farther in on account of the rope, which was taut and had apparently gone its length. However, he was more than satisfied with what he saw, and presently he returned to the ledge and, tugging at the rope, was assisted up the step ladder. Watkins sighed with relief as he stood beside them once more.

'Rather an aimless journey, wasn't it, Sir Leonard?' asked the Commissioner.

'On the contrary,' replied Wallace, 'I have discovered where Dorin and Levinsky have been hiding, I think. Now all you have to do is to capture them.' He described the cave-like apartment and what he had found therein.

After Watkins had recovered from his surprise he decided to see the place for himself and, carefully instructed by Leonard about the ladder, he swung himself over the edge of the hole and descended, followed by Batty, who had asked and obtained permission to view the hiding place. When the two returned, the Commissioner asked Wallace what he proposed to do next.

'Nothing at present,' was the reply. 'We'll just put these boards in place and return to your house.' The planks were carefully adjusted, and the trio returned the way they had come, and were soon back in the Commissioner's bungalow. A bearer placed chairs for his master and Wallace on the veranda, and brought tea.

'There is one thing that I am suspicious about,' said Wallace, as he lazily helped himself to sugar, 'and that is, where were Levinsky and Dorin during our investigations? Knowing, as they must know, that the whole police force is looking for them, one would expect them to hide in the cave in the daytime and move about, if they wanted to, at night. Possibly that is explained by the fact that they are keeping a watch on the aeroplane, but then one would be sufficient for that purpose. Then where was the other?'

'Do you think he was somewhere in the tunnel?'

'That is exactly what I am wondering. He may have been listening to us all the time – he may have been hiding under that heap of bedding even, or those clothes in the cave. Unfortunately the rope prevented me from getting near enough to look.'

'Dash it all!' exclaimed the Commissioner. 'I never thought of looking.'

'No, but Batty did, because I gave him the hint.'

'Then why do you say unfortunately you couldn't?'

'Simply because he could easily have got out of the cave, and gone somewhere else in between the time that I ascended and you descended.'

'But there was nowhere else to go.'

'To men of resource like Levinsky and Dorin there was. For instance they could easily have dropped into the water, and held on to a ledge until you had gone. You didn't look in the water, of course?'

'No!'

'Well, it doesn't matter. If they saw us it will only make them the more desperate to recover the plans and get away. If we were not seen then there is plenty of time to capture them. Now listen! I have here an envelope which looks very official and which I am guarding with great care.' He took from his pocket the long envelope, which Batty had sealed carefully in the morning, and showed it to the Commissioner. 'When I go to bed I am going to do so with the curtains of my room wide open, so that anybody who happens to be watching from amongst those bushes outside can see every movement. I shall wrap, or rather get Batty to wrap, this envelope inside one of my bandages, get into bed, the lights will be switched off, and I shall await events.'

'Then you think you are being watched?'

'I don't know. But if Levinsky or Dorin, or both, know of our investigations of this afternoon, I shall be watched tonight, and I hope this packet will act as the bait necessary to make two desperate men enter even the Commissioner's house. As soon as the light is out, I want you and Batty, and a couple of your men to come into my bedroom and wait with me.'

The Commissioner nodded grimly.

'And in the meantime,' went on Leonard, 'send half a dozen men down to that underground hiding place with orders to arrest anybody who enters it. As their wait down there may be lengthy, tell them to take some food with them, and also to go well armed.'

'I'll go down to headquarters myself and give orders,' said Watkins, 'so that there will be no mistake.' And sending for his car he left immediately.

Wallace sat for a long time thinking so deeply that he quite failed to notice that his pipe was empty. Rousing himself, at length, he took out his pouch and started to make awkward efforts to fill it, but Batty was on the spot in a moment and, taking the pouch and pipe, performed the necessary operation. Then holding the match carefully until the tobacco was burning evenly, he threw the stump away and looked at Leonard quizzically.

'I'm wondering, sir,' he said, 'if you can go down on a rope with them burns, an' one arm, what you'd do if you had both yer arms, an' was quite fit.'

'But I didn't altogether go down on the end of a rope,' said Wallace. 'You forget the ladder!'

'Well, you didn't know of no ladder when you started, sir.'

For a moment there was silence, and then Leonard smiled at the sailor.

'If we don't get Levinsky and Dorin this time,' he said, 'it will be a caution!'

CHAPTER TWENTY-NINE

Levinsky and Dorin Again

Wallace went to his room, and prepared for bed just after half past nine. Everything was done exactly as he had decided. The curtains were not drawn, and with all the lights full on it would have been an easy matter for a watcher, if there was one, to see everything that took place.

When he was in his pyjamas, Leonard directed Batty to unwind the outer bandage on his arm, put the long envelope in place, and rewind the bandage over it. That done, he smiled with satisfaction.

'It would be hard to find a safer place for these – er – plans, Batty,' he said. 'The bait is prepared, the scene is set, and now all we have to do is to await events.'

Batty grinned.

'When you talked about them papers as bait this morning, sir,' he said, 'I thought you really meant you was goin' fishin' with 'em.'

'So I am!'

'Arter proper fish, sir?'

'Well, what fish could be more proper than Levinsky and Dorin?'

'I mean fish wot swims in the sea, sir.'

'Batty, I gave you credit for more intelligence. Considering our long association in crime, your wits should be keener by now!'

The mariner stared at his employer with perplexity.

'Long 'sociation in crime, sir!' he exclaimed.

Leonard laughed.

'Oh, Batty, Batty, wake up, or I shall have to pension you off and employ somebody in your place.'

The sailor certainly woke up at that announcement.

'Belay,' he said, and then added hastily: 'Beggin' yer pardon, sir – but don't let thoughts like them get adrift in yer head. I don't want ter be pensioned off nowise, no'ow and never, an' if it's all the same to you, sir, I ain't goin' ter let no other craft take my place, until I 'ands in me papers, an' sails away nice an' taut on me last voyage to Davy Jones's locker.'

Leonard put his bandaged hand affectionately on the startled man's shoulder.

'Don't worry, Batty!' he said. 'I was only joking. You and I will never part company until death comes to one or other of us.'

'Bless yer, sir! That's 'ow I likes to 'ear yer speak – them other words made me old timbers shiver just as if I'd got out o' me bearings an' run ashore.'

'And now,' said Leonard, 'I'm going to get into bed. Put out the lights, and call Major Watkins!'

The Commissioner arrived quietly and, feeling his way to an armchair, sank into it. Batty at Wallace's command sat in another, while two policemen squatted on the mat at the door.

'I wonder if we will have to wait long, or if anything will happen at all,' said Wallace. 'It is going to be pretty tedious anyway – I hope you won't get hopelessly bored, Watkins.'

'Rather not!' replied the Commissioner. 'I feel keyed up to top pitch, as a matter of fact, and I shall be deucedly disappointed if nothing happens.'

'Brien will feel very annoyed if anything does and he is not here to share in it,' chuckled the other softly. 'Poor old Bill, he always complains that he misses most of the real excitement.'

'He doesn't seem to have missed much since the two of you started operations in India. That must have been a thrilling chase of his after Levinsky from Lahore.'

'Yes, and I missed that. I hope he'll get through to Delhi safely, though I don't think there is much fear on that score.'

'None at all!' decided the Commissioner. Thereafter there was very little conversation, and after a while Watkins came to the conclusion that Wallace had fallen asleep, for he made no movement, and his breathing was very regular. But Leonard was very far from sleep. He lay there thinking deeply, and turning plans over in his mind – plans of action to bring into operation, if the night passed quietly and nothing transpired.

Time passed slowly, and in spite of his assertion the Commissioner began to feel rather bored, while Batty found the waiting very wearisome, and gave vent every now and then to prodigious yawns suggestive of the desire for action of some sort. No sound of any kind came from the policemen – Indians seem to have the gift of complete inaction, and can wait for hours in the same position, almost without movement.

A clock somewhere struck ten then after what seemed an interminable period, the half hour. Still nothing happened and the minutes crawled by to eleven and then half past. Batty, with a grunt, began to rub his left leg, which had gone to sleep, and Watkins, who for the last half hour had found great difficulty in keeping his eyes open, could do so no longer and fell asleep.

Another twenty minutes must have gone by when suddenly there came a sibilant whisper from Wallace.

'There is a scratching sound coming from the window of the dressing room,' he said.

Watkins woke up, and Batty forgot to rub his leg. The two of them listened intently but heard nothing, and another few minutes went by. Then there was a faint noise, as though somebody was pushing back a curtain.

'Stand by!' came Wallace's tense whisper.

There was no further sound, but Wallace, lying in bed with all his senses on the alert, had an uncanny sensation that something had entered the room and was gradually, noiselessly, approaching his bed. Minutes went by: minutes that seemed to be fraught with peril, and presently even the iron nerve of the great chief of the Secret Service began to fret a little with the apprehension of the unknown. He almost felt that some satanic force was at work, and that he was dealing with a power that was inhuman and cruel beyond conception. He longed to bring this terrible suspense to an end, but still he waited. And then something touched the bed – very gently, but something that was undoubtedly solid, and without hesitation he acted.

Sliding out of bed he at the same time called to Batty to switch on the lights, and immediately all was confusion. They caught a glimpse of what appeared to be a gigantic form, and in a moment Watkins had sprung from his chair, and grappled with it. Batty went to his assistance, and a terrible fight ensued. Hither and thither the combatants swayed, and Watkins was thrown against the bed with a force that testified to the intruder's strength, but Batty hung on, and the two policemen sprang across the room and tackled the man in rugby fashion, the four of them coming to the floor with a crash that shook the furniture. Watkins joined in again, and they gradually began to get the fellow under control. He was a man of enormous strength, and fought like a veritable demon, biting, kicking and scratching in his efforts to win free.

Watkins and his companions had almost mastered him, when suddenly two other men entered the room with levelled revolvers. One of them fired, and a policeman rolled over with a groan. The revolver made no sound, and Wallace noticed that both weapons had silencer attachments.

'So, Dorin, we meet again!' said Leonard, addressing the taller of the two newcomers.

'We do, Sir Leonard,' replied the Russian, 'and not for the last time either.'

'Oh, I'm glad to hear that. But don't you think you had better surrender quietly – you won't get away.'

'That is where I differ.' He turned to the four men on the floor. 'Release that man!' he said to Watkins and Batty.

'Stay where you are!' commanded Wallace.

'If they do, Sir Leonard,' replied the other, 'we shall shoot your friends, and you as well. You must admit that we have the upper hand. When we saw your preparations for bed, it appeared to us that it might be a trap, therefore we made arrangements accordingly. So the tables are turned, you see.'

'And do you expect to get away from here safely?'

'Certainly! We have made our plans for that also. Come on,' he added, changing his tone, 'we have no time to waste, so release my friend!'

'All right, Watkins,' said Leonard. 'Let him go!'

The Commissioner and Batty reluctantly released the big man, and shaking off the remaining policemen, he rose to his feet, and joined his companions.

'Curse you!' he said, glaring at Wallace. 'I'll get you yet.'

'Not so, Levinsky,' replied Wallace. 'But I'll get you.'

'And now, Sir Leonard, we'll have those plans,' put in Dorin.

Wallace shook his head.

'You won't,' he said.

'Then I shall shoot you like a dog!'

'Very well, shoot away!'

There was a tense pause, while Batty looked from his master to Dorin, and back in an agony of apprehension.

Then the latter spoke again.

'You seem to value your life cheaply,' he said. 'I shall count to three! If you do not hand them over, I will fire on the word three.'

Wallace bowed mockingly, and Dorin pointed his revolver straight at his heart.

'Keep the others covered,' he said to his companions, 'and if they move, shoot them! Now – one – two—'

Then Batty with a sob threw himself in front of Leonard.

'Give 'im wot he wants, sir,' he pleaded.

'You'll get shot, if you're not careful, Batty,' said the other.

'He very nearly did,' said Levinsky. 'But he has sense! It will be to your advantage, Sir Leonard Wallace, to do as he suggests.'

'I seem to have no choice,' said Wallace. 'Undo this bandage, Batty.'

The sailor commenced to do as he was directed, when suddenly with incredible swiftness Leonard drew a revolver from where he had noticed it in the inside pocket of Batty's coat, and fired. In spite of the bandages on his hand it was a remarkably good shot, and Dorin dropped his revolver, and clasped his other hand to his wrist with a cry of pain. At the same moment Leonard dropped on the floor behind the bed and pulled Batty with him. However, Levinsky grasped the sudden disadvantage that had come to his friends and himself, and instead of firing at his opponents he smashed the two electric bulbs with rapid shots, plunged the room into darkness, and shouted to his companions to get outside.

'After them!' roared Leonard, and Batty and Watkins needed no second bidding, following the three through the window.

Struggling into a dressing gown and slippers somehow or other, Leonard got outside just in time to meet Watkins running back.

'They had a car in waiting,' gasped the latter, and ran on to get his own car out of the garage. This was soon done, and Batty and Wallace climbed in. The policeman was told to stay behind and attend to his wounded companion. Then they were off in full chase of the other car.

They sighted it tearing along ahead of them, for it was a beautiful moonlit night and everything could be plainly seen for some distance around.

'Where are they making for?' asked Leonard.

'Goodness knows!' replied the Commissioner, who was seated crouched over the wheel.

'This road leads to the Oyster Rocks and if they keep on in this direction they'll end by dropping into the sea.'

'Perhaps they'll double round somewhere.'

'They can't! We're bound to get them!'

'I hope so!'

They lost sight of the car ahead for a minute, but swinging round a curve they saw it again making its way along a headland jutting out into the sea.

'They must be mad,' cried the Major, 'they'll be over in a minute.'

Almost as he finished speaking the car disappeared from view, and a minute later they drew up within a few feet of the edge of a cliff, which dropped straight down to the water twenty feet below. The three of them walked quickly to the place where the car had gone over and looked down. There was no sign of either machine or men.

'Well, that's the end of Levinsky and Dorin,' muttered Watkins in an awe-struck tone. 'They hadn't a chance going over in a car. Fancy their committing suicide like that!'

'Can we get down?' asked Wallace.

'Batty and I can, but you can't, Sir Leonard. There is very little foothold, and nowhere to stand down below. As you see the water comes right up to the rock.'

'Is it deep?'

'Fairly.'

'Deep enough for a car to sink out of sight?'

'Yes.'

'Well, will you and Batty climb down and have a look round. Perhaps you may find some trace of them.'

Watkins and the sailor immediately did as he requested. The Commissioner found the undertaking somewhat hazardous, but Batty made light of it and was soon down to the level of the water. The moonlight enabled them to see for some distance, but at first there appeared to be no sign of the missing car or its occupants. Eventually, however, they saw one of the cushioned seats floating a little way away, and one or two other objects that obviously had come from the machine. After waiting for some time in the hope that one of the bodies might rise to the surface, they climbed back to Wallace who was seated patiently awaiting them at the top. They reported what they had seen.

'We'll have to search for the bodies in the daylight,' added Watkins, 'that is, if there is anything left to search for. There are plenty of sharks round here.'

They returned to the car and got in. Wallace appeared very much preoccupied, and did not speak until they had reached the place where they had lost sight of the other car for a short while; then he bade Watkins stop, and getting out, he strolled about, apparently in a very aimless manner. The Commissioner and Batty watched him curiously, but said nothing. Presently he disappeared in the midst of a clump of stunted trees and after a few seconds emerged on the other side going away from them. Then he vanished altogether for fully five minutes, and Batty began to grow anxious. He sighed with relief when Wallace suddenly reappeared walking quickly towards them, his dressing gown giving him the appearance of a monk. When he once more reached the car:

'Those fellows are devils of ingenuity,' he said.

'Why?' asked Watkins. 'Don't you think they are drowned?'

'No, and I never thought they were. Obviously as soon as they got round that curve they strapped the wheel, so as to keep the car heading for the rocks then as soon as we were lost to view, they opened the throttle, jumped out and hid among those trees, after which they made their way towards that side of the promontory. Over there is a steepish pathway descending towards some rocks. I couldn't manage the whole way, but I am perfectly convinced that there is a hiding place below, very likely near the mouth of that underground river.'

Watkins whistled.

'By Jove! he said. 'That's an idea! Perhaps they'll make their way back to the cave, and they'll be taken there.'

'No, they'll hide somewhere else. Levinsky and Dorin are not the sort of flies to walk into the parlour of the spider. Who is the third fellow? Did you recognise him?'

'No, I've never seen him before.'

'Well, will you go back and fetch a few of your men to keep watch here. Batty and I will guard the place until you return.'

The Commissioner nodded and drove back towards Karachi, leaving Wallace and Batty together. The two made their way to the place that the former had recently discovered and sat down to wait.

'Wot about me goin' down an' 'aving a look round, sir?' asked Batty.

'Not now. It is quite likely that they are nearby, and you might end your days suddenly. Up here we can see both ways, and cannot be surprised.'

'Then you think there are more than three o' them, sir?'

'It is quite likely. At any rate we'll search the place thoroughly in the morning, and try to rout them out.'

'You took a mighty risk goin' down there by yourself, sir,' said Batty reprovingly.

'I didn't go far, Batty.'

'But yer would 'ave done, if yer could.'

'No; I realised that I might be walking into danger.'

Watkins came back after twenty minutes with four policemen and an English sergeant. The latter was fully instructed by Wallace, and also told to send a couple of men to search for the car as soon as it was daylight. Then the three returned to the Commissioner's bungalow and went to bed.

When he awoke, Wallace felt the effects of the excitement and his exertions of the previous day, and found himself with a high temperature, and very little ability to move. In spite of this, however, he was early on the scene of the previous night's – or rather early morning's – adventure. With the help of Batty and the sergeant of police, he got down to the bottom of the path and discovered, as he had half expected, a tunnel-like opening from which the water was running out almost fiercely.

'I should say that this is obviously the mouth of the underground river,' he said to Watkins. 'Now the question is: did they have a boat hidden down here, and thus get away altogether, or are they in the tunnel? You notice there is a narrow ledge in there. It looks a bit precarious, but that wouldn't stop our friends, and as it wouldn't stop them, it won't stop us. Have you brought that flash lamp of yours, Watkins?'

'Yes, but I don't think you had better make the attempt, Sir Leonard. I don't think you are too fit this morning – I've noticed you stagger once or twice, and your face is flushed.'

'I'm all right, don't worry! Take the torch, Batty, and lead the way! You're the most sure-footed for a job like this.'

Watkins handed the electric lamp to the sailor, the latter stepped on to the ledge, and made his way into the tunnel, followed by Leonard and the Commissioner, who anxiously kept his hand on the former's arm. The sergeant brought up the rear with another lamp, which he had borrowed from one of the policemen.

'Keep your revolvers ready,' said Leonard. 'You may need them before very long.'

The ledge was exceedingly slippery and once, if it had not been for the steadying influence of Watkins' arm, Leonard would have fallen into the water. In places they walked along almost at the same level as the rushing, bubbling stream; at others they were high above it, but there appeared to be no cave, or gap in the wall of rock, large enough to afford a suitable hiding place, and after they had traversed some distance Leonard called a halt.

'Go ahead by yourself, Batty,' he said loudly, in order to be heard above the sound of rushing waters. 'If you come upon anything that looks suspicious, come back and report, but be careful, and hold your revolver ready for use.'

'Aye, aye, sir!' replied the sailor, and went on.

'I must confess to a certain ridiculous feeling of weakness,' said Leonard to Watkins, 'so I am going to sit down and wait till Batty comes back.'

The part of the ledge on which they were then standing was some feet above the water, and although it was very damp Leonard sat down with his feet dangling over the edge. The rays of the sergeant's lamp made ghostly shadows on the surrounding rock, and the whole scene looked weird and unreal. Crawling, loathsome-looking things clung to the wall, and as the light reached them scuttled affrightedly into the darkness to which they belonged. The Chief of the Secret Service smiled grimly to himself as he thought how his present surroundings seemed so appropriate a hiding place for such men as Levinsky and Dorin – reptiles that should be trodden on and destroyed, like any other noxious creature of the dark.

There was too much noise to permit conversation to be carried on with much success, and after one or two attempts both the Commissioner and Leonard lapsed into silence, and became deeply absorbed in their own thoughts. Batty was away a long time, and when half an hour had passed they began to grow anxious. The sergeant suggested that he should follow and see what had become of the sailor. Leonard was about to agree to this when they saw a tiny light in the distance, the reflection of which appeared to be dancing about like a will-o'-the-wisp, and they knew that Batty was returning. He arrived presently.

'Well, Batty,' said Wallace, 'any luck?'

'Not wot you might say was useful like, sir. I went a 'ell of a distance – beggin' yer pardon, sir; I mean a long way, sir – when suddenly I couldn't go no farther.'

'Why?'

'Because this 'ere ledge ended, sir, an' there was nothin' but wall with no place to put me feet nowhere. I switched the light dead a'ead an' about four feet across was another bit o' ledge, so I 'itched up me slacks, sir, an jumped over, an' wot dyer think, sir? It was that there ledge outside the cave, wot we found yesterday.'

'Good Lord! What did you do?'

'Looked in an' said "'ow do" to the Injun coppers wot was there, sir. An' you should 'ave seed their faces – they just got the surprise o' their lives, but when they sort of come to their senses, they all started layin' 'longside an' arrestin' me. It took me a long time to explain who I was, but one feller understood English, an' 'e decided to come with me an' see for 'imself if I was me, so ter speak, sir.'

'Where is he, then?'

'Well, beggin' yer pardon, sir, but 'e couldn't jump acrost the gap, an' fell overboard. I left 'is mates 'aulin' of 'im out.'

His hearers laughed.

'I'm afraid men like that wouldn't have held Levinsky and Dorin,' said Wallace to the Commissioner, 'when Batty could walk into the middle of them and out again with such ease.'

'They're a lot of fools,' said Watkins irritably.

'Was there no hiding place at all on the way, Batty?'

'None whatsoever, sir. Not even an 'ole big enough to 'isle a baby's bottle, sir.'

'H'm! Well, let us get out of this place!'

They made their way to the entrance and thence up the side of the cliff. Wallace gave orders for a watch to be kept for the Russians until further notice, and then they crossed to the place where the car had fallen into the sea. It was low tide, and the shattered body of the machine could be plainly seen. It had turned a complete somersault apparently, and was resting on a rock with the front raised almost at the perpendicular. The steering wheel was visible and, as Leonard had guessed, it was tied in position. There was no further information to be gained there, and presently they returned to the Commissioner's bungalow.

'We seem to have come to an *impasse*,' said Watkins.

'What are you going to do now, Sir Leonard?'

'I'm going to rest for a few hours – I feel a decided susceptibility to make a complete fool of myself by fainting, and I think a little quiet will allay such womanish tendencies.'

At once Watkins was all alarm and wanted to send for the doctor there and then, but Leonard would not hear of it and presently went to bed. He fell into a troubled sleep, but it did him good, and when he awoke at two o'clock he felt much better.

He sat on the veranda with Watkins after tiffin, and discussed matters.

'It is rank bad luck losing Levinsky and Dorin again,' he said. 'I begin to feel that I am fated never to catch them, but I'm not going to give up until they are back in Russia.'

'They must have got away in a boat,' said the Commissioner. 'Shall I send the police launch to search for them?'

'No. I feel convinced that they are in that tunnel somewhere.'

'But Batty was very definite about there being no hiding places.'

'I know, but if he could walk right into that cave without being challenged, it is likely that they could walk past it, mount the ladder, and hide above somewhere.'

'Great Scott! I'd better have the whole passage searched again then!'

'It is not necessary, and besides you would never find them, they're as slippery as eels. They want those plans, and while I have this dummy package on me, I feel convinced that they'll hang round in the hope of getting it. The only thing to do now is to pretend to leave for Delhi, and bring them into the open for one last desperate attempt.'

'But you are in danger while they think you have the plans on you.'

'All the better – that's the way we'll eventually get them.'

'Then Batty and I will have to watch you like hawks, Sir Leonard.'

'Good! It is encouraging to add you to my bodyguard.'

A telegram arrived from Delhi during the course of the afternoon announcing the safe arrival of Brien and the plans, much to the relief of both Leonard and the Commissioner.

At four o'clock came an urgent telephone message from the police depot for Watkins, and he hurried away. Leonard called to Batty to give him a pipe, and was puffing away deep in thought, when a ragged-looking native came on to the veranda, and with many salaams handed him a letter. Opening it Leonard read the following:

Dear Sir Leonard,

I should be much obliged if you could come down to the old bus for a few minutes. I have an individual here who, as far as I can make out, says we are on his land, and wants to charge a fee. I can't get rid of him. Perhaps the Commissioner will come with you and settle him. I am sorry to bother you.

Yours respectfully,

G. Hallows

Wallace lay back on his chair and laughed.

'Poor Hallows!' he said. 'Here, Batty, get out the Commissioner's little two-seater. We're going to take a run down to the aeroplane.'

He gave the man who had brought the note a few annas. Batty drove the small car round to the front porch, and getting in Leonard was driven rapidly to the ground on which the aeroplane rested. Except for the machine the place had a deserted appearance.

'I wish Hallows would not interview people of this sort in the saloon,' murmured Leonard to himself, as he got out of the car, and walked across to the plane. Batty remained behind, sitting at the wheel with the air of an official of great importance – he rather fancied himself as a chauffeur.

Leonard reached the machine, and pushed open the door of the saloon.

'Well, Hallows,' he said, entering, 'what is the trouble?'

The next moment a sickly-smelling cloth was wrapped round his nose and mouth, and he felt strong arms grasping him. He struggled fiercely, then feebly as the fumes of the chloroform overcame his senses, and presently sank to the floor unconscious.

'Splendid!' said the voice of Levinsky. 'Now for the other!'

CHAPTER THIRTY

A Terrible Situation

After he had waited for a quarter of an hour and there was no sign of Wallace returning, Batty began to feel rather bored. When half an hour had gone by and still his employer did not come, he became fidgety, and getting out of the car started to walk about. A few urchins watched him with great interest, as though he were a strange and legendary being they had heard about, but never expected to see. He tried to enter into conversation with them, but his efforts at Hindustani only made them stare the more and presently he gave it up in disgust and, leaning against the car, contemplated the aeroplane, anxiously waiting for the door of the saloon to open, and Wallace to appear. But nothing whatever happened, and it struck him as curious that there was no sign of life anywhere about the machine. At last he decided to go across and see if Wallace was likely to be delayed much longer. He reached the door of the saloon and pushed it gently open, but no sound reached him and, his curiosity by this time getting the better of him, he stepped inside. Immediately the door was snapped to behind him;

he found himself contemplating three revolvers pointed steadily at his head, while the malignant eyes of Levinsky, Dorin and another man looked at him mockingly from behind them. Two other men stood by, and Batty suddenly realised that he was caught in a trap. With a heart full of foreboding he looked round and saw his master lying on the floor. For a moment Batty thought he was dead, and with a cry of agony he hurled himself upon Levinsky. The latter was taken by surprise; he fired, but his shot missed – and he went down before the bull-like rush of the sailor. He would have had very short shrift had not the others flung themselves on Batty and pulled him off. The latter fought like a tiger, and even the combined efforts of the five seemed at first doomed to failure; but numbers told, and at length they had him safely trussed up and gagged, and threw him into a corner like a sack of potatoes, where he lay impotently glaring hatred and murder at them.

Levinsky contemplated him sardonically.

'If I had known you were going to be so troublesome, my friend, I would have killed you off-hand; as it is, you are lucky to be alive.'

'Why not shoot him, and have done with it?' said Dorin.

'No, we'll reserve a better fate for him than that,' said the other. 'I think that we might take him and his master well up into the clouds, and as soon as we have secured the plans, drop them overboard. It will be a modern variation of the game of walking the plank – what do you say?'

The other laughed, and one of them clapped Levinsky on the back.

'You always were a man with a very pretty humour,' he said.

Levinsky shook his hand off, and spoke in a rapid, commanding manner in his own language.

'We have already wasted too much time,' he said. 'And now the sooner we get away the better. Have you the letter for the Deputy Commissioner?' he asked Dorin.

The other nodded and handed it to him.

'Georoff must take the car back, and hand this to the Commissioner's servant – let us hope that he will not have returned yet, or there may be awkward questions asked, but it is hardly likely that he can have done so. Then, Georoff, you must get out of this country as soon as possible and return to Moscow; do you understand?'

The man addressed as Georoff bowed his head in acquiescence. Levinsky handed him the letter.

'Now go, and we will depart.'

Georoff immediately left the saloon, and the chief of the spies turned to one of the others.

'You have had a look around, and are sure that everything is in readiness, Alexieff?'

'Yes!'

'Everything depends upon your skill, and Polunin here knows enough about aeroplanes to be of use to you. So let us start at once.'

Alexieff and Polunin immediately started the great propeller whirring, and in a few minutes the aeroplane rose from the ground and Karachi was left behind.

Lying helpless in his corner, Batty felt the vibrations of the machine and gave himself up for lost. He forced himself into a more comfortable position and looked about him. Wallace was lying face downwards and looked as though he were a dead man; but after watching intently for some minutes, Batty noticed that he was breathing and a sob of thankfulness rose in his throat. On the other side of the saloon Hallows and Woodhouse were laying together, both breathing stertorously after the fashion of drugged men. Batty, if he could, would have ground his teeth together with rage, to think that after all Wallace's endeavours his efforts should end like this.

After watching him for some time Levinsky stooped and removed the gag.

'You can shout and call as much as you like up here, my friend, and nobody will hear you. What do you think of my other three captives? Their attitudes suggest that they don't care where they are. But what an unpleasant surprise Sir Leonard Wallace will experience when he realises that after all he has lost the game and I have won!'

'You swine!' roared Batty. 'You damnable swine! If I could only lay me 'ands on yer, you'd never know 'ow yer died.'

'Just so, but I have no intention of permitting you to lay your hands on me.'

'Yer needn't think you've won yet, 'cos you 'aven't, an' you'll 'ave the whole bloomin' Air Force sailing on yer tail afore long.'

'Brave words, my lad, but quite unconvincing. I have taken precautions to prevent such a thing happening, at least for several days, and by that time we will be safely away, and the vultures will have cleaned you and your master's bones, and left two very respectable skeletons to testify that it is dangerous to try conclusions with me.'

'Belay!' said the sailor. 'You make me fair sick. You'll grin t'other side o' your face afore long.'

'You are impertinent, my man!' and Levinsky savagely kicked him.

'What about bringing the others to their senses?' queried Dorin.

'Oh, let them lie. They'll come round by themselves before long.'

He proved to be correct, for presently Hallows began to stir. Levinsky and Dorin tied his hands behind his back, and did the same to the other two. After a few minutes the airman opened his eyes and looked about him.

'Where the deuce am I, and what has happened?' he asked. Then he caught sight of his companions, and looked at Batty wonderingly. At the same time he became aware that his hands were tied behind him.

'What am I tied up like this for?' he demanded.

Levinsky laughed.

'We thought it safer,' he said. 'You notice that all your friends are treated alike. As a matter of fact we are taking you for a little trip in your own machine.'

'Good God! Do you mean to say—'

'I mean to say that the tables are completely turned on Sir Leonard Wallace, and that you are my prisoners.'

Hallows whistled.

'What are you going to do with us?' he demanded.

'You will know in good time – at present it were best if you behaved reasonably and philosophically.'

''E says 'e is goin' ter chuck us out of the aeroplane,' said Batty.

'What? You fiend!' exclaimed Hallows.

'That is the fate I reserve for Sir Leonard Wallace and his servant. I may have other plans with regard to you.'

'What?'

'I may offer you service in the Air Force of the Soviet. There are vacancies for a few good pilots, and if you behave yourself you may be offered one of them.'

Hallows laughed.

'You're very kind,' he said mockingly.

During this conversation Woodhouse had recovered his senses, and had listened in a dazed, uncomprehending sort of manner. Now he glanced across at Batty.

'Hullo!' he said. 'We seem to be in a hell of a mess!'

'You've said it, mate,' said Batty; 'but it won't be for long. You just wait until Sir Leonard comes to and starts to think a bit.'

Dorin smiled cruelly.

'Sir Leonard Wallace's thinking days are nearly over,' he said.

Batty looked at him fixedly.

'Blow me!' he said, 'but I've got a feelin' that your thinkin' days are just beginnin'!'

It was some time later before Leonard recovered consciousness and, as with the others, some minutes after that before he realised the position he was in. He looked very weak and ill, but he smiled from between the bandages that enveloped his head and face.

'So I have walked into the trap like a young innocent!' he remarked. 'It was a clever touch your suggesting in your letter that I should bring the Commissioner along with me, and you made a good guess in thinking that I did not know Hallows' writing. I must be getting into my dotage, but in extenuation of myself I must admit that I never thought you would have the daring to capture the aeroplane in broad daylight. I apparently did not know my Levinsky as well as I thought.'

'You do not know him at all,' said the Russian. 'During the short while that remains to you of life I hope you will discover a little!'

'No doubt I shall. But, if it is not boring you, I should be glad to hear how you got the better of Mr Hallows and Woodhouse.'

'That was a simple matter, just as everything was simple, except perhaps the capture of your man.'

'Good old Batty!' said Wallace, and smiled at the sailor. 'But how did they take you?' he asked.

'Came along to see wot 'ad 'appened to you, sir,' said Batty, 'and walked into the five of them.'

'So there are five!'

'Not now, sir — one o' them was left be'ind to take the car back.'

'And now there are four. It reminds me of the ten little nigger boys. But, pardon me,' he went on to Levinsky, 'you were going to tell me how you took the plane!'

There was a dangerous glint in Levinsky's eyes. He resented Wallace's levity – he had expected him to be overcome with despair, and perhaps fear, when he found out the terrible situation he was in. Instead of which he treated the whole matter almost as a joke. The Russian looked at him savagely.

'You will soon find this is no laughing matter!' he said.

'No, I expect not; but you haven't told me what I asked yet!'

'Two of my friends came along and, finding Mr Hallows and the other at work, introduced themselves as British officers, and during the course of conversation offered each a cigarette.' He shrugged his shoulders. 'The cigarettes were drugged!'

'I see! But you must have been very desperate to have taken such a risk – out in the open, too!

'Desperate ills require desperate remedies,' said Dorin.

'Don't be sententious, Dorin,' said Leonard. 'And now, where are you taking us, and why?'

'We shall eventually reach Russia,' said Levinsky, 'but you will be dropped over the side. Your unfortunate habit of interfering must be stopped once and for all, and the only way to do that is to kill you. Therefore I much regret that you will end your days in a short space of time. Have you any last requests to make?'

'Don't be more of a hypocrite than you can help, Levinsky. If you are going to drop me over, get on with it. It is the sort of thing that would appeal to you and Dorin. You certainly were both born to dangle at the end of a rope! I am sorry I shall not be there to see you dangle.'

Levinsky kicked him in the side with savage force. Batty roared with anger, but Wallace merely smiled.

'I wish I could find a word expressive enough to describe you,' he said. 'Cur and cad are much too good!'

This time Dorin kicked him.

'All right, Dorin,' said Leonard, 'you need not be jealous. Whatever I have said to Levinsky equally applies to you.'

'Let us take the plans from him, and get it over!' snapped Dorin to Levinsky, and the latter nodded.

With rough hands they commenced to search, and Dorin tore the bandage from his arm. Leonard gritted his teeth with the pain, but still smiled.

'You won't find them there,' he said.

Levinsky found the packet in his pocket and gave a cry of triumph.

'So, Sir Leonard Wallace, you lose your plans and also your life. You must wish now that you had never left England.'

'Not in the least,' replied Leonard. 'The plans don't worry me at all.'

'What do you mean?'

'Open that package, and see for yourself!'

A look of dawning doubt came into the two Russians' faces.

Levinsky tore the envelope open and took out the contents. When he and Dorin saw that they were nothing but plain sheets of paper their rage was terrible to behold. Frantically they searched the prone man before them, tearing his clothes and pulling his bandages off with such force that they tore the flesh off with them. Then finding nothing, they kicked him until they tired. Batty, Hallows, and Woodhouse struggled to free themselves from their bonds to go to Wallace's aid, but in vain, and the sailor swore and sobbed in turn, as he watched the fiendish cruelty of the two Russians. At last they ceased kicking and belabouring him, and he lay a bleeding, bedraggled object, horrible to behold, but not a groan came from him, and even in his agony he smiled.

'You fools,' he gasped. 'Major Brien delivered the plans and your photographic copies to the Viceroy this morning. You will find the telegram assuring me of that fact among the letters you have taken from my pockets.' And he fainted.

Levinsky sat down trembling with rage, while Dorin stood with his hands tightly clenched, grinding his teeth. Presently the former spoke in Russian.

'What fools we were to think that the other was burnt too badly to leave his bed. While we were doing nothing the plans were on their way to Delhi.' He raised his arms and cursed for several minutes.

'Well, we've lost them now,' said Dorin, 'so let us throw him out and make for Russia.'

'Not while he is unconscious,' said the other. 'Let him walk out with all his faculties about him, so that he will suffer the more.'

He looked through the letters and papers they had found in Leonard's pockets; among them was a cablegram which he read two or three times.

'This is from his wife,' he said to Dorin. 'She is on her way out to join him!'

'Well, what does that matter to us? She won't see him.'

'No, but it is interesting to know that she is travelling all that way to hear that her husband is dead.'

'When was that sent?'

'On the eighteenth, from Marseilles. That means that she is somewhere in the Red Sea by now. She mentions the yacht, so that must be his father's yacht – the *Greyhound*, isn't it?'

'I don't know, and it is not a matter that interests me!'

Levinsky crushed up the cablegram, and put it into his pocket.

'I wish I could think of a death that would make the Englishman suffer more than by merely falling from an aeroplane,' he said.

Leonard recovered from his faint, and as soon as the two spies noticed it, they compelled him to stand. He was so injured and ill, however, that he nearly sank to the floor again, and Dorin was compelled to hold him up.

'We shall open the door,' said Levinsky, 'and you will walk through. If you hesitate, or attempt to resist, you will be pushed through.' He raised his revolver menacingly.

'You needn't worry,' replied Leonard, swaying against him in his weakness. 'The sooner I get away from the two of you the better I shall be pleased, even if I do fall a few thousand feet. I suppose I can have my hands untied to shake hands with my friends before I go.'

'No!'

'Very well!' He turned and looked at the three men lying on the floor, and smiled once more. He looked a pitiable object standing there, swaying drunkenly between the two Russians, with blood streaming from the corner of his mouth and great clots of it on his face. His clothes were torn, his collar burst apart, with a large vivid scratch on his throat showing where one of the Russians had brutally torn it open.

'Goodbye, Hallows, and you too, Woodhouse; I hope you get out of this all right!' Then he turned to Batty, down whose face tears were streaming. 'Hallo, old chap,' he said, 'what's all this? Pull yourself together and, when you are free again, give Lady Wallace and Adrian my love, and tell them I went out thinking of them. Also give Major Brien a hearty handclasp and all my cheerios. Goodbye, and thanks for your faithful service!'

Not one word could any of his companions utter, so stricken with emotion were they.

'Your servant will be following you shortly,' said Levinsky.

'Don't be a worse cad than you can help,' said Leonard. 'What harm has the man done you? You can, at least, let him go when you arrive in Russia!'

'Perhaps! We'll see!' answered Levinsky.

'Remember me to the Russian Soviet! I don't think your reception will be very good, when they know how you have failed in India.'

Levinsky let out an oath, but Dorin smiled.

'They will, at least, thank us for ridding the world of you,' he said. 'Come! Enough of this!' He threw open the door of the saloon.

Leonard gave one glance round, and stiffened himself. Batty found his voice and cried out.

'Go on!' said Dorin.

With his head held high, and gathering all his remaining strength to save himself from stumbling, Leonard walked to the door. He had reached it, and the next second would have dropped into space and eternity, when—

'Stop!' shouted Levinsky, and grabbed him by the arm.

He swayed dizzily, and would have fallen out even then, had not the Russian, with a herculean effort, dragged him back into safety. The three Englishmen gave great sighs of emotion and relief.

'What did you do that for?' demanded Dorin angrily.

'I have thought of a far better idea,' replied Levinsky, shutting the little door and speaking in English, so that Wallace could understand him.

'His wife is on her way out to join him, so why not *let* her join him?'

'What do you mean?'

'She is travelling out by the *Greyhound*, so we will get into touch with her by wireless in Sir Leonard Wallace's name, and request her to join him at Bushire. There you or I will meet her in the guise of a police officer, and tell her that Sir Leonard has sent you, or me, whoever it happens to be, to escort her up country to him. When we get her safely in the wilds where the aeroplane will be waiting, and where there is no fear of our being interrupted, we will kill him, and she will be able to see him die. I always heard that Lady Wallace is a great sportswoman, and naturally, she will want to be in at the death!'

'A masterly plan, my dear Ivan,' said Dorin.

'You infernal scoundrel!' ground out Leonard. 'You wouldn't dare!'

'Oh, but we shall, and it will be quite an easy matter. Your death will then be satisfactory from every point of view, and will recompense us for the many ignominies you have put upon us.'

For the first time Leonard showed real emotion.

'Oh, God!' he groaned. 'If only I could get at you.'

Stark horror showed in the faces of Hallows, Woodhouse, and

Batty, and each of them strained at their bonds in great efforts to get free. But Levinsky and Dorin had done their work only too well, and their endeavours were in vain.

'What do you propose to do with the woman once she has seen her husband die?' asked Dorin.

'That remains to be seen!' replied Levinsky. 'We may take her to Russia with us. She is a beautiful woman, and would be highly welcome to certain members of the Soviet!' He shrugged his shoulders. Hallows watching his face, saw the coarse, horrible leer that came over it, and shuddered.

'What are we to do with these fellows until she arrives?' asked Dorin. 'It will be several days before she can do so.

'We'll find a suitable place, as I said, for the aeroplane to rest out in the wilds, and give them food enough to keep them alive. It would spoil matters if any of them died of thirst or starvation, especially the respected Sir Leonard Wallace. As soon as we alight for the night, you and I will study a map and decide upon the spot.'

The aeroplane came to rest just before nightfall on a deserted spot close to the sea at the extreme end of Baluchistan. The Russians could not have chosen a better place, for they were scores of miles from the nearest habitation in a district that appeared to be deserted by man and beast. It was a wild mountainous region, which would have given one the impression that it was impossible for an aeroplane to land anywhere in the neighbourhood, but the pilot, Alexieff, had found a place, and showed very great skill in bringing the machine to earth.

The four prisoners were left in the saloon with Polunin to guard them, while the others made a fire and cooked some food, which they had brought with them. The Englishmen were given sparingly of the slender stock of tinned provisions carried by the aeroplane, but none of them felt like eating, especially as their captors refused to untie their hands, and attempted to feed them. Leonard aching in every limb, with the stinging pain of his burns throbbing all the time, and worn out in body and mind, eventually fell into a restless, tortured sleep, while the others, lying in their uncomfortable, cramped positions, dozed and lay wide-awake alternately; and so somehow the night passed.

Early the next morning the flight was resumed, Levinsky and Dorin having decided that they would land in the desert between Shiraz and Ispahan, and there await the arrival of Lady Wallace; Dorin in the meantime being dropped at a spot within twenty miles of Bushire, where he could easily find his way to that port, send a wireless to the *Greyhound* and wait until she reached there. In a week's time the aeroplane was to go back to the place where he had been left, and hang about in the neighbourhood until he returned with Lady Wallace, when she would be taken aboard, and carried well into the desert, there to witness the death of her husband.

The aeroplane made good progress and at half past four landed near Bushire, where Dorin alighted and set off for that city. Then flying north for fifty miles, Alexieff at length noticed an ideal place for the machine to rest. It was a spot between two sand hills, away from the beaten track, so that it would have been possible to remain hidden for months without being discovered. Within a distance of five miles, too, there was an oasis set in the desert like a beautiful green island. There the plane came to earth, and remained for a week.

The privations suffered by Leonard and his companions during that week are beyond description. Every possible insult and indignity was heaped upon them, and Wallace's sufferings were hideous. They were made to lie out in the open without any cover, and in the daytime the fierce heat of the sun caused them endless agony. None of them was ever able afterwards to think of that week without a shudder.

Levinsky offered to free Hallows, and Woodhouse, if they would agree to serve the Soviet, and promise on their honour to make no attempt to help the other two. The suggestion was of course received with the utmost scorn by both of them, and Woodhouse was so outspoken in his denunciations of the Russians that they almost kicked him into unconsciousness.

The four made plans to escape, but they were too well watched, and their hands were never once untied. At last, they were compelled to give up any idea of freeing themselves. Thus day after day passed slowly, agonisingly by.

Major Watkins reached his office in reply to the telephone message to find that the officer who had apparently sent for him had been called out suddenly to the outskirts of Karachi. Nobody in the office knew anything about the reason for the call he, therefore, decided to wait until his subordinate returned. The latter came back a very puzzled man, and informed the Commissioner that he had been on a wild-goose chase, as when he reached his destination he discovered he had not been sent for. He further informed the Major that he had not telephoned to him. After talking the matter over, the two decided that they had been hoaxed, and a very annoyed Commissioner returned to his bungalow.

Arrived there, another surprise awaited him. His bearer handed him a note, which he said had been delivered by an English sahib who had come back in the little car in which the Excellency and his servant had gone out. Tearing the envelope open and extracting its contents, Watkins read the following, written in very scrawling characters:

> *My dear Watkins,*
>
> *Some information has reached me, which I think may help us to lay Levinsky by the heels. I am off in the aeroplane, and may not be back for a couple of days. Keep a good watch your end – I think we are coming to the finish of the chase at last. Excuse the writing, but Batty is doing his best on account of my damaged hand, and he has many virtues, one of which is not penmanship.*
>
> *Kind regards,*
> *Wallace*

For a long time the Commissioner studied this document. Then he slowly put it into his pocket.

'I don't like it!' he said. 'I don't like it at all!'

CHAPTER THIRTY-ONE

Lady Wallace Arrives

A beautiful white yacht, every line of which seemed to denote speed, steamed gracefully past the isle of Perim in the Red Sea. It was one of those very hot days when travellers are apt to wish almost that they had not been born. There was not a ripple on the surface of the sea, and its very oiliness seemed to suggest heat.

Under a double awning two ladies lay in deck chairs, striving with the help of large fans to cool themselves slightly. Nearby, in the same attitude of listlessness, sat two nurses and four children, who spent their time in wiping the perspiration from their faces, and sighing for a little air.

Presently a burly, bronzed man, in the white duck uniform of a marine captain, strolled along the deck and, raising his hand to his cap in salute, smiled at the two ladies.

'Do you find it warm, ladies?' he asked.

'Warm!' exclaimed one of them. 'I personally find it unbearably hot. Shall we have this heat all the way to Bombay, Captain?'

'No, Lady Wallace. It will probably be much cooler tomorrow.

The change will come as soon as we are past Aden and in the Arabian Sea.'

'Well, it's a relief to hear that,' said Molly.

'It is exceptionally hot for this time of the year,' said the Captain. 'I suppose you do not feel inclined for any deck games this morning. I noticed the quartermaster putting up the net for tennis as I came along.'

Molly laughed, and looked at her companion.

'He's an optimist,' she said. 'What do you say, Phyllis?'

'My dear, I'm too hot to talk, let alone play games! It's even too hot for the children – just look at them!'

They all looked at the four sprawling scraps of humanity, and laughed.

'As it is Sunday,' remarked the Captain, 'perhaps they thought they had better have a day of rest.'

'Rest for you and the officers I should think, Captain,' said Molly. 'Why, you must be thoroughly tired of children by now!'

'By no means,' said the Captain. 'It has been a great treat to have the little ones aboard. We don't very often have such a pleasure and my officers and myself have thoroughly enjoyed it, while the quartermasters go about now with grins on their faces and are always devising new games.'

'They have been wonderfully good,' said Phyllis. 'They seem to understand children so well.'

'Most of them are family men and have kiddies of their own, so they are experienced.'

Just then the wireless operator, an alert young man, ran down the gangway from the deck above and, coming up to the others, saluted smartly.

'A wireless message for Your Ladyship,' he said.

'Oh, splendid!' said Molly and, taking the buff-coloured envelope from his hand, she tore it open and read the contents, then handed it to the Captain.

'My husband wants us to go to Bushire,' she said. 'Isn't that somewhere in Persia?'

'Yes,' said the Captain and read the marconigram before handing it back. 'Then I'm afraid you will have to put up with more heat.' he smiled. 'The Persian Gulf has the reputation of being one of the hottest parts of the world.'

'Oh dear!' said Phyllis. 'Why on earth should Leonard choose to go there?'

'I can't think,' said Molly. 'What connection can there possibly be between the Indian Government and Persia!'

'Have I your orders to set my course for Bushire, Lady Wallace?' asked the Captain.

'Oh yes, of course, please!' said Molly. 'Is it nearer than Bombay?'

'No, I'm afraid it is not. Roughly speaking, I should think we will be there on Friday morning. That is, if we make as good time as we have done since leaving Marseilles.'

Presently he left them, accompanied by the wireless operator, and Molly turned to Phyllis with a pout on her pretty lips.

'Leonard doesn't send his love,' she said. 'I have never known him send a cablegram or telegram without it before.'

'Perhaps he is hard up,' smiled Phyllis, 'and couldn't afford the extra amount!'

'But he even signs himself "Wallace" and not "Leonard". Look!' She leant across to her companion, and showed the wireless message to her. '"*Meet me at Bushire – Awaiting you there – Wallace*",' read Phyllis. 'It is a bit abrupt, isn't it?'

'Perhaps he got somebody else to send it for him.' Molly cheered up.

'That must be the explanation,' she agreed. 'But I'll pretend to be very hurt and annoyed with him all the same.'

'Don't be cruel, Molly!'

'That isn't cruel It does husbands good to keep them in their places – you spoil yours!'

'I couldn't spoil him half as much as you spoil Leonard. I really should be very jealous of you, because after all, you have a message from Leonard, even though it is abrupt – I haven't even a teeny one from Billy.'

'I suppose he is at Bushire as well, so you can have half the marconigram.' And laughingly she tore the paper in halves and gave one of the pieces to Phyllis.

Since leaving Marseilles the yacht had experienced beautiful weather, with the result that she had made splendid progress and was nearly a day ahead of her expected time. Owing to the presence of the children the trip had been a very merry one, and had been thoroughly enjoyed by all on board from the Captain down to the ship's boy. All had vied with each other in giving the children a good time, and little Adrian had become a special favourite. His greatest enjoyment was to play pirates, and the good-hearted Captain had proved himself a first-rate actor when, brought to bay on his own bridge, he was forced to surrender his ship and to descend a prisoner and, apparently, a heartbroken man to his cabin. Adrian would have liked to have made his captives walk the plank, only as he naïvely put it, 'they would have got rather wet'.

As the Captain predicted, the next day was much cooler, a nice head breeze making all the difference, and games were resumed with redoubled energy. At noon another marconigram arrived, this time for Phyllis, and it proved to be a rather lengthy one from Billy.

'*Looking keenly forward to your arrival,*' it read, '*Let me know date and time of reaching Bombay. Am at present in Delhi, but will come to meet you. All love. Billy.*'

Phyllis perused it with surprise, and handed it to Molly.

'They are not together,' she said, 'and Billy apparently doesn't know that Leonard wishes us to meet him at Bushire.'

'That's strange!' said Molly, after she had read the message. 'I suppose Billy did not know Leonard's plans when he sent this. You had better send a reply at once, so that there will not be any muddle.'

The two girls went to the wireless cabin and composed a message for Billy, which was duly sent off to Viceregal Lodge, Delhi. Phyllis asked her companion if she was going to send a marconigram to Leonard, but the latter shook her head.

'No,' she said. 'He doesn't deserve one. Billy doesn't forget to send his love, but my husband does, and if he did not actually dispatch it himself, he could have told his messenger to send his love, couldn't he? And the very idea of signing it "Wallace".' Molly stamped down the gangway in great indignation, followed by the laughing Phyllis.

The yacht continued to make rapid progress and at seven o'clock on Friday morning sighted Bushire and took aboard the pilot to conduct her into that exceedingly noisy and evil-smelling port. An hour later she was snugly anchored with a crowd of native boats round her, like chicks round a hen. The port authorities had come and gone, and the quartermaster's time was occupied in keeping off the crowd of shrieking natives below, who were bent on selling fruit, and wares of all descriptions and seemed determined to climb on board. Some succeeded, but were sent over the side again in double-quick time by the indignant sailors, much to the amusement of Adrian and his little friends, who found everything highly interesting and exciting.

Molly looked in vain for Leonard or somebody representing him, and as time went on and nobody appeared she began to feel very doleful and worried.

'The poor man doesn't know we've arrived yet,' said Phyllis. 'We're ahead of time as you know. You should have sent a marconigram and not been so unkind.'

'Don't rub it in, Phyllis!' said Molly. 'Let us go and have breakfast! Perhaps there'll be a message by the time we have finished.'

Dorin had employed a couple of men to watch for the arrival of the yacht, but had no idea that she could possibly arrive so soon. His astonishment was great therefore when on Friday morning they came to the small hotel in which he had taken a room under the name of Spencer and announced that she had entered the harbour. He was just about to get up when a message was brought to him that they were waiting to see him. So, hastily dressing, he had them sent in.

'Arrived already!' he exclaimed. He spoke Persian fluently, as he did several languages. 'Surely you have made a mistake?'

'Not so, Excellency. She is the *Greyhound*, for the name was signalled!'

Dorin swore. This was an unexpected *contretemps*. The question was, how could he keep Lady Wallace waiting until the morrow, for, not expecting the arrival of the yacht before Saturday, the aeroplane would not reach the rendezvous until then. But he was a man of action and, dismissing the two Persians, he hurriedly bathed and shaved and, spick and span, set off to the harbour where he hired a boat and was rowed out to the yacht.

Molly and Phyllis had just concluded breakfast, when a message was brought to the former that a Mr Spencer had come aboard and was waiting to see her. She went on deck and saw a tall man with a fair beard, wearing spotless ducks, awaiting her. He bowed deeply.

'You have come from my husband?' she asked.

'I have, Your Ladyship,' he replied, 'and I deeply regret that I am so late. But we did not expect the ship until tomorrow.'

She smiled.

'We have come out very quickly,' she said, 'so it is really our fault for being here so soon.'

'Nevertheless I feel deeply guilty, and Sir Leonard will be annoyed I fear.'

'Not at all. Why should he be? Is he in Bushire?'

'No, madam. He is some miles up country in chase of some people he has followed from India. He arranged to return to a spot within twenty miles of this city tomorrow morning, and left me here to take you to him.'

'Then I shall not be able to see him till tomorrow,' she said in disappointed tones.

'I'm afraid not.'

'Why cannot he return here? Surely if he can come within twenty miles he can come here!'

'He does not wish to lose time in following these people, so he asked me to bring you out in a car and await the arrival of the aeroplane.'

'Then he is flying?'

'Yes!'

'And does he propose to take me with him after these people?'

'I believe so!'

'Oh, how exciting!' And she turned to Phyllis, who had just come on deck, introduced Dorin to her, and then told her the news.

'But, my dear,' said Phyllis, 'how extraordinary it all sounds! I really don't see why he couldn't have come the other twenty miles. Surely twenty miles is nothing to an aeroplane.'

'You may be sure Leonard has some motive,' said Molly.

'I suppose so, but I can't see it!' Phyllis shook her head doubtfully. 'Why was Major Brien left at Delhi?' she asked Dorin.

The latter started. So this was the wife of the Major! He had not hitherto connected the names. Certainly, he thought, this complicates matters, and how did she know that her husband was at Delhi. He showed no signs of his uneasiness, however, and smiled.

'Major Brien returned to Delhi with some very important documents for the Viceroy, and we came up here,' he said.

'Are you connected with the Indian Police?' asked Molly.

Dorin bowed.

'I am the Deputy Commissioner of Karachi,' he lied.

'Oh, I see. And are these people you are after political criminals?'

'Yes! In fact they are more than that, they are spies of the Russian Government!'

'Dear me! How thrilling! Are there many of them?' asked Molly.

'Three or four!'

Molly and Phyllis asked several more questions, all of which were answered by Dorin without hesitation and with an absolute disregard for the truth. Then he suggested that the two ladies should accompany him ashore, where he would endeavour to show them round the city. Molly shook her head.

'No, thank you,' she said, 'it is much too hot for one thing, and the look of the place does not appeal to me for another. What do you say, Phyllis?'

'I agree with you, dear. I am not at all keen on leaving the boat.'

'I really think you are wise,' said Dorin smiling. 'There is very little to see here and it is a pretty dirty hole.'

'Perhaps you will dine with us on board tonight, Mr Spencer?' invited Molly. 'We generally have dinner about eight.'

'It is very kind of Your Ladyship,' said the Russian.

'Then we shall expect you!'

He bowed, and a minute or two later took his leave. Molly and Phyllis sought their chairs under the awning.

'I don't like that man,' said the latter. 'He is too smug.'

'Neither do I,' said Molly. 'I dislike excessively polite people, and he is one; besides which his manners are un-English and over-elaborate. Poor man, I hope we are not making his ears burn with our criticisms; and he is probably quite a nice fellow. Isn't it awful to think that I have to wait a whole day before I see Leonard?'

'What about me?' exclaimed Phyllis. 'I may have to wait several days before seeing Billy.'

'Yes, poor dear, I forgot that. It was rather selfish of me.'

Dorin went ashore deep in thought. The fact that Mrs Brien was on board the yacht rather worried him, and for the first time he had doubts about the wisdom of sending a wireless message for the *Greyhound* to come to Bushire. He returned to his hotel and spent several hours thinking things over. At first he was inclined to take both women with him to meet the aeroplane, but on second thoughts he decided that to include Phyllis in the party might be unwise and cause complications, so he determined that if she wished to come he would have to prevent her doing so by saying that Wallace had sent his regrets, but was definite on the point that only Lady Wallace was to go.

As a matter of fact Phyllis had no desire to make the trip at all, and when Molly suggested it at dinner that evening she said she would rather stay on board and look after the children. Dorin proved himself such a genial companion during the meal that the two girls almost revised their opinion of him. He was a splendid conversationalist and a great traveller, and he interested them very much with his vividly drawn pictures of the various countries he had been in. In fact, laying himself out to obtain Molly's confidence, he very nearly overdid it, for she asked him how it was that he, an Indian police officer, had visited so many countries, and he was constrained to invent a long story of secret missions to different parts of the world on behalf of the Indian Government. Dorin, in truth, was a versatile man, and he might have made a name for himself as an author of romantic fiction, if he had not chosen to be a rogue.

At ten o'clock the next morning he returned to the yacht, and escorted Molly ashore. Adrian was very anxious to go with her, and coaxed and cajoled his mother for a long time before she eventually persuaded him that he could not go. It was a very disappointed little face that watched the boat leave the vessel's side. The Captain had been informed of her proposed trip at breakfast, and seemed rather doubtful about it. He turned up later on with a small loaded revolver, which he handed to her. At first she refused to take it, but he was so earnest and persistent that at last she laughingly consented, and hid it in her dress.

An antiquated car was waiting at the landing-stage, and entering it with Dorin, they were jolted out of the city in the direction of Shiraz. The heat was intense and presently, when they left the road and took to a mere track across the desert, the dust rose round them in clouds, and Molly thought she had never had such an unpleasant experience in her life. At last they reached their destination, and a desolate spot it was. For miles round nothing was to be seen but a waste of sand, a few stunted trees, and some cactus plants. The solitude began to frighten her a little, and she almost wished she had not come. It occurred to her as strange that Leonard should have wanted her to meet him in such a place, and for the first time, she began to have misgivings about the genuineness of the rendezvous and her companion, who was doing his best to cheer her with his conversation. She studied him covertly, and noticed how anxiously he scanned the sky for any signs of the aircraft. She wondered what she should do if, after all, this bearded stranger had not been sent by her husband, but that, hearing of her arrival, he had kidnapped her for some reason of his own – things like that had happened even in this extremely law-abiding twentieth century, and the driver of the car was a particularly villainous-looking individual, she thought. Then the humour of such an idea occurred to her – a very important and respectable member of the Indian police, turning kidnapper! – and she laughed. Dorin looked at her curiously, and politely asked why she laughed, but she gave him an evasive answer, and thereafter there was silence – a deadly silence which, to Molly's imagination, seemed to suggest some impending disaster. The stillness of a desert is unlike any other quiet – there is something intense, almost frightening about it, and to anyone in Molly's position it has a sense of evil in it, as though all the forces, of wickedness are gathering their strength for some terrible outburst of sin.

At last the tension was broken, a distant hum could be heard, and with an exclamation of satisfaction Dorin pointed to a speck in the sky which rapidly grew larger, and Molly recognised the great aeroplane in which her husband had left Croydon eighteen days before. The big figures and letters on it, denoting the squadron of the Royal Air Force to which it belonged, gave her a great sense of relief, and she turned to Dorin with a smile.

'It was rather desolate waiting, wasn't it?' she said. 'I cannot see where the fascination of a desert comes in; it gave me rather a feeling of dread.'

'I agree with you, Lady Wallace,' replied the Russian. 'Deserts are most uninteresting places.'

The aeroplane sank lower and lower, and presently planed down to the earth, and came to rest about twenty yards from them. Dorin at once helped Molly to alight from the car, and escorted her across to the huge machine. A smart young fellow came to meet them, and saluted her respectfully.

'Sir Leonard Wallace's compliments Lady Wallace,' he said. 'He is awaiting you about fifty miles from here.'

Molly hesitated. Again a doubt assailed her; again she thought Leonard's behaviour to be strange. Why had he not come to meet her now! But the young man before her looked to be so obviously an English officer, and after all this was the same aeroplane.

She smiled.

'You are not the pilot who was in charge when my husband left England, are you?' she asked.

'No, Lady Wallace. I have taken over from him for the present.'

He helped her into the interior of the machine, then turned to Dorin.

'The others are guarding the prisoners,' he whispered in Russian, 'so I came alone. I suppose you did not think to bring any petrol with you?'

'No; why?'

'I am running very short. There is not enough to carry us as much as a hundred miles.'

Dorin muttered an oath under his breath. He paid the driver of the car and turned back to Alexieff.

'We'll have to obtain some somewhere, after Wallace is finished with,' he said. 'Let us get back now!'

He joined Molly in the saloon and the aeroplane rose in the air again. Then Dorin cast off all pretence. He bowed to her mockingly.

'I am sorry to have deceived Lady Wallace,' he said, 'but in the circumstances it was necessary. It is my duty to inform you that you are in the hands of the Russian Soviet – my real name is Dorin, and I am one of their chief agents!'

Molly started back and went white to the lips.

'Surely you are—you are joking,' she said.

'By no means! I am deadly serious!'

'Then my husband—?'

'Is also a prisoner with two of his companions – I am taking you now to witness his execution.'

A great cry of terror rose to her lips.

'You wouldn't dare!' she gasped.

'Pardon me! The execution was determined upon by my colleague and myself. We were only awaiting your arrival to carry it out.'

Stricken with fear and a great grief, Molly sank into one of the cushioned seats. It had come upon her with overwhelming force that this man Dorin meant every word he said, and the shock deprived her for the time being of all her faculties, all her strength. But she was a brave woman and came of a family of soldiers, and presently her brain commenced to work again. She thought of every means she could to get the better of this man, who was now sitting opposite her, watching her with a cynical smile on his face. At first her inclination was to draw the revolver the Captain had pressed upon her, and hold him up. But further reflection showed her how useless such a proceeding would be, and she decided to keep the weapon hidden in the hope that it might prove of assistance to her husband.

As she thought of Leonard she could not repress a sob. So this was the explanation of what she had considered his strange conduct. He was all the time a prisoner in the hands of these fiends, and had not sent the wireless message. No wonder it was signed 'Wallace'; no wonder there had been no message of love in it. Striving to keep her voice firm she asked Dorin what harm her husband had done him and his companions, that they should desire to kill him. She was answered by a passionate outburst from the Russian.

'In one week,' he said vehemently, 'Sir Leonard Wallace has destroyed our power in India: he has caused all the efforts of years to be of no account. Our hard work, our careful propaganda has gone for naught, and we have had to leave the country. Not only that, but he also upset our efforts to influence opinion in England four years ago. Is it any wonder that now he is in our power we mean to destroy him? And it is a sweet revenge to force his wife to see his end. We have failed in India through his interference, but we will rid the world of him, and our great country will be proud of us and grateful to us. After his death you will be handed over to be dealt with by the members of the Soviet themselves – they admire pretty women!'

She shuddered. The horrible smile with which he accompanied his last words brought a terrible picture before her mind and suddenly she felt weak, almost paralysed; but her womanhood reasserted itself, and she sat proudly up with a dignity that impressed Dorin in spite of himself.

In the seclusion of the desert retreat, Wallace lay in agony. It was not so much the torture of his numerous sores under the burning heat of the sun that was troubling him, but the fact that Molly should be in the power of these inhuman fiends, who had staged such a terrible drama to wreak their vengeance on him. Close to him lay Batty, and a little farther away the two airmen. Levinsky and Polunin were seated smoking under the shade of a tarpaulin, which they had erected to protect themselves from the fierce rays of the sun. With feelings of dread the four Englishmen had witnessed the departure of the aeroplane for the rendezvous, where it was expected that Molly and Dorin would be awaiting its arrival. Presently Batty spoke.

'I've managed to loosen this rope wot ties me 'ands, sir,' he said hoarsely. 'If yer turns over on yer side, an' I wriggles to yer, d'you think yer can make shift to get me free?'

'I'll try, Batty,' replied Leonard, 'but be careful! They are watching every movement.'

'Aye, aye, sir!'

By imperceptible degrees the sailor wriggled nearer and nearer to Wallace, and after some time they lay back to back, and the latter's fingers could just reach the cord that tied Batty's wrists. Watching the Russians from the corners of his eyes, Leonard's fingers found the knot and slowly, painfully began to work at it. Whenever Levinsky's or Polunin's eyes strayed in their direction, he stopped and held his breath in apprehension, but to the Russians it only appeared that the two men were lying together, and no suspicion was raised. At last, after what seemed an eternity, Leonard found the knot give in his fingers, and he pulled the strands of rope apart.

'I've done it, Batty!' he whispered in exultation, between his closed lips. 'Draw away! You can do the rest.'

At that moment Polunin came across to them.

'Get apart!' he growled, kicking Batty. The latter, without a word moved aside, but there was a triumphant gleam in his eyes, at which the Russian would have wondered, had he seen it.

In a short while the aeroplane arrived, and Leonard got to his feet somehow. Standing there swaying drunkenly he watched Dorin alight followed by Molly, and a sob of emotion shook him from head to foot. Levinsky advanced to the machine and raised his hat to the girl with ironical politeness.

'Welcome to our little retreat, Lady Wallace,' he said.

But Molly took no notice of him, she was searching for her husband. At first she failed to recognise him in the terrible-looking object, covered with clotted blood, who stood swaying so weakly a few yards from her. Then with a cry of anguish that should have softened the most hard-hearted, she ran to him and put her arms round him.

'Oh, my darling,' she moaned, 'what have they done to you?'

Levinsky strode forward with the intention of pulling her away.

'You shall have one lover-like scene before he dies,' he said, 'but at present—'

He never completed the sentence, for suddenly Molly swung round with a cry, and in her right hand she held a wicked-looking little revolver.

'Move a step more,' she said, 'and I will shoot!'

Her face was deadly pale, but there was the light of an

unflinching courage in her beautiful eyes. Levinsky stopped dead, and stared at her. Dorin, with an oath, drew his own revolver, but in that moment Batty shook free the cord which had bound his wrists and, with a roar that contained all the pent-up sufferings of days, sprang upon him. A crashing blow from the sailor's right fist found its billet, and Dorin went down with a groan.

Then, in the stillness of that desert atmosphere, could be heard the sound of an aeroplane's engine, and all looked upwards; the Russians with a deadly fear, the others with the hope of deliverance.

An aeroplane appeared in view, then another, and another.

The group below was sighted, and one by one the machines glided down.

CHAPTER THIRTY-TWO

Brien to the Rescue

Having handed over the plans and told his story to the Viceroy, Brien spent a couple of days in sheer laziness, as he described it, attended with great care by Lord Oundle's own physician. The rest and attention did him a lot of good, and he began to feel quite fit again. But after a while the lack of news from Leonard bothered him, and he longed to be up and doing. As his chief showed no signs of returning, he had a vague idea of going back to Karachi to help him, but the doctor, aided by the Viceroy, Muir, Lady Oundle and Doreen, appealed to him to stay where he was, and at last, very reluctantly, he decided to remain for a couple of days longer.

On the Sunday that the *Greyhound* passed the island of Perim and made her way towards Aden, he and Sir Henry Muir spent some time in calculating the yacht's position, and having satisfied himself that she was somewhere in the Red Sea, Billy decided to send a marconigram. He wasted several forms in an effort to say what he wished to say in a reasonable number of words, but at length he was satisfied and the message was dispatched early on Monday morning. Having sent it, he gave himself up to pleasurable anticipation of the arrival of his wife and children, and spent the morning in a long cane chair in a shady part of the garden. After tiffin he was joined by Doreen, whose gay spirits and light chatter prevented him from becoming dull.

They were engaged in the not very exciting game of Halma, and Billy had just been beaten for the fourth time, which says more for his gallantry than his ability, when a message was brought to him that he was wanted on the telephone.

He entered the house and after some difficulty, succeeded in hearing the voice at the other end of the wire. It was the Deputy Commissioner of Karachi, and a very agitated man he appeared to be. Having made himself known, Watkins surprised Billy by asking if he had heard from Sir Leonard Wallace.

'No,' replied Billy. 'Isn't he with you?'

'He hasn't been here since Friday afternoon!'

'Where has he gone?'

'Goodness knows! I had a message calling me to the office, and when I returned he and his manservant, Batty, had disappeared. They had apparently taken my small car and gone down to the aeroplane. A stranger, whom I have been unable to trace, brought back the car, and a note from Sir Leonard saying that he was after Levinsky and might be away a couple of days. That was Friday; since then I haven't had a word from him, and I am very worried.'

'That's strange!' said Billy. 'But I don't think you need worry. Sir Leonard very often disappears like that, and there cannot be any question of foul play if he has gone in the aeroplane.'

'But he took no baggage! I have all along thought there was something wrong. You see, in the first place, the telephone call that took me to my office turned out to be a hoax, and when I got back I found Sir Leonard's note awaiting me.'

'Then you did not see the man who brought it?'

'No! And although I have made enquiries nobody has come forward.'

'It certainly sounds rather extraordinary!' said Billy.

Watkins went on to describe the way in which Dorin and Levinsky had got into the house in an effort to recover the plans, and had escaped, and how he and Wallace had searched for them.

'The more I think of it,' he added, 'the more I feel convinced that the telephone message, calling me away on Friday afternoon, was sent on purpose to get me out of the way while Sir Leonard went down to the aeroplane.'

'You've made me feel very worried,' said Billy. 'I tell you what – I'll get the Air Force here to place a machine at my disposal, and fly to Karachi. Then we can go into the matter together.'

'I shall be very glad if you will,' said Watkins, and a second later rang off.

Billy went along to see the Viceroy and was lucky to find him disengaged. The latter listened to him thoughtfully, then said:

'I think you are wise in going to Karachi in the circumstances. I'll arrange for an aeroplane to be placed under your orders early in the morning. Will that do?'

'Quite, sir, thank you!' said Billy.

By now he had become very anxious and returned thoughtfully to the garden, where even Doreen's bright chatter failed to disperse the foreboding that had upon over him. He had tea with Lord and Lady Oundle and of course Doreen, and they had just finished, when Muir came across the lawn with a paper in his hand.

'A wireless message for you, Brien,' he said. 'It was telephoned from the telegraph office to save delay.' And he handed the slip to Billy.

The latter read it and started to his feet.

'It is from Phyllis,' he said, 'and she says, "*Have received wireless from Leonard asking us to meet him Bushire so have changed course and are going there. Love, Phyllis.*"'

'What on earth is he doing in Bushire?' asked the Viceroy

'I don't know,' said Billy grimly. 'There is something wrong somewhere, and I am going to find out what it is.'

Early the next morning he left for Karachi in an aeroplane lent by the Royal Air Force and piloted by Forsyth, but owing to engine trouble they were compelled to make a forced landing near a place called Didwana, where they were held up until Wednesday afternoon. The trouble was found to be too serious to repair in a hurry and, in reply to their frantic telephone messages to Delhi, another machine was sent, which Forsyth took over, leaving the damaged one at Didwana. Eventually they arrived at Karachi at noon on Thursday.

Billy went straight to Major Watkins' bungalow where the Commissioner received him with relief.

'Thank Goodness, you've come!' he said. 'I haven't had a word from Sir Leonard yet.'

'I received a marconigram from my wife in which she said that he had asked the yacht, which is bringing her and Lady Wallace to India, to meet him at Bushire.'

'At Bushire! Then he must have tracked those Russians up

there. Well, it's a relief to know where he is and what he's doing. I began to think that something had happened.'

'And you were right,' said Billy. 'I feel certain that something *has* happened. Sir Leonard Wallace is not the man to go off in this manner without leaving a clue behind him.'

'But you said that he often disappears like this.'

'I know I did, but he always informs some member of his department. In this case I thought a note would have arrived for either you or me, and the only information we have about his whereabouts is an accidental mention in a marconigram. And knowing him as I do, I am sure he would not have asked his wife to meet him at Bushire if he was engaged on any serious business.'

'Then do you think the wireless message was a fake?'

'I don't know what to think, but I'm off to Bushire tomorrow morning. Can I have another couple of aeroplanes?'

'Good Lord! What for?'

'I've got a very fantastic idea in my head that the aeroplane was stolen by Levinsky and Dorin, and Sir Leonard and Batty kidnapped.'

'But that is ridiculous. You forget that Hallows and the mechanic would have had to be kidnapped as well, and how do you know that Dorin, or the other, knew how to pilot a machine?'

'I don't, but it's quite likely they can; and as for Hallows and Woodhouse . . .' He shrugged his shoulders. 'I know the whole thing sounds mad, but I am quite willing to believe almost anything possible to those two Russians.'

'But how about the yacht? Why should Levinsky and Dorin want it to go to Bushire? I presume they are the people you suspect of sending the faked marconigram – if it was a fake?'

'Please don't ask me questions which I can't answer. My brain feels confused, and I hardly know what I *am* thinking! Probably I am searching for a mare's nest, but I'm not going to take any risks – there is just a chance that my fantastic ideas may be right. Can I have those aeroplanes?'

'Of course, if I can fix it. I'll get in touch with the Commandant of the Royal Air Force depot here at once.'

There was some delay in getting the additional machines, and it was past noon on the next day before Billy left for Bushire, with the result that they were still four hundred miles from their destination when darkness came on and they were compelled to descend. They were away again very early in the morning and, at last, just after eleven o'clock, alighted on the outskirts of Bushire. Leaving his companions to explain matters to the Persian officials who arrived to ask the reason for this air invasion by British aeroplanes, Billy commandeered a car and was driven to the harbour, where he found a man who agreed to row him out to the yacht for a sum quite ten times the usual hire.

Phyllis, who was sitting on deck, saw him coming, and awaited him at the top of the gangway with the children. There were an emotional few minutes; then holding him from her:

'What on earth has happened, dear?' she asked in great anxiety. 'Why are you covered with bandages?'

'Don't trouble about that now, Phyllis!' he replied. 'I'll tell you all later on. Where is Molly?'

'She's gone ashore with Mr Spencer to meet Leonard.'

'Mr Spencer! Who is he?'

'The Deputy Commissioner of Karachi.'

'My God!' exclaimed Billy. 'What was he like?'

Phyllis stared at him in surprise.

'What is the matter, dear?' she asked.

'Tell me what he is like for God's sake! It is a matter of life and death!'

Frightened by his vehemence, Phyllis did as she was asked.

'He is very tall and fair, and has a beard,' she said.

'Dorin!' ejaculated her husband, and added, 'I shall have to leave you, dear: Molly is in grave danger. Which way did they go?'

Full of anxiety, Phyllis told him that Dorin had said that they were to meet Wallace at a rendezvous twenty miles north of the city.

'That's all I can tell you,' she concluded.

He kissed her and the children.

'I must get after them as soon as possible,' he said. 'I hope it won't be very long before I'm back with both Molly and Leonard.'

'God grant it, dear!' she replied earnestly, and she ran down the gangway and jumped into the waiting boat.

He presently turned to wave his hand. She was still standing where he had left her, her right hand caressing the curls of her eldest son's head, her left plucking nervously at her handkerchief in the dread lest some danger should befall him.

Heaping vituperations on the head of the unfortunate driver of the commandeered car, in order to get him to go quicker (not a word of which the man understood), Billy soon rejoined Forsyth and the others. They were still engaged with the Persian officials, who were making copious notes. He gave orders to start at once, telling Forsyth in which direction to go. As the officials saw these foreign airmen making ready to depart, their indignation knew no bounds, and one even drew a revolver, thinking that such an act would show the strangers that they could not come and go on Persian territory with impunity. Forsyth immediately pulled it from his hand and flung it away.

Then commenced a deafening babel, in the midst of which the three aeroplanes rose one after the other and flew away, leaving a crowd of angry men waving notebooks and pencils in their impotent wrath.

It was some time before the trail was picked up, and then Forsyth saw a car below apparently making its way in the direction of Bushire. At Billy's suggestion he descended, and the driver of the car, who was very startled, informed them that a lady and gentleman had left his car a quarter of an hour before, and had gone away in a very large flying-machine. He appeared impressed by the size of the other aeroplane, for he repeated that it was a very large one several times, and looked with contempt at Billy's small fighting machine. But the latter had obtained the information be required, and his small flying force headed away due north. Brien sat in his seat with a pair of field glasses glued to his eyes, and at last discerned his quarry between a group of sand hills. He gave the signal, and the three machines sank to earth.

As he jumped from the plane a dramatic scene met his eyes.

A terrible-looking figure, whose clothes were torn in shreds and whose face was a mass of dirt and clotted blood, stood swaying weakly next to a woman, and with a gasp of horror Billy recognised him as Wallace. The woman was Molly, who stood, her little head proudly uplifted, facing Levinsky with a revolver. Farther on was Batty with clenched fists, standing over a man who lay on the ground at his feet. Two other men were huddled together by the great aeroplane which had served Leonard so well and, in the end, almost proved to be his undoing, while near them lay Woodhouse and Hallows with their hands tied behind them.

All this appeared like a cinema picture before Billy's eyes as he dashed forward with drawn revolver, followed by Forsyth and his companions of the other machines.

Levinsky swung round with a snarl.

'So I lose after all,' he said. 'Then Sir Leonard Wallace and his wife die first.' And suddenly he drew his revolver and fired point blank at Molly.

But Leonard had guessed what was coming, and a fraction of a second before the shot he threw himself against Molly, and the two of them fell to the ground, the bullet passing harmlessly over them. At the same moment Billy's revolver spoke; Levinsky staggered drunkenly, sank to his knees, and rolled over with a bullet through his heart.

'So much for you, Levinsky,' muttered Brien. 'It was a better death than you ever deserved to die.'

Batty had allowed his attention to wander from Dorin during the events that ended with Levinsky's death, and now the Russian, springing to his feet, dashed the sailor to the ground with a blow of his left fist and fired two shots in rapid succession at Billy. Both missed, and he fell riddled with bullets fired by the airmen. Alexieff and Polunin made a feeble attempt at resistance, but were soon overpowered and, skilfully bound, were thrust into the interior of the big aeroplane. Hallows and Woodhouse were relieved of their bonds, and Molly who, now that everything was over, looked as though she were going to faint, shakily cut the cord that tied her husband's wrists together. Batty procured water and half sobbing, half laughing in her utter relief, she bathed Leonard's face with tender care. He smiled up at Billy.

'Thanks, old chap!' he said, and there was a wealth of meaning in that simple little phrase. 'So we got them both in the end, and it's due to you and Molly here. By Jove, darling!' he added shakily, 'I'm proud of you. But – but I'm sorry you found me in this state.' He smiled. 'I'm a frightful mess, I'm afraid!'

A sob escaped Molly, and Billy turned away.

Impatiently he brushed something damp from his eyes, then blew his nose vigorously.

'I'm an idiot!' he muttered to himself.

NEXT IN THE SERIES

THE DEVIL'S COCKTAIL